Altars of Stone

Also by Corinne Brixton

THROUGH MARTHA'S EYES
published by Matador

All profits to Tearfund
Registered Charity No.265464 (England & Wales)

Altars
of
Stone

Book One of
The Line of Shem Trilogy

Corinne Brixton

Scriptures taken from the Holy Bible, New International Version®, NIV®. Copyright ©
1973, 1978, 1984, 2011 by Biblica, Inc.™ Used by permission of Zondervan. All rights
reserved worldwide. www.zondervan.com The 'NIV' and 'New International Version' are
trademarks registered in the United States Patent and Trademark Office by Biblica, Inc.™

Matador
9 Priory Business Park,
Wistow Road, Kibworth Beauchamp,
Leicestershire. LE8 0RX
Tel: 0116 279 2299
Email: books@troubador.co.uk
Web: www.troubador.co.uk/matador
Twitter: @matadorbooks

ISBN 978 1789017 076

British Library Cataloguing in Publication Data.
A catalogue record for this book is available from the British Library.

Printed and bound by CPI Group (UK) Ltd, Croydon, CR0 4YY
Typeset in 11pt Aldine401 BT by Troubador Publishing Ltd, Leicester, UK

Matador is an imprint of Troubador Publishing Ltd

*In loving memory
of my mother,
Iris Wyngate Brixton MBE,
who taught me my first words
and so much more.*

'Corinne Brixton is a wise and experienced guide to the Christian life. This is a book which I hope will introduce many to the riches of the Bible, and help them to understand it better.'

Rt. Revd. Graham Tomlin, *Bishop of Kensington and President of St Mellitus College;*

author of "The Seven Deadly Sins and How to Overcome Them" and "Looking Through The Cross"

'A good story, based on the Best and Biggest Story the world has known. Caught up in the lives of Shem and his line, I absorbed a thousand small details of history, culture and theology by osmosis and came away not only knowing more but remembering again the startling ways in which the struggle of human life can be turned to good, and the good become better, in the company of God.'

Revd. Hilary Edgerton, *Assistant Priest in the Benefice of Saddleworth and prison chaplain.*

'A gripping read—the Old Testament stories are brought to life in a new way through the lives of eyewitnesses. True to Biblical and historical details yet told in an accessible and personal way. Can't wait for the next book.'

Christine Fry, *Member of Church of England General Synod.*

'The first book of the Bible comes to life in Altars of Stone. As the author imaginatively tells these timeless stories in an accessible way, fascinating details are revealed that many Bible readers would miss. Remaining utterly faithful to Scripture, this is an ideal book for anyone who wants to get to grips with what life was like in Old Testament times, and wants to be excited afresh by God's actions in the world.'

Revd. Clive Gardner, *Team Vicar of St Mark's, Wimbledon*

'Corinne Brixton's book has some similarities to the historical novels of Hilary Mantel, such as "Wolf Hall". Mantel has brought parts of English history to life for many people; Corinne takes us on a much more ambitious journey back thousands of years into the world and stories of the Old Testament. Drawing on her knowledge of the ancient world, she weaves a story on the basis of the Old Testament narrative, imagining with us how our spiritual ancestors experienced God in a world so different from ours, but equally real. A creative and thought-provoking book.'

Revd. Dr. David Wenham, *MA, PhD, Tutor in New Testament, Trinity College Bristol;*
author of "The Parables of Jesus" and "Paul and Jesus: The True Story"

Acknowledgements

I could not have written this book without the careful study of the Biblical text previously accomplished by others, who have published their scholarly findings in commentaries and other books. Many of their insights have been incorporated into *Altars of Stone*, and I am indebted to them for sharing their learning. The main sources of information are listed in the Bibliography at the end. Thanks also go to Clive Gardner and Angie Blanche, who read and commented on the manuscript as it was evolving, to Sue Dowler, Hilary Edgerton and Cairine Hart for their excellent proof-reading, and to Peter Warne for using his extraordinary artistic gifts to create the cover design. And I will always be grateful to and in awe of the God who has revealed Himself in Scripture and in the lives of flawed men and women down through history.

Foreword

The Line of Shem trilogy does not seek simply to retell stories that Scripture has already made memorable. It has a two-fold aim. Firstly, to provide background to and commentary on some of those stories, set in a world far removed from our own culture and time and involving many customs and details with which modern readers may be unfamiliar. Secondly, to build up, over the course of the three books, an overview of the main characters and events of the Old Testament. It will do this by taking ten 'bit-part players' from pivotal stories across the fifteen hundred years or so of Old Testament history.

Generally, story-telling in Scripture differs in a number of ways from modern styles. One particular difference is that the Bible is fairly scant when it comes to the internal feelings and thoughts of those involved. *The Line of Shem* has, therefore, deliberately chosen characters peripheral to the main stories to lessen the risk of any unintended misrepresentation of the 'main players' in Scripture. In *Altars of Stone*, we meet the first three of those characters: Shem, one of the sons of Noah; Eliezer of Damascus, a servant of Abraham; and Asher, one of the lesser-known sons of Jacob. The events described all occur in the first book of the Bible, and each chapter starts with a quote from Genesis to enable the reader to find the original story in Scripture.

The Biblical accounts on which this book is based have been taken as history. This is, after all, what much of the Old Testament claims to be (the text generally making it clear when it is not). Its events are set in a real geographical setting, with plenty of historical details that relate to the times and places in which those stories are set.[1] As one writer has helpfully pointed out, 'the Old Testament has consistently been shown to be a reliable guide in those areas where it can actually be tested. The accounts of personalities and conflicts are often corroborated by sources outside the Bible.'[2]

Shem's story is likely to be the one giving rise to the greatest number of questions about historicity. The flood narrative is taken by scholars in different ways. Here, it is an imagining of how it might have been, if taken on its own terms.

Every effort has been made to be as accurate as possible in the historical details included. However, various assumptions have had to be made at times. Notes at the end of each chapter have therefore been included to indicate, as far as possible, where and why any assumptions or choices have been made. This will hopefully enable the reader to distinguish more easily between what comes directly from Scripture and what is artistic licence or conjecture. The notes also contain, where appropriate, historical or archaeological details. It is not necessary to read the notes to enjoy the book, but hopefully they will enrich the experience and enlighten the reader.

A few additional comments are also worth making. Firstly, the personal name of God, *Yahweh* (which translates the Hebrew YHWH), has been used throughout. In most modern Bible translations, YHWH is rendered *the LORD*, reflecting the Jewish practice of reverencing the name of God by not speaking it. It is not clear when this became common practice among the Jews, but certainly there is nothing within the Scriptures themselves to imply that this was the practice during Old Testament times. Therefore, the characters in the stories use the actual, revealed name of God, although *the LORD* is used in the Bible references at the beginning of each chapter.

Secondly, the stories are set in a culture without clocks. The word *hour* does not occur in the Old Testament, and so the passing of time has had to be referred to in terms that would be more appropriate. The language employed throughout the book has attempted to avoid all anachronisms, not only those concerned with time. Any scales on the included maps are in miles for the convenience of the reader.

Thirdly, although women may not be the main focus of many of the Biblical narratives, they are there throughout. It has been easier, however, to 'get closer to the action' through men. Two of the ten 'bit-part players' in the trilogy, however, will be women.

Fourthly, there is, of course, only one place where these stories are told with complete reliability and without error: the Word of God. Any thoughts, words or actions beyond the Biblical narratives are a work of imagination.

Finally, a comment on the stories themselves, using the words of a favourite author:

'The Bible begins with the book of Genesis, written when primogeniture—the passing of all the family's wealth and estate

to the eldest son—was the iron law in virtually all societies. Yet the entirety of Genesis is subversive of this cultural norm. God constantly chooses and works through the second sons, the ones without social power. He chooses Abel rather than Cain, Isaac rather than Ishmael, Jacob rather than Esau, Joseph rather than Reuben. And when he works with women, he does not choose the women with the cultural power of beauty and sexuality. He does his saving work through old, infertile Sarah, not young Hagar, through unloved and unattractive Leah, not lovely Rachel.[3]

Hopefully the stories in this book will leave readers with what has been gained in the writing of them: a deeper love for the Scriptures and for the God who inspired them to be written down.

Notes

1. *See, for example, Kenneth Kitchen's extensively-researched book, "On the Reliability of the Old Testament" (Grand Rapids: Eerdmans, 2003).*

2. *Chris Sinkinson, "Time Travel to the Old Testament" (Nottingham: IVP, 2013), p. 29. He also adds, 'Of course, the further back we go, the less evidence remains, but there is still enough to remind us that we are dealing with some form of history, even in its earliest writings.'*

3. *Tim Keller, "Making Sense of God" (London: Hodder & Stoughton, 2016), pp. 206-207.*

Shem

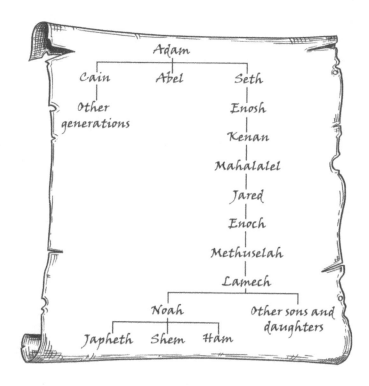

Adam

Cain   Abel   Seth

Other generations

Enosh

Kenan

Mahalalel

Jared

Enoch

Methuselah

Lamech

Noah   Other sons and daughters

Japheth   Shem   Ham

I

*The L*ORD *saw how great the wickedness of the human race had become on the earth, and that every inclination of the thoughts of the human heart was only evil all the time. (Genesis 6:5)*

Stupid! Stupid! Stupid! Shem cursed his folly as he lay motionless in the long grass. He tried to breathe as silently as possible, despite his chest demanding large gulps of air after his desperate flight through the night. An unseen tree root had brought him crashing to the ground, his wrenched ankle forcing him to abandon escape in favour of hiding, although he almost feared the thunderous beating of his heart would give him away. *Why on earth hadn't he been more careful to heed his father's warning about returning well before sunset? Stupid!*

'We know you're there,' shouted a voice, the mere tone of which knotted Shem's already twisted stomach more tightly. The voice in the darkness was immediately followed by several others, all taunting him or jeering.

'You won't get away—you're ours!' shouted another.

Shem raised his head slightly, grateful for the cover of darkness, and peered through the tops of the grass in the direction of the voices. His every sense was sharpened by fear. He saw a couple of flaming torches being held aloft, and in their light he could see five or six shadowy shapes moving around. He knew that they were all out for gain, for blood and for sport. *If they found him, he would be stripped of every item of value, and then, if he was fortunate, he would be killed outright. But if not…*

Shem wrested his thoughts away from a path that went to a very dark place, and forced them deliberately in the only direction in which help might be found. *God of my fathers, of Adam, of Seth, of Enosh…* His lips moved silently, naming as many of his ancestors as his terrified mind could remember and ending finally with the name of his own father, Noah. He had prayed to his father's God before, but never with the fervency of that moment. *If you will deliver me this night, O Yahweh, then I vow that you will be my only God and that I will serve you all the days of my life as my father has done. Hear my prayer, O Lord Almighty!*

Shem, with his heart still beating furiously, laid his forehead against the earth, prostrating himself before the unseen One to whom he had prayed, surrendering himself fully—and in desperation—to Him. And then he strained his ears and listened.

For a long time, nothing changed as Shem remained as still as death. The shouting continued, and although the direction from which it came altered from time to time, it never came any closer. Then—eventually—the voices became more distant. Anger replaced the mocking tone as the men realised they were to be denied their sport for that night. Or at least with Shem as its victim. And finally the night was quiet once more, except for the sound of the breeze blowing through the grass and the occasional cry of a faraway fox or jackal on a night-time hunt of its own.

Shem pushed his body—now cold from lying on the ground, unmoving, for so long—up into a kneeling position. He peered around. Not that there was much

4

to see. The beginning of the month, marked by the new moon, had fallen only two days earlier. The moon, which would very soon disappear below the western horizon, was still only a thin crescent, providing little if any light. Very close by there was a jagged black shape that obliterated the starlight in part of the sky, and Shem knew it was the tree whose root had—maybe providentially— sent him flying headlong. He finally raised himself to his feet, though keeping his weight off his left ankle. When he did shift onto his injured leg, he was relieved to find it could bear him, although his first hesitant steps were more of a limp.

Standing a short distance away from the tree, the full extent of the night sky was laid open to him. He tilted his head back and gazed up into the grandeur of the heavens. It was as if someone had taken a handful of dazzling sand and cast it across the black expanse. Something approaching a sense of peace descended upon him, and although he had only recently risen from the ground, he dropped to his knees, touching his forehead to the earth once more. He whispered a prayer of thanks to the unseen Creator who had heard and answered his prayer, and delivered him from those who had sought his life.

Once on his feet again, he studied the darkened landscape. He wasn't sure if he was seeing, faraway to his right, some fires in the settlement he had visited earlier, or whether his eyes were playing tricks on him. Whatever the truth, Shem knew that he had no real option other than to wait for dawn in order to find his way back to the family tents. His thoughts lingered there. *His mother and father would have become anxious when he didn't return before sunset from the errand.* He limped back to the tree and sat down with his back against it. He pulled his outer woollen cloak around him against the chill of the night. His recent terror had driven all tiredness from him, and his mind returned to the events of the day…

Shem studied the animal that his younger brother, Ham, was leading. He muttered under his breath as they walked along.

'What?' said Ham, turning towards him.

'Your donkey—it's hobbling.'

Ham looked back over his shoulder for several paces—and then groaned. They both stopped, and with them, their donkeys. 'What shall we do?'

Shem thought for a few moments. 'It will go ill for the donkey if we push it too far, and we're only halfway to the town. You will have to return with it.'

'Why should I be the one to go back?' protested Ham. They had both been eager to make the trip to the town to trade barley from their recent harvest for olive oil. Their small family encampment felt too quiet at times.

Shem gave his brother a withering look. 'Because you're younger than me and *I'm* the one Father entrusted with the bartering.' Ham started sulking. 'It is better that one of us goes on than neither, and we're halfway there already. *And* we need more oil.' There was a small voice in Shem's head cautioning him that his father would not want him to go alone. But he told himself that all would be well. Like Ham, he was reluctant to forego the visit. He went over to the lame animal. 'Here, help me move one of these sacks onto my donkey.'

His brother grudgingly gave in. 'Well don't stay too long,' he grumbled, unknotting a rope. 'Remember what Father said.'

Soon the brothers and their donkeys were walking in opposite directions. Shem was grateful for the thin woollen covering over his head as noon came and went. There was little shade on the tracks leading towards the town of mudbrick houses, which lay to the south-west of their camp. When the settlement, surrounded by scattered tents, finally came into sight in the distance, Shem pulled on the rope harder, urging the donkey on and quickening his pace.

He was soon among the houses and found a stall set up in one of the town's narrow streets, with various sizes of stoppered jars set out upon it. 'You have oil?' began Shem.

A swarthy man broke off from a conversation with two others. He looked Shem up and down in a manner that left him feeling uncomfortable, and then nodded.

'Can I try it?' continued Shem, trying to sound confident.

The man, still not speaking, took a stopper out of a jar and poured a little out into a cup. He set the cup down and pushed it towards Shem. He tested the oil as his father had instructed him, and then, after showing his barley, the bartering began over the size and number of jars the grain was worth. When both were finally satisfied—though neither showing it—Shem began unloading the sacks. He turned to see the man bringing out some different jars. Shem fixed him with his gaze and pointed to the original jars. 'Those are the ones I'm taking.' He was thankful that a beating heart remained unseen, but wished that Ham were there.

The man held his eyes and shrugged. 'It is the same oil.'

'Then it is the same if I take the first ones.' It was only when he was leading the donkey away, the jars tied firmly to its back, that he allowed himself to breathe freely once more.

But then, having carried out the job his father had entrusted to him, he tarried. *After all, it was one of the summer months, and nightfall would be slower in coming.* He wandered around the small town, seeing what other goods were being offered: pottery of all shapes and sizes, flint and bronze tools for working the ground and working wood, woollen cloaks and waterskins. But there was more that a man could buy. Veiled women stood on corners, sometimes accompanied by boys, or by girls who were yet to reach their womanhood. More than once he saw men taking their pick, and then following the object of their desire from the bright sunlight into the dark beyond the doors of small houses.

As he lingered by a stall selling dates, a commotion suddenly erupted nearby. Shem swung round—and immediately hauled madly on the donkey's rope. Had he been a moment or two later, two men brawling and cursing each other loudly would have careered into the creature and its load. As it was, they crashed into the stall, sending it and the baskets of dates flying. And judging by the smell, Shem guessed the fight was fuelled by an excess of beer.

The irate voice of the trader rose above the turmoil. 'You idiot! May the gods rain down disaster upon you!' When Shem turned, he saw the curse was directed against him. *He was being blamed for the men colliding with the stall!* He hurried off without looking back, with more curses assaulting his ears. By the time he had turned into another narrow street, the sound of the fight had all but faded. Although he had intended to set off home, he soon came upon a pair of elderly men playing some sort of game on an engraved wooden board with small, smooth stones. He stopped to watch.

Two grey-haired heads turned towards him. 'What are you staring at?' spat out one of the men, inspecting him with disdain.

'I was interested in your game,' replied Shem, hastily adding, 'my lords.' *There was no harm in honouring them with a title they almost certainly didn't deserve.* They both stared at him, and then—without a further word—returned to their contest. But just when Shem thought he might finally have some vague idea about how the game was played, it degenerated into a dispute.

'You are a cheat!'

'And you are blind!'

The insults flew back and forth, becoming increasingly vulgar, until one player tipped up the board and hobbled away, muttering curses. He gave a backward glance, heavy with contempt. Shem bent down and helped pick up the small stones, but despite his polite request for the rules of the game—should he wish to teach it to his brothers—the other player just dismissed him rudely.

His stomach suddenly rumbled and he looked up at the sky once more. He realised with a jolt that he'd left his departure dangerously late, with the sun already out of sight behind the houses. But before he'd even left the town, one of the ropes holding the jars of oil to the side of the donkey became loose. More than once the jars slipped down again just when he'd thought he'd secured them. He finally left the settlement and set off to the north-east, acutely aware that the many locals and travellers who had earlier been scattered around the outside of the town had all but disappeared.

He'd only gone a comparatively short distance when a quick look over his shoulder told him that he was no longer alone—and that he was in trouble. In the rapidly fading light he could see a small group of men who appeared to be armed with clubs and staves. His heart quickened and he began hurrying, urging the donkey into a trot. A second glance behind. They were now running towards him. *They were after him!* The speed of the animal was no match for their pace. His only hope of escaping with his life was to abandon his donkey and the oil and flee. He let go of the rope and bolted, hitching up his tunic so that he could lengthen his stride. He desperately hoped that the donkey and its wares would be a sufficient prize. When he stole another brief look, terror filled him, as if an icy river had suddenly coursed through his body. The animal and the oil had been left in the safe-keeping of one of the gang whilst the others continued the pursuit.

Shem wasn't sure how long or how far he'd run, but when he finally had to pause for breath in the deepening twilight, he ducked behind a tree and listened. He couldn't hear the sounds of a chase. He dropped onto his haunches and warily peered around the tree. He could just make out the men, standing far enough away to ease his terror slightly but not enough to make him feel safe. Any momentary relief, however, dissipated when he realised that the pause was not because they'd abandoned their hunt. What he guessed to be the repeated crack of flint upon iron was followed by a sudden burst of flame as one torch and then another was lit. When a cry of *Let's get him!* followed, Shem didn't wait to find out if they were coming in his direction. He only stopped running when his foot finally encountered the hidden tree root and he was flung, face-first, into the grass.

The memory of how close he had come to disaster sent both a shiver of fear and a fresh sense of gratitude through him, and he mouthed another silent but heart-felt prayer of thanks. As the sliver of young moon disappeared completely, the hunger that had been banished by his terror returned with a vengeance, and his growling belly only served as a reminder of how ravenous he was. And with that, his thoughts returned to the family tent. *Had his parents and brothers eaten that evening, or had fear for his safety taken their appetites?* Somehow he couldn't imagine either Japheth or Ham foregoing their evening meal, even if they *were* concerned about him. That would not be true of his mother, Naamah. *She would be sick with worry.* A wave of guilt washed over him.

He eventually nodded off, but not before a final thought drifted through his mind: *Stupid!*

Shem awoke as the first grey light of dawn was streaked across the far horizon. The short night had been punctuated by fitful sleep, troubled by at least one dream of being chased whilst weighed down by sacks of grain. He rose to his feet and rubbed his limbs. They were stiff and aching from the cold and discomfort of a night spent outside, sitting against a tree. He shivered. Although he was eager to get moving and for the warmth it would bring, he had to content himself with once again wrapping his cloak more tightly around him as he waited for the light to strengthen and—hopefully—reveal to him the direction in which home lay. Faint pinks and oranges began to creep into the early morning sky. Some distance away, he spotted a familiar hill. Running for his life had clearly taken him further than he'd imagined and he was not as far from home as he'd feared. He began walking as quickly as his painful ankle would allow him.

He hadn't taken many paces, however, before he came across several large birds feeding—scavengers tearing flesh from carrion. They only lifted their heads when he was almost upon them, reluctant to abandon their prize. *Maybe a rabbit or a deer.* As the birds rose from the carcass into the air, Shem froze, his mouth suddenly dry. The part-eaten corpse of a naked man lay there prone, not a single item of clothing either on it or nearby. The head, hands and feet had been hacked off, and were nowhere to be seen. Putrefaction had not yet set in on the small amount of flesh that was still intact. *The kill was a recent one.* Shem's stomach rolled and he bent over and retched, though his empty belly had nothing to offer up. *That could have been him!* When he straightened up, still heaving, he glanced around nervously, though he guessed the culprits were long gone. He turned his head towards the corpse, but could not bring himself to look upon it again. *The ground was dry and hard and there was no way to bury it. He would have to leave it for the vultures.* Shem hastened his uneven strides, tracing out an arc around the body before continuing in his previous direction. As he hurried on, he did his best to purge his thoughts of the horror he had stumbled upon.

Unknown paths soon became recognisable ones, and before the sun had risen too far above distant mountains, Shem finally spotted the familiar dark outline of their tents—and, with it, the even more familiar outline of his father. Not that Noah was either standing or moving. He held himself erect, despite his kneeling position, his head tilted upwards and his arms held out in front of him. And Shem knew his father was praying for him.

As he continued walking unevenly, his eyes remained fixed on the man who had given him life. And he was absolutely sure of one thing: *the only reason he, Japheth or Ham were different from those in the town was because of their father. It was he alone who had taught them the ways of Yahweh and shown them how to live.*

'Father!' shouted Shem when he judged himself within earshot. For a moment, he thought he hadn't been heard. But when Noah dropped his hands and turned his head, Shem guessed that a prayer of thanksgiving had been offered up as his father's first response. Noah rose to his feet and approached the tent. *Presumably passing on the news of his return to his mother.* She emerged moments later, wiping tears from her cheeks. The cost of his folly—beyond the loss of the donkey and oil—suddenly jolted him, and he couldn't meet his father's eyes as he came to embrace him. 'I'm sorry, Father,' he began. 'The donkey—'

'—the donkey can be replaced,' interrupted Noah. 'You can't.' And Shem knew that he was forgiven.

The small family of six were soon gathered by the freshly kindled fire. As Japheth's wife, Arisisah, kneaded dough for the first bread of the day, Shem recounted to them all that had happened the previous evening. The story was told between mouthfuls of lentil stew. Shem was more than happy to eat it cold rather than wait for it to be warmed.

Ham's eyes widened as they listened to his story of escape. 'What would the men have done to you?' he asked.

Shem hesitated. *Was his brother so ignorant of the nature of the world in which they lived?* The details of the corpse were best left unspoken—and forgotten.

His father intervened. 'That is not a question to be either asked or answered,' he said sternly, leaving his youngest son in a chastened silence. 'Yahweh delivered your brother from those who intended evil, and that is all that we need to know.'

'It is not safe to live so close to that place!' exclaimed Naamah suddenly to her husband.

'It is the same everywhere,' replied Noah gravely. 'Nowhere is safe. The earth is full of violence every way you turn. Greed and deceit, raiding and murder.' He shook his head, and then spoke forcefully. 'Men have forgotten the Creator who gave them breath. And they forget that He can just as easily take that breath away! They think He doesn't see their deeds or care about what they do. But they are wrong!'

It wasn't the first time that Shem had heard his father say such things. His own gradual entry into manhood had enabled him to see the world through more enlightened eyes, and he knew his father's words to be true. He sometimes wondered if his father was alone upon the earth in truly knowing the God of their fathers, as there seemed precious little evidence of it elsewhere.

'But let us speak no further of these things this day.' His father's words brought Shem back to the present. 'As I spoke with Yahweh about you, my son,' he continued, turning to face him, 'and was assured that He would return you to us safely, I also became certain that now is the time for me to provide you with a wife.' Shem stopped chewing the mouthful of stew, and stared at his father, dumbfounded. Noah then added, 'And I know where I will find the right choice for you.'

It took a few moments for Shem to swallow the spiced lentils that his mother had cooked the previous evening. When his mouth was finally empty, his stunned words were few. 'Now? Where?'

The journey some days later to Noah's father, Lamech, took Shem and Noah three days. The care of the fields, the sheep and the goats were left to Japheth and Ham. In addition to the donkeys on which they rode, there were three others carrying gifts for Lamech and for the family of Shem's future wife—whoever they might be. On the second day of their journey, Shem finally told his father of a detail of his recent story that he'd kept close to his heart and unsaid. 'I didn't only pray to Yahweh for deliverance when I was being chased that night,' he began, his eyes fixed ahead of him.

'No?' replied Noah, inviting him to continue.

'I vowed that if He rescued me, then I would serve Him as my only God all my days—as you have done.'

'And did you mean it, my son?'

'I did.' Shem finally turned towards him. 'And I do.'

His father's face was radiant with pride and joy. 'Then Yahweh shall also be known from now on as *the God of Shem.*'

Whilst Noah had chosen a life far removed from the corruption of the dwellings of men, his father and siblings had not. They had remained close to a large settlement on a tributary to the east of the River Tigris, pitching their tents within sight of its stone walls. As they neared their destination, Shem stared at the city, which had been known to his father in his youth. 'What's it like?'

Noah turned his head slightly towards his son. 'Crowded.' He then added after a pause, 'And not a place I would want any of my family to be.'

'How many live there?'

'Who knows? Several hundred—maybe more.' As the donkeys walked steadily forward, Noah continued: 'What else can I say? There are brick houses, filthy streets and small market places, storehouses for grain, a temple—'

'They worship Yahweh?' interrupted Shem, but his father shook his head.

'They worship many things, but the true Creator is not among them.'

'Do they not know of Him?'

'They do not wish to hear of Him,' said Noah grimly. 'I know that much from when I lived here. They would rather follow gods of their own design who demand little of them and leave them to do as they wish. And so they bring violence and corruption to the ordered and good world that Yahweh created.'

'But what of your father's family?' asked Shem, somewhat bemused. 'Surely *they* follow Yahweh?'

'My father does—and my grandfather. But beyond that...' Noah looked steadfastly ahead. He finally added, 'Only the Almighty truly knows the answer to that question.' Whether deliberate or not, any further discussion was curtailed by Noah pointing to a particular cluster of tents. 'Over there.' And Shem's heart gladdened at the prospect of a proper meal and a softer, warmer bed that night.

As they neared the small camp, his father hailed those outside. Men, women and children hurriedly approached them or emerged from tents. Shem recognised some but by no means all. And foremost among them was Noah's elderly father, Lamech. After the customary greetings and introductions, they were soon sitting on rugs in the front, communal area of Lamech's tent, with bowls of hot food and platters of fresh bread before them. Various uncles and cousins of Shem sat with them, not to mention his ancient great-grandfather, Methuselah.

When news had been exchanged—not all of it good— and the bowls of food emptied, Lamech finally turned to Noah and asked, 'So, my son, what brings you back to us?' He paused and turned pointedly towards Shem. 'Or does the presence of my grandson tell me all that I need to know?'

And Shem felt himself redden as every eye fell upon him.

For the rest of the evening, Shem sat and listened in silence as his older male relatives discussed his future wife, and the suitability—or otherwise—of the possible girls within the wider family. Their opinions both fascinated and terrified him.

'She certainly has the look of her mother!' *Was that good or bad?*

'Her meals are like no others.' *What was that supposed to mean?*

'It was a shame about the oxen.' The others all nodded sagely. 'But it should not stop her marrying.' Shem didn't even want to think about it.

He did notice during the evening, however, that his father's questions had little to do with a girl's appearance or abilities. Her virtues and worship seemed of far more interest to him.

After the mention of too many names for him to remember, one name started to be spoken more than any other. And when one of his cousins finally ran off to find and summon the mysterious Salit, Shem once again prayed a silent prayer to the God who had so recently delivered him: 'Please don't let her be ugly.'

When Shem and Noah departed seven days later to begin the journey home, all their spare donkeys were devoid of the gifts they had previously carried. Two were now loaded with the materials for a new tent, and the third bore a new burden in the form of Salit, Shem's wife of three days. Shem had been relieved to find that the men had chosen well—and that his prayer to the Almighty (however unworthy) had been answered. Her dark eyes and abundance of raven-coloured hair met with his approval. After he had presented her with embroidered garments and gold jewellery, including several bracelets which he had placed upon her wrists, a simple covenant had sealed the marriage. A covenant *and* their first somewhat awkward night together.

It was near noon of the third day when their own tiny settlement finally came into view once more. The sides of the tents had been hitched up so that air could move freely though them, dissipating their otherwise stifling heat under the summer sun. Even though they were still some distance away, Shem recognised the familiar sight of his mother kneeling on the ground, performing the daily task he had seen a thousand times or more: grinding grain for bread by rolling a handstone backwards and forwards over a handful of grain placed on the curved surface of the oblong quern-stone. She must have seen them out of the corner of her eye, for she suddenly rose to her feet and came out to meet the newest member of the family.

As Shem and Salit left Noah's tent after a long and lingering meal that evening, to return to their own newly-pitched tent that stood nearby, Shem said quietly, 'You go ahead. I'll follow shortly.' Despite the desire that rose within him, there was something about the coolness of the night that made him pause, particularly after the stuffiness of sitting inside. His gaze lingered on his new wife as she disappeared into the darkness of their tent with the small clay lamp she was carrying. He watched as the light inside strengthened slightly, as other lamps were lit from the one in her hand. Shem finally tore his eyes away from the place where they would lie together that night, and turned them upwards to the expanse of the star-filled sky.

The moon that had begun to wane when he and his father had departed on their quest had disappeared completely the night before, but now had waxed to a thin crescent that was about to set. Shem suddenly recalled the night a month earlier when he had last seen the moon that thin, and he shivered slightly with a coldness that had nothing to do with the night air. The joy of the recent days had, for a while, overtaken the memory of his near disaster—and what he had seen.

As he looked up at the vastness, he felt very small. He pondered his father's belief, that Yahweh saw not only every deed done but every thought of the heart—and that it all mattered to Him. *What was it that his father had said?* *'Men have forgotten the Creator who gave them breath, and they* forget that He can just as easily take that breath away.' That was it! And Shem stared up at the stars in silence, wondering about the Creator whose power had placed each of those stars in the heavens—and whether they would see such power at work again.

They would.

Notes

1. There is no indication within Scripture of where Noah lived before the flood. It has been assumed that it was around Mesopotamia. A location to the east of the River Tigris has been chosen, and this becomes significant later in the story.

2. Even before the Iron Age, there was some use of iron obtained from meteorites. Hence the reference in this chapter to its use in fire-lighting.

3. Genesis 10:21 can mean that either Shem's older brother was Japheth or Shem was the older brother of Japheth. The former meaning has been chosen. Genesis 9:24 states that Ham was the youngest son, despite the sons being listed as 'Shem, Ham and Japheth'. It has been suggested that this order may be more to do with the priority of Shem or the rhythm of the words. Another possible pointer to Shem not being the firstborn is that Genesis 5:32 breaks the pattern of the genealogy that it ends, listing Noah's three sons rather than just the firstborn as happens with all those previously listed. That Shem is born second may also be implied by the fact that Noah became a father at 500, but Shem was 100 years old two years after the flood (Genesis 11:10), when Noah would have been around 603. It is also common in Scripture for God to choose to work through a younger son rather than the firstborn.

4. *Whilst Exodus 6:3 is often translated in such a way as to imply that it was only from the time of Moses that their God was known by the name of Yahweh (rendered as 'the LORD' in modern Bibles), the verse can also be translated as a question in the negative, to be read, 'I appeared to Abraham, to Isaac and to Jacob as God Almighty, and by my name the LORD did I not let myself be known to them?' Given the fact that the name 'Yahweh' is frequently on the lips of many in the book of Genesis, including Noah (see 9:6), it has been assumed that the patriarchs knew God by this name, and that the verse in Exodus should be rendered in the alternative translation.*

5. *Although the names of the four wives on the ark are not mentioned in Scripture, the ones used in this account have been drawn from early Jewish and Christian writings (among which, however, there is no particular consensus as to what those names were).*

6. *It is clear that Noah had brothers and sisters (Genesis 5:30). Nothing is said of them (or of their faith), however, at the time of the flood. The implication of Genesis 6:9 is that Noah alone found favour with God, although Lamech does speak of Yahweh (5:29).*

7. *The saddle quern was a very early form of stone for grinding grain. The upper, cylindrical handstone is rolled over the grain which sits on the lower stone, the quern—an oblong stone which is curved like a saddle.*

2

God said to Noah, 'I am going to put an end to all people,
for the earth is filled with violence because of them.'
(Genesis 6:13)

'A WHAT?' exclaimed Shem, unsure whether he'd heard his father correctly. Each person seated around the evening meal had suddenly ceased eating, even if they were mid-mouthful. Any hand reaching towards the bowls of food had suddenly frozen in mid-air. And every eye was fastened upon Noah.

'An ark,' replied Noah calmly, as if there were nothing unusual in what he was saying. 'Yahweh has told me that I have to build an ark—a boat. And He has told me its size. It must be three hundred cubits long, fifty cubits wide and thirty cubits high.'

Shem stared at his father in stunned silence—as did his brothers and all the wives, who now numbered four. The size was beyond anything he could conceive, its height alone as tall as a tree. Shem finally opened his mouth to voice the question that was demanding to be asked, but Japheth was quicker.

'Why?'

Noah sighed deeply. Shem had never before seen his face so grave or his eyes so full of sadness. 'The Almighty is going to bring an end to all the violence and evil done by man,' he explained. 'He is going to bring a flood on the earth and destroy all life. Everyone will die. But we are to be spared—the eight of us. And we are to take two of all living creatures—a male and female—so that life may continue after the flood.' His answer only deepened their shock, and when none of them spoke, Noah continued. 'The ark is to be made of gopher wood and is to have three decks. We are to make rooms and a door in it, and cover it with pitch.' But neither Shem nor anyone else was paying attention to the details.

'Everyone?' echoed Naamah quietly. Shem wondered if she was thinking of her father's family.

Noah nodded. 'All life belongs to Him. It is His to give, and His to take away. But do not think that He brings this judgment lightly or because He is cruel. He is grieved by—'

'Grieved?' interrupted Japheth, clearly astounded. 'You mean Yahweh feels pain?'

Noah did not speak for a moment, regarding his firstborn steadily. 'How could the Creator *not* care about His creation? If we can be pained by the world around us, how much more the One in whose image we are made. Yes, he is grieved, Japheth. He is grieved by the continual wickedness of men. Their hearts only ever incline towards one path.' His eyes swept across the gathering. 'Each one of you has seen it with your own eyes—the bloodshed and depravity, the deceit and evil—and you know just how close it has come to us in the past.'

Noah turned his head towards his second son, and Shem suddenly remembered the feeling of terror that had gripped him that night some six years earlier. He had encountered the depths of evil first-hand, and never wanted to do so again.

Noah went on, 'It is the Lord's will that the world *He* created should continue—but *not* the world of violence that men and women have made, where nothing now is as it should be.'

The enormity of what his father was saying was almost more than Shem could take in, and—apart from his father—each person seemed to have been, like him, struck dumb.

'The Lord God did not intend death for us,' continued Noah, 'but our father Adam's disobedience brought it upon him and all his descendants, down to this day. Yet we continue to defy our Creator. He has therefore already spoken of how the lifespan of men will now be limited to a hundred and twenty years, so that the likes of my years may not be seen again. But now the Lord God will destroy those who have destroyed his earth, and there will be a new beginning.'

A few more heartbeats of silence followed. Then everyone was talking at once, asking the many questions suddenly forming in their minds. 'Can we build such a boat by ourselves, Father?' asked Shem, even as his two brothers were asking about where they would find enough wood and pitch for something so huge. The women meanwhile were voicing questions about the supplies that would be needed and how the animals would be assembled—and whether the Lord truly intended snakes and bears to be aboard the ark. More and more questions tumbled into Shem's mind and out onto his lips, until his father eventually held up his hand to bring order back to their meal, though all food had been forgotten.

When silence had been restored, Noah lowered his hand and spoke: 'The Lord has not told us everything we will need to know. But He will guide us. And,' said Noah pointedly, 'he has given us minds.' And for the first time since informing them of the impending judgment, there was a hint of a smile on Noah's face. 'And that means…?' he said, directing his gaze to his youngest son.

'That he intends us to use them,' replied Ham. Shem smiled to himself at the reply that Noah had instilled in each of them from the time they had started seeking him for answers, when their legs had been much shorter and their questions incessant at times. Not that Ham was a child any more. He had been married the previous year to Nahlat, who had been chosen from among their numerous cousins, as had his own wife.

'And with our minds enlightened by Yahweh's help, we will find all the answers to the questions that need to be addressed, so that we can do exactly what Yahweh asks of us,' responded Noah. 'And we must content ourselves with that knowledge tonight.'

But there was still one question burning in Shem's mind that could not wait. 'But Father,' he began, '*when* will this happen? When will Yahweh flood the earth?'

And once again, Noah's mood seemed to lighten. 'Presumably not until we've finished.'

Shem lay awake that night and, despite his best efforts, sleep persistently evaded him, like an errant but nimble goat refusing to be caught. His mind was too full of unanswered questions. He tried to lie as still as he could, so as not to disturb Salit.

But his mind was clearly not the only one troubled. A soft voice broke the silence. 'Are you awake, Shem?'

He turned towards the voice. 'You can't sleep either?'

'No,' she answered quietly, adding after a pause, 'I'm scared.'

Shem reached out in the darkness until he could feel her warm, smooth body, and he slid himself closer to her, wrapping his arm over her and pulling her close, until he could feel the beat of her heart against his chest.

For some time they lay quietly together. Then Salit suddenly spoke again. 'Noah tells us what God says. But how does your father hear Him? How do you know that he hears His words truly?'

Shem didn't reply immediately. He thought back to a time when he had asked his father a very similar question—and to the answer that had been given. 'He says that when Adam first walked in the garden in Eden, he and Eve could speak with Yahweh face to face, because He walked with them in the cool of the day.'

'They saw God as well as hearing his voice?'

Shem nodded, despite Salit not being able to see him in the dark. 'Yes, but Father says it is different for him. He says it is like hearing the wind. You hear the noise that it makes, whether that is the whisper of a breeze as it moves through the leaves of a tree, or the howling of a gale as it sweeps over the plain. In both cases you do not see the wind itself, yet its sound is unmistakeable. He says that for him, the same is true when he hears the voice of Yahweh.' Shem paused, but when Salit remained silent he added. 'Maybe it is like you hearing my voice now, even though you do not see me…'

'But I can feel you,' replied Salit's gentle voice, and Shem then felt her laying her face on his chest as she drew in a deep breath. 'And I can smell your scent.' He stroked her hair as she remained there, but then felt her lift her face: 'Have *you* ever heard the voice of Yahweh?'

Shem shook his head, 'No—but I have vowed that I will serve Him all my days, and one day I hope to hear Him speak as my father has done.'

'But you *do* trust that your father speaks truly the word of God?'

Shem thought for a moment. 'Did anyone ever tell you the story of Enoch?' He felt her shaking the head that was now resting upon his chest again.

'Who's Enoch?'

Shem wondered— at that moment—how many of his father's brothers and sisters did indeed worship the Creator, if they seemed to care so little about the one life that had been truly pleasing to Him. 'Enoch was my father's great-grandfather,' explained Shem. 'Methuselah's father. But Enoch only lived on earth for three hundred and sixty-five years.'

'Why did he die after so few years, if he was pleasing to God?' asked Salit. 'Methuselah is over nine hundred and sixty—and still lives!'

'But Enoch *didn't* die!'

'What do you mean?'

'My father tells me that he walked with God—as our father Adam did before he sinned—and that Enoch's life was so blameless that Yahweh took him to Himself. Wherever Yahweh is, Enoch now walks with him there.'

There was a pause, and then Salit asked, 'So why do you tell me of Enoch?'

'Because I believe my father walks with God in the same way Enoch did. Do you know any man alive who lives such a blameless life?'

There was another pause: 'Not you, for certain!'

Shem could feel his wife gently shaking with laughter and he allowed himself to smile.

When Salit was still again, she added, 'You are right, Shem. I know of no man who knows Yahweh as Noah does or lives as he does.'

'And that is why I trust that he hears the word of God truly,' said Shem softly.

And with her head still on his chest, Salit whispered, 'Then I will trust him too.'

Notes

1. *Although some have taken the flood narrative as myth, the Scriptures in general and Jesus in particular treat Noah and his family as actual people. It is also noteworthy that there are flood narratives in other ancient cultures, possibly pointing to a shared memory of an event from a time pre-dating written records.*

2. *The genealogy in Genesis 11, if taken as complete, would date the flood to only 300 years before Abraham (maybe around 2500 BC). Many, however, believe that Biblical genealogies may not always be complete records. However, given the earlier, pre-flood reference in Genesis 4:22 to bronze, it has been assumed here that it occurred at some point in the Early Bronze Age (3300-2100BC).*

3. *Scripture does not normally indicate exactly how prophets and others heard God's voice. It does, however, show that there were occasions where God appeared in a human form and spoke (e.g. Genesis 18:1, 2, 22). It also seems that at other times no visible form was seen despite an audible voice being heard (e.g. 1 Samuel 3:1-10).*

4. *Nick Hiscocks helpfully comments, 'The doctrine of total depravity is based on verses like Genesis 6:5. We are not as bad as we could possibly be in every area. But we are not as good as we should be in any area.' (Explore Bible-reading notes)*

5. *The longevity recorded in the early chapters of Genesis has always raised questions, but it does find parallels in other ancient Near Eastern accounts. Whether these ages are symbolic or more literal is still debated. It has been suggested that the ancients possibly aged more slowly, possibly as a result of being closer to Eden and therefore less affected by the cumulative effects of sin. It should be noted, however, that post-flood the ages recorded in Genesis decrease fairly steadily (if not entirely smoothly), until—at the end of the book— Jacob says to Pharaoh, 'The years of my pilgrimage are a hundred and thirty. My years have been few and difficult, and they do not equal the years of the pilgrimage of my fathers' (Genesis 47:9). Genesis ends with Jacob's son Joseph dying at the age of 110. After those living at the time of Genesis (and excluding Job, the dating of which may also be very early), only five people are recorded as living longer than a hundred years: Miriam (125+), Aaron (123), Moses (120), Joshua (110) and Jehoiada (130 – 2 Chron 24:15)—a possible fulfilment of Genesis 6:3 ('their days will be a hundred and twenty years'). As it is difficult to resolve whether these ages are purely figurative or not, they have been left unchanged with an assumption of a slower rate of ageing. Of the three people currently recorded as having lived longest in the modern era, the oldest is 122, followed by 119 and then 117.*

6. *A cubit is approximately 0.5 metres.*

3

Noah did everything just as God commanded him.
(Genesis 6:22)

'In a few days,' began Noah, 'we will be moving from here to pitch our tents near those of my father, Lamech.' He was standing with Shem and his brothers in the middle of their small camp.

'Why there?' asked Ham.

'Look around you, dear brother,' replied Japheth, a slight mocking tone in his voice. 'How many trees do you see?'

'I know we need wood!' said Ham defensively, scowling at his eldest brother. 'But why *there* in particular?'

'The mountains and the forests that cover them,' said Noah, 'come near to the river there. But the city will also be close at hand, and we can barter for tools and stores when we need them. Whilst we cut wood and build, the women will take care of the herds and plant crops—there is good ground there where they can do both. We will also be able to gather reeds from the river to caulk the ark, and nearby there are also pools of pitch where it oozes from the ground.'

Japheth turned to Ham. 'Satisfied, little brother?' he taunted. Moments later the two of them were locked in a bout of wrestling, as Ham attempted to bring his brother to the ground.

'I'd save your strength, if I were you,' called out Shem in amusement. 'You're going to need it!'

'Leave them be,' said Noah. 'There will be precious little time for sport when we start.'

As Shem and his father stood watching the struggling of the two evenly-matched young men—both of them, like Shem, closer to a hundred than fifty—yet another question formed in Shem's mind. 'What of your father's family? Will they help us?'

Noah was silent for a moment, and then said quietly, 'I don't know. My father or grandfather would, of that I'm sure. But neither of them is of an age now where that is possible. But my brothers...' Noah's voice trailed off. He sighed before continuing. 'If they are not willing, then maybe the ark itself will be a warning to them—and to those in the city. They will ask why we are building it, and we will tell them and speak of the righteousness of God. And who knows? Maybe they will heed our words and turn from their wickedness and the Lord may yet be merciful...' As his words trailed off again, Shem turned to look at his father. His eyes seemed to be set on some far horizon, but he spoke no more. The silence that followed was broken several moments later by Japheth's triumphant cry, as Ham found himself yet again flat on his back in the dust.

The journey north-west was a slow one. The extensive herds of sheep and goats were not easily or quickly moved. The progress of the donkeys was also slow but steady. Each was loaded with grain, rugs, clay jars or pots, or was pulling one of the small carts carrying the four tents and their poles. Their new camp, when it was

31

finally in place, lay—out of necessity—closer to the forest than to the city on the banks of the river, but not far from either. As the rest of the family continued ordering their new communal life, Shem wandered over to a sheep that had somehow managed to get its wool thoroughly caught in a nearby thorn bush. He crouched down beside the distressed animal, and began the awkward task of trying to free it whilst it continued thrashing about. 'How can such a small creature get itself into so much trouble in such a short time?' he muttered to himself, as the animal finally calmed down enough for him to effect its release.

'The same could be said of mankind,' said a familiar voice. Shem straightened up and stood next to his father as they both watched the sheep scampering off to rejoin the rest of the herd. Noah sighed, shaking his head. 'O that the trouble that we have created could be untangled so easily.' He then looked around. 'But this is the right place for us to begin.'

They stood for a while, gazing eastwards towards the forest, and shading their eyes against the sun that had not yet risen to its zenith. Tall, majestic trees ran north-west to south-east for as far as Shem could see, rising with the mountains beneath and behind them. He knew that it was from these trees that the wooden beams needed for their task would come.

'Enough wood for you?' said Shem lightly.

Noah chuckled. It was the first laughter of any kind that Shem had heard from his father in many days, particularly since discovering on their arrival that Lamech had died the previous month although Methuselah still lived. 'You will be sick of the sight of trees by the time we have finished,' said Noah. 'And not only that. Your hands will be blistered, your arms and back will ache, and you will have suffered more splinters than you care to number. And I do not doubt that more than once you will wonder if what Yahweh asks of us can indeed be done.'

'And can it?' asked Shem, turning from the trees nearby to his father.

'He would not ask it of us if it couldn't.' Noah continued to look steadily at the forest and the tall, upright trees, and for a few moments his brow was furrowed as if contemplating some difficult question. 'How many trunks will be needed, do you think, to run the length of the ark?'

Shem stood squinting up at the trees for a moment, trying to guess their height. 'Three...four, or maybe even five?'

Noah chuckled again: 'We'll find out soon enough. We will choose our level ground tomorrow, and mark out three hundred cubits in one direction and fifty in the other. And then we will fell our first tree and find the answer to our question.'

'And today?' asked Shem.

'Today we will barter for axes!'

Shem stood staring at the shape they had measured out on the ground and marked with wooden pegs and cord. Its length was greater than any structure he had seen other than a city wall, and he was certain that no boat on earth had ever measured more than a tiny part of it. The first tree that they felled took longer than Shem had imagined it would, largely because of their inexperience with the bronze axes.

'Swing it like that, and you are likely to kill yourself— or more likely, someone else!' shouted out Irad, one of

Noah's brothers who had agreed to share with them his skills in working wood.

Shem grinned as Ham replied in exasperation, 'I'm only trying to do what you told me!'

'More care and a little less frenzy,' shouted back Irad.

Shem leant on the long wooden handle of his axe and watched as his brother slowed his pace and tried to concentrate his blows on the same spot on the trunk of the tree. His gaze drifted onto his uncle and he wondered what was going through his mind. *Probably something between mild amusement and outright incredulity.* It was clear, to Shem at least, that Irad thought they were mad but had decided to humour them, and he suspected that most of the rest of the family also thought they had taken leave of their senses. *Still,* thought Shem as the tree finally began to creak, *better to have their help than not, even if they doubted their reason.*

'Keep back!' warned Irad. Moments later, a loud *crack* split the air and the tree crashed to the ground. The earth beneath Shem's feet shook from the impact.

The lessons that day and in the days that followed included splitting the long trunks (using mallets to drive wooden wedge-shaped pegs in along the length of the wood), shaping the wood using a bronze adze, and lashing beams together closely and tightly. And when they eventually rested on the seventh day, Shem finally had the answer to the question that he and his father had pondered: there were more trunk lengths to three hundred cubits than he'd thought.

His father had been right. Shem unwound the coarse cloth protecting his hands and looked down at his thumb. The skin was red and raw and a fresh blister was forming. He sat down on the log next to Ham in the shade and gratefully accepted the skin of goat's milk that Salit was offering to him. Many months had passed since they had started building in earnest. Although the speed of their progress was increasing as they became more proficient with their tools, they had only recently finished the flat bottom of the boat, complete with its cross-beams, caulking and coating of pitch. They had begun on the sides of the boat, but that was proving to be more difficult, and the advent of the summer heat had also slowed the ark's growth.

Shem gave a sigh of satisfaction after wiping away the drips of the slightly sour milk that were whitening his lips. He handed the skin on to Ham, who began downing the warm drink as if his life depended upon it.

'Leave some for me, you glutton!' exclaimed Japheth in a way that only an older brother could. He dug his elbow into Ham's ribs and then grabbed the skin, leaving a little rivulet of milk running down his brother's beard. The lilting sound of Salit's laughter brought a smile to Shem's face. She handed Ham one of the rounds of fresh bread that she had also brought for them, as they rested for a time while the sun passed its zenith. *She was kinder than them!*

Although Noah was usually with them as they worked, he had taken some of their tools to be sharpened by Irad and his sons, and so Japheth was left in charge—*although that was a debatable term.* Salit sat next to Shem and the four of them stared in silence at the wooden edifice that lay in the sunshine not far from the log on which they sat.

'Is God really going to destroy everyone with a flood?' asked Ham suddenly. 'What if our father's hopes come to pass, and men and women—at least those here—heed the warning and change their ways? Might not God spare them and relent, and not send the flood?'

Shem turned his head towards the city and shrugged. 'Who knows?' For a moment he tried to imagine what it would be like if everything as far as the eye could see were under water. It was not a thought that brought him any joy, despite the evil he had encountered. *God was merciful. Maybe, as Ham was suggesting, there might yet be a staying of God's hand and deliverance from judgment... if men turned from their wickedness.* Shem's eyes returned to the beginnings of the boat nearby. He smiled wryly. 'Whatever happens, we're not going to need any more firewood for the rest of our lives.'

If Shem had held out any hope of a change in those who witnessed their labours, then what actually happened was—if anything—a change for the worse. He returned to the camp one evening with his father and brothers to find Ham's wife, Nahlat, in tears and being comforted by Naamah. Salit and Arisisah stood nearby, clearly concerned. When Nahlat looked up, her face was not only wet with tears. Blood trickled out from a gash on her cheek as she lowered the cloth she had been holding against it.

'What happened?' asked Noah gravely.

'Nahlat and I had gone to the river to wash clothes,' Salit began. 'There were other women from the city there. They started jeering at us, accusing us of behaving as if we were better than them. They shouted, *Do you really think the gods favour only you?* Then they told us we weren't welcome. We remained silent, but then they began throwing stones at us. Some hit us, and as we were quickly gathering up our washing to leave, a sharp flint struck Nahlat's face. And even when we were hurrying away, they kept hurling abuse and stones at us.'

Shem felt anger rising within him as he heard Salit's voice begin to waver. There was thunder on Ham's face and his hand went to the axe tucked in his belt.

Noah laid his hand over his son's. 'We will not meet violence or scorn with our own. We will entrust ourselves to Yahweh. He has promised that each of us will enter safely into the ark. But we will also conduct ourselves carefully and wisely, and if that means doing washing elsewhere, then so be it.'

But it was not only the women who met with derision. As well as the brawling, drunkenness and depravity that Shem was used to encountering in the city, he began to see something new. Many stared or pointed as he and his brothers walked by. Insults were sometimes whispered but often flung at them. *Deranged as fevered dogs. Bloodsucking leeches. Impotent issue of a crazed old man.* He had heard them all—and worse. For the safety of the women in particular, the camp was moved right next to the boat, so that the wives were never alone when the men were working.

Bringing the camp closer also brought new challenges. 'Oi!' Ham's voice rang out across the deck. As Shem turned, he heard the slap of a hand followed immediately by the bleat of a goat. 'Get away you stupid animal!'

'Another one chewing the bark off the wood?' called Shem, amused.

'The stupid creatures will probably still be eating the boat when we're on it! And if this boat sinks—' Ham broke off and pointed at the retreating animal. '—I'm blaming that goat!'

On another occasion, a new piece of wood had just been put in place when Shem turned to find a pair of sheep peering at it, as if they were inspecting his workmanship. 'Good enough for you?' said Shem with a wry smile, before chasing them away.

Sheep and goats were not the only visitors, however. They got used to the sight of men and women from the city standing a safe distance away and watching. Usually they would jeer, but occasionally they just stared in bafflement. But another reaction—or lack of it—also became clear. As Shem walked through the city one day with Japheth, it suddenly struck him. 'They behave as if their lives will go on forever,' said Shem in a low voice. 'Trading, pursuing pleasure, eating and drinking. As if disaster were not dangling over their heads.'

Japheth nodded. 'We build a huge barge on dry land and they carry on regardless.'

They looked around at the familiar sights. Women grinding grain on their quern-stones or holding babies on their hips. Men drinking or playing their gambling games in the streets. And everyone seemingly utterly oblivious of the coming judgment. Only recently, their uncle Irad had told them of one of his daughters being given in marriage to a man in the city. 'They continue marrying and having children,' muttered Shem, 'and all the while they see us not as a warning but as amusement.' And as if to prove his point, three elderly men seated on stools around some form of gaming board suddenly looked up and, seeing Shem and Japheth, shared some whispered comments. Shem bristled as they both walked away with the sound of cackling in their ears.

Months became years, and the ark gained decks, rooms and a door, as well as height. The women began to spend time cutting grass with their sickles, together with any other nearby plants that could be used as fodder. Once dried in the sun, it was bundled up tightly and stacked in what had been set aside as storerooms on board. The women also began stitching together the covering for the ark from goat skins. And eventually there came a day when the last of the pitch had been applied both inside and out. The ark's height finally measured thirty cubits, including the gap left all around the top for air and for light, just below the frame over which the ark's covering had been stretched.

Shem put his arm around Salit, as the eight members of the family stood together in silence and stared up at the huge boat, shining slightly in the evening sun, as the warm orange light fell on the lustrous surface of the dark pitch.

'I have to say,' said Japheth finally, 'it looks like no boat that I have ever seen.'

'It's more like an enormous black chest,' added Arisisah, cocking her head to one side slightly.

But their inspection was interrupted as Ham suddenly whispered, 'Look!' Their attention shifted away from the boat and towards the city. An elderly man, wizened by the passing of innumerable years, was slowly making his way towards them on a donkey.

'Methuselah comes,' said Noah, recognising his grandfather even from a distance. They began making their way towards him.

When they finally met, Methuselah dismounted with the help of Noah, and in a voice cracked by age, said simply, 'So you have done it.' For a long time he didn't speak further, as his watery eyes surveyed the huge craft which, even at some distance, still appeared vast. He finally nodded, as if in approval. 'I'd hoped I would see it finished before my walk on this earth is over—as it will be not many days from now. And Yahweh has allowed it.' With that, Methuselah raised his hand and began to give them his blessing as the patriarch of the family. When he finally lowered his arm, he turned to Noah. 'Now walk with me, son of my son.'

They were soon out of earshot, and the remaining seven turned back to look at the ark. After a few moments, Shem felt a slight nudge at his side, and bent his head downwards to hear Salit's whisper. 'I know there is no way to steer the boat, but...'

Shem caught the strain in his wife's voice as it trailed off. He smiled gently. 'The boat will drift, yes, but it will be guided by the hand of Yahweh. And we shall entrust ourselves to Him.'

And trust was spoken of again as night fell. They were sitting together around the evening meal, with the tent flaps pulled back and the fire burning low outside. The ark loomed large beyond it, like some huge, black shadow. 'We do not know how much longer we have before the flood,' began Noah, 'and we still have work to do. Stocks of grain and oil are needed, and vegetables and fruit must be gathered and dried where possible. All will have to be stored on the boat, and we will barter our herds for all that must be bought. You have seen how the Lord has blessed our flocks since we have been working on the ark in obedience to His command. He has provided us with great wealth in our goats and sheep. Now we will use that wealth to stock the boat. We will need to store as much fodder for the animals as is possible, but we will trust that the Lord will give us the time that we need to complete the task before He brings those animals to us.'

Noah paused and then smiled at them all. 'You know of covenants. Each of you seated here is in a covenant relationship with another. Japheth and Arisisah—you are bound together by a covenant. You have vowed to live faithfully together as husband and wife for all the days that you share on this earth. Shem and Salit, Ham and Nahlat— the same is true of you, as it is of Naamah and me. And Yahweh has graciously promised to establish His covenant with us. We are bound to Him as His people, but He also binds Himself to us as our God. We must continue to walk before Him in trust and obedience. But He will be faithful to us, keeping us safe through the judgment that will soon come. And His blessing will be upon us.'

Something stirred deep within Shem, and before the night was out, he had—once more—knelt silently and alone under the stars, with the vast shape of the ark visible in the moonlight, and committed himself to serve the God of his fathers, *his* God.

Shem never discovered what had passed between his father and Methuselah on the day the ark was finished. But within two months, his great-grandfather's walk on the earth had finally come to an end. And one morning, after a further month had passed, Noah emerged from his tent with Naamah, and called his sons and their wives to him. 'Yahweh has spoken once more…' he began.

Notes

1. *Although the Scriptures speak of 'gopher wood' being used for the ark, the meaning of the Hebrew word is uncertain (some translations use 'cypress' instead), and so we have no definite knowledge of what type of wood this was, let alone the methods or details of the ark's construction. Any descriptions here are based on research into the Bronze Age, the tools that were used then, and modern-day attempts to replicate Bronze Age boat-building. The story here cannot be anything more than educated guess-work.*

2. *There is no indication in the Bible how long it took to make the ark. It seems fair to assume that it would have taken several years at least.*

3. *It has been assumed that the covering of the ark was not made of wood but of animal skins (which would have also been used for tents). Genesis 8:13 speaks of 'removing the covering' of the ark, and it is hard to see how this could have been done if the roof was solid wood and they were still inside.*

4. *Although popular images of the ark are of a conventional, traditional boat-style, with a curved hull and a shaped prow, it is unlikely that Noah and his sons had the capability to build this sort of boat. Also, this type of boat was unnecessary. The ark did not need to be steered in a particular direction. It merely needed to float and be stable in water, and was therefore probably more like a box with a flat bottom. It is note-worthy, however, that the ark's dimensions produced a similar shape to modern super-tankers, with their associated stability. The Gilgamesh Epic, another ancient flood story, had a boat with the dimensions of a cube, which would have been unstable and more easily capsized.*

5. *Although we know that Noah had brothers and sisters (Genesis 5:3), we do not know their names.*

6. *A general location to the east of the Tigris is the setting chosen for this story. In ancient times, pools of pitch are documented in this area. It is also near to the Zagros Mountains, which were at one time covered in forests (before extensive deforestation in the first two millennia BC), and would have therefore been a possible source of wood for the ark.*

7. *Although there is no indication in the flood account in Genesis of those under God's judgment having an opportunity to repent, New Testament texts (1 Peter 3:19,20, 2 Peter 2:5, 3:9) do speak of Christ preaching (most probably of salvation through repentance and faith) through Noah whilst the ark was being built. These texts also refer to God patiently waiting, Noah being a preacher of righteousness, and God not wanting any to perish but all to come to repentance.*

8. *The age of Methuselah given in Scripture (Genesis 5:27) implies that he died in the same year as the flood. Although it is possible that he was killed by the flood, the reference to his death is no different to that of the others in the genealogy, so it has been assumed here that he died shortly before the flood.*

4

*Noah was six hundred years old when the floodwaters
came on the earth. And Noah and his sons and his wife
and his sons' wives entered the ark to escape the waters of
the flood. (Genesis 7:6-7)*

'Seven days?' exclaimed Shem, with a strange mixture
of fear and exhilaration.

Noah nodded, 'That's what the Lord said. That is
when the flood will come. He has told me that it will rain
for forty days and forty nights.'

'Is that how long we are to be on the ark?' interrupted
Ham.

Noah shook his head. 'It will certainly be longer
than that, but exactly how long Yahweh has not told us.
But there is more. There is to be a distinction between
the animals on the ark. We are to take one pair of every
unclean animal, but seven pairs of those that are clean.'

'Will the ark be big enough?' asked Salit anxiously.

'And what about food?' added Naamah.

Noah smiled. 'The Lord Himself knows the number
of animals that will be coming and therefore how much
space they will need. He has not told us how many there
will be, but He has given us the measurements for the ark,
and the number of decks. We can therefore be assured that
it *will* be big enough. As for food, we have worked hard
to collect it, and Yahweh gave us flocks to barter for more.

We will trust, again, that He has given us time and wealth enough to feed all that will come to us—for however long we will all be on the ark.' When silence followed, Noah said, 'Good! Then we go to the ark to make our final preparations.' And with that he disappeared into his tent, followed by Naamah, to ready himself for the tasks ahead.

Shem and his brothers lingered outside with their wives, and all were looking towards the ark. 'So this is it,' said Japheth with an air of gravity.

'But what does Noah mean by clean and unclean?' asked Nahlat, looking to her husband for enlightenment. 'Surely he isn't talking about those that groom themselves and those that wallow in the mud?'

When Ham hesitated, Shem answered instead. 'Clean animals are ones that we may offer to Yahweh in sacrifice—as Adam's second son Abel did, offering the fat of firstborn sheep and goats from his flocks. Unclean animals are those, like pigs, that are unacceptable for such a holy purpose.'

'But,' began Japheth slowly, 'we only know which are clean and which unclean among the animals we know. What if the Lord brings us beasts we have not met before? How are we to know whether they are clean or not?'

The three couples stood in silence for a moment, and then Ham grinned. 'It's easy!' He was clearly relishing the chance to triumph over his eldest brother for once, although Shem was also intrigued as to what he was about to say. 'The Lord said the animals will come to us, didn't He? If seven pairs of a beast turn up, then they are clean. If only one pair, they're not!'

The triumphant expression was still on Ham's face as Noah emerged from his tent moments later, and the way he was looking at Ham made it clear that he had heard the exchange that had just taken place. 'The Lord Himself would be pleased with that answer,' chuckled Noah as he clapped his youngest son on the shoulder. The moment of humour quickly passed, however, and Noah became serious again. 'And now to work...'

Shem stood at the top of the large wooden ramp (that was also the door to the ark) and looked up at the sky. It was clear and cloudless. There was no sign of any change, and it was hard to believe that a flood was coming. The end of the seven days was not far off, and yet still the ark was empty, save for fourteen goats and fourteen sheep (the best—and all that was left—of their flocks). They had now done all the preparations possible, except packing up their tents to take onto the ark. That would be their last task before finally entering the ark themselves. All they could do now was wait—and trust. Salit stood at Shem's side, as the eight of them kept watch together. Nobody spoke. The day wore on, but then, all of a sudden, there was a change in the wind. Shem felt it, and could tell by the way the others suddenly stirred that they had sensed it too. Noah turned his face upwards, eyes closed. He drew in a deep breath, let it out slowly and then opened his eyes. 'It begins,' he said.

The first sign that anything was happening was, however, an unexpected one. All their eyes were suddenly drawn in the direction of the city. There was a growing commotion. 'They come,' said Noah. But he wasn't referring to the men who were angrily shouting—almost screaming—at what were (or had been) their animals. 'Fourteen cows and two pigs,' said Ham, after a quick count of the livestock which were making their way slowly and steadily towards the ark. The animals could not be diverted from their course, no matter how much the men swore at them or pulled on their tethers or coats. By now, every man in the mob was livid, either trying to block the animals' path or thrash them into submission.

Just as Shem began to wonder what the hostile band would do when they reached the ark, the men suddenly stopped in their tracks. They were no longer looking at their animals, but over towards the forest behind the ark. The shouts of anger froze on their lips and then transformed into cries of fear. Their animals were abandoned as they turned and began fleeing back to the city. *What was happening? What was on the other side of the boat?*

Shem waited, puzzled. But then the hairs on the back of his neck bristled. Around both ends of the ark came a stream of creatures—including lions—moving slowly like the cows and pigs. As if an unseen herdsman were driving them along, steering them this way and that between invisible boundaries beyond which they could not stray. And all of them moving towards the ramp. Shem had experienced God's hand at work on the night when he had been hunted. But this was different. Some might have seen his deliverance on that night as merely good fortune, but what was happening now had no explanation other than the mighty hand of the Creator. And he knew that if Yahweh had not been his God, then he, too, would have been fleeing.

'I can't even get a single goat to go where I want it to,' murmured Ham, as he stood transfixed by the ever-increasing stream of animals.

'The beasts know the voice of their Creator,' responded Noah, 'and obey unquestioningly. We are the only ones of God's earthly creatures who dare to defy His command.'

Shem felt Salit stiffen at his side, and he knew the reason. The pair of lions was now not far from the bottom of the ramp, and her eyes did not move from them. 'Just be grateful,' whispered Shem, mindful of Ham's recent comments, 'that lions appear to be unclean.'

'You needn't fear them,' said his father (although his eyes were on them too). 'They will not harm us.'

They had all worked hard at making pens and cages and perches on the three decks for the different animals and birds that there might be, and they had planned (as far as they were able) for where livestock should be kept and where predators should go, for the violence of mankind had spread to the wild animals. But at that moment Shem had no idea how easy—or otherwise—it was going to be to separate and guide the creatures in the way they had planned. They all stepped back, and eight pairs of astonished eyes followed the male and female lion as they moved gracefully and slowly past them, seemingly oblivious to their presence and their scent, and went into the ark of their own accord. The Divine Hand, it appeared, was still guiding them.

'Japheth—follow them and shut the cage behind them,' said Noah. 'It may be that the Lord pacifies them for the whole time that they are on the ark—but He may not. The rest of you—be ready to do the same as the other animals arrive.'

The whole day was spent—as was the next—following the animals as they entered the ark. The familiar arrived alongside those that Shem had never seen before and whose names were unknown to him. He constantly marvelled at how they all miraculously went where required. Birds flew obediently onto perches in their cages, predators walked in beside prey, as if totally disinterested in the smaller creatures that would normally be their next meal. The lesser and the greater and everything in between crawled, slithered, hopped, trotted or flew into the ark, as the silent Voice called to them all and the vast, unseen Hand guided them to their place of safety. The ramps inside the ark to the different decks held the weight of the heaviest animals, and the smallest insects found the dark corners in which to nest.

From time to time, Shem also spotted in the distance men and women from the city who had come to watch the strange procession. None came near, however, and none stayed long. The way in which they quickly scurried away made Shem suspect that they viewed what was happening with deep fear, supposing it to be some work of either sorcery or a god whom they did not want to know. *If only they feared what they should fear,* thought Shem as another small group hurried back to the city. And beyond the city, far away to the west, Shem could see storm clouds beginning to pile up, seemingly reaching to the heavens.

'How are we going to raise the door?' asked Ham, interrupting Shem's thoughts.

'Father says that Yahweh will take care of that,' answered Shem, though not fully understanding what that meant exactly.

'The animals are far fewer now,' said Ham, as the two brothers stood at the top of ramp, watching the procession of animals that had dwindled from a steady stream to a trickle.

'It is almost time,' said a deep voice behind them.

Shem turned to face his father. 'Should we bring the tents aboard now?'

Noah nodded. 'Japheth and I will take care of the rest of the animals. I will send the women to help you bring everything into the ark.' As Shem and Ham began their descent down the ramp, Noah added, 'Make the most of it. It will be the last time your feet touch dry ground for many days.' And Shem suddenly realised that everything familiar, everything he had known for the whole of his life—apart from his family—was about to be taken from him. *He was about to make an uncertain and unmapped journey into the unknown.* And his mouth felt strangely dry.

As the last of the tents were finally packed away in the ark—for how long, Shem knew not—Noah called his family to the door. The storm clouds that had seemed distant were now alarmingly close and beginning to fill the sky in every direction. The late afternoon sun was already obscured by the clouds, giving them a strange orange tinge. Shem shivered slightly as a cold breeze blew across from the river.

'Take a last look,' said Noah grimly. 'When you next set eyes upon earth, it will be very different.' None of them spoke. Shem placed his arm around Salit's shoulders and pulled her close to him, as she wrapped both her arms around his chest. Noah finally drew in another deep breath. 'It is time.' And with that he stepped back from the top of the ramp, and Shem and the others followed his lead.

Once again Shem felt his hairs prickling, as the huge and heavy door began to rise, silently and easily, as if it were made from feathers rather than weighty beams of wood. The Hand that closed the door remained unseen, and Noah said simply, 'Yahweh shuts us in.' The light of the world outside dimmed as the huge door rose to meet its frame, and soon the only light that remained was from the small lamps that the women had lit.

As soon as the door was in position, Shem and Japheth lifted between them solid wooden bars and dropped them into their slots across the door, to hold it in place. Any gaps around the tight fitting door were then caulked with reeds—as the rest of the boat had been—before a layer of pitch was added from the bucket that was standing beside the door.

'All is now ready,' said Noah, as the black brush was finally returned to the almost-empty bucket. 'Come. We will go to our own corner of the ark and call on the name of the Lord.' Noah led them silently up the ramp from the middle to the top deck where the light from the gap under the roof had dwindled to an eerie, orange glow. As the small family gathered together, Noah looked upwards, raised his hands and prayed, praising Yahweh for His righteousness, thanking Him for His mercy, and committing themselves, the ark and each creature within to the sovereign care of their Creator. And when Noah finally lowered his hands, even the faint glow had faded into darkness. As they stood in silence, Shem strained his ears. He soon heard what he was listening for: the beginning of the slow beating of rain upon the ark. It soon became faster.

By the time they were sitting silently in the light of lamps eating a small evening meal with bread that had been baked earlier, each taken up with his or her own thoughts, the rain was hammering down onto the roof and sides of the ark. Suddenly they all stopped eating and looked at one another. A new, faint sound was now mingling with that of the torrential rain. They could just hear, almost imperceptibly, the shouting of voices and a series of faint *thuds*, as if large implements were being used against the ark. Shem shuddered to think of who might be outside in the storm. The face of Irad came suddenly and unbidden to his mind. *There was nothing they could do. It was too late.*

'They are in the Lord's hands,' said Noah quietly, as if answering Shem's thoughts. 'And we must leave them there.' Those were the only words spoken, and the meal was finished in silence.

As Shem and Salit lay down together in the darkness in their small area that night, pulling the goats' hair blanket over them for warmth, the almost-deafening sound of the rain continued. The only other sound that Shem could now hear was the faint crying of animals. He once again pulled Salit close and wrapped his arms around her, caressing her softly and kissing her head. He continued to hold her in his arms until her breathing became slow and steady. Before he finally fell asleep, however, he felt the ark shudder a few times, as if it were being hit by powerful waves.

At some point during the night, he woke abruptly. Above the sound of the rain he could hear the ark creaking. It then juddered for a few moments, and suddenly Shem felt the sensation of movement. The ark was afloat. The flood had come.

Notes

1. There are no details given in Scripture of what happened when the flood began, other than Noah, his family, and all the animals entering the ark, the Lord shutting them in, and 'all the springs of the great deep' bursting forth and 'the floodgates of the heavens' being opened (Genesis 7:11). This verse implies that it was not rain alone that was the cause of the flood upon the earth, and hence the reference in this chapter to waves hitting the ark.

2. Four physics graduate students at the University of Leicester conducted a study which found that a boat with the dimensions of the ark that was full of huge numbers of animals would be able to float. They estimated the boat would weigh 1.2 million kilograms (the Titanic weighed about 53 million kilograms), and would have been able to support up to approximately 50 million kilograms—the equivalent of 2.15 million sheep. See http://physics.le.ac.uk/journals/index.php/pst/article/view/676/475

5

*And the waters flooded the earth for a
hundred and fifty days. (Genesis 7:24)*

'Another notch?' called out Shem across the ark and
above the noise of the rain. Ham was furiously whittling
away at one of the ark's wooden beams with a small knife.
'How many does that make?'

'Twenty-nine!' shouted back Ham. Shem wandered
across to inspect his brother's work. Ham had decided
on the day that the door of the ark had been shut that
he would keep a record of the days as they passed. Two
blocks of ten notches had already been carved, and the
third (making their first month) would be completed
the following day—although day and night were, in fact,
difficult to distinguish, as the difference in light between
the two was minimal at best. 'Eleven more days of rain,'
added Ham with a certain amount of satisfaction, as he
stepped back to admire his efforts.

Shem nodded. *How good it was going to be to be free of the
incessant drumming of the rain!* He was glad the notches were
marking the passing of time, for days had already become
monotonous and largely indistinguishable from each
other. It was an endless round of feeding, watering and
cleaning up after the animals—the latter, as best as they
could under the circumstances. Then there were cows,
goats and sheep to be milked. Most tasks were done by the

limited light of small lamps, especially on the lower decks of the pitch-black ark. Their own meals were far more limited than they had been used to before, and Shem was grateful that they at least still had some (relatively) fresh fruit and vegetables. His gratitude also extended to the divine declaration that cows, goats and sheep were clean, ensuring that fourteen of each were on the ark (though only seven of each, females), so there would therefore be plenty of milk and curds for the duration—however long that might be.

Shem took a couple of paces towards the window and opened it a little, breathing in deeply the fresh air outside, deliciously untainted by animals. The torrents of rain prevented him seeing any distance. *Not that there was much to see any more.* When the ark had begun to float, they had felt from time to time dull *thuds*, presumed to be the ark drifting against trees on the mountains nearby—or the mountains themselves. They had even caught sight of these from time to time, if they had ventured to peep through the window and through the rain that lashed against the ark, and into the gloom beyond. As sudden jolts could come from any direction, Shem guessed that the ark was drifting and turning as the winds and water currents buffeted it. He kept telling himself that Yahweh ruled the whole realm of nature, that He was Lord over every drop of water and breath of wind. But his heart still wavered when the ark juddered. *Surely Yahweh would not allow any shortcomings in their workmanship to despatch the last creatures that drew breath to a watery grave.* At least, that was what he told himself.

But as the days slipped by, any remaining contact with the solid world that they had left behind lessened and then dwindled to nothing, as the world of water engulfed all they had known.

By the time there were sixty notches on the beam, Shem was sick of spending most of the day in near-darkness, sick of the all-pervasive smell of animals, and sick of cold meals. Even when they gathered together as a family in the dark evenings, there was no roaring fire to gather around. As Ham had pointed out at the start, a pitch-covered wooden boat and fire was not a good combination. Particularly if you happen to be on the boat. And there would be no easy escape for any smoke. The only things that cheered them as they sat together were the telling of tales and the singing of songs, especially when Noah spoke (for no one told a story quite like him) or when Naamah's sweet voice rang out. But even these were bitter-sweet, reminding them of a world and its people that were gone forever.

Although the rain had, as God promised, ceased twenty days earlier, there was no sign of the water abating—not that there was any way to judge that. They had long since ceased to feel or see any sign of the mountains, and now they were simply drifting unobstructed.

Shem put down the leather bucket he had been carrying, and joined his father by the window. Seeing the sun again was, at least, one consolation. It also gave some sense of east and west, north and south, in an otherwise featureless world. He looked out on the cloudless blue sky. It was as if the floodgates of heaven had opened and utterly emptied their stores, as if every cloud had vanished after giving every last drop of rain, so nothing was left in the sky but sunshine. Neither Shem nor Noah spoke. Shem could faintly hear Naamah singing somewhere on the ark as she carried out her daily tasks. Although he couldn't make out the words of her song above the ever-present noise of the animals, he'd known them from his youth. The melody was a familiar but haunting one. A wave of desolation suddenly swept over him. *They were so alone.* He looked out upon the emptiness of their world—there was only water as far as the eye could see—and he wondered how Adam and Eve had felt when they were the only two. *Did it not matter to them because God also walked in the garden? Did they even know what it felt like to be alone?* Shem's thoughts, however, were suddenly interrupted.

'It is as if Yahweh has uncreated the world.'

Shem briefly looked across at his father, but then followed his gaze back out to the blue again.

'All the waters above and below the sky are separate no longer,' continued Noah. 'They are together again and the earth is formless and empty once more, as it was on the first day of His creation.'

'You speak of Yahweh making the world,' said the familiar voice of Nahlat. Shem and his father turned to face her. 'I would very much like to hear about it.'

'I will tell you that tale,' replied Noah with a smile. 'It is a good story—a very good story.' But at that moment, they heard Japheth hailing them as he emerged up the ramp from the lower deck. Noah sighed. 'But I think it is a story that will have to wait until tonight.'

Japheth approached the three of them with a look of perplexity on his face. 'Father?'

'Yes, my son.'

'Rabbits are counted as unclean before the Lord, aren't they?'

'That is correct.'

'So there should only be one pair of them.'

'Yes. Why do you ask?'

'I think you'd better come and see…'

As Shem finished yet another cold meal, he couldn't help but think of the warm, fresh bread he had eaten almost every day of his life—up until they had entered the ark. *What he wouldn't give for a mouthful of that bread now! Or, come to that, anything warm.* The small lamps scattered around flickered in the darkness, sending huge, dancing shadows of the family onto the black walls of the ark as they sat on woollen rugs or fleeces together.

'Now,' said Noah, diverting Shem's thoughts away from images of steaming food, 'it is time for another tale. But this is the greatest of all tales, for it is the account of God's creation, passed down by each generation from Adam himself.' Salit snuggled back against Shem, seeking a comfortable and warm place from which to enjoy the story. Although Shem and his brothers had already heard it many times, it was new for each of their wives. Before Noah began, Japheth and Ham whispered together briefly, and then laughed and nodded, but Shem thought nothing of it. He looked back towards his father. His face seemed to be etched more deeply with lines than even just a few years earlier, although whether that was simply a trick of the shadows cast by the lamps' dim light, Shem couldn't be sure.

Salit finally stopped wriggling and Noah began. 'In the beginning, there was only God Himself. Nothing or no one else. He created the earth and the heavens above it, but there was still no form to the earth. It was dark, empty and covered with water, but God's Spirit was moving over the waters.' Noah paused, and in the silence that followed, Shem was oblivious to the faint bleating of sheep and goats and the barking of a dog. 'And then God spoke,' said Noah, in barely more than a whisper. '*Light be!*' he then boomed out. 'And there was light, and it was good. God separated the light and darkness, and that was the first day.' Noah paused again, and then his voice boomed out for a second time. '*Sky!* said God, and there was. And it separated the waters above the earth from the waters below. And it was good. That was the second day.'

Shem smiled to himself as Noah used his voice, his hands and his face to bring the story to life, just as he'd done when he and his brothers were small. Noah clearly still relished recounting the greatest story of all, describing vividly the rest of the six days of creation. Dry land and plants came next, then the sun, moon and the stars, followed by fish and birds. Then, on the sixth day, all beasts on the earth. And finally, the crowning work of God's creation. 'Even after He had created all creatures of the land—those we now have in the ark—Yahweh had not finished,' said Noah dramatically. He then lowered his voice, as if sharing a momentous secret. 'His best was yet to come. For He then created man and woman to be the pinnacle of His creation, to be different from the beasts.' His voice rose again—rich, majestic, solemn. 'For mankind alone was made in His image, to be like Him—to rule over the world and subdue it.' Noah extended his arms, as if embracing the whole of creation. 'And God looked at all that He had made and it was very good. And He then rested on the seventh day and made it holy.'

Hearing the word *good* proclaimed again and again, like a steady, life-giving heartbeat throughout the story, stirred a sadness within Shem. For a moment he wondered how God had felt, seeing His beautiful world made ugly by the violence and evil of men. But the sorrow was dispelled by the sound of his wife's soft and sweet voice. 'But what does it mean to be made in God's image? How are we like Him?'

'Ah, Salit! That is a good question,' replied Noah, 'and maybe we can answer it by pondering how Yahweh has made us different from the animals.' He looked around at the small gathering, inviting them to respond.

'We build and we make things?' offered Shem.

'Indeed, yes—we create! Like this ark. It was not before, but now is. But unlike God, our hands can only work with what He has already created.'

'And we are in charge?' suggested Japheth.

'We rule, yes, but only over the animals. Yahweh rules all things, including the sun, and the moon—'

'And the rain!' added Shem.

His father nodded. 'And we owe our lives to that.'

'We also speak, as God does,' continued Shem. He then added with a wry smile, 'The animals know only how to make noise—although they know that well!'

'But Yahweh not only speaks,' responded Noah. 'He also makes Himself known to us and shows us His love. And so *we* can speak and love and know each other too.'

'But what about laughing?' asked Ham. 'The animals don't do that. Is Yahweh humoured by anything?'

'Well, He made you,' said Japheth.

When the laughter died down, Noah spoke again, but with sadness. 'We were made in God's image, but we have marred that image—His light in us does not burn as it once did.'

Shem felt Salit suddenly move her position, and she sat up a little. Noah's words had clearly sparked a fresh question. 'You spoke of God creating light on the first day...' she began hesitantly.

Noah nodded. 'That is correct.'

'And yet the sun and the moon and the stars were not created until the fourth day. So where did that first light come from, and how were there days before the sun was made?'

Noah laughed. 'The Almighty has blessed my second son with a wife who listens carefully! The Lord tells us all we *need* to know, Salit, but not all the mysteries we might like to know. But just think! Maybe if we were telling our story of the flood and the ark, we would not say how many trees we cut down, or the tools we used, or how we cut the beams and bound them together. We might not say where the pitch came from or list every animal that came on board. Maybe we would just tell others what God told us to build—'

'And how long and high and wide He told us to build it!' interjected Japheth.

'Yes, maybe that,' said Noah with a broad smile. 'What is important is that Yahweh told us to build it, and that we obeyed Him—not how we built it. So you see, Salit, Yahweh tells us what is most important, but not every answer to every question. And if He did tell us, would we understand? For He is God Almighty and we are just tiny creatures on His earth, small as ants! What we *need* to know is that it is He, and no one else—no gods that others may speak of—who created the world in which we live. And that is also why we are accountable to Him. Men and women thought this was *their* world, to do with as they pleased, but they were wrong. It is Yahweh who has brought, by His hand alone, order from chaos and life from the dust. Only He can do that.' Noah paused and his eyes were bright. 'Ah, but such life from that dust! There is more to tell. The Lord not only gave us the story of His creation; He also gave us the story of how life was meant to be. And that tale doesn't *end* with the creation of mankind—it begins with it!'

And once again Shem and the others listened with rapt attention as Noah spoke of how God fashioned Adam from the dust of the ground and blew His life-giving breath into him. They heard of how God planted a garden in the area of Eden, and how it was watered by four rivers, one of which was the Tigris near which they had so recently lived. Then Noah recounted how God placed Adam in the garden to work it and take care of it, and how Adam named each of the animals and birds, as part of his dominion over them.

'But,' continued Noah, his eyes wide, 'in all of Yahweh's creation, there was one thing that was not good.'

Shem felt Salit stir in his arms as Noah paused, building the drama of the story. *She was intrigued!*

Noah cast his gaze over each of them in turn. 'It was not good for the man to be alone, and so Yahweh determined to make a helper fit for him. But none of the animals whom Adam had named were suitable.' Noah smiled broadly. 'And so Yahweh created the perfect companion and helper for Adam. He fashioned Eve lovingly from his rib as he slept, creating her from him to be like him, but separated from him to be different—to be not only his companion but his wife, their bodies joining them together to be one again.'

Shem gently caressed his wife as Noah spoke of Eve's creation, but much as he had been enjoying his father's story, he suddenly hoped that he wouldn't continue for too much longer. But before Shem could retire that night with Salit, there was more that Noah needed to say, and he listened as his father told again the tale that explained the presence of so much evil and pain in God's good world.

'In the middle of the garden, there were two particular trees,' continued Noah. 'The tree of life and the tree of the knowledge of good and evil. God gave the man and woman complete freedom in the garden, and permission to eat of *any* of the trees in the garden—except just one. There was only one command from the Lord, one thing they were not to do, and that was to eat from the tree of the knowledge of good and evil.'

Shem's heart was drawn back into the story—of how the snake's lies led first Eve and then Adam to eat from the fruit of the tree. *How could Eve have been so stupid to take the fruit that God forbade?* thought Shem. *After all, God had warned them they would die if they ate the fruit!* But even before Noah had spoken another word, a memory rose in his mind: a picture of a dark night when he had stupidly ignored his own father's warnings. Shem quickly lowered his eyes to the ground, rebuked by his own conscience. *Would he have behaved any differently if it had been him in the garden and not his first ancestors? Maybe the story of Adam and Eve's sin was his story too.* His chastened mind was, however, quickly brought back to the present by the voice of his wife.

'But did Adam and Eve not know the meaning of right and wrong before they ate the fruit?' asked Salit, clearly perplexed.

'They knew they were going against the will of their Creator,' replied Noah, 'and that is the very nature of sin itself. They were trying to take the place of God—ruling their own lives and deciding for themselves what they would and would not do.'

'But Yahweh said they would die when they ate of the fruit,' said Arisisah, sharing her own perplexity, 'but they didn't.'

'They now feared Yahweh and hid from Him,' said Noah quietly. 'They no longer enjoyed His presence and were banished from His garden. *That* is a death itself.' He shook his head sadly. 'And they were barred from the tree of life, condemning them to a mortal life like that of the animals, so that they too would one day die. But their disobedience left nothing untouched,' continued Noah. He then began to describe the shame that the man and woman felt before each other, and also the curses on the snake and on the land. Finally he spoke of the pain for all women that would blight every birth.

'You will each know that for yourselves one day,' said Naamah, looking at each of her daughters-in-law in turn. 'You have watched sheep and goats giving birth, and have been on the ark long enough to see the birthing of many other creatures—'

'Especially the rabbits,' interjected Ham. The eyes of his father reproached him.

'And you have seen,' continued Naamah, 'how giving birth seems a small thing to them. As if they barely feel it. It will *not* be like that for you.' She paused, and then added with a knowing smile, 'Japheth was the worst.'

'I remember it!' added Noah, grimacing.

'And it is like that for every birth we go through,'

continued Naamah. 'The seed of our offspring may be sown in love and delight, but no child comes into the world without bringing great pain.'

'That is indeed the story of our world,' said Noah. 'And each new generation brings fresh pain upon God's earth.' And he finished the evening's tale by briefly recounting the generations that had passed since the days of Adam, until their own.

The oil in the lamps had all but been consumed by fire by the time that Noah's voice fell silent. No one spoke for a while, as each pondered the story they had been told. Until, that is, Nahlat broke the silence, perplexity in her voice. 'Where did Cain's wife come from?'

The quietness was suddenly and unexpectedly shattered by an eruption of rowdy laughter and an animated exchange between Japheth and Ham. Shem stared at them in bemusement. He was not the only one.

It was only when Noah purposefully folded his arms that they finally calmed down. 'Well?' he said, raising an eyebrow.

'When we heard that you were going to be telling the story of creation,' explained Japheth somewhat sheepishly, 'I said to Ham that I wouldn't be surprised if one of our wives asked about Cain's wife, as we did ourselves when we heard it for the first time…'

Shem knew his brothers only too well. 'And so *Ham* suggested you make a wager on which wife it would be,' he said with a withering look. Japheth nodded.

Noah, with his eyebrow still raised, asked, 'And the nature of this wager?'

'Japheth lost, so he gets to do my chores tomorrow,' replied Ham hesitantly.

'And for suggesting the wager in the first place,' replied Noah with a mischievous smile, 'you will do *his* chores tomorrow, and then you will *both* muck out the pigs—which may or may not dissuade you from future wagers. And as it is late, Ham will also give his wife in his own good time the answer that I gave him when *he* asked the same question of me.'

Shem felt Salit stir once more. She twisted her head so she was facing him and whispered with curiosity, 'Which was?'

Shem quickly moved his body away from his wife's so that he could stand. He pulled her to her feet, leant over to her and said softly, 'Come with me and I'll tell you…'

Notes

1. *The chronology of the Biblical record of the flood is remarkable in its detail. It is recorded as beginning on the 17th day of the 2nd month of the 600th year of Noah's life (7:11), the ark resting on the mountains of Ararat on the 17th day of the 7th month (8:4), and the tops of the mountains becoming visible on the 1st day of the 10th month (8:5). On the 1st day of the 1st month of Noah's 601st year the water had dried up from the earth (8:13) and by the 27th day of the 2nd month, the earth was completely dry (8:14). A basic assumption would be that normally months would be marked by the moon, and as a new moon occurs on average every (approximately) 29.5 days, lunar months would either be 29 or 30 days long. The statement in 8:3 that implies that the 17th day of the 7th month (i.e. 5 months after the rain began) is 'at the end of 150 days' also implies a 30 day month.*

6

*'Come out of the ark, you and your wife and your sons
and their wives…' Then God blessed Noah and his sons,
saying to them, 'Be fruitful and increase in number and
fill the earth.' (Genesis 8:16, 9:1)*

When Ham's notches reached and then passed seventy-
five, Shem began to wonder whether God had forgotten
them. Apart from the ark, the earth was still devoid
of anything except water. And nothing seemed to be
happening. They continued to drift, and the days dragged
by with nothing except the notches on the beam to
distinguish them.

'The Lord has accomplished His will,' said Shem, as
he stood next to his father by the window once again, 'and
yet the flood still prevails.'

Noah seemed to hear the unspoken question behind
his words, and turned to face him. 'And you wonder,
Shem, why Yahweh's hand does not act?'

Shem nodded. He suddenly wondered if the ark was
nothing more than a speck on the vast and featureless
waters to God—and easily overlooked. 'Have you heard
His voice again, Father? Has He said anything more to
you?' And before Noah had a chance to answer, Shem
blurted out, 'Does He forget us?'

Noah sighed, shook his head, and then said quietly,
'No, no… and no. The words Yahweh spoke before the

flood, He has fulfilled exactly. The flood came after seven days as He said it would, and then it rained for forty days—no more, no less. And finally every creature outside the ark that had the breath of life in it died, just as He said. The Lord perfectly fulfilled His word on each occasion. But He did not tell us how long we would be on the ark. All we can do, therefore, is patiently await Yahweh's time. However, what He *has* said is that He will establish his covenant with us.'

'Meaning?'

'Meaning we are His people and He continues to be mindful of us. You committed yourself to the Lord, Shem, and now you must trust Him—regardless of what your eyes do or do not see or what others may or may not say. Trust and obedience are seldom easy, but are always best. So we will be steadfast in our confidence that Yahweh has *not* forgotten us and that, in His time, the flood will be no more.'

Shem stared out at the waters again and wished he had a faith as great as his father's. *Still, there wasn't exactly any alternative* but *to wait, so he would trust the Lord as best he could.* But as he lay beside Salit that night, there *was* a change—a new sound. That of a wind blowing. And Shem had the uncanny feeling that God had heard every word of his earlier conversation with his father—and had responded.

It was on the day that Ham completed his fifteenth block of ten that they felt it. There was an unmistakable juddering, and a sudden jolt. Shem steadied himself against a beam and then waited, every sense alert. *The boat was no longer drifting!* If he had any doubts about it, they were dispelled when the decks of the ark began to take on a small but noticeable tilt across the width of the ark. The list increased for a while and then became fixed— thankfully whilst the slope was still relatively shallow.

'The waters recede,' said Noah to the whole family, gathered beside the open window which happened to be on the slightly lower side of the boat. 'We must be resting on a mountain, behind us.'

Shem looked out, but there was still nothing to see but water. Land was tantalisingly close, but out of sight. By his side, Japheth asked, 'What do we do now?'

And although Shem knew that the question was directed to his father, he also knew the answer—and gave it. 'We wait. And we keep trusting Yahweh—'

'And eating cold meals,' added his younger brother with a sigh. 'Still, it surely won't be for too much longer if the water is going down!'

But Ham's optimism was ill-founded.

'How many times have you had to sharpen your knife?' asked Shem, as Ham once more carried out his daily assault on the wooden beam.

'Less times than the number of notches but more than I'd care to remember,' he replied, carving another groove in the wood. He grunted as a final shaving of wood parted company with the beam, and then stood back, tucking his knife into a small leather pouch hanging from his belt. There were now thirty-seven blocks of ten notches. Ham had grouped the blocks into sets of three, making twelve complete sets and one single block of ten. 'More than twelve months,' said Ham. 'Three hundred and seventy days.'

The waters had receded with what felt like an agonising sluggishness. It had taken almost three months after their grounding for the tops of the mountains to finally emerge above the watery expanse. Forty days after that, Noah had sent out a raven and then a dove to test the extent to which the waters had abated. And when Ham's notches numbered three hundred and fourteen, they had pulled back the heavy covering over the ark, enabling them (with the aid of ladders) to establish that the surface of the earth was visible as far as the eye could see. Although Shem and his brothers had been keen to open the door of the ark, Noah insisted that they wait for Yahweh's command. 'For He alone knows when the earth is ready,' he said firmly, 'not just for us, but also for all the creatures on the ark.' And Shem had remembered his father's words about obedience seldom being easy—and now a further fifty-six days had passed.

'A year and ten days,' sighed Shem.

'But that will be the last notch you will ever carve—' They turned to see Noah folding his arms and surveying Ham's handiwork. '—at least on this ark.'

'Yahweh has spoken?' asked Shem excitedly, scarcely allowing himself to believe that their long ordeal might finally be over.

'He has told us to leave the ark—and to bring out all the animals with us. The earth is ready.'

It took some time for them to gouge out the pitch and caulking from around the huge door of the ark. 'What happens if it breaks as it hits the ground?' called out Ham. He was balancing somewhat precariously on a ladder held steady by Shem, using his knife to ease out the tar-covered reeds packed along the small gap at the top of the door.

'Then we use the ladders,' said Shem, attempting to avoid the bits of blackened reed that were cascading down around him.

'Have you ever seen sheep trying to climb down ladders?'

'Not for the animals, idiot!' replied Shem, grinning. 'We would use them to reach the ground, and then mend the door sufficiently for it to be used as a ramp again. But we won't have to. The beams making up the door run lengthways and will hold firm. Japheth and I fixed more than enough cross-pieces to keep them together, and the hinges are strong.'

'Do you want to make a bet?' said Ham mischievously, as he descended the rungs.

'No!' laughed Shem, 'but not because I don't trust my work!'

Moments later all were gathered by the door. 'Ready?' asked Noah. Shem nodded, and he and Japheth lifted one bar from across the door, whilst Noah and Ham lifted the other. The four men then took the two bars and, in unison, swung them against the door. The loud *thud* was accompanied by creaking and a small shower of dust and reed fragments. They hit the door a second time— and there was movement. The door juddered, daylight suddenly peeking in around it. The cracks of light widened as the weight of the door began to work for them. The huge wooden slab rapidly gathered speed as it swung on its hinges down towards the ground, flooding the middle deck of the ark with daylight that it hadn't seen for over a year, and hitting the rocky earth with a resounding *crash*. But its beams held.

'Told you so,' whispered Shem to his younger brother with just the slightest hint of smugness.

Shem stood for a moment at the top of the ramp to catch his breath and take a short but well-earned rest from herding the animals out of the ark. The largest ones (and those most prone to hunting other beasts) were still to come, giving the smaller animals plenty of opportunity to run or fly away before the predators emerged. The last to leave would be their own sheep, goats and cows, all having multiplied whilst on the ark. From these animals they would build up herds again. Noah had told them, however, to keep back a male—the best one—of every clean animal and bird. When Shem had asked him why, Noah had simply replied, 'They are for Yahweh.'

Shem chuckled as he listened to a good-natured dispute between his brothers about the final number of rabbits that had hopped or scampered down the ramp. He then silently surveyed the scene before him, the like of which he knew he would never witness again. Animals were dispersing in every direction down the mountain and towards the lower ground, whilst the sky was dotted with birds of various sizes stretching their wings unhindered for the first time in many long months. They soared and swooped in the blue sky, exulting in their newly-found freedom, many of them already no larger than black specks of dust, as they rose up towards the clouds which had also returned to the skies.

As his father encouraged a pair of dogs down the ramp, closely followed (or obstructed) by a litter of five enthusiastic puppies, Shem couldn't help but smile. He had only known such creatures as roaming scavengers before, but somehow, in their year with eight humans on the ark, they had gradually become somewhat comical and almost endearing.

'A new life for all of us,' said Noah as he stood beside Shem, watching the dogs as they began to romp away from the ark together into a world that the puppies had never known. Noah then turned to his second son. 'I have a job for you and your brothers, Shem,' he began. 'A job that, for a change, does not involve animals. Do you know where your tools are—the ones used to build the ark?'

'I stowed them carefully away before the rain started.' He was intrigued by his father's question.

'Good! We are going to need firewood,' explained Noah. 'Dismantling one of the roof beams will probably be a good place to start.' He smiled wryly. 'We won't, after all, be needing the ark again. I will send Ham and Japheth to help. And whilst you do that, I will build an altar to Yahweh from some of the stones scattered here. We will then sacrifice the clean animals to Him as burnt offerings.'

Noah gazed across the new world before them. 'There will, in time, be evil again on this earth—of that I am sure.' He turned to Shem. 'But the first blood to be spilled on the newly-cleansed earth will not be an act of violence, but of worship. We will present an offering of our best in thanksgiving to the Lord. He has been faithful, and we will begin our lives on this new earth as we will continue them—honouring our Creator.' And with that, Noah left Shem's side, and made his way down the ramp.

Shem followed the path of the smoke as it spiralled upwards from the fire that licked around the animal carcasses on the stone altar. In the end, he had not only prepared wood to burn but had also helped Noah finish the sizeable square stack of rocks and stones on which the sacrifices were to be offered. It needed to be large enough for a bull, gazelle, sheep and goat, as well as other smaller animals and birds. Ham's freshly-sharpened knife had been used for a new and very different purpose, and the ground around the altar was stained dark by the blood of the animals that had been quickly and efficiently slaughtered. With reeds that had been used in the caulking of the ark as kindle, the first fire they had lit in over a year soon took hold, its flames rising high above the lifeless sacrifices. Although none of them had ever killed to eat, Shem had to admit that the smell of the meat as it burned on the altar was highly appealing.

Noah's eyes had also followed the smoke high into the sky, but they remained there, his stance attentive, as if listening to a voice from beyond their world. 'It is a pleasing aroma to Yahweh,' he began, and Shem knew that he was passing on what he had heard. 'He promises never to destroy every living creature again, even though the heart of man is inclined to evil from childhood. For as long as the earth remains, there will be seedtime and harvest, cold and heat, summer and winter, day and night.'

Silence fell once more, broken only by the cracking of wood and the roaring of fire.

But then Shem heard it. The reactions of the others told him that they heard it too: a voice like the wind, but with words that captured his heart and held him in rapt and unwavering attention, as if it were the only voice in the world. 'Be fruitful and increase in number, and fill the earth.' The Voice then spoke of the animals—how they would now fear them and also be permitted as food. It spoke of the sanctity of human life, made in the image of God, and again commanded them, as at creation, to multiply.

Suddenly, rain began to fall softly and silently upon them, no longer a powerful judgment but a gentle shower to cleanse and refresh them after their year of confinement on the ark. Awe gripped Shem as he looked around in wonder and listened to God reaffirm His promise to never again destroy the world with a flood. And there was to be a sign. As the sun, which had been obscured by the rain-clouds, suddenly broke through, Shem heard God's final words to them. 'This is the sign of the covenant I have established with all living creatures on the earth.'

Although Shem's eyes were drawn towards the sun in the west, Noah suddenly exclaimed, 'Look!' Shem turned and followed his father's gaze eastwards—and gasped. Every colour under heaven was displayed in a huge arc that rose from the earth, high into the sky before curving back down to earth again. 'God's bow,' said Noah. 'He has set His bow in the clouds—His battle with evil is over.'

Shem sat staring into the flames of the family's campfire, feeling the warmth not just of the fire but of Salit's body as she sat against him. His stomach was full of hot food and warm bread, and he was out in the cool, fresh air, under a star-lit sky. A feeling of deep contentment settled upon him, but for reasons that ran deeper than just comfort and beauty. *He had heard the voice of Yahweh—his God. The same God had, under a different star-lit sky, rescued him some years earlier—and had now rescued him again, together with the seven others sitting around the fire.* Shem's heart whispered a silent *thank-you*, heard only by divine ears.

'Have you any clearer idea of where we are?'

Japheth's question drew Shem's eyes away from the mesmerising fire and back to their father to whom the question was addressed. The landscape around them was nothing he recognised, and Shem was interested to hear what Noah had to say.

'Judging by the sun and the stars, I would say we are north of where we began. There is no sign of the plain between the great rivers, and the mountains run in different directions to the ones we knew before. We may well be in the region of Urartu.' He paused. 'But more importantly, we are tonight in the centre of Yahweh's will—and at the beginning of a new world. We will spread out from here, find lands for pasture and for crops, and fulfil His command. The Creator's earth needs to be filled once more, so you, my sons, must now have sons and daughters of your own.'

Shem's eyes wandered away from his father to the large stone altar, where the fire had long since died down. Embers still glowed in the darkness, however, causing smoke to curl up slowly into the night air. His eyes then fell on their newly-pitched tents where they would sleep that night. And only one thought went through Shem's mind as he wrapped his arm around Salit and pondered Noah's words: *that sounded like an excellent plan.*

It was not until two years after the flood that Salit gave birth to their firstborn. 'What have you named him?' asked Noah, as Salit sat on a sheep-skin rug cradling their newborn son.

'Arpachshad,' replied Shem, with a heart brimming full of pride and joy.

'Then it is Arpachshad who will receive my blessing,' said Noah. He then leaned down and gently picked up the small bundle, and gazed for the first time upon the face of his grandson. Noah smiled as he gazed down upon the tiny new life, and began his prayer. 'May you be blessed by the God of Adam, the God of Noah, and the God of Shem…'

In the years that followed, however, Shem began to see the ugliness of sin marring his own children. It was a sinfulness that he knew was still lodged deep within his own heart and one that had not and could not be erased by the waters of the flood. Many times he thought of Yahweh's words on the day they'd left the ark: *the heart of man is inclined to evil from childhood.* And he knew those words to be true.

On a day when a rainbow appeared once again in the sky, he asked his father, 'Will there ever be a day when the earth is truly free from evil?'

Noah seemed to be studying the rainbow, and was silent for so long that Shem began to wonder whether he'd heard his question. But just as he was going to repeat it, Noah drew in a long breath, which then came out in a deep sigh. 'The Lord only knows, my son. We know that His purposes are loving and good, and that the presence of evil in this world grieves His heart even more than our own. He has also shown that He can recreate the earth—so why not also the heart of man? I believe that He will have a plan to put *all* things right, including our hearts. But we also know that He does not always work as quickly as we would like.'

Shem remembered the interminable days they had spent on the dark and often foul-smelling ark, and had to agree.

But Noah hadn't finished. 'His plan for this earth and for us will be good—very good—but how long it will take, only He knows. It may take many years and many generations.'

Their conversation was suddenly interrupted by the sounds of a squabble erupting. They both looked over to where Shem's two young sons were each protesting loudly. 'Maybe His plan will start with Arpachshad,' said Shem with a little laugh.

But Noah turned to his own son. 'Maybe His plan has *already* started—with Shem.'

Notes

1. *Urartu is the Assyrian name for the ancient country in the mountainous region southeast of the Black Sea and southwest of the Caspian Sea (which is today divided between Armenia, eastern Turkey, and north-western Iran). The name became Ararat in Scripture, and the Bible records the ark coming to rest on the mountains of Ararat (plural).*

Eliezer

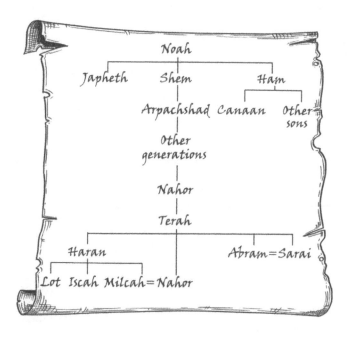

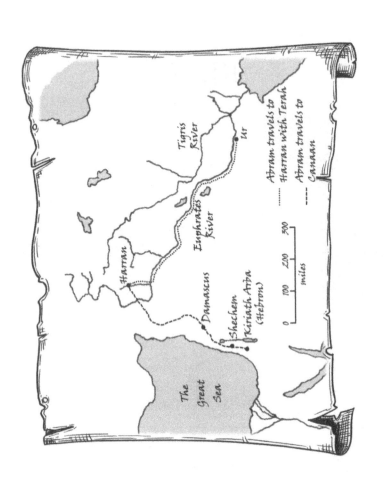

I

*The LORD had said to Abram, 'Go from your country,
your people and your father's household to the land I will
show you.' (Genesis 12:1)*

'Eliezer!'

The young man who had been sitting—forlorn—amongst the roped sack-cloth bundles looked up. The paraphernalia of a long journey was scattered on the dusty ground nearby: rolled rugs and animal skins, clay jars of various shapes and sizes, tents and their poles. Eliezer pulled himself wearily to his feet. Despite his dejection, however, he couldn't help being somewhat curious at his uncle's apparent—and uncharacteristic—good mood. But if the previous three years had taught him anything, it was that questioning his uncle was never a wise idea, however great his confusion or justified the cause.

Since the untimely deaths of his parents when he was barely ten years old, his uncle, aunt and numerous cousins had been his only family. From the outset, though, it had been clear to him that his presence was, at best, simply that of an extra labourer. On darker days, he was made to feel like an unwelcome burden. He'd always suspected that his uncle disliked him, believing him to be too clever for his own good. More than once during the time under his uncle's care, he'd found himself beaten with a cane after an injudicious response.

'Don't just stand there like a donkey waiting for me to come to you. Move yourself!'

Eliezer, still holding his peace, picked his way through the baggage, donkeys and cousins, the latter showing no desire to make his passage any easier, moving neither legs nor bodies out of his way.

'Well, you have your wish,' began his uncle when he'd reached him, though Eliezer was at a loss to know of any wish that had passed his lips, and quite clearly his parents were not suddenly going to be alive again. 'I know you had no desire to leave Damascus and travel with us here, to the Land of the Rivers. So I have found a way for you to return west, rather than continuing with us. There is a man—a rich man—who is planning to travel in that direction. He needs another servant and is willing to take you on. You will do well with him. Collect your things, say your goodbyes, and I'll take you to him.'

Eliezer suspected that *You will do well with him* would be more truthfully rendered as *I am free of my duty.* As he gathered his meagre possessions—the most treasured of which was his father's wooden staff—he wondered if any money had changed hands between his uncle and this rich stranger. *Money going in either direction was possible.* He'd learned from bitter experience that there was nothing to be gained from asking his uncle for the silver that was rightly his from the sale of what had been his father's small herd. The only items of value he had been able to keep within his grasp were his mother's thin gold bangles, rings and earrings, which he always carried in a small leather pouch on his belt.

There was little warmth in any of the farewells, except that of his aunt, who had been his mother's sister. The sight of her tears suddenly made his throat tighten, as he left the embrace of possibly the only person on the face of the earth who cared for him.

'My lord!'

Eliezer was not used to hearing such deference upon his uncle's lips, and it stirred a curiosity within him for the second time that day. He put down his small bundle and stood at his uncle's side by the open door of the sizeable house, as they waited for its owner to appear. Eliezer's gaze wandered from the mud bricks of the house to the narrow, bustling street in which they were standing. The city of Harran was at the northern end of the Land of the Rivers. The Balikh, the smaller river on which it stood, flowed into the mighty Euphrates some distance to the south. Their waters then continued flowing towards Ur, the great and prosperous city on the southerly reaches of the Euphrates, only a few days' journey from where the river merged with its equally mighty counterpart, the Tigris. A greeting immediately tore his attention away from the nearby traders and their wares. In the open doorway stood the man in whose hands his future lay.

Eliezer's first impression was of an air of calm authority. *He must be a man of some standing.* He judged him to be forty to fifty years old—a guess that he was shortly to discover was surprisingly on the low side.

His uncle's voice interrupted his thoughts. 'This is Eliezer, the nephew of which I spoke.'

As the stranger's eyes came to rest upon him, Eliezer rapidly cast his own to the ground. But it was not only out of customary respect for his elders. He suddenly felt unsure of himself in the presence of a man whose riches and power were clearly far in excess of those of his own small family. He felt a hand upon his shoulder, inviting him to raise his eyes, and he found a kindly face smiling at him. 'And I am Abram.'

Eliezer and his uncle followed Abram into the house for the hospitality that custom dictated, turning right immediately after entering the tiny entrance chamber, and into the living areas that were out of sight of those passing along the street. The richly-coloured rugs and the wall-hangings spoke of wealth, and they soon found themselves in a spacious room. Rugs and cushions were generously scattered on the floor, and a large window and door opened out onto a courtyard with an assortment of small trees in terracotta pots.

Abram invited Eliezer's uncle to sit. Eliezer was unsure whether the invitation extended to him—*he was, after all, going to be a servant in this man's household*. He glanced at the tray in the middle of one of the rugs and, seeing only two cups on it, decided to remain standing. Given Abram's next words, Eliezer thought he'd probably made the right decision.

'Let us see how your nephew pours beer.' And he gestured towards the tray. Eliezer was conscious of Abram's scrutiny, and so took utmost care in pouring the thick brown foaming liquid. Having filled the cups, he offered the first to Abram. 'Guests first,' he said in a firm but gentle voice, adding, 'but it is an understandable mistake.' Having handed the men the cups, Eliezer waited for them to drink, and then picked up the platter of figs and dates that was also on the tray—and offered it to his uncle first. 'He learns fast!' said Abram with a smile, and Eliezer felt himself flushing slightly at the unexpected praise.

'Yes, he's a clever lad.'

Eliezer couldn't help smiling to himself. It was the first time his uncle had ever spoken positively about his agile mind. He then stood and patiently listened as the two older men spoke politely of their travels.

'And which route did you travel from Damascus?' asked Abram.

'We made our way north through Hamath, until we reached the Euphrates,' answered his uncle. 'We then joined the trade route running west from the Great Sea, and we arrived in Harran yesterday.' Abram then asked a number of questions about the roads and places on them, which Eliezer assumed was probably because he intended to go that way himself.

'And will you continue westwards to the Tigris and to Nineveh?' asked Abram.

His uncle shook his head. 'No. I intend to travel south, following the Euphrates to Ur. That is, I understand, where you have come from, my lord.'

Abram nodded. 'When we left Ur, it was to travel further west, but when we reached Harran several years ago, my father wanted to settle here instead. But I will continue my journey when the time is right.'

'I hear much said of the city of Ur. Merchants speak of its splendour and learning, its music and art.'

'The land is fertile and their crops more than they need,' said Abram, before pausing to take a sip of beer. 'Some are therefore free to follow such pursuits.'

His uncle seemed to ponder the point for a moment. 'Most travel—as we do—towards Ur and not away from it,' he commented, his interest clearly piqued.

'They do.' But Abram did not elaborate, and his uncle knew enough manners not to press him further.

The conversation rapidly moved on to the route to Ur, although Eliezer remained intrigued by Abram's journey. 'And how many dwell there?' asked Eliezer's uncle, after eliciting details of the city's wealth and grandeur.

'Some say fifty-thousand or more.' Abram smiled. 'But has anyone ever counted them? I cannot say.' Eliezer suddenly found the older man's eyes upon him. 'I understand you are able to not only count, but also write numbers.'

Eliezer nodded, 'Yes, my lord.' A lump suddenly came to his throat, as he remembered the father who had taught him such things.

'And what of reading and writing?'

'He knows some already,' interjected his uncle, though Eliezer considered his words to be something of an overstatement. 'And he is not yet fourteen. You have already seen, my lord, he is a quick learner.'

'Good!' Abram then addressed Eliezer directly. 'It may be that you will be more use to me counting and recording flocks rather than keeping them. Tomorrow I will see what you are capable of.'

It felt strange to be waking up in a house rather than the tent that had been his home since leaving Damascus—and with other servants whom he had known for less than a day. His uncle's farewell had been brief. There had not even been a backwards glance as he had disappeared down the street, leaving Eliezer in the care and service of a man he barely knew. But there was something about Abram that Eliezer instinctively felt drawn towards, and he found that, rather than feeling desolate or afraid, he was unexpectedly excited about the prospects of his new life.

The other servants had, of course, been more than willing to share all they knew of their master with someone who was eager to listen. 'He's over seventy years old,' said a woman called Ninlil. 'And Sarai is over sixty!' Eliezer had considered Abram a fortunate man when he'd met his wife the previous day. That Sarai was beautiful was not in dispute. But his face must have shown surprise, because Ninlil then added, 'You are not the first to find that difficult to believe—they both carry their years well.'

'The master says that longevity runs in his family,' added an older man named Burrukam, whom Eliezer soon learned was Ninlil's husband. 'His father, Terah, is around twice his age! And Sarai is actually Abram's sister too—born of Terah but to a different mother.'

A man marrying his half-sister was a practice Eliezer had encountered before. 'And what of their children?' he asked. No one spoke. The servants looked at one another uneasily, their eyes darting back and forth. *He had clearly crossed a boundary that should not have been crossed.*

As the most senior servant, Burrukam finally broke the awkward silence. 'Sarai is barren. They have no children. You would do well to avoid any talk that reminds them— and particularly the mistress—of that.'

'But what of the young man I saw? I supposed him to be their son.'

'That was Lot, their nephew,' replied Burrukam. 'He is the son of Abram's brother who died in Ur.'

'Lot has his own sizeable flocks and possessions,' interjected another servant, 'inherited from his father.'

'There is another brother, Nahor, who still lives in Ur,' continued Burrukam. 'But Lot came with Abram when he left the city.'

'And why *did* they leave?' asked Eliezer.

Another short silence followed, but this time it was Ninlil who broke it. 'He says that his god spoke to him—and told him to go to a land that would be shown to him.' And for a second time, Eliezer's expression was one of surprise.

'Correct—again!' said Abram, as Eliezer held out the clay tablet on which he had impressed a number against the single word, *goats*. It was the last number in a column which already had figures for camels, donkeys, cattle and sheep. Each word, however, had had to be read and explained by Abram. 'You have both counted and recorded the animals without error,' Abram continued. 'There are few among my servants who would have done so well as you. I will make sure you are taught how to read properly—I have seen enough to believe it is within your capability.'

Eliezer was not used to such praise, and his heart warmed as it had not done for a number of years. He also had the strange but distinct impression that Abram liked him. *Although maybe he was just like that with everyone.*

They were standing a little distance out of the city, downstream on the Balikh River, where Abram's herdsmen were taking care of his flocks and livestock. The lush vegetation and ample water made for good grazing, and the dark tents of his servants, woven from coarse goats' hair, were scattered around. Not for the first time, Eliezer had to agree with his uncle's assessment. Abram was indeed a rich man. He followed his master's lead, and turned back in the direction of Harran. 'I think you will be of more help in the house than the field,' continued Abram, 'although we may not be here for much longer.'

The formalities of the previous day were gone. To his surprise, Eliezer found himself in a conversation with his new master, as they walked back to the city together along the river, passing women washing clothes in the shallows at the water's edge. After Abram had enquired about his family, Eliezer summoned up the courage to ask about the city to which his uncle was heading. 'I've heard of the Ziggurat at Ur built by King Ur-Nammu to honour Nanna,' he began, using the newly-learned Akkadian name for the moon god, rather than the name *Sin* he'd grown up with. 'Does it really reach half way to the sky?'

Abram raised an eyebrow. 'If you have heard that, then the rumours have added much to its height between Ur and Damascus!' After a moment, he added however, 'Although truthfully, there is none like it, and it towers above Ur.' Abram then paused again and shook his head. 'Such a waste of bricks and labour!'

Eliezer was puzzled. *Surely such a magnificent building would be pleasing to the gods!* 'My lord?'

'They think their tower, made by the hand of man, helps their god come down to earth.' Abram grunted with contempt. 'The Creator does not need our help to see the people and the earth He has made!'

His master spoke with such feeling and conviction! Eliezer felt a sudden desire to know more of the beliefs of the man who—according to the other servants—claimed to have heard the voice of a god. *Not that he was about to ask Abram directly. But how to broach the subject?* His quick mind flitted to what he'd been told the previous night. 'Do most in Harran worship Nanna? Is it not meant to be the main centre of his worship after Ur?'

'That is true enough—and my father still worships him.'

Abram's words were telling, as much for what they didn't say as for what they did. The silence that followed seemed pregnant with meaning, and Eliezer longed to know why. It would be impertinent, however, to ask his master too bluntly about his own beliefs. So he began hesitantly. 'But you speak of the creator, my lord…'

'Indeed. And do those in Damascus also speak of One who made the heavens and the earth?'

'Yes, my lord. They call him *El,* the supreme god, who also fathered other gods, such as Hadad, the god of storm and rain, and Yam and Mot.'

'And your name—Eliezer—comes from the name of your creator god?'

'Yes, my lord.'

'I know El too—but also by another name: Yahweh. But He is not one of many. He is the one true God, who rules all of creation.'

The name was completely new to Eliezer, and he was fascinated. 'Do many worship Yahweh?'

'My ancestors of long ago did: Shem and his father Noah, and right back to our first forefather, Adam.' They had already passed the numerous tents that lay close to (and were an extension of) the city, and were approaching the first of the city's brick houses. Abram let out a little laugh. 'But that is another story for another day.'

'I would like to know more of your god, my lord!' Eliezer said suddenly and with sincerity. Even if Abram hadn't mentioned this god speaking to him, there was something about Abram and the way that he spoke that stirred a longing deep within: a longing to understand the world in which he found himself—and the god who created it.

Eliezer revelled in the next two years. Although there were features common to most days—notably his lessons in reading and writing—there were a wealth of tasks to carry out (often at Abram's side) that kept him both busy and interested. He learned how to buy and sell livestock, as well as butcher and prepare animals for a meal, and how to barter in the markets of Harran for anything from a new woven rug to a jar of olive oil. He became acquainted not only with all those who served in Abram's household but also with his numerous possessions. And Eliezer had a keen eye for anything that went missing—for whatever reason.

From his first days with Abram, he had sought to be conscientious and careful in everything, working hard each day and seeking to please his master in even the smallest of jobs. And he'd watched with delight as his master's trust in him had grown. Abram began giving him responsibilities, even if it was only conveying a message to the herdsmen—or finding Terah. Abram's father seemed to spend most of his days amongst the older generation of Harran. They passed much of their time hunched over clay gaming boards, throwing dice made from bone and moving their clay cones and pyramids around the board in ways that Eliezer never mastered. He often thanked the gods for the day his uncle had happened to meet Abram. His uncle's words *You will do well with him* were probably far truer than either of them had ever dreamed.

Not that *thanking the gods* was entirely true anymore. Eliezer had made a decision within days of his first conversation with Abram that had changed that. If Abram's life reflected even in a small way the god that he followed, then Eliezer decided that Yahweh would also be his god. But not just as one of many. He would acknowledge Him, as Abram did, as the true God. And so any prayers that were prayed began to be directed towards the God of Abram and his first ancestors—the Creator who not only made men from the dust, but also spoke to them.

But as Eliezer began his third year in Abram's service, when he had just turned fifteen and his master was seventy-five, an announcement came that was to change everything. Ninlil burst into the room where he and others were beginning to prepare food for the evening meal. 'The master is calling us together. He says he has something important to tell us all.'

There was an air of anticipation as they crammed into the open-air courtyard. The bright blue sky overhead was framed by the four plastered walls. Although they stood in shade, the late afternoon sun formed a bright band along the top of the west-facing wall. The low chatter rapidly petered out as Abram walked out to address them. An expectant hush fell over the assembled men and women, both old and young. Eliezer craned his head to see his master better.

Abram did not speak immediately, but first cast his gaze across the servants—his own and those of his father and nephew. 'For those of you who are part of my father's household,' he began, 'little will change for you. But for those of you who serve me or my nephew, Lot, you will shortly be leaving Harran, and setting out with us to travel west. The God of my fathers has spoken. It is time to leave. We will make our preparations, and depart at the new moon. There will be much to do, and tomorrow we will begin to put our plans in order. But you should know this one thing: I do not plan to return here.' As low murmuring filled the courtyard, Abram concluded, 'Burrukam, Eliezer—come with me.' And then he was gone.

The murmuring became an animated babble as Eliezer began weaving his way through his fellow servants. His mind was reeling. Countless questions were tumbling into it as he scurried after his master and back into the house. *Did it mean that Terah was staying behind? Did Abram's loyalty to Yahweh come above his family? And did that really mean he was now preparing not only to leave Harran but also his father? And when exactly had Yahweh spoken to him—and how?* Eliezer's heart thrilled with excitement.

Burrukam, however, clearly felt differently. He muttered out of Abram's earshot, 'We are the fly leaving the rump for the hair on the tip of the cow's tail!'

'You speak as if all lands beyond the Euphrates are home to savages,' countered Eliezer. 'Savages who are incapable of making even a clay pot!'

'They are compared to Ur,' said Burrukam under his breath. He then grunted. 'What god sends men away from perfectly good houses to live in tents?' The last word was said with contempt.

Eliezer smiled to himself as Abram stopped and turned around to face them both. *Extra work and the life of a wanderer! Months of Burrukam grumbling could lie ahead!*

The time until nightfall was spent listening to Abram's instructions for all that would need to be done for the journey, including the purchasing of tents, grain and oil. They would also have to separate his possessions—which were many—from those of his father. Meaning (as Eliezer had supposed) that Terah was staying in Harran.

Burrukam, being older in years and longer in service with Abram, felt more at liberty to air both his questions and his displeasure. 'What is so wrong with Harran?' he asked their master.

'There is nothing wrong with it—except it is no longer where Yahweh wants me to be.' When Burrukam muttered something, Abram added, 'You knew when we left Ur that we were heading further west.'

'But we barely know anything of where we are going,' replied Burrukam with little grace.

'I am familiar with Canaan, my lord, if we travel that far!' exclaimed Eliezer. 'Or I can tell you at least something of the land. My father travelled there from Damascus and told me much about it.' His enthusiasm earned him a scowl from Burrukam.

Abram, however, seemed amused. 'That would be of great help.'

But mentioning his father suddenly brought a question to Eliezer's mind: *would their departure mean that Abram would never see Terah again? If his own father had still been alive, would he have been willing to leave him behind to obey a command of the Creator?* Eliezer couldn't be sure.

'And will we find a suitable city to live in when we get there?' asked Burrukam, pointedly directing his comment to Abram rather than Eliezer. 'Wherever it is we are going.'

'The Lord will direct us.' But Abram then added, 'I have lived in a house of brick for too long.'

And (particularly as it involved no hard decisions for him) Eliezer's heart was gripped once more by the prospect of following his master's God—a God who acted and spoke in the lives of men—wherever He might lead.

Notes

1. There is only one brief reference to Eliezer of Damascus in Scripture, in Genesis 15:2. His story here, apart from him being a servant of Abram (that is, Abraham), is entirely imagined. He is taken to be 60 years younger than his master.
2. There is no widely-used term in the Bible for what we would call Mesopotamia (literally, in Greek, '[land] between rivers'). The Septuagint, the Greek translation of the Old Testament, and various English Bible translations do use 'Mesopotamia' to translate 'Aram Naharaim' which occurs only five times in the Old Testament (once each in Genesis, Deuteronomy, Judges, I Chronicles and Psalms). Aram Naharaim is "A region somewhat ill-defined... Aram-Naharaim, literally, 'Aram of the two rivers', suggested to the ancients the region between the Euphrates and the Tigris... If plural, it was no doubt the country called by the Egyptians 'Naharin', an Aramaic name, meaning 'the land of the rivers'. It embraced a considerable extent on both sides of the Euphrates, extending east as far as the Tigris and west to the Orontes... All the Biblical references are to places in this region" (from www.jewishencyclopedia.com). Hence the use of the term 'the Land of the Rivers' in this story.
3. Abraham was not necessarily the oldest of Terah's sons, despite Genesis 11:26 listing Terah's sons as 'Abram, Nahor and Haran'. This may be, as with Shem, because of Abraham's significance rather than because he was the firstborn. It has been assumed that Haran is the eldest. He is certainly likely to be older than Nahor, as Nahor marries one of his daughters. Haran also dies first, even before their father. As happened in Genesis 5:32 (with Shem, Ham and Japheth), Genesis 11:26 also breaks the pattern in the wording of the genealogy preceding it.

4. *Harran (the name of the city) is, in Hebrew, slightly different from the name of Abraham's brother. Harran is widely thought to be an ancient city (of that name), the ruins of which are located in modern-day Turkey. Although some Bible translations use 'Haran' rather than 'Harran', the NIV translation uses the latter, as has this story, if only for the reason that it avoids confusion with Abraham's brother.*

5. *It is most likely that Abraham, coming from Ur, would have used the cuneiform script for writing, if (as is assumed here) he was literate.*

6. *Acts 7:2-3 states that God's first call to Abraham came whilst he was still in Ur and it therefore seems that Genesis 12:1-3 is a further call he received in Harran, particularly as it includes the instruction to leave his father's household. It is not clear how long they had been in Harran—only that Abraham was seventy-five when he left there. It is difficult to harmonise this with Acts 7:4, which states that Abraham left Harran after the death of his father. Genesis 11:32 says that Terah died in Harran at the age of 205. The only way to harmonise these figures would be for Abraham to be born when Terah was 135. This, however, begs the question of why Abraham would be surprised at becoming a father at 100.*

7. *It is not clear exactly when Abraham knew that Canaan was the land to which God was sending him. In Genesis 12:1, he is told, 'Go...to the land I will show you.' In 12:5, it says that he set out for the land of Canaan, but it is not clear if that is written from the perspective of later knowing where he went, or because Abraham knew that Canaan was his destination. 12:7 could, however, be the point at which he finally knows that that is where God is sending him. It is assumed here that Abraham knows he is travelling west, but only that Canaan is the promised land when he arrives there. Hence he sets out from Harran in faith, trusting that God will lead him.*

8. *The problem of foreign languages being spoken does not present itself in Genesis (other than in chapters 11 and 42:23), and so is not dealt with here. The roots of the Hebrew language are also debated by scholars.*

9. *Joshua 24:2 says that Terah and others of Abraham's forefathers 'lived beyond the River and worshipped other gods.'*

10. *As with Shem, it has been assumed that Abraham knew God as 'Yahweh' (see note at the end of the first chapter of Shem).*

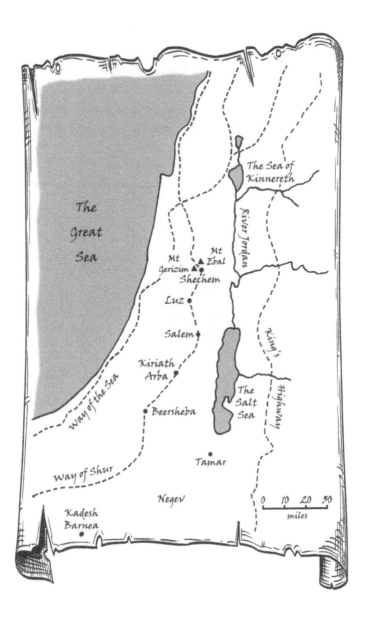

2

The LORD appeared to Abram and said, 'To your offspring I will give this land.' So he built an altar there to the LORD, who had appeared to him.' (Genesis 12:7)

'Is that the place?' asked Abram.

Eliezer nodded. 'It is.' They both stood in silence for a few moments, looking south towards the plateau on which Damascus stood. The snow-covered peak of Mount Hermon was visible to the south-west, beyond the fertile green land around the city. 'It means nothing to me now,' said Eliezer simply and truthfully. The old life that he had lived there with his parents now felt a distant memory. *Another life.* His left hand, however, instinctively rested on the small pouch hanging from his belt and containing his mother's meagre gold, whilst his right hand grasped more firmly the staff his father had once held.

A sound to his left interrupted Eliezer's thoughts. He and Abram both turned to see Lot approaching. 'We reach Damascus at last, Uncle?' he began, as he stopped beside them.

'So Eliezer tells me.'

'And will we camp near there tonight?'

'Yes, and we will rest the animals for a few days and replenish our supplies. We should easily reach the city by sunset.'

'Good!' And then Lot was gone, presumably to inform his herdsmen of the plans.

The prospect of several days without travelling was welcomed by Eliezer. The previous six weeks had been spent retracing the journey that he had made with his uncle more than two years earlier. Then it had been their small family with their donkeys; now it was a tide of livestock and people sweeping into the land, in numbers akin to those of a village. The speed of the donkeys bearing the family possessions had determined their pace before; now it was the movement of sizeable herds. The animals had certainly slowed their progress from Harran. They had initially travelled west from Harran to the Euphrates, and then south and further west for many days on the trade route that ran all the way to Egypt. From time to time, they had encountered merchants and their camel trains travelling both south and north, and more than once lengthy bartering with the traders had ensued. But, whatever other tasks occupied Eliezer, his mind kept drifting back to the God who had spoken to his master—and he wondered what had been said.

As they descended slowly towards Damascus, whose brick houses and palm trees still seemed tiny in the distance, Eliezer found that he was—unusually—alone with Abram. For a while they both walked slowly and steadily, the only sound apart from the scuffing of their feet on the dusty ground being the dull *thud* of their staffs hitting the earth with every second pace. 'My lord?' began Eliezer hesitantly.

'Go on…'

'Will Yahweh tell you when and where to stop?'

'He will—though He hasn't done yet.'

Eliezer's brow furrowed. 'But how do you…I mean,

when He…' He glanced at his master and was surprised to find amusement on the older man's face.

'I am guessing you are intrigued by the idea of the Creator speaking to a man.'

Eliezer grinned. 'My lord is wise, and knows not only what his servants say but also what they think!'

Abram laughed. 'Sometimes!'

'Please do not think me impertinent, my lord, but I would like very much to know how you hear His voice and what it sounds like.'

'It does not surprise me,' said Abram, 'for if I walked in your sandals I am sure I would have the same questions.' His gaze returned to the city. 'You are one of the few, Eliezer, who, rather than thinking me mad, wishes to know more of the God whom I follow. And not out of idle curiosity.'

'I do, my lord!'

'That is good, and a hunger for such knowledge deserves to be fed.' Abram paused, and for a few moments his thoughts appeared to be elsewhere, as if he were suddenly in some distant place or time. 'But how do you explain a voice that has no body, or words that come with such might and authority that they drive you to your knees? I do not know. But that it was Yahweh I have no doubt. For He spoke words that would never have entered my mind, telling me to leave my people and my father's household for an unknown land that He would show me. But He also promised to make me into a great nation and to make my name great. He said He would curse those who curse me, and that not only would He bless me, but also that I would be a blessing to all peoples on earth.'

Eliezer stared at Abram. It was hard not to. *A great nation? A blessing to all people? His master's words made it sound as if Yahweh had singled him out from all those on earth.* He waited.

After another pause, Abram turned towards him and said, 'You look at me, and you wonder how it could possibly be so?' Eliezer was unsure how to respond, but thankfully Abram didn't wait for an answer. 'Well, I wonder that too.'

After a few more moments of silence, Eliezer suddenly spoke. 'But I see a very great people already, my lord! We number more than three hundred, if you count the women and children.'

Abram laughed. 'Ah! I should have guessed that you would have counted them, as you have counted everything, my young but faithful servant! Three hundred, you say? And yet hardly a nation, Eliezer.'

'But it is certainly true that Yahweh has blessed you greatly! He blesses your family and yourself with long life, and with much wealth.'

'Those are blessings indeed,' said Abram, before falling silent.

Eliezer guessed they were both thinking about the one blessing he lacked—that of a child. *And it was a great puzzle. A puzzle and what seemed like a curse. How was it that the God whom Abram served so faithfully kept Sarai barren? Surely it was within the power of the Creator to grant them a son?* Eliezer was, after all, perfectly aware of what was known to all: that childlessness was a disaster, and a source of great shame to a wife. Sarai had failed to perform the most important task of a wife, and Eliezer had been in the household long enough to see the hidden looks of pity or disdain from other women when she walked by. But he also knew his master well enough to glimpse his pain. *And who would care for both Sarai and him in their old age? Who would be there to perform the necessary rites for them in death?* The promises that God had given to Abram seemed strange. *How would Abram's name become great without descendants?* And Eliezer desperately hoped that at that moment Abram couldn't discern his thoughts.

'Do you know why this is called the land of Canaan?'

Eliezer looked up from tightening one of the ropes on the tent, and realised that Lot was speaking to him. He shook his head, 'No, my lord.' It wasn't often that his master's nephew paid him any heed, and he stopped what he was doing to give his full attention to the young man standing nearby, mallet in hand. It had been around ten days since they'd left Damascus. After passing west of the Sea of Kinnereth, they had travelled through hill country, until they arrived at a crossing with another main route, at the town of Shechem, near where they were now making camp. A fertile valley lay to the west of them, cradled between two mountains—Mount Ebal on the north side, and Mount Gerizim to the south.

Lot brought the mallet down on one of the wooden tent pegs. He muttered something under his breath—directed at the peg—before speaking again. 'One of Terah's ancestors was called Shem,' he continued, straightening the peg before bringing the mallet down once again, even harder. The sound seemed to echo off the nearby rock.

'I have been told that, my lord.'

Lot repeated his blow. 'Shem had two brothers, one of whom was called Ham, and Ham had four sons, one of whom was called Canaan. And this is the land where his descendants settled—and where they still live. So now you know.' And with that, all of Lot's energies were returned to the tent peg, and Eliezer was left slightly bemused by the sudden attention.

The lesson in family history now seemingly over, Eliezer returned to pulling the tent ropes taut, although still thinking of the land around them. If this was the land Yahweh was sending his master, it was already occupied.

'Eliezer!'

He glanced up to see Abram standing nearby. 'Master?'

'Finish what you are doing and then go and choose two young kids from the flock. In Shechem they will trade wheat, grapes and olives for livestock. We will go there.'

'Yes, my lord.'

As Abram left them and returned to the tent that he and Sarai shared, Lot fixed Eliezer with his gaze once again. He raised an eyebrow. 'I never knew my uncle to have favourites…until now.'

Eliezer flushed and suddenly became very interested in the tent peg near his foot. 'I…I only try to please my master,' he stammered.

'Well, you'd better be quick then,' replied Lot, and Eliezer hurried off, avoiding Lot's eyes.

The smell of baking bread met Eliezer as he approached his master's tent. He was carrying a wooden bowl filled with curds made the previous day by leaving some goat's milk to sour and pouring off the whey. Plump grapes to add to the simple early morning meal were brought by Burrukam, who was grumbling as was his custom. Sarai retrieved the flat bread—now cooked—from the top of the pottery oven standing over the fire. Making the bread could, of course, have been done by a servant. In most families, however, it was done by the wife and mother. Eliezer suspected that both grinding the grain—the wheat so recently bartered for in Shechem—and then baking the bread helped Sarai to feel more like the provider for the family. Even if there were no children to feed.

'It makes a welcome change from barley bread,' said Lot, after taking a large mouthful of the fresh round that he had dipped in the curds. He was sitting with Abram on rugs in the entrance to the tent, the front flaps of which had now been raised, to let in both air and the light of the new day.

'I am surprised my brother's son notices the difference, given the haste and abandon with which he eats,' said Sarai with a wry smile, offering him the woven basket in which the rounds of fresh bread were piled. She then joined them, cross-legged, on one of the rugs.

'Haste need not mean a lack of attention,' replied Lot, as he broke another piece of bread, 'nor a man's reasonable hunger, a lack of restraint.'

'*Reasonable?* That's not the word I would use…' muttered Burrukam.

Eliezer lowered his face to conceal a grin; Lot's voracious appetite was a source of humour amongst them all. Such comments were, of course, not for the ears of the family. He glanced across at Abram, but his thoughts were clearly elsewhere.

The light morning meal shortly after sunrise was usually the time when Abram gave Burrukam and Eliezer their tasks for the day. But not only that; he also told them what he expected of the rest of the household, be it preparing to move camp, going to any local markets, pasturing the animals, or investigating the surrounding countryside. But that day was different. Although both servants stood patiently waiting, Abram barely spoke as he ate, and seemed to be deep in thought for most of the time that Sarai and Lot continued their exchange.

'Today, I will build an altar.' Abram's sudden pronouncement immediately silenced everyone. 'An altar to Yahweh,' he continued, 'for He appeared to me in the night.' Eliezer stiffened and Lot's half-full mouth remained open. All were as still as the air in the tent as they waited for him to continue. 'He promised in Harran that he would show me the land to which he wanted me to go. This is that land.' He paused, letting the momentous truth sink in. But he had not finished. 'Yahweh has not only sent me here to Canaan, however. He has now promised to give the land to my offspring.'

Sarai flinched. Judging by her ill-disguised surprise, Eliezer guessed it was the first she knew of what had happened and a momentary look of pain darkened her face. Abram leaned over and whispered something to his wife, and Eliezer was too respectful to strain his ears to hear. Lot's reaction was to studiously avoid the eyes of all and start eating again, pressing the last torn piece of bread into a bowl that now held only a few smears of goat's curd and consuming it whilst staring down at the rug. But Eliezer's mind was racing. *Appeared to him rather than just speaking? What did that mean? How could the Creator appear to mortal man? What form did Yahweh take? Nanna, the moon god, was shown as an old man, with a beard made of lapis lazuli, riding on a winged bull. Was Yahweh like that?*

'Eliezer!'

He started. 'Yes, my lord.'

'I want you to choose a lamb from the herd—the best and the most healthy. Tether it nearby, so that it is ready for the sacrifice.'

'Yes, master.'

'And Burrukam—bring two or three strong men from the household. I will need their help in building the altar.'

'Master,' he replied, bowing his head. But as Eliezer left the tent moments later at Burrukam's side, the older servant muttered, 'Maybe Abram's god is blind, and hasn't noticed that the land already belongs to others and that our master has no offspring.'

Eliezer was shocked. 'You must not talk of our master's God in that way!'

'So you say. But maybe if he honoured Nanna, as his father did, the gods would open Sarai's womb and grant her children.'

'You should not say such things!' insisted Eliezer. But mainly because he could not think of a reply.

The altar, standing at the centre of the land that God was giving to Abram, was complete by noon. Rocks had been gathered and stacked in a square pile that was two cubits long, wide and high. As the altar was being built, Abram had sharpened the knife that he would use, scraping bronze upon stone. The year-old lamb stood quietly nearby, nibbling any green shoots within reach, oblivious of the fate that awaited it.

'The killing must be swift and clean,' said Abram, running his finger along the bright edge of the long knife as Eliezer untied the lamb. It was the best one he could find, unblemished and healthy, and he brought it to Abram. Lot stood nearby with a lit torch, Sarai at his side, with a number of the other servants watching.

One swift slash rendered the vulnerable creature lifeless. Eliezer then helped his master lift the lamb with its blood-soaked throat onto the sizeable pile of wood and kindling that Abram had gathered and carefully arranged on the stone altar. Lot stepped forward and lit the dried hay and sticks at the base of the wood, and flames were soon licking around the motionless sacrifice.

'Great Creator of all that is,' cried out Abram in a loud voice, with his hands and face raised to heaven, 'You have given each creature the breath of life, and we now offer the life of this creature back to You. This land and all the earth and its people are Yours. You have led us to this place, which we dedicate to You. You are sovereign, O Yahweh. May Your great name be known and praised in this land and in our lives. Accept our worship, O Mighty God, whose greatness cannot be shown in wood or stone or metal. May we, Your faithful servants, honour You. Protect us, and guide our steps, O Lord Most High.'

As Eliezer watched the lamb being engulfed by the fire, he thought once again about the words Abram had spoken that morning. *Was it really true that Abram would have descendants of his own? Was that what Abram meant by God's greatness being shown in the lives of men?* To Eliezer, it seemed obvious that if Yahweh had created both the heavens and the earth, then all things must be possible for Him. *But if he were Abram, would he be able to trust God to do the impossible for him?* He tore his eyes away from the mesmerising flames and looked across to Abram and Sarai—and wondered what words his master had whispered to his barren wife that morning.

The acrid smell of burning hair and skin was soon replaced by the pleasing aroma of roasting meat, and long after Eliezer had followed his master away from the place of worship, the smoke and the smell of the lamb continued to rise up to heaven.

There was always a cost involved in sacrifice, thought Eliezer, passing the smouldering remains much later, as the sun finally dipped below the town of Shechem to the west. And as he thought of the journey that Abram had begun in Ur, he knew that, however much Yahweh had blessed his master, there was a cost to obedience too.

To Eliezer's surprise, their journey began again the following morning. At the end of the second day of travelling, however, they found themselves pitching their tents between a place called Luz to the west and Ai to the east. And the first thing that Abram did was build another altar.

'The cities all seem to rule themselves,' said Lot to Abram, as Eliezer was being taught by his master how to arrange the stones in the best way, so that the altar kept its shape as more stone was added.

'We will undoubtedly soon discover where allegiances lie and what alliances have been made,' replied Abram. He suddenly exclaimed, 'Watch your fingers!'

Eliezer glanced up. He was about to place a particularly heavy and jagged rock on the growing pile. 'Yes, master.'

'It will help neither of us if they end up crushed or bloodied.'

Lot nodded towards the unfinished altar. 'You still stake your claim on this land wherever you tread.'

'Before it is my land, it is God's,' said Abram. He turned his attention away from his nephew and back to the stones. 'Every altar declares that this is, and has always been, *His* land.'

'That went well,' said Burrukam, his voice heavy with sarcasm. Several weeks had passed since the sacrifice near Luz, and the servants (now including some Egyptians) were sitting together around a fire. It was the first evening after leaving Egypt.

'And you would have done better, I suppose,' replied his wife with no less sarcasm.

'Hush, woman. I would have done better because I would not have been in the master's predicament in the first place.'

'Meaning?' demanded Ninlil.

'Meaning that although Pharaoh may be particularly attracted to foreign women, as he was to Sarai, those foreign women still have to be attractive.'

The men around the fire laughed, but Ninlil's face was like thunder. 'Ha!' she replied. 'Pharaoh may have many wives, but you have only one! You would do well to remember that.' This time it was the women's turn to laugh.

Eliezer had witnessed many times the lively exchanges between Burrukam and his wife, but it was their daughter who now held his attention. Lilith's eyes seemed to sparkle with mirth as she, too, laughed. Her dark curls fell beautifully around her face, but when her eyes happened to meet his, he looked away swiftly, flushing—and found instead her father scowling at him.

Some weeks earlier, their tents had been pitched in the Negev, the drier region at the southern end of Canaan. Purchasing barley, wheat and oil had become increasingly expensive, however, as a famine began to take hold of the whole land, and Abram had decided that they would travel further south and on to Egypt. But although its well-watered lands offered a more certain supply of grain, it presented other challenges.

'The master's plan was a good one,' began a servant named Bazi. 'Many Egyptians may have seen Sarai and wanted her. To say that he was her husband may have put the master's life in danger.'

'Yes, and saying that he was her brother was clever,' began another. 'He could put off any who wished to take her as their wife. And Sarai is, after all, the master's half-sister.'

However, to Eliezer, the half-truth had still felt like a half-lie—saying Sarai was his sister was not the same as saying she was his wife. His master's seeming lack of trust in God's protection had surprised him.

'But he could not put off Pharaoh himself,' responded an Egyptian named Hagar, gazing out under her long, dark eyelashes. She had been given to Sarai by Pharaoh as her maidservant when, much to everyone's alarm, he had taken her as his wife. If the question of whether Pharaoh had lain with Sarai was in any of the servants' minds, it remained unspoken.

'And the master did very well,' replied Bazi. 'Pharaoh gave him sheep, oxen and donkeys, and even camels.'

Eliezer finally spoke up. 'Yes, but he would have given them back in the blink of an eye—together with his own flocks—to free Sarai!'

'But he did not need to,' said Hagar.

'No,' replied Eliezer, 'because Yahweh rescued Sarai, by sending that plague on the Egyptians—and taking it away when Sarai was returned.'

'He left Egypt far richer than he arrived,' said Ninlil. She then looked at her husband and shrugged her shoulders. 'It ended well.'

Suddenly, both Hagar and Burrukam's names were called from the tent of Abram and Sarai. And Burrukam added, with a note of finality, 'And this evening has ended too.' The most senior servant had spoken.

All knew it was time to return to return to their tents, but Eliezer lingered. Before Burrukam made his way over to tend to Abram's needs, Eliezer asked, 'Now do you believe that Yahweh sees his servants and protects them?'

Burrukam just scowled. As the older man turned his back to leave, Eliezer grinned. *If there was one thing Burrukam hated more than living in a tent, it was being proved wrong.*

Notes

1. *A study of the Exodus has shown that the people of Israel, with large herds, moved at between 9-18 miles (15-30km) per day. This seems a reasonable equivalent to use for the movement of Abraham and his herds, allowing time for pitching tents, etc. A conservative rate of roughly 10 miles a day in travelling with herds has been assumed. Harran to Shechem is roughly 400 miles, so that would take 40 days or approximately 7 weeks, if Abraham rested on the Sabbath. Given that they might also have had some stops, that figure has been rounded up to 2 months. Damascus is something over 100 miles from Shechem.*

2. *The exact route that Abraham took from Harran to Shechem is not clear—they could have travelled through Damascus or been on a route further west.*

3. *Genesis 29:27, telling the story of Jacob, uses the word 'week', so it is taken to be a valid unit of time for the patriarchs to use.*

4. Part of the significance of the land of Canaan is that it is where Europe, Asia and Africa all meet, forming a land bridge between them. Major trade routes (such as the King's Highway and the Way of the Sea) would therefore have to pass through the land or nearby.

5. Although, through Moses, specific instructions were given as to how burnt offerings were to be done, i.e. cutting the animals in pieces, it is not clear if that would have been done by Abraham, or whether he would have simply laid the animal on the altar whole (see, for example, Genesis 22:9).

6. Both in Genesis 12 and 13, Abraham visits Bethel. However, later in Genesis it tells of how Jacob stays at a place called Luz, and renames it Bethel (Genesis 28:19). The earlier name of the city, Luz, is therefore used here in the story of Abraham. The Sea of Kinnereth (or Chinnereth in some versions) is an earlier name for the Sea of Galilee, and the Salt Sea (or Sea of the Arabah) is an earlier name for the Dead Sea.

7. Just because the Bible describes something doesn't mean that it approves it. This applies, for example, to Abraham's deception during the stay in Egypt.

8. Canaan was not a nation with fixed borders before the Israelites arrived there after the Exodus. Many cities operated independently, under their own rulers.

3

Now Lot, who was moving about with Abram, also had flocks and herds and tents. But the land could not support them while they stayed together. (Genesis 13:5-6)

It was difficult to count accurately whilst there was an altercation going on. Eliezer sighed as he stood in the shade of the acacia tree. Its feathery leaves gave some shelter against the sun, and had he not been distracted by goat kids and quarrelling, he might have taken time to admire its blossoms, which hung on the tree like tiny yellow orbs. He glanced up from the clay tablet on which he was trying to record the number of newborns in the flock. The herder, Hanish, had been standing by his side keeping the goats in order. Until, that is, one of Lot's shepherds appeared nearby, bringing his sheep into the same grazing area, and Hanish had swiftly departed to remonstrate. Although Eliezer couldn't initially hear what passed between them, as their voices became louder he clearly heard *oxen dung* and *wits of a dead donkey*. By the time the insults had descended to the level of *useless as a camel's fart*, and they were shouting loud enough for Eliezer to hear every word, he decided it was time to run back to his master.

It was the third time since the new moon that he had witnessed such strife between the herdsmen, and the moon hadn't even waxed full yet. When he reached the camp, however, Abram was nowhere to be seen. 'Idiot!'

muttered Eliezer, chiding himself, as he remembered too late that his master had gone to the nearby town of Luz with Burrukam. He hesitated near Abram's stone altar, to which they had returned after leaving Egypt. A movement in the corner of his eye made him turn his head. *Well, at least there were some benefits to be gained from his mistake.*

'Is that heavy?' he asked casually, as Lilith walked nearby, bearing a large bundle of washing destined for the nearby stream. She paused.

'Are you offering to carry it for me?' she replied, her dark eyes filled with merriment.

'Do you need me to carry it for you?'

'*Need* you?' she replied with laughter. 'What do you men think we do, then, when you are not around?'

'Are you making fun of me?'

'Would I make fun of one of my master's favourite servants?' Eliezer was momentarily struck dumb. 'And are we forever to talk in questions?'

Eliezer thought furiously for a moment. 'I don't know. Would you like that?' He felt pleased with his reply when Lilith laughed again. 'You remind me of your mother,' he continued, and then felt the need to hastily add, 'in a good way.' Her raised eye-brows flustered him slightly. 'What I mean is, you aren't afraid to say what you think.'

'So you would not want a wife who never answered you back?'

Not if it was you! 'Er…no.' Eliezer felt himself flushing. *That sounded weak.* 'No, I definitely wouldn't.'

'With all this standing and idle chatter, this washing *is* now getting heavy.'

'Then I *will* carry it for you,' said Eliezer, 'whether you need me to or not.'

'Eliezer!'

The presence of his master, so recently desired, now felt like an unwelcome intrusion, although Eliezer was glad that the arrival hadn't been moments later, when he would have been seen taking Lilith's washing from her. As it was, Burrukam was already scowling at him. *It was always a scowl when it concerned him and Lilith.* It was a scowl that said, *Keep away from my daughter*. But Abram seemed amused.

'Yes, my lord!' Eliezer hurried over to the donkeys from which the men were now dismounting, as Lilith scurried away with her dirty clothes towards the stream.

Abram pointed to some other donkeys, laden with supplies. 'As you are here, you can help Burrukam unload the animals.'

'Yes, my lord.'

'But I had not expected you back so soon. Did you visit all the herds, as I instructed you?'

'No, master. Because I need to speak to you about the herdsmen.'

'Trouble again?'

Eliezer nodded. 'I'm afraid so. Even the patience of Hanish wears thin.'

Abram sighed. 'I have been giving the matter much thought. This, I believe, decides it. I will speak with Lot. Yahweh has blessed us both, but the land cannot support such great numbers of animals, particularly with others living nearby. The time has come for our companies to part.'

From where they were standing, Eliezer had a good view of Canaan. He and Burrukam had followed Abram to a hill-top near Luz. Lot and his servant Zambiya were also there. They were in the hill country, which ran from north to south through the land, and their current vantage point enabled them to see some distance in every direction. To the west, the land sloped down towards the plain that ran, again north to south, along the coast of the sea. To the north, in the distance, he could see Mount Ebal and Mount Gerizim, near the town of Shechem. To the south, the hill country continued down to the city of Salem and beyond. But it was to the east that Eliezer's eyes were drawn. The ground sloped down again, but at the bottom lay a wide, flat valley through which the Jordan river flowed. The land there was well-watered and green. His attention was suddenly drawn back to Abram as his master began addressing Lot.

'Let us put an end to any quarrelling. You are my brother's son, and we must be at peace. Look around you—we can see the whole land from here. It is time for us to separate. If you go to the left, then I will go to the right. If you go to the right, then I will go to the left. Choose which way you will go.'

Eliezer couldn't quite believe what he was hearing. *Surely it was to Abram that God had promised this land! It should be his choice!* But his master seemed unperturbed.

It didn't take long for Lot to make his decision. He and Zambiya whispered together for several moments, and then Lot raised his arm and pointed towards the lush Jordan valley. 'I will take my herds eastwards.'

'Very well,' said Abram. And that was all he said on the matter.

Whilst Abram and his nephew said their farewells, Eliezer kept a respectful distance. 'I could have told the master which way Lot would go without having to come up here,' grumbled Burrukam at his side. 'Never mind the protection and help his uncle has given him, he was always going to pick the best for himself, given the choice.' Although Eliezer agreed, his loyalty to Abram meant that he wasn't going to admit as much, at least to Burrukam. 'We could even have settled down in the valley, and not had to move so much.'

Ah, so that was it, thought Eliezer, understanding the deeper reasons for the other servant's grumbles. Eliezer kept his peace as Burrukam continued to lament their lot, until Abram finally called them to himself as his nephew departed.

'You may return to the camp now, but I will stay for a while.' Burrukam quickly ambled off, but Eliezer hesitated. 'You have something you wish to say?'

'It's just…well…Lot has chosen the best grazing land for his flocks.'

'I gave him the choice.'

'But…'

'You believe I have been treated unfairly by my nephew?'

'I mean no offence, my lord, but…' Eliezer trailed off, not quite sure how to express his sense of injustice to his master.

Abram looked directly at him. 'Eliezer, it is not the first time I have put my future in Yahweh's hands. And it probably will not be the last. The Lord has been good to me, and I do not expect that to stop just because Lot has chosen to go east.' He paused, sadness in his eyes. 'He has chosen, however, to live at the very edge of the land that God has promised—maybe even beyond it. And I hear rumours of what happens in the cities of the valley. And the rumours are not good.' Abram fell silent again as they both looked down towards the Jordan, with the Salt Sea just visible at the southern end of the long valley. He finally shook his head and sighed. 'But I will stay and speak with Yahweh.'

'What, here?' replied Eliezer, surprised.

Abram once again appeared amused. 'No man needs an altar or a temple to be able to speak to the God of Creation. Yahweh cannot be confined to a house of wood, brick or stone, made by the hands of men.' Abram regarded Eliezer for a few moments, and then added, 'And any who believe in Yahweh may speak to Him. And though He remains hidden from their eyes, He will still hear them.'

'But, my lord, you also said that Yahweh appeared to you!' Eliezer desperately wanted Abram to describe what he saw. And his master seemed to understand that.

'You are eager to know more of the Lord's ways, and that is good. But can I explain Him adequately to you...?' Abram gave a little laugh. 'All I can tell my young servant is that I know not whether I slept or was awake when the Lord appeared to me. And that he appeared to me in the form of a man. But One whose presence would make any on earth tremble and any king throw himself down at His feet.' Eliezer's eyes widened, and Abram continued. 'And now I must stand before Yahweh, and hear if He wishes to speak to me.'

'I will leave you, my lord.'

'Yes, that is good. But you needn't go far.' And once again, Abram looked at him steadily. 'And do you believe, Eliezer, that Yahweh is the one true God?'

'I do, my lord, and I have pledged myself to your God.'

'Then He is your God also, and you may speak to Him too.'

'What do I say?'

'You say what is on your heart.'

And so, a short while later, Eliezer was standing out of sight of Abram, hands lifted to heaven, as he'd seen his master do, and he spoke to the unseen God. He asked for protection for Abram's household, for guidance and for God's continued blessing. And he prayed for Lilith, for, of all that he knew, she was the one who was chiefly on his heart.

'Eliezer!' His master's familiar summons raised him swiftly to his feet. It hadn't taken Eliezer very long to run out of things to say to Yahweh. The lack of any immediate response from heaven meant that he was soon sitting on a large stone, tossing smaller stones at a nearby tree, having decided to wait for his master. Not that he had any idea how long Abram might be. *What if he spent whole days speaking with the Lord?* In the event, he clearly didn't—at least not on that occasion.

'Master?'

Abram strode across to him, staff in hand. Any previous sadness was gone, and there seemed to be a new air of determination. 'We will be moving camp tomorrow.'

'The Lord has told you to leave?'

'He has told me to walk through the length and breadth of the land. All that we saw from the top, He is giving to me. To me and my descendants, who will be as numerous as the dust of the earth.'

Not for the first time, Eliezer felt unsure of what to say, given Abram's lack of a single heir. He knew that the Creator could do anything, but... *as numerous as the dust of the earth?* Eliezer quickly decided on the only safe response. 'So where are we going first?'

'I have built an altar here, and one to the north, in Shechem. We will now travel south—to Kiriath Arba—and I will build an altar there also.'

Eliezer darted between the guests who were seated on the rugs scattered around Abram's tent, offering trays of fruit as he did so. The sides of the tent had been let down against the advancing chill of the night, and although the fire that could still be seen through the open tent flaps provided some light, other lamps were carefully (and safely) positioned around the tent. Eliezer tried not to stare too much at the three sizeable brothers who seemed like small giants in comparison to him. Their Amorite dress was not unlike their own: woollen tunics, held in place by belts, and larger, looser over-garments, with long scarves wrapped around their heads. Although they looked formidable, Eliezer guessed that Abram was better to their neighbours as an ally rather than a rival. Not only had the Lord blessed his master with livestock and silver and gold, but he also had something approaching a small army. There were three hundred and eighteen men who could, if necessary, bear a sword. Of this Eliezer was sure—he had counted them, and he was one of them. He'd also helped barter along the way for weapons, and then watched as Lot had taught those same men how to use them.

'Yahweh will protect us,' Abram had explained. 'But He may do that by protecting us in battle. And if any who oppose us know of our strength, then they may think twice about meeting us in the first place.'

And looking at the three men seated there that evening, Eliezer understood his master's wisdom.

'You have travelled far,' began the brother named Mamre, whose territory was closest to their camp. 'And was Egypt to your liking?'

'It is not a place I would stay longer than I had to,' replied Abram. 'Their gods are many and strange, as are their customs.'

'It is not only their gods who are strange!' exclaimed another of the brothers, Eshcol. 'Their men have no beards and they paint their eyes like women.' He then belched loudly.

'But at least they don't wear their food on their face,' said Aner—who appeared to be the eldest—as he flicked Eshcol's beard to dislodge the crumbs that lingered there. Mamre roared with laughter.

'It was a fine meal,' retorted Eshcol, adding, 'and it still is,' as he took some more figs from the platter Eliezer was holding.

When Mamre had stopped laughing, he turned to Abram. 'And speaking of gods, I see you have built an altar in your camp. Do you plan to stay here?'

Eliezer wondered how Mamre would view Abram's presence. *Yes, grazing land would have to be shared, but the protection of a powerful and well-armed ally was not to be ignored.*

'If the flocks need more pasture we will move. And we will move if my God directs me,' replied Abram. 'But what of the others beyond Kiriath Arba? What can you tell me of the cities and their rulers?'

'You need to know first that soon there may be trouble nearby,' began Aner. Eliezer's attention was immediately wrested away from sheep and onto their guest, dressed in his colourful red and blue outer garment. Burrukam's expression of boredom had swiftly disappeared.

'How so?' asked Abram.

'There was an alliance of four kings from the east—from the Land of the Rivers—' continued Aner.

'And even beyond that,' interjected Eshcol, 'from Elam, to the east of Ur. Its king, Chedorlaomer, led the alliance.'

'I do not know the name,' said Abram. 'It is many years since I left Ur. But what of the alliance?'

'Some twelve or thirteen years ago,' said Aner, 'those kings invaded this land. They came from the north, travelling south along the high plateau to the east of the Jordan. They made war with five of the kings around the valley of Siddim, near the southern tip of the Salt Sea, and conquered them. They and their cities have lived in subjection to Chedorlaomer since then.'

'Which cities?' asked Abram. And Eliezer presumed that his master, like him, was thinking of the land into which Lot had travelled.

'Sodom and Gomorrah, Admah and Zeboiim, and Bela,' answered Aner.

'And why the trouble?' asked Abram.

Mamre shook his head slowly. 'Foolishly or bravely, the five kings have rebelled against the alliance in recent months, refusing to pay the tribute demanded of them.' He then added, 'At least, that is what we have heard.'

'And you expect the kings from the east to return?'

Mamre glanced at his two brothers and then met Abram's eyes. 'That would not surprise any of us. Though who knows when they might come.'

Abram paused long enough to take grapes from Eliezer's platter and to nod to Burrukam to refill the men's cups. As the beer was being poured, he asked, 'And you have dealings with those five cities?' Eliezer thought of the rumours that his master heard.

'Traders come from there,' replied Mamre, whilst his brothers drank deeply from their cups. 'But we ourselves care not for the cities or their people.' He then put his own head back and drained his cup, which Burrukam immediately refilled.

'And why is that?' asked Abram, feigning ignorance.

'I am surprised you have not heard of their reputations,' began Aner. 'Particularly Sodom and Gomorrah. They do many detestable things. They consider rape a sport. Men, women, travellers—it matters not to them. All are fair game.'

'I would not consider myself or my family safe near them,' muttered Mamre. 'They show no pity to any in need.'

'And such immorality is not hidden. I am told they parade it, as if they have no shame,' added Eshcol. 'I would not live near there either.'

The visitors were offered a tent for the night, but before they left Abram's presence, he pledged allegiance to them, and they to him. 'An attack against you is an attack against us,' Mamre declared in his deep, gruff voice. And Abram replied in kind.

After bidding goodnight to his guests, but before he retired behind the curtain into the back of the tent where he slept with Sarai, Abram tarried under the stars. As Burrukam, Ninlil and Lilith collected up the dirty cups and plates, and straightened the tent, Eliezer slipped outside into the cool night air. Abram was standing by the embers of the fire.

'My lord?'

'What do you wish to say or ask?' said Abram, his features clear in the light of an almost-full moon.

'Is Lot safe?'

'Safe from the kings of the east or from the men of the five cities?'

Eliezer had only really been thinking about the cities of Sodom and Gomorrah. *But Abram had a point.*

However, before he had time to answer his master's question, Abram continued. 'He will be safer from both if he stays away from the cities. Of that I am certain. But will he? Of that I cannot be so sure.' And with that, he turned and headed back into the tent, and Eliezer knew that their conversation was over.

Notes

1. *In Genesis, Abraham's location is not always specified.*
2. *As is said on a number of occasions in Genesis and Joshua, the town of Hebron was previously known as Kiriath Arba (see, for example, Genesis 23:2; 35:27; Joshua 14:15; 15:54). It is not clear when this change of name occurred, or whether it is related to the tribe of Levi (one of whose descendants was called Hebron). However, it does seem likely that it was its previous name of Kiriath Arba that was in use at the time of the Patriarchs, so that name has been used here.*
3. *Although Sodom and Gomorrah have not been located with any certainty, many assume that their location is now under the Dead Sea, at the southern end. In the story, they are assumed to be across the Jordan, at what was the south-western end of the Dead Sea. There are, however, some Bronze Age city*

ruins located on the eastern edge of the Dead Sea, one of which (to the north-east) was certainly destroyed by a catastrophic fire. However, the date for this seems late for the most likely date for Abraham.

4. *In the Book of Deuteronomy, the Amorites are described as the last remnants of the giants who once lived on earth (3:11). Hence the references here to their size.*

5. *Isaiah 3:9 says, '…they parade their sin like Sodom. They do not hide it.' This implies that Sodom's sin was blatant. Ezekiel 16:49-50 also states: 'Now this was the sin of your sister Sodom: she and her daughters were arrogant, overfed and unconcerned; they did not help the poor and needy. They were haughty and did detestable things before me.' Their sins were clearly not just of a sexual nature.*

4

When Abram heard that his relative had been taken captive,
he called out the 318 trained men born in his household
and went in pursuit as far as Dan. (Genesis 14:14)

Eliezer came hurtling down the hillside towards the camp, with little thought for either his safety or those in his path. He didn't even notice Lilith standing at the well, drawing water. 'Master! Abram!' Eliezer glanced around him as he slowed his pace, searching for one person only. His cries were clearly heard, as moments later Abram and Sarai came into view, walking around the edge of a tent.

'What is it, Eliezer?' asked Abram.

Eliezer could only speak in short bursts, as he tried to catch his breath. 'We need...a donkey!...You must come...master!'

'Where have you run from?'

'Beyond...Kiriath Arba.'

'No wonder your face is like a ripe pomegranate.'

Sarai turned and gestured to Lilith. 'Bring some water for him.'

Eliezer was not sure he had ever run so far and so quickly. His chest felt as if a camel were sitting on it. He bent over and put his hands on his knees. He only looked up when he felt Abram's hand on his shoulder. Lilith was standing there, holding a cup of water out to him.

'Drink some water,' said Abram, 'and catch your breath. And then explain to me what's happened.'

Eliezer gratefully took the cup from Lilith's hand, even managing a quick if rather sweaty smile, and downed the water in one. He handed it back, nodding in thanks, and then took several deep breaths.

'Now, start again.'

'I was with Damuzi and his sheep when a man suddenly seemed to appear out of nowhere. It was Zambiya.'

'Lot's servant?' said Sarai, surprised.

'Yes. He was injured and was asking for you, my lord. He said he had an important message, which he had to give to you in person. He looked exhausted. He drank all the water we had, and asked for food, but we had none. I wasn't sure he would make it back here, particularly with an injured leg. So I left him with Damuzi and ran back here to get help.'

'And you have no idea what his message is about?'

'No, my lord.' Eliezer paused. 'But I did learn one thing. There has been a battle.'

Abram looked grim but determined.

The animals were soon trotting along, carrying Eliezer and his master, with a spare donkey for the injured man.

'Master, do you think this has anything to do with that rumour?'

'It is possible, and that is what I fear.' Abram fell silent, looking steadfastly ahead.

Eliezer was left with his own thoughts, as he jerked up and down on the donkey's back. Almost a month earlier, they had heard reports of either a raiding party or a small army moving south along the trade route—the King's

Highway—that ran along the high plateau to the east of the Jordan. The route began in the Land of the Rivers, and eventually wound its way to Egypt. But nothing of what they'd heard gave any indication of the army's intended destination—or, if it was heading further south, whether it would return the same way at some later time.

'We're almost there now, my lord,' said Eliezer finally, as he guided their donkeys round a rocky hill covered with both clumps of yellowing grass and scattered sheep.

Moments later, he heard the voice of Damuzi. 'Master! Over here.' He waved madly at them. Eliezer spotted Zambiya sitting in shade, his back against a tree.

The sheep scattered as the donkeys approached, and Abram and Eliezer dismounted swiftly as soon as they had come to a halt. Zambiya immediately tried to rise to his feet. 'No, do not try to move,' said Abram. 'I'm told you are wounded.'

'I have news for you—' began the servant in a croaky voice.

'It can wait until we have given you water,' said Abram firmly. Eliezer swiftly took the waterskin from his donkey and offered it to the man, who drank deeply and eagerly. 'Are you able to speak now?'

'Yes, my lord. I have come from Lot and his wife in Sodom.'

Eliezer's eyes widened. *A wife—and in Sodom! But that would not be the news that Zambiya was bringing.*

The servant continued. 'They and all that they own have been taken—'

'*Taken*? By whom?' asked Abram, his questions urgent. 'And when?'

'By Chedorlaomer and his army—two days past. I managed to escape, but most didn't.'

'And do you know which way they went?'

'They were seen heading north.'

'That is all I need to know for the moment. We will get you back to the camp and dress your wounds. Then you can tell us more.' Abram turned to Eliezer. 'Give Zambiya the bread and cheese you have brought.' As Eliezer hurriedly extracted the provisions from the bag slung over his shoulder, Abram continued to give him instructions. 'I will wait with Zambiya and ride back with him, but I want to you go as fast as you can to Mamre. Tell him that I am going to need his help and that of his brothers. Ask him to meet us at our camp as soon as he is able. Go—now!'

Within moments, Eliezer was trotting round the hill again, and heading towards the tall oak trees that marked Mamre's camp near Kiriath Arba. He wondered what Abram thought of Lot living in Sodom. *Maybe he, like Burrukam, had tired of living in tents. Or had his wife been the cause of Lot moving to a brick-built house? And if she was from Sodom, then he was surely in some way allying himself to the men of that city.* He remembered Aner's words and shuddered. *Surely Lot was playing with fire, if what the brothers had said was true.*

Eliezer offered a silent prayer of thanks to the God of Abram when he arrived, finding not only Mamre but also his brother Eshcol there. Having briefly told them what he knew, they quickly decided not only to accompany Eliezer immediately but also to send a message to summon Aner.

Eliezer felt dwarfed by the two men as they all urged their donkeys on. He noticed the swords that both of them now carried—and was glad that the brothers would be fighting with them and not against them.

With what Eliezer decided must have been Yahweh's blessing, they arrived at the camp only a short while after Abram, and just as Burrukam had finished applying oil and bandages to Zambiya's wounds. They all remained on their feet. As Ninlil and Hagar served them all beer and bread, Abram turned to Lot's servant who was seated on a small wooden stool. 'Now, tell us everything you know. What has happened since you parted from us?'

'For some months, we pitched our tents among the cities of the valley. We met men from Sodom, and it wasn't long before the master had taken a wife called Hurriya from among their daughters. We then moved into a house in the city. Then, almost a month ago, we saw signs of an army passing south—'

'Along the King's Highway?' asked Abram.

'Yes. We feared it was Chedorlaomer and the kings allied with him. But they didn't turn aside from the Highway, and disappeared to the south. Then, four days ago, fugitives came from a town called Tamar—'

'Some from our tribe are there,' interjected Mamre. 'They are Amorites, like us. The town lies—what?— probably a day's journey south-west from the far end of the Salt Sea.' He stood with his powerful arms folded and his sword hanging from his belt, looking every part a warrior.

Zambiya continued. 'They said their town had been overrun by men from the Land of the Rivers. It seems that each place the kings have been, they have conquered— first towns to the north, along the King's Highway, then south as far as El Paran on the sea. They then turned back,

131

travelling north again. Bera knew that if they'd reached Tamar, they would be coming to attack Sodom also—'

'Bera?' queried Abram.

'Sodom's king,' replied Zambiya. 'He summoned the other kings of the cities by the Salt Sea, and they came out together, prepared for battle, planning to meet Chedorlaomer in the valley of Siddim. 'I was with Lot and his wife in the city. I do not know what happened in the valley, only that our king did not return and, before we could flee, the city was being overrun that night by the armies from the east. We quickly decided to hide. Lot and Hurriya ran back into the house, but I climbed down into a well, injuring my leg. I stayed there a long time. I could see the light of fires burning above me, but I stayed there until the city was finally quiet and the light of day was dawning. I returned to the house, but it had been stripped bare. My master and his wife were nowhere to be seen. The only ones I found were those like me, who had managed to escape capture. They were saying that many from Sodom had been taken—and that Lot and Hurriya were among them. I then knew that I must come and find you—and it has taken me two days. Now I have told you all that I know.'

Mamre spat contemptuously onto the dust. 'So the kings of the east now take their tribute in cities and in lives.'

'If all I have heard of Sodom is true,' began Abram, 'then Lot has been foolish to make his home there. But I will not abandon my nephew. I will pursue the armies north and, with the help of Yahweh, rescue Lot and all that is his.' He glanced over at Eliezer. 'How many armed men are there within the household?'

'Three hundred and eighteen, my lord.'

Abram then turned to Zambiya. 'And do you know how many Chedorlaomer and his army number?'

'No my lord, though I fear it is many more than you have.'

'No battle is won by strength of numbers alone,' replied Abram. He then turned to Mamre and Eshcol. 'And will you, your brother and your men join me?'

'We have not forgotten our vow of friendship, Abram,' answered Mamre. 'An attack against you or your family is an attack against us. And Aner will say the same.'

Eshcol nodded in agreement. But to Eliezer's surprise, a shrewd smile suddenly appeared on his face. 'If what Zambiya says is true, there will also be much plunder with them.'

Mamre, with a smile not unlike his brother's, added, 'And plunder and captives will slow them down.'

Eliezer had never been so scared. His heart was racing and his throat felt tight. His palms were clammy though his mouth was dry. He was used to holding a writing stylus not a sword. He was lying on the ground in the dark, and he and those around him were crawling as quietly as they could, whilst listening for the signal that would begin their attack. They had been pursuing the army north for five days. It hadn't been difficult to follow them. The route was strewn with empty sacks, jugs and broken pottery, with the occasional animal carcass, corpse or wounded (and abandoned) slave. The latter were especially useful in determining details of how many they were, how they travelled, and—of particular interest to Abram—how they camped at night. And their scouts had finally spotted them that morning.

Abram and the three brothers had been spying on the armies since midday, and had determined to ambush the camp that night. Their own forces, numbering around five hundred, had been divided into four groups under them. They had waited until the prolonged feasting and drinking was over, supplied undoubtedly by ample spoils. Only the first watch of men remained out under the stars, after the rest had returned to their tents—with or without captured women. The four groups were now slowly and silently moving into position so that they surrounded the camp. The group to the north, led by Aner, had furthest to go, and it would therefore be Aner who would give the signal to attack when he and his men were in place.

The plan was a simple one. At the signal, they would rush into the camp while most were sleeping (or indulging themselves), making as much noise as possible. The plan was to shout and bang shields, giving the impression in the night of a much greater number, and catching the camp unawares.

If Eliezer's previous prayers to the God of Abram had been beset by a wandering mind and too little to pray for, his silent prayers now were utterly focused and unceasing. *Great God of Abram! My master has followed and served you faithfully. Protect us now, I pray. Give us success and victory. Defeat our enemies. Let them be so drunk that they can't lift a sword. Please help me to be brave and to do what I must. And, I beg you, Yahweh, please do not let me die!*

The cry of a fox—or a very good imitation of one—broke the stillness of the night. When it was repeated twice moments later, Eliezer knew that it was the signal. His heart was pounding as he quickly scrambled to his feet. Dark figures rose around him, like shadows in the night.

And suddenly the still air was riven, as if by thunder, as a mighty clamour erupted. Eliezer started running, gripping his sword more tightly as he began to bang it on the shield. He wasn't sure what he was meant to be shouting. What came out was *YAAAAAAAAAHHHHHHH!*

He could never remember afterwards exactly what had happened—or how long they'd fought. He remembered the smell of blood, the metallic clash of sword upon sword, the cries of men and animals, and the terrified faces illuminated by the burning tents and fires in the camp. And he knew that his own sword found its mark more than once. Then, in the dark, they were suddenly running. Not away, but in pursuit of the four kings and their men, as they fled north. They were still running when the grey light of dawn became a sunrise to the east. And they only stopped when the sun began to sink in the west, the remnants of the invading army having melted away into the hills of the north, heading back to the land from which they had come.

Eliezer sat on the ground, dazed and utterly exhausted. A hand thrust a skin of water into his own, and a voice urged him to drink. He found he was trembling when he tried to raise the skin to his lips, and the strong hand of the stranger—presumably one of the men of Mamre or his brothers—helped him to lift it so he could drink. 'Now eat this, and eat it all,' said the same voice, taking the skin from his hands, and replacing it with a small loaf and a cake of figs. 'You will feel better with bread inside you. They had plundered widely and there is plenty.' Eliezer bit a piece off the loaf and chewed, staring blankly at a bush some ten paces away. He was too tired to even think. And when he had finally finished eating, he leaned forward and rested his arms on his bent knees. He laid his forehead on his arms, and closed his eyes. He only stirred again when he felt a hand upon his shoulder; he had no idea how long had passed—only that it was now dark.

'Eliezer?' said the familiar voice of his master. He lifted his head. 'Yahweh be praised! You are safe!' exclaimed Abram with relief as he held up a torch.

'Master?' he answered wearily, waiting for any command that he might be given, though not sure if he was actually capable of doing anything, should his master ask.

'It is over. Tomorrow we will return to all those who were rescued, but tonight we rest here, and refresh ourselves with bread, meat and beer.'

And that night, as the appetising smell of roasting meat filled the air around the huge campfires, and songs were sung from hearts stirred by the joy of victory and an abundance of beer, Eliezer whispered the simplest of prayers into the darkness: 'Thank you.'

Eliezer assumed that Abram had met with Lot and spoken with him. But he had not witnessed it—and did not want to ask. All he knew—from Burrukam—was that Lot intended to return to Sodom, and had taken his possessions from the spoils taken from the kings of the east. Eliezer guessed that the decision would not be one of which Abram approved. They passed Shechem and then Luz and Ai on the southward journey back to Kiriath Arba. But late one afternoon, as they traversed the Valley of Shaveh near the city of Salem, its king came out to meet them. Eliezer watched his master with fascination. Melchizedek, the king, had brought out, not bread and water for them, but bread and wine.

Refreshments fit for a king! And Abram seemed to show him great deference.

Eliezer suddenly understood when Melchizedek lifted up his hand in blessing and spoke. 'Blessed be Abram by God Most High, Creator of heaven and earth. And praise be to God Most High, who delivered your enemies into your hand.'

So he was also a believer in the true God! Here was a king who had also rejected the deities of the land and worshipped the God of Abram. And Eliezer wondered whether there were others in Canaan who did the same. As the two men stood talking, Eliezer's eyes wandered over the nearby hills. Olive trees were dotted over the sloping rocky ground. Here and there, clusters of bushes darkened the hillside, and higher up, a young herder sat among scattered goats, his staff resting across his knees, watching them with interest. But suddenly the herder's attention was drawn by something to the south. Eliezer followed his gaze. His brow furrowed. A group of men were coming in their direction. *But who were they?*

The voice of his master suddenly broke into his thoughts. 'Eliezer!'

'Yes, my lord,' he replied, hurrying over to him.

Abram had also noticed the men approaching, but clearly had other matters he intended to deal with first. 'I want you and Burrukam to take a tenth of the spoils—the food and goods we retrieved. Then load it onto donkeys. It will be our offering to the priest of God Most High, thanking Yahweh for our deliverance.'

'The priest?' asked Eliezer, confused.

'Melchizedek. He is not only the king of Salem, but also a servant of the one true God. He has given his blessing, and, as is customary, I will give the priest of Yahweh my tithe.'

'Yes, my lord.' But before Eliezer could carry out the task, they were interrupted.

Burrukam hurried to Abram's side. 'My lord, Mamre tells me that it is Bera, the king of Sodom, who draws near.'

'Thank you,' said Abram, fixing his eyes on the group of men. 'You were right to tell me.' He did not, however, walk towards them to meet them.

Burrukam stepped aside, and Eliezer joined him. 'How did he escape Chedorlaomer?' he whispered to Burrukam.

'Rumour has it he fled the battle—and hid,' replied Burrukam drily under his breath. 'And now he is in our master's debt.'

But if there was any sense of indebtedness, it was not apparent. The king strode up to Abram with neither deference nor manners. 'Give me the people of my city,' demanded Bera. 'You may keep the goods for yourself.'

Burrukam spat into the dust. '*Give!* He insists on what is Abram's by right!' he whispered with contempt. He then added sarcastically, 'No wonder Lot feels at home in Sodom!'

Eliezer remained silent, waiting for his master's response. Abram held Bera's eyes and, after a few moments, replied, 'I have sworn an oath to Yahweh, God Most High, Creator of heaven and earth. I will not accept anything belonging to you, not even a thread or a sandal strap. I will never allow you to say, *I made Abram rich.*' But Abram had not finished. 'I will accept nothing but what my men have already eaten. And the men who went with me—Aner, Eshcol and Mamre—let them have their share of the spoils.'

And Burrukam chuckled softly beside Eliezer. 'That put him in his place.'

As Eliezer stood by himself a little way from the fire that night, grateful that only half a day's journey remained, his thoughts drifted to Lilith. Not that she had ever been far from them. He longed to see her pretty face again and hear the laughter that brought joy to his heart. *Would she be relieved and glad to see him safely back? Would she now think more of him for having held a sword, and for having helped liberate Abram's nephew and defeat the four kings?* Although he had to admit, his part in the victory had not been a significant one. His thoughts continued to wander happily until he suddenly felt a presence at his side. 'My lord?'

'Ah. Just one more night. It will be good to be home, will it not?'

'Yes, my lord. And Yahweh blessed us with a great victory!'

'It was a blessing indeed.' Abram paused for a moment. 'Yahweh blesses us in many ways. And one of the first blessings that He gave to our forefather Adam was the gift of a wife.' Eliezer suddenly stiffened, acutely conscious of where their conversation might be about to go. 'How long is it that you have been with me now, Eliezer? Five years?'

'Yes, my lord. Two years in Harran, and it is almost three years since we left there.'

'And you are how old now?'

'Eighteen, my lord.'

'A good age to marry.' Eliezer remained silent, though his heart was beating faster. He had known almost from the start that it would be his master's decision as to whether he married. And if so, when—and to whom. 'There are a number of girls within the household who would be suitable for you.'

Eliezer still didn't dare speak—except silently to heaven. *Please, God, let it be Lilith!*

'But after giving it some thought, I have made my decision.' The pause that followed felt like the passing of many seasons, and Eliezer could barely endure it. 'Lilith will make you a fine wife.' Eliezer released the breath that he didn't realise he had been holding. It was all he could do to keep himself from shouting for joy. 'Does this choice gladden your heart?'

'Yes, my lord!' exclaimed Eliezer, but then suddenly feared that he might have appeared too eager. He began again, in a more sober tone. 'She is a fine woman. She serves you faithfully, my lord, and I am told that she both cooks and weaves well. She is also good with camels.' *She is also good with camels? Idiot! Could he not think of anything more sensible to say?* 'And goats.' He told himself to stop speaking.

But Abram seemed amused by his inept attempts to disguise his pleasure. 'And you like her.' It was not a question from his master's lips. It was a statement.

It finally dawned on Eliezer that his observant and wise master would have been well aware of his feelings, for he had always been different whenever Lilith was near. He finally admitted the truth. 'Yes, my lord. Your choice could not have gladdened my heart more, and I am more grateful that I can say. There is no other gift that I would have desired.' And he fingered the pouch holding his mother's gold jewellery. *They would be his gift to Lilith.*

But suddenly a small but rather dark cloud obscured the sunshine flooding his mind. 'But...'

'What is it?'

How could he say this? He must choose his words carefully. 'Maybe not all will welcome the match.' *He wasn't about to name Lilith's father!*

'Ah, yes,' replied Abram, seeming to understand what lay behind his words. 'That could be difficult.'

And Eliezer suddenly panicked. *Great God of Heaven. Please don't let him change his mind! Do not let him suggest Ninki or Sisili instead.* He then thought of the servant by the name of Humusi and panicked even more.

'However,' continued Abram. 'I am convinced that Burrukam will be delighted with your marriage to his daughter when I also tell him of another decision.' He fell silent for a moment and looked away, fixing his eyes elsewhere. 'If I remain childless, then you are to be the one to inherit all I possess.'

Eliezer knew what he *thought* his master had just said. *But Abram couldn't possibly mean that! How could he? What did he mean?* 'I don't understand, my lord...' began Eliezer slowly.

'Your uncle claimed you were quick of mind,' replied Abram with a smile, though Eliezer thought there was sadness in his eyes. 'My words were clear enough. But let me say them once more. You are to be my heir.'

Eliezer still could barely comprehend what was being said. Eventually, he managed to stutter out, 'But... but what about Lot? He is your nephew, one of your own flesh and blood.'

Abram's smile faded. 'Lot returns to Sodom. He must know that the city sins greatly before Yahweh. And yet he still remains.' Abram's eyes finally met Eliezer's, his features sharp in the light of the fire. 'A heart that is turned towards Yahweh and desires to serve Him is closer to mine. Lot has made his choices—and he has chosen to live outside of God's promise. So you will be my heir.'

Despite knowing the extent of Abram's riches, Eliezer's response was one of shock rather than delight. His mind darted back to words that Abram had spoken near Shechem. *The land He has promised to give to my offspring.* He felt confused. *If Abram thought he might remain childless, then what had happened to Yahweh's promise? Or was this his master's attempt to see that promise fulfilled?* But Eliezer had no answers.

Notes

1. *A day's journey without flocks is estimated to be around 20-25 miles on foot.*

2. *The trade route, the King's Highway, is named as such in Scripture in Numbers 20:17.*

3. *It is not clear what form the night attack took, whether it was done silently and by stealth, or with noise and shouting. Here it is assumed to be like that described in Judges 7:19-23, when Joshua attacks the Midianites at night.*

4. *The Hebrew of Genesis 15:2—'the one who will inherit my estate is Eliezer of Damascus' (NIV)—is notoriously difficult to translate. However, most translations have the same sense as the NIV, which seems to be borne out by the following verse, which implies that a member of his household (rather than a son) will be his heir.*

'This is my covenant with you and your descendants after you, the covenant you are to keep: every male among you shall be circumcised.' (Genesis 17:10)

Nine months after Eliezer lay with her for the first time, Lilith gave birth to a healthy son. Eliezer named his firstborn after his father, Kemuel. He had been wed to Lilith within a week of their return from battle. He had also immediately noticed the difference in how he was treated after being declared as Abram's heir. There was greater respect, and he found himself listened to more readily, even by Burrukam.

By the time their second child—another son—arrived, they were still living in the hill country. The cooler air ensured that there was pasture for the animals for a greater portion of the year. Eliezer frequently thanked Yahweh for the life, security and family he had been granted. But, as he continued to serve his master, he still puzzled over Abram's lack of offspring. He knew that if, at some point, Abram adopted him, then his own children would be counted as Abram's descendants. *But was that truly what Yahweh had promised? Why would the God of all creation not grant his master children of his own? Surely that would be a small matter for the One who had created all things!*

But one summer morning, Eliezer was given a very different task by Abram for that day. 'I need you to go to the herds, Eliezer. Select for me a heifer, a goat and a ram. Each must be three years old and flawless—the best that you can find. I also need some birds. Are any of the herdsmen or servants good at catching or shooting them?'

Eliezer thought for a moment. 'Zuzu, my lord. He sets a good snare.'

'Excellent. Send him to me. And bring the animals back here. Oh, and before you leave, fetch me the whetstone and two of the best knives.'

'Yes, master.'

'Take help if you need it, but I want you and you alone to select the animals.'

Having Abram's trust often made Eliezer's days full and varied, but he relished any responsibility placed on his shoulders. As he worked quickly to fulfil his master's orders, he wondered what he was planning. That sacrifice was involved, he had no doubt. *But why so many animals? Surely they would not all fit on the nearby altar Abram had built when they had first reached Canaan, seven years earlier.*

Noon had passed by the time Eliezer returned, leading a heifer on a leash. Two other servants accompanied him with the goat and ram. Zuzu returned shortly afterwards, with a dove and a young pigeon in a wicker cage. 'Good!' declared Abram. 'We are ready.'

Eliezer and his two helpers were soon following Abram out of the camp with the animals, the wicker cage now in Abram's right hand. Eliezer's curiosity only increased as they led the animals away from the altar and further from the camp. It was only when they reached a flat, open space on a nearby hill that Abram finally stopped. There was a solitary tree and a stream running nearby. 'Tether the animals over there,' said Abram, pointing to the tree. 'Then you may return to the camp—except Eliezer. I need you to stay.'

'Yes, master.' Having tethered the heifer, Eliezer hurried back to Abram, who was by now unsheathing the knives that had been tucked into his belt. *Maybe now he would at last be given some idea of why they—and the animals—were there.*

'Yahweh appeared to me in a vision last night,' began Abram after the others had disappeared from sight. 'He told me that I will not only take possession of this land, but also have a son from my own body—the first of countless descendants. And I believe Him.'

Eliezer stared at him, both awed and exhilarated. He had never felt right about being titled as Abram's heir. *And this was why! His master was to have a proper heir—somehow…* 'I am glad, my lord,' said Eliezer—and meant it. But he was still mystified as to what they were doing there.

'I asked Yahweh to give me a sign,' Abram continued. 'A sign to confirm that what He had spoken would come to pass. And this is where He will do it.'

'Master?'

'I will explain. But we have work to do. The Lord told me to bring these animals, but we must now prepare them. And we will start with our most difficult task.' He handed Eliezer one of the freshly-sharpened knives, its keen, bright blade catching the sun. He wielded the other himself. The heifer's throat soon bore the scarlet gash that had, in a moment, robbed it of its life and sent it crashing to the ground. 'And now,' explained Abram, 'we must cut the animal in half.'

Eliezer stared at the substantial carcass. *It was going to be challenging!*

'We will cut it behind the ribs,' said Abram. 'Then its backbone should be our only hindrance.' And as they worked together on the bloody task, he continued. 'You understand what a covenant is?'

'Yes, my lord. It is a solemn and binding agreement between two parties—like marriage.'

'Marriage is indeed a covenant. One between a man and a woman. But others may also enter into covenants, and there is a custom of how that is done. Animals are slaughtered and cut in two. The halves are laid in two lines, opposite each other. Those making the covenant then pass together between the halves.'

'But why, my lord?'

'It is a custom that says, *May this happen to me if I break the covenant that I am making with you.*'

They paused to catch their breath for several moments, and then continued carving until eventually the heifer was cleft in two, their hands bathed in the animal's blood. Abram nodded to himself, as if approving the results of their labour. 'Now we must wash both parts before laying them out.'

Dragging the substantial dead weight of the two halves to the stream and back was not going to be possible, even with two of them. A number of trips back and forth with their waterskins sufficed instead, dousing the carcass to cleanse it. Then they dragged one of the halves away from the other. *His master certainly would not have been able to do the task himself.* Even with two of them, it took all their strength, and the smell of blood filled Eliezer's nostrils as he breathed heavily. The goat and ram then met similar fates, though their halves were carried to the stream, turning its waters red as they were immersed and cleansed. The halves were then added to what became two lines. The birds, once their necks were broken, were left whole, the dove added to one line, and the pigeon to the other.

As the two men crouched by the stream, both cleaning their knives and resting after the exertion, Eliezer asked, 'Now what, my lord?'

'Now we wait.'

'For what?'

'For Yahweh to perform whatever is His wish.'

Excitement and fear suddenly coursed through Eliezer. *Was he to witness the hand of God for himself?*

As both men began their vigil a short time later, Eliezer eagerly surveyed the deserted landscape, as if at any moment something unusual might occur. The sense of keen anticipation began to wane, however, as the afternoon dragged past. The only visitors were vultures, kites and ravens swooping down onto the carcasses. They were swiftly chased away.

As the sun neared the tops of the hills in the west, Eliezer began to wonder if anything was actually going to happen. But then, when the light began to fade, he sensed something different. The world around him suddenly seemed unnaturally still. His heart quickened and his eyes darted around. Had his master not been there, he might have fled—though Abram, who had moments earlier been awake and alert, appeared to have abruptly fallen into a deep sleep. Then Eliezer felt it. Though afterwards he couldn't quite describe what *it* was. *A heaviness. As if something else were filling the air. Someone. Someone wonderful and terrible and vast.* Eliezer suddenly felt tiny and fragile and naked. He threw himself down and knelt with his forehead touching the ground, breathing heavily and shaking. He stayed there, silent, aware only of the powerful Presence surrounding him and the rapid fading of the twilight into a darkness as terrifying as it was complete. He shut his eyes tightly.

He wasn't sure how long he had been kneeling trembling in the dirt, but suddenly his name was spoken softly. Relief washed over him at the sound of Abram's voice. *He was no longer alone in the dark.* But when he finally lifted his head, his whole body flooded with fear once more. It was no longer black as pitch. Above and between the two lines of pieces was a flaming torch hanging in mid-air, as if borne by an unseen hand. Beside it was a smoking brazier, and both were moving slowly and silently towards them. Then Eliezer heard a voice that was not his master's above the thundering of his heart, and his fear turned to terror.

'To your descendants I give this land, from the Wadi of Egypt to the great river, the Euphrates—the land of the Kenites, Kenizzites, Kadmonites, Hittites, Perizzites, Rephaites, Amorites, Canaanites, Girgashites and Jebusites.'

And then all was silence. The smoking brazier seemed to melt into thin air, but the torch gently floated down to the ground. Eliezer knelt, as if turned to stone, staring at the torch, his heart still pounding. Eventually Abram spoke. 'He leaves us a torch, to light our way back.' And as the cry of an owl pierced the night, it was as if they were suddenly back in their familiar world, where the air simply felt cool and fresh, and the gentle crackling of the flaming torch was the only sound. 'You can pick it up.'

Eliezer swallowed. He summoned his courage, raised himself to his feet and walked warily over to where the torch lay burning on the ground. He paused and then slowly and gingerly reached down. He felt its heat upon his face and arms. The rough wooden handle was like any other to the touch. His fear finally melted into wonder as he picked it up and carried it back to Abram.

'Yahweh came, didn't He, master?' he said, awed.

'Yes, He did. You saw the brazier and heard His voice?'

'Yes, my lord. I heard Him promise to give to your descendants the land of Canaan—and more.'

'I knew not whether I was dreaming or not.'

'You *were* sleeping as the sun set.'

Abram's brow furrowed. 'Yes,' he began slowly. 'And the Lord spoke of my descendants being enslaved for four hundred years in a foreign land, but of them then returning here.'

'I did not hear those words, my lord.'

Abram seemed lost in thought for a moment.

'What now, master?'

Abram suddenly drew in a deep breath, as if awakening from sleep. 'We must return.' And with that, they began walking in the direction of the camp.

For some time they walked in silence, Eliezer scarcely believing what he had seen. But eventually, he spoke. 'Master?'

'Yes, Eliezer.'

'What was the meaning of what we saw?'

'The Lord has made a covenant.'

'With you?'

'Yes, that is right. He alone passed between the carcasses, because it is *His* purposes. His decision and

His power alone will bring these things to pass. He has assured me of his promises, and that all He has spoken He will surely fulfil.' But once again, Eliezer—despite his longing to know the answer—still would not ask how a childless man was to have many descendants.

In the darkness of the tent, Eliezer felt Lilith snuggling up to him. The night on the hill with Abram was long past. They had now been in the land of Canaan for ten years. And Abram still had no son. 'I have something to tell you,' she whispered. He didn't have to see her face to know that she was excited. Her voice alone told him that. He could feel her swollen belly against his stomach. It would only be two months more until their third child was born.

'You are going to tell me that our next child is *definitely* going be a girl. Despite you also telling me that before Eldad was born.'

Lilith's laughter spilled out, as sweet as any birdsong. Eliezer smiled to himself. *He could always make her laugh.*

'No! It's about Abram. Though it does concern you too. My father overheard him talking to Sarai in their tent.'

Eliezer always felt a fierce loyalty towards his master, even when it was his wife talking. 'If it is something I need to know, then Abram will tell me himself when the time is right.' Although he suspected—for his seven years of marriage had taught him as much—that she was going to tell him anyway.

'You will probably find out soon enough, so you may as well hear it from my lips now.' She lay her arm across his chest and laid her head close to his.

Had they been outside in the day, he could, of course, have followed his principles and walked away from the gossip. *But there was no escape here.* He sighed resignedly. 'What did your father tell you then?'

'It wasn't my father. It was my mother. My father heard it and then told her and she told me.' Eliezer sighed again. But he was not surprised. 'Anyway, Sarai told Abram that the Lord had kept her from having children. So she told him to sleep with Hagar. Then she said that if Hagar has children by him, they will be counted as her own!'

'And presumably counted as Abram's also,' said Eliezer drily.

'But that's right, isn't it? I have heard of men who have raised up families through the maids of their wives.'

'It is, indeed, done.'

'Sarai clearly thinks her idea is better than Abram appointing you as his heir.'

Eliezer did not wish to comment. 'And did he agree to Sarai's idea?'

'If he did, it was not in my father's hearing. But he didn't hear him disagree either. Still, we will soon know, if Abram does lie with Hagar and she falls pregnant.'

'And you think that the Lord will open Hagar's womb when He keeps Sarai's closed?' asked Eliezer.

'If she does conceive,' replied Lilith, avoiding his question, 'it will mean that you no longer inherit all he has!'

Eliezer already knew his response—and had told Lilith before. 'If my master has a son, I will rejoice that the Lord has fulfilled His promise to him. And I will want my wife to rejoice with me.'

They were both silent for a few moments, and then Lilith added, 'We will just have to wait and see, won't we?'

And as Lilith eventually slipped into sleep, Eliezer stared into the darkness. *Why was he about to become a father for the third time, aged twenty-five, whilst his seventy-five-year-old master, who served Yahweh so faithfully, remained childless?* But he remembered the flaming torch. *Maybe this was the way in which the Lord would fulfil His promises. After all, Abram had not been told that his descendants would be through Sarai. Maybe he would consent to her suggestion for that reason.* Eliezer closed his eyes. *Lilith was right. They would just have to wait and see.*

No-one could escape Hagar's swelling belly. She paraded it around for all to see, and there was not one person in the camp who hadn't heard that she was bearing Abram's child.

'She flaunts it,' said Lilith with disdain, 'and behaves as if she is the favoured one. I have seen the way she looks at Sarai, as if her mistress were below her! It is painful enough for Sarai as it is. And mother says she refuses to do as Sarai tells her. It is shameful! Abram ought not to allow it.'

Eliezer sighed. Although he would never say such things about Abram and Sarai, even to his wife, he had to agree with every word Lilith had spoken. *It was to be expected that Hagar immediately falling pregnant would be hard for Abram's wife.* Bearing children was a wife's role, and it was always difficult for wives who failed in that task. *But if the Lord kept women from having children, what could they do?* Eliezer sighed again. He knew that, despite Abram's joy at the prospect of being a father, his master was not blind or indifferent to his wife's pain. Only that morning, he had overheard Sarai blaming Abram for what had happened with Hagar. Abram had then given Sarai permission to do what she felt best. *Not that he was about to tell Lilith of that conversation.*

But Eliezer didn't need to tell Lilith. Everyone saw the consequences soon enough. Sarai made sure that Hagar's head was no longer held high, but was bowed in shame instead. She seemed to take every opportunity to humiliate her maid, shouting at her harshly or treating her unkindly. And Abram did nothing. Eliezer constantly puzzled over this seeming fulfilment of God's promise to Abram. That he was about to become a father was not in doubt. *But like this? Was this Yahweh's intended purpose?* Eliezer wondered what his master thought about it all. *Whatever he thought, it still felt wrong.*

'Eliezer!' Abram's tone was urgent. Eliezer immediately stopped counting the jars of oil within the stores, and rushed out of the tent.

'Yes, master?' He had never seen Abram so distressed.

'Have you seen Hagar?'

Eliezer thought quickly. 'Not since last night.'

'She is missing. No one has seen her this morning, and her tent is empty. Find ten others and send them out to search for her beyond the camp. And see if you can find anything out from the herdsmen.'

That Hagar might have run away was no surprise. She may have been carrying Abram's child, but the way in which Sarai had treated her over the previous ten days had, in Eliezer's mind at least, been cruel. But wherever Eliezer went, and to whomever he spoke, no one had anything to tell him. By the time the afternoon was almost spent, and the ten men had returned, Eliezer had only one thing to report to Abram.

'My lord, no one has seen Hagar. But I am fairly certain that one of the donkeys is missing—unless someone else has borrowed it and not told me.'

Abram looked grim. 'If she has fled, then at least it would mean that no accident has befallen her. But it is too late in the day now to send others out to search further afield.'

'Where might she go, my lord? Do you have any ideas?'

'If she were with others, then I might guess that she would head towards Egypt. But to try to make that journey herself…?'

'It is not a journey that any would want to make by themselves.' Eliezer paused. 'So what do we do, my lord.'

'We wait and hope that, wherever she has gone, she will return by night-fall.'

But by the time darkness had fallen, she was still missing. Despite further searches, there was no sign of her (or the missing donkey) the next day—or the nine days that followed. Abram was driven to distraction. *It was hardly surprising, given that Hagar—wherever she was—was carrying the only child from his eighty-five years of life.* And Sarai seemed strangely quiet and subdued. *Maybe she knew it was her cruelty that had driven her maid to desperation.*

But on the twelfth day after her disappearance, Eliezer heard a sudden commotion. He looked up sharply from the goat carcass that he was butchering for the evening meal. Hagar was quietly and meekly riding a donkey into the camp. Eliezer rushed to Abram's tent, his hands still bloodied. 'My lord! Hagar returns!'

Moments later his master was at her side, helping her down from the beast. 'Eliezer—bring food and drink to my tent. Quickly.'

And so it was that Eliezer, as he served milk, bread and curds to Hagar, heard her story. But even before she spoke, he wondered what had happened to evoke such a change in her. The recent desperation in her eyes had gone, but neither the haughty air nor the belligerence had resurfaced. *Something had happened to her.* Of that Eliezer was sure.

'Where have you been, Hagar?' began Abram.

'I ran away, master.' Although Hagar had dropped her eyes to the floor, she glanced up quickly at Abram. She avoided looking at Sarai, and Eliezer guessed that she was choosing her words carefully. She lowered her gaze once more. 'I was unhappy.'

'Where did you go?'

'I followed the Way of Shur south, master. I was planning to return to Egypt.'

Abram shook his head and sighed. 'That was foolish. But what changed your mind and brought you back?' Sarai kept silent, content to let her husband ask the questions.

'It was the fifth day after I left. I had travelled beyond Kadesh Barnea and stopped at a spring to refill my waterskins. But a man seemed to appear from nowhere.' Hagar raised her eyes again, but now there was wonder in them. 'I had never seen him before. But he knew my name and knew that I was the maid of Sarai. I knew at that moment that it was Yahweh's angel!' Abram looked steadily at her but Sarai drew in a sharp breath. 'He asked where I had come from and where I was going. So I told him that I was fleeing. He told me to return to my mistress and submit to her. But he said more.' Her eyes were shining. 'He told me I would bear a son, and that his name should be called Ishmael, because the Lord had seen my troubles and heard me!' It was now Sarai who was staring at the ground. But Hagar hadn't finished. 'He said that my son would be like a wild donkey, at odds with everyone, and that he would live to the east of all his brothers.'

Brothers? The word did not slip by Eliezer unnoticed.

Hagar fell silent. 'And then?' asked Abram.

'And then he was gone. And I wondered that I should be allowed to see the God Who Sees and yet live. So I named the spring, *the Well of the Living One Who Sees Me.* And then I turned back, and here I am.'

No one spoke for several moments, but eventually Abram said simply, 'So his name will be Ishmael. *God hears.* It is a good name.'

But before the day was out, Eliezer overheard an exchange that only added to his perplexity about the ways of Yahweh. He was about to hail his master from outside his tent, when he heard the unmistakable sound of sobbing and the pained voice of Sarai. 'She bears your child and now the Lord has appeared to her. What wrong have I done that Yahweh withholds his favour from me? Why does he not see *me*?' His master gave no answer. *What was there to say?* Eliezer crept away quietly as the sobbing continued. *He would return later.*

Ishmael was born the following year, when Abram was eighty-six years old. Lilith was asked to take over much of Hagar's role as Sarai's maid. Eliezer suspected that it had little to do with the amount of Hagar's time that was taken up with the new baby. After all, Lilith had usually managed to continue serving Abram and Sarai when their own children had arrived. *Although Lilith also had her mother and siblings around her, and Hagar had neither.* It wasn't difficult to guess that Sarai found it painful to see, every day, Abram's son—a son that wasn't her own. Despite her earlier claim that she would obtain children through her maid, she did not treat Ishmael as such. And the years of pain had taken a toll. She may, like Abram, have been blessed with longevity and seemed much younger than she was, but her seventy-six year old face was beginning to show signs of age, and her dark hair was flecked with grey.

So this is the fulfilment of the Lord's promise to Abram, thought Eliezer, as he watched Hagar nursing the child one day. *But was this birth—that had brought so much joy to Abram but such pain to his wife—the way that Yahweh worked? But what else could it be?* And this thought was only strengthened when Lilith some time later, in her role of serving Sarai, reliably informed him that Sarai was now beyond the age of child-bearing.

'How do you know?' asked Eliezer.

His wife looked at him as if he was stupid. 'She no longer bleeds every month.'

Of course! He flushed slightly and added defensively, 'I did not grow up among women.'

'And yet you have a wife. Has that not taught you such things?'

Eliezer just smiled. 'My wife has taught me many things.' And he kissed her.

And so, as the years slipped by, Eliezer watched—or so he thought—the promised child grow. But then, when Ishmael was thirteen and Abram ninety-nine, everything changed.

Eliezer, as usual, deferred to his now-ageing father-in-law, allowing him to enter Abram's tent ahead of him. When he had ceased being Abram's heir, Eliezer had thought Burrukam might revert to his attitude of benign disapproval towards him. He had, however, remained friendly enough—*in his own, grumbling, sardonic way. But then again, he and Lilith had given him five healthy grandchildren.* He followed Burrukam inside. They had both been summoned shortly after dawn. But Eliezer was perplexed to find—unusually—Sarai standing at Abram's side. He couldn't quite fathom the expression on Abram's face. *Was it excitement or even shock?* Sarai stared straight away, giving nothing away.

'You have much work to do today,' began Abram, smiling. 'After many years, Yahweh has appeared to me once more. He has told me that every male in the household must be circumcised—no matter how young or old, and no matter whether born in this household or not.' Eliezer's eyes widened. 'It is to be the sign of His covenant,' Abram continued, 'showing that all who are mine are His people. Our flesh will bear the sign that we belong to Yahweh, and from now on, any male born into the household must be circumcised on the eighth day.'

Even as Abram was still speaking, Eliezer was contemplating with some trepidation his own three sons having their foreskins cut away. *Kemuel, now twenty, would bear it like a man, as would his second son, Eldad. But his youngest, Asriel—aged six—would more than likely scream his way through the whole ritual.* And Eliezer wasn't too keen on the idea either. Circumcision was not unusual among the peoples around them, but it was generally performed to mark entry into manhood or as a fertility rite. *This was different.*

'Eliezer.'

His attention suddenly snapped back to his master. 'Yes, my lord.'

'How many males are there in the household now?'

'Three hundred and ninety-four men, my lord, but I am not sure of the number of children and infants.'

'I want every male circumcised today—and that will include myself and Ishmael. You will need to make sure that we have enough sharp flint knives for the purpose, and you will need to tell every servant and herdsman to come to the camp today. You must tell them that any who refuse will no longer be part of my household.' Abram paused, and both Burrukam and Eliezer nodded. 'But there is something else that everyone must know, and not just the men.' He took a deep breath. 'I am no longer to bear the name *Abram*. Yahweh has declared that, from now on, I am to be known as *Abraham—father of a multitude*. For he has promised that many nations and kings shall come forth from me.' He paused. 'But not only that.' He looked at his wife. 'The Lord has also said that Sarai is to be known as *Sarah*. For *she* will be the mother of those nations and kings. For in this season next year, she will bear me a son, whose name shall be called Isaac. He will be the one, not Ishmael, with whom Yahweh will establish His covenant.'

Eliezer stood with his mouth open—until Abraham looked at him, and he quickly shut it. He looked at Abraham and then at Sarah, dumbfounded. And, for once, Burrukam had nothing to say either. Eliezer opened his mouth again to speak. But despite the multitude of questions suddenly swirling around in his mind, he shut it for a second time.

'Now you have work to do,' said Abraham, and Eliezer shook himself out of his shock.

'Yes, master,' he replied. Burrukam nodded.

'And I would suggest you begin straightaway. You both handle knives well, so the three of us will perform the rituals. Ishmael will be circumcised first, and then we will be circumcised last of all.

It was only as Burrukam was about to leave the tent ahead of him, that Eliezer paused, turned, and finally spoke. '*Isaac*, my lord. What does it mean?'

'It means, *he laughs.*' He smiled wryly. 'For I laughed in disbelief when Yahweh told me of the son that Sarah will bear.'

Eliezer nodded. 'My lord,' and followed his father-in-law out of the tent.

And as they emerged into the bright morning air, the sun finally rising above the eastern hills, Burrukam muttered under his breath, 'I don't know which is worse. Being expected to suffer the insufferable or believe the unbelievable. Either way, he asks too much.'

'Yahweh or Abraham?' asked Eliezer with a grin. Burrukam just grunted.

'And will my husband lie with me tonight?' whispered Lilith mischievously, as Eliezer finally walked into the tent— painfully and wearily—when Abraham's instructions had finally been carried out. She was comforting their six-year-old, who was still grizzling from his own painful ordeal.

Eliezer groaned in reply. 'No—and I never want to see another foreskin again.'

'Well, you certainly won't be seeing your own again,' laughed Lilith.

But later, as they lay beside each other in the dark, waiting for sleep to overtake them, Lilith asked quietly, 'What Abram…I mean Abraham…said about Sarah—that she would bear him a son. Do you believe that?'

Eliezer stared into the darkness, breathing in the familiar smells of their tent, and thought for a moment. He pictured once again the flaming torch and brazier he had seen years earlier. 'I have seen Yahweh perform deeds that I cannot explain. I have also seen you holding each of our newborn children in your arms, and each time, that has also seemed a miracle to me. Surely nothing is too difficult for the Creator who gives life in the first place.' He paused. 'But maybe that is easier for me to say than for my master to believe.' He thought for a moment. 'Would I believe it if I were him—'

'And I were ninety years old—'

'And had not been fruitful, as you have been?' Eliezer paused again. 'I cannot answer that. But as to whether it will happen…'

And as she had said once before, Lilith concluded, 'We will just have to wait and see, won't we?'

Notes

1. *Circumcision became a sign for all Jews—descendants of Abraham. But initially, as shown here, it was simply given to all in Abraham's household—all those linked to him, rather than descended from him.*
2. *A wadi is a dried-up river bed. It flows with water (and with great intensity) when it rains in the winter, but possibly only for one or two days.*

6

*The L*ORD *appeared to Abraham near the great trees of*
Mamre while he was sitting at the entrance to his tent in
*the heat of the day…the L*ORD *said, 'Shall I hide from*
Abraham what I am about to do?' (Genesis 18:1,17)

The first thing that caught Eliezer's attention was Abraham running. It was not a sight to which he was accustomed, particularly when it was so close to noon. The whole camp was quiet, as was normal in the heat of the day, when the morning's work was finished and most rested. He stopped beating the last of the rugs he was ridding of dust, and looked in the direction in which his master was running—and suddenly wondered how he had not noticed the arrival of three strangers. He was equally surprised to then see Abraham kneeling and lowering his forehead to the ground before them. He listened with interest.

'My lord,' began Abraham, 'if I have found favour in your sight, please do not pass by without stopping and resting. Please, let water be brought for you to wash your feet. Rest yourselves in the shade under the tree, and I will bring you a little bread to refresh you. You have visited your servant—please stay before going on.'

One of the men nodded. 'Very well. Do as you say.'

Eliezer put down his beater and readied himself to serve. As the three men walked towards the oaks nearby, he followed Abraham as he hurried back to his tent. Sarah was sitting in the shade of its entrance, with the door flap pulled back. His instructions to her were brief but clear. 'Quick! Take three measures of fine flour! Knead it, and make bread.' The large quantities far surpassed, of course, the humble offer of a little bread. As custom dictated, what was served would generously exceed what had been promised. Eliezer was puzzled by his master's haste, and soon found himself receiving similarly brief instructions. 'Take water to our guests, then meet me at the cattle.'

'Yes, my lord.' But Abraham had already gone.

As he carried a large pottery bowl of water to the men, freshly filled with cool water from the well, Eliezer was curious. He wished he could look upon the faces of the guests, but kept his eyes low out of respect for them. 'My lords,' he said simply, as he set the bowl and a cloth down before them, backing away, before turning to hurry to his master. The haste made him glad that the recent wound inflicted by the flint knife had healed and he could move freely—and painlessly—once more.

By the time Eliezer reached him, Abraham already had a noose around the neck of one of the calves. 'That is the best calf, my lord,' said Eliezer, guessing that Abraham wanted to serve his guests the finest he could offer. 'There is none better in the herd.' *Although surely a lamb or a goat would have been more than sufficient for only three.*

Abraham placed the rope in Eliezer's hand. 'Take it and prepare it. Cook it as quickly as you can, then bring the meat to me on a platter. Place the best and most tender portions on top. Now hurry.'

'Yes, my lord.' But, once again, his master had gone. He was used to Abraham's generous hospitality to all, even when it was, like this, at an inconvenient time. But the amount of flour Sarah was using was huge. It would make a small mountain of the finest of bread. And it would be more than matched by his mountain of meat. His curiosity grew. *He had never seen his master so eager to please guests, lavishing on them his very best.*

Although Eliezer would normally have boiled the meat from the calf, he decided to roast it over the fire in smaller pieces, so it would be ready as quickly as possible. Meat was not often part of their meals, and its presence was another sign of his master's desire to honour these men. *Were they strangers to Abraham, or did he know them?* Eliezer couldn't be sure. But one thing of which he *was* sure, when the succulent, rich-smelling meat finally lay in a steaming pile on a wooden platter, was that no guest could fail to be flattered by such extravagance.

He stood nearby, should he be needed, as Abraham waited on the men himself, serving not only the meat and bread, but also curds and milk to go with the meal. And then Abraham also stood in the shade of the tree as they ate. *As if he were a humble servant and not the mighty prince he was.*

Abraham refilled the men's cups with milk more than once, and offered them water to wash their hands when the meal was over. As Eliezer cleared the platters, one of the men finally spoke. 'Where is Sarah your wife?'

So the men did know Abraham! Eliezer was sure that his master had not mentioned her name.

'She is in the tent,' he replied.

'I will surely return to you about this time next year, and Sarah your wife will have a son.'

And suddenly Eliezer remembered Abraham's words from some years before, about Yahweh appearing to him in the form of a man. The hairs on the back of his neck bristled.

But the man spoke again. 'Why did Sarah laugh and say, *Will I really have a child, now that I am old?*' Eliezer started. He had not heard Sarah speak. The visitor continued, 'Is anything too hard for Yahweh? I will return to you at the appointed time next year, and Sarah will have a son.'

Sarah slowly emerged from the tent, pale, with a look of fear on her face. 'I did not laugh.'

The man turned to face her. 'No, you did laugh.'

The men then rose, all looking in the same direction, towards the south-east. Eliezer assumed that that was where they were heading. As they left, with Abraham accompanying them, Eliezer bowed low. It was only when they had passed him that he stared dumbfounded. From the back, with scarves covering their heads, they looked almost indistinguishable from Abraham. *Had he really just witnessed Yahweh among them?*

He looked towards his master's tent, but Sarah had already disappeared inside again. *The men had known that she hadn't believed their words.* Despite his sense of wonder, he suddenly chuckled, raising an eyebrow. *If Abraham believed the words he had heard, there was one thing his master would have to do in three months' time to demonstrate his faith.*

Eliezer had expected Abraham simply to accompany his guests to the edge of the camp, to send them on their way. But Abraham didn't return—at least, not straightaway. He finally spotted his master approaching the tents late in the afternoon. But before entering the camp, Abraham paused and turned round to look back in the direction from which he had come—the south-east—as the men had done earlier.

'Master?' began Eliezer, when he reached his side. Abraham remained silent for so long that he began to wonder if he had heard him. But instead of replying, Abraham finally turned slowly towards him. And Eliezer did his best to hide his surprise. *He'd been given news of a son to be born to him. So why was his expression now so grim?* Eliezer waited for him to speak.

'You did well with the meal earlier.' And that was all that was said before Abraham walked back to his tent, and disappeared inside.

The sun had barely risen above the horizon when Eliezer emerged from his tent the following morning. Lilith was already at work, baking the first bread of the day, cooking the flat rounds on the outside of the pottery dome that sat over the fire. Other women, including Sarah and Kemuel's new wife, were performing similar tasks nearby.

His hand received a short, sharp slap as he reached towards the growing pile of freshly baked bread. 'Ow!'

'I haven't finished yet!' said Lilith, without moving her eyes from the dome. She seemed to see everything, whether she appeared to be looking or not.

Eliezer smiled. 'But it smells so good.'

'And it will still smell good when you return from speaking to the master.'

He sighed, knowing he wouldn't win. So whilst the bread baked, he strolled across towards Abraham's tent to receive his orders for the day. But even before he reached her, Sarah glanced up and said, 'If you are looking for Abram…' She stopped to correct herself; she had used the old name longer than any. 'Abraham is not here. He left before sunrise.' But no explanation was given regarding his whereabouts.

'Then I will stay near our tent until the master returns,' replied Eliezer, his gaze resting briefly on the large oaks nearby, under which the guests had sat the previous day and reiterated the promise that Sarah would have a son.

Apart from Abraham's absence, however, the day continued like many others. Eliezer was teaching their youngest son, Asriel, to recognise and write numbers, whilst Lilith and their two girls started milking the herds, beginning with the goats nearby.

'That's right,' said Eliezer, as his son traced out first *one* and then *two* and then *three* in the dust with a stick. By the time he reached *seven*, Eliezer had his hand on the stick, guiding him.

He heard, several paces away, the voice of his youngest daughter, Jael. 'What's that?' *As if she was asking Lilith what she was cooking.*

But Lilith did not reply. Several moments of silence passed, then, 'Eliezer.'

The fear in Lilith's voice tore him instantly away from the incomplete character in the dust, his hand still on the stick. 'What is it?' he asked, apprehension growing as he saw the fright on her face. Both her hands were clasping the shoulders of Jael. But she was not looking at her daughter or him. Her eyes were fixed elsewhere.

'Come over here, quickly,' answered Lilith. Eliezer hurried to her side, with Asriel trotting behind him. 'There.' He followed her pointing finger, between the tents and beyond—and froze. For in the sky to the southeast was a sight so strange, so unearthly, that he couldn't make sense of it. 'What's that?' she asked, echoing Jael's question.

'I don't know…' he began slowly. 'Wait here.' He ran through the camp and then up a slope beyond it to the north, to get a better view. But as he turned, he found Lilith and the children behind, either curious or too frightened to be left.

'What's happening?' asked Lilith in a strained voice, clutching Asriel to her, as Eliezer stood with his arms around their two daughters.

Eliezer could see more clearly now, but that did nothing to help his understanding. It looked to him as though a vibrant sunrise of oranges and reds in the south-east was melting in the sky and dripping down upon the earth. As if the sky itself were raining fire. And then he felt his throat tighten and his mouth go dry. For it suddenly dawned on him that that was *precisely* what was happening. He could now see dark smudges above the ground, and guessed it to be smoke. *What evil device was this?*

'It is fire falling upon the earth,' he finally replied. But even as he said the words, he remembered how Abraham's visitors had looked in that direction the day before. *Was this the hand of God?*

'How is that happening—and why?' whispered Lilith.

'I don't know,' said Eliezer for a second time. 'But it falls upon the cities of the valley—upon Sodom and Gomorrah.'

After a moment, she asked quietly, 'And what of Lot?'

'It is—what?—almost twenty years since we have seen him. Maybe he has moved on from Sodom.' But Eliezer said that more to comfort her than because he thought it might be true. *Surely Abraham's nephew had a family by now*. But he also remembered the reports of violence and depravity of the cities that Lot had chosen to live amongst. *Was this God's judgment?* Eliezer watched the smoke rising higher.

More and more people from the camp were streaming out to see the strange and alarming sight. Some cried with fear, whilst others spoke quickly and loudly, or called upon their gods—or the One True God. Burrukam and Ninlil were there, and his own son Kemuel and his wife. Sarah stood slightly apart, by herself, whilst Hagar stood beside Ishmael. And each was staring at the unnatural destruction. Eliezer wished for the presence of the one man who might be able to explain better than any other. But Abraham was still nowhere to be seen.

It was as if a gigantic furnace had descended upon the valley. The unwelcome image of the meat that he had roasted the day before came into his mind. Before he could help himself he was thinking of human flesh, charred and black. *Surely none could have escaped, let alone endured, such devastation!*

Eventually, sometime after noon, the rain of flames began to subside, and then stopped, although the smoke and flames on the ground continued. And still they all watched. Until, that is, Abraham, walking with his staff, came over a ridge to the south-east, his back to the smoking valley and his face grave. Any talk rapidly dwindled away, and a hush fell over the entire company. No one spoke. No one rushed away, ashamed at being discovered away from their work. *For how could one work when fire fell from the sky!* All stood expectantly—waiting, hoping, for some form of explanation, something that would make sense of the inexplicable.

Abraham stopped in front of them, and surveyed the faces of both young and old. And then he spoke. 'Yahweh has sent His judgment upon Sodom and Gomorrah, for their sin was exceedingly great.' He paused. 'And now it is ·over.' And with that he walked forward, the crowd parting for him, but also following him, for it was clear to all that they were now expected to return.

As the afternoon melted into twilight, a breeze from the south brought the stench of brimstone into the camp. It was the smell of destruction. Eliezer finally plucked up the courage to voice one of the questions that burned in his heart, as he spoke with Abraham later that evening beside the fire outside his tent. 'My lord?'

'Speak freely, Eliezer.'

'The men who visited us yesterday—was Yahweh one of them? You said He had appeared to you as a man before.'

'Yes, and I guessed that you would realise when you heard His words.' Then Abraham, staff in hand, suddenly said, 'Come, walk with me.' And together they made their way once more to the edge of the camp, and away from the light of the fires and clay lamps. They stood under the stars in silence for a while, their eyes fixed on an eerie red glow that broke the darkness.

'Did you know yesterday that Yahweh was going to destroy Sodom and Gomorrah?' asked Eliezer suddenly.

'I knew that they were going down to the cities, to see if all that was spoken against them was true.'

'And Lot, my lord?'

'Yahweh assured me that he would not sweep the righteous away with the wicked,' said Abraham quietly.

'And if Lot and his family have escaped, then it will only be with their lives. My nephew has lost everything by choosing to live among the depraved.'

After a pause, Eliezer—mindful of stories told by Abraham in the past—asked, 'Is this like the time of Noah?'

'It is both like and unlike. Then the Lord judged the whole earth, but He also promised that He would never again destroy every living thing. He did not say, however, that His judgment would never fall. This time, He destroyed only the cities against which the outcry was greatest. And this time He judged with fire rather than water. Make no mistake, Eliezer: however terrible the destruction of those cities may seem, their sin was so heinous and despicable that Yahweh could not let it continue fouling this land. And He has already told me that He will also judge the Amorites in this land, four hundred years from now, when their iniquity will have grown.'

'Why does the Lord destroy some cities and peoples and not others? Surely there is wickedness elsewhere?'

Abraham responded with a little *Hmm*, as if his words had struck a chord deep within his master. 'When we speak with Yahweh, He allows us to ask the questions that are on our hearts. We need never fear being honest with Him, Eliezer, for He already knows our thoughts. He may not answer all our questions, but we can be assured that He is the Judge of all the world, and that He will *always* do what is right.'

And Eliezer did not doubt his words.

Notes

1. *It has been assumed that these events occurred shortly after Yahweh appearing to Abram in Genesis 17, as on both occasions Abraham is told that Sarah would bear him a son the following year (17:21 and 18:14).*

2. *Brimstone is an ancient name for sulphur. It is said that the area at the south end of the Salt Sea smells of sulphur. That area would also have been barren after the disaster.*

3. *Normally, a reference to sitting in the city gate (as Lot is recorded as doing in Genesis 19:1) means a person having some sort of recognised authority or standing in the city. Lot disappears completely from the narrative after the pitiful description of what happens in Lot's family after they fled from Sodom (Genesis 19:30-38). It is not clear whether Abraham ever saw him or heard from him again—there is certainly no mention of it in the Biblical narrative.*

7

*Now the LORD was gracious to Sarah as he had said…
Sarah became pregnant and bore a son to Abraham in his
old age. (Genesis 21:1-2)*

I suppose that didn't end too badly, thought Eliezer.

'That was a disaster!' exclaimed Lilith under her breath, as she gave a sharp tug on the rope of a heavily-laden donkey. Eliezer was glad that at least she lowered her voice when expressing opinion about their master and mistress when the children were around. Most of their offspring were leading similarly-laden donkeys just ahead of them. Asriel, however, was walking with his hand in that of Eliezer, but at six, their conversation was above him in every sense. 'How could Abraham have been so stupid?' she continued. 'Telling a ruler that Sarah was his sister did not work well in Egypt. So why did he think it would work with Abimelek?'

Only days after the destruction of Sodom, they had left Kiriath Arba and travelled along the Way of Shur to the southern border of Canaan. Then they had turned north-west and travelled to the plains and foothills nearer the coast, and to the vicinity of the city of Gerar where Abimelek was king. Eliezer pulled Asriel's hand slightly as he began to dawdle. 'The master presumed that the king did not fear God—'

'Which was clearly *not* the case from all that I have heard!'

173

'Abraham was wrong,' said Eliezer with a sigh. 'He should have trusted Yahweh to protect him.'

Lilith glanced over at him, her eyebrows raised. 'That is a rare admission of fault from your lips.'

Eliezer smiled. 'I am not entirely blind to my master's failings, few though they may be. But,' he continued, 'although Abimelek took Sarah into his household, the Lord *did* protect her once again, making His displeasure clear to Abimelek and ensuring he didn't lie with her.'

'Abraham was still foolish,' declared Lilith, with a note of finality. 'Even if for a second time he left richer because of it.'

Eliezer fell silent, content to give his wife, as usual, the last word. *It was strange, though.* God had closed the wombs of the women of Abimelek's household, until Abraham had prayed for them. *God had heard his prayers for these women and answered immediately, and yet had not opened Sarah's womb in all the years that he must have prayed for her.* But Eliezer contented himself with the knowledge that Abraham and Sarah were together again. *Which, after all, they needed to be, if a child was to be born to them in less than a year.*

The sun continued to make its slow and almost imperceptible journey downwards. Soon it would be behind the low hills to the west. It was almost five months since they had left Gerar. They'd travelled south-east, and onto higher ground, although they were still in what was considered Abimelek's land. Eliezer was glad to be back amongst the hills. It reminded him of the land around Damascus where he had spent his earliest years. A wadi nearby spoke of water flowing from the mountains in the winter down into the valley where they had made their camp. But a dry riverbed was of no use to herds or to those who owned them. The steady *thud, thud, thud* meant that the men who were digging the well were still making progress—as did the basketfuls of earth and rocks that were being hauled up to the surface with ropes by those standing near the edge of a large hole. Eliezer hailed them. 'How goes the work?'

Jushur, one of Burrukam's sons, grinned back at him, covered in dirt. 'The earth we pull up is no longer dry.'

'It is a good sign, my brother!' exclaimed Eliezer with a smile. 'I will tell Abraham. He will be glad to hear it.' Eliezer stopped by the edge and leaned gingerly over. He could only just make out those digging below in the murkiness of what would hopefully soon be a water-filled well. He stepped back, and put down the small sack. 'The master sends bread for you…and meat.' His news was greeted with broad smiles. The portions of boiled goat meat were a rare treat, but Abraham had insisted that morning that those working on the well should be rewarded for their efforts that day. He'd seemed in an unusually cheerful mood.

'And how is my sister today? Is she bearing you any more children at the moment?'

Eliezer laughed. 'Not that I know of! But I can tell you that she was happy enough when I left her.' They continued to talk about their families and children for a while, before Eliezer said his farewells and made his way back towards the tents.

'I have something to tell you,' said Lilith, her eyes shining. Eliezer had barely reached their tent before she was dragging him inside.

'And what news has my wife for me today?' he asked, a wry smile on his face, before kissing Lilith. After more than twenty years of marriage he was quite familiar with her desire to pass on to him any and every piece of news or gossip that she had acquired. Which, he had to admit, was quite useful for knowing what was happening in his master's camp.

Lilith peeked out through the tent flaps, making sure there was no one outside, then turned back to Eliezer. 'Sarah's belly swells!' she said, wide-eyed. 'I saw it for myself when I was helping her make a new tunic earlier.'

Eliezer stared at her, momentarily struck dumb. *Could this finally be the fulfilment of Yahweh's promises?* 'Did you say anything to her—or she to you?' asked Eliezer.

'No, I don't think she realised what I saw.'

Eliezer thought for a moment. 'If she is carrying, how long do you think she has been with child?'

'She might be in her fourth month.'

Eliezer's mind rapidly counted the months. *Yes, the timing of a birth would be as Yahweh had said!* But he suddenly became serious. 'Lilith—have you told anyone else?'

'No. You are the first.'

'And I must be the only one. You must not speak of this to anyone else. Not even your mother. *Especially* not your mother! You cannot be wrong about this. We must wait until the matter is sure and Abraham is willing to speak of it.'

'Maybe she is not sure herself yet. After all, she has not had her monthly bleeding for many years, so will not be able to know in the way that most women do—at least to start with.'

'It will show properly soon enough if she is with child. We must be patient and wait.' But Eliezer suddenly remembered Abraham's mood that morning. *Maybe he already knew.*

'It is a good well, my lord. They have built it with care and I'm sure it will last many years.' Eliezer was standing with Abraham next to the well, which, after several months, now had a low wall of stone around it. A large wooden cover with leather straps to lift it leaned against the wall. Abraham took the leather bucket that sat on the wall, and tossed it into the well. They watched as the rope to which it was attached unravelled as the bucket fell. A *splosh* told them it had reached the water. Abraham's hundred-year-old but still-vigorous arms then pulled up the rope, hand over hand, until the container cleared the stone circle. He carefully rested it on the wall, and drew some water out with a cupped hand. He looked at it for a few moments and then drank. A smile came to his face.

'The water is good!' He then tipped the bucket into a low wooden trough nearby, from which animals could drink. 'You are right. The men have done well. They must be rewarded.'

'I will see to it, my lord.' Abraham glanced back to the camp, anxiety briefly crossing his face. 'All will be well, master,' said Eliezer. 'Ninlil and Lilith will care for Sarah well, and they trust the midwife completely. She has helped many women bring children to birth, and she will help Sarah now.'

'You are right, Eliezer,' said Abraham with a sudden smile. 'This baby—this boy—has been promised by God, and He who spoke that promise will surely fulfil it completely…despite the father being a hundred and his wife ninety. He said that Sarah would be a mother, so He will keep her safe as well.'

'Yahweh is faithful,' replied Eliezer simply.

'Faithful and good. But I have a mind to hurry back to the camp, for I would see the tiny face that reflects His goodness as soon as I am able.'

Eliezer began hauling the wooden cover back over the well with a grin. 'Then hurry we will, my lord!'

They didn't need to hear Ninlil's proclamation of the child's birth as she emerged, smiling, from the tent. They had already heard the sound of a baby using its first breath to cry out to the world it had entered. Eliezer marvelled. *Yes, the child had been promised by God some twenty-five years earlier, but the birth was still a great miracle.*

'My lord,' Ninlil began, as she approached Abraham, 'we are still attending Sarah, but will tell you as soon as she and the baby are ready for you. You have a son!'

'I know,' replied Abraham. 'And his name is Isaac.' And he put his head back and laughed.

'It is just as well this child is weaned only once—and that he has no younger brother,' grumbled Burrukam, as he drained the beer off the tub, where mashed barley bread had been fermenting in water.

'Do not complain, my husband' responded Ninlil. She slapped another round of wheat dough on the side of the heated pottery oven. 'For you will get to drink the beer and eat the food at the feast.'

Eliezer smiled to himself. Lilith's parents, by now over seventy, had become his own. Twenty-seven years had passed since he joined Abraham's household, and he was now forty. Through Lilith, he had five children and a grandchild on the way through Kemuel and his wife. Yahweh had blessed him with a family after he had lost his own flesh and blood. And now Abraham and Sarah had a child of their own—the beginning of the many descendants God had promised him. And only the finest of feasts was a suitable celebration for his weaning at two years old.

'Eliezer! Do not stand there day-dreaming,' chided Lilith. 'We only have until sunset to finish preparing the food. The meat on the spit needs turning or else it will burn. And,' she added, 'there are many onions that still need to be peeled and sliced.' She turned to their daughters. 'Jael—do not chop those melons too small. And Inanna—you only need a little of that fig syrup in the dough.'

Most of Abraham's servants who weren't herders were involved in preparing the feast. Eliezer knew that to be the case because he and Burrukam had had to organise most of them. *But then, they were preparing enough choice food for hundreds of mouths!* The whole camp seemed to be filled with cooking pots and delicious aromas. Goat stewing with coriander and cumin, and whole lambs roasting on spits. Barley, wheat and sweet fruit breads baking. Lentil and onion stew bubbling, smelling of garlic. And besides all that, there were cheeses and dates and figs and grapes. Eliezer had never seen such a feast, and wondered how much the young Isaac would sample, now that he was no longer fed by Sarah's breast.

The celebration was one he would never forget, with music and dancing around the great fires that had been built in the camp, as well as feasting until well into the night. And at the centre of it all, a proud mother, whose hair was streaked with grey, and her son, who waddled around on his chubby legs—when he wasn't, that is, being lifted high into the air by his beaming elderly father.

But if it started well, it ended on a sour note, though Eliezer knew not why. All that was clear to him was that Sarah was displeased by the time the evening ended. She may have hidden it from most, but Eliezer saw the anger in her eyes, as she and Abraham disappeared into their tent, with Abraham carrying their sleeping son. He did not have to wait long, however, to discover the cause. For a raised voice in a tent seldom went unheard, particularly when there were female ears nearby that were ready to listen.

'My mother heard it clearly!' whispered Lilith, as she lay beside Eliezer under the woollen blanket in the tent.

'Can't it wait until morning,' groaned Eliezer. Beer and a good meal after a day of hard work had left him longing for sleep. *But that was never going to happen until Lilith had her say.*

'Ishmael mocked Isaac during the feast,' continued Lilith softly. 'Sarah was furious.'

'What was Ishmael supposed to have done?' asked Eliezer sleepily.

'She didn't say. But she did hear Sarah telling Abraham to drive out Hagar and Ishmael. Not that she could bring herself to use their names. It was *this maid and her son.* Can you believe that?' But before Eliezer could reply, she continued, 'What do you think Abraham will do?'

'We'll see…' murmured Eliezer. If Lilith said any more, he was unaware of it as he finally yielded to oblivion.

As Eliezer picked up the discarded cups and meat bones the following morning, he kept looking for Ishmael and Hagar, but didn't see them around the tents as he usually did. Sarah appeared tight-lipped and Abraham subdued. When he hadn't seen either the sixteen-year-old or his mother by the time the sun was overhead, Eliezer finally plucked up courage to ask his master, before they all retired to the shade of their tents in the heat of the day.

'Master?'

'Speak, Eliezer.'

'I have not seen Ishmael and Hagar this morning. Did the feast make them ill in any way?'

Abraham sighed, and sadness filled his eyes. 'I might as well tell you now, for you will know soon enough anyway. I have thought it best, for Isaac's sake, to send them away. Yahweh assured me last night that He would watch over them, and bless Ishmael. It will be for the best.' There was no mention of the quarrel or the mocking, and Eliezer certainly wasn't going to be the one to bring it up.

'A hard decision, my lord,' said Eliezer gently. 'But the Lord is faithful.'

'Faithful and good,' replied Abraham, as he had done before. But this time, his voice was weary.

Eliezer thought of his second son Eldad, only a year or two older than Ishmael. *How would he feel, sending him off, knowing that he might not see him again?* His master's words echoed in his mind: *Faithful and good.* But that did not mean that Yahweh kept His people from pain.

Eliezer was barely out of his tent when Abraham approached him. Although the darkness of night had passed, the sun had not yet risen above the hills near

Beersheba. They had named the place *the well of the seven* after the well they had dug out some nine years earlier, just before Isaac was born. 'My lord?'

'I must undertake a journey. To offer a sacrifice. Isaac will be coming with me, and so will you. Choose another of the younger men to come too. We will be gone for probably five or six days. See to it that we have enough provisions.'

'I will ask Kemuel—'

'No.' The forcefulness of Abraham's response took Eliezer by surprise.

'Has my firstborn offended you in some way, my lord?'

'He has not,' replied Abraham quickly and more gently. 'He serves me well.'

Several alternatives flitted through Eliezer's mind. 'I know he is young, my lord, but Asriel—'

'Not Asriel!' If anything, Abraham's reaction was even stronger. Eliezer hadn't even had the chance to suggest that he would be good company for Isaac, since he was only seven years older than him. 'Bring Jushur,' said Abraham, deciding the matter.

Eliezer did not question Abraham's judgment, but remained puzzled by his insistence that he should not bring one of his own sons on the journey. *Still, his brother-in-law was a good enough choice.* He was also puzzled as to why they were travelling such a distance to make a sacrifice. *Maybe Abraham was simply choosing a new part of the promised land to dedicate to Yahweh?* Eliezer didn't trouble himself too much. *They would find out soon enough.*

It had been seven years since Isaac was weaned, and Eliezer had seen the delight that he brought to Abraham and Sarah. To have a son was blessing enough, but to know that the promises of the Almighty rested upon him made him a child like no other. But as he watched Abraham chopping wood for the burnt offering that morning, his master appeared strangely distracted, as if some matter of great moment troubled his mind.

A further mystery as they set out was the absence of an animal to be sacrificed. There was a sheathed knife tucked in Abraham's belt, but no goat or lamb tethered to the donkey which was carrying the wood and their bedding. *But his master knew what he was doing. Maybe there was a town near their destination from which they would purchase a suitable beast.* And so he did not ask.

For two days they travelled north through the hill country, passing through Kiriath Arba on the second day, and for two nights they slept under the stars. They travelled largely in silence. Abraham rarely spoke, and still seemed preoccupied. When Isaac did speak to him, his answers were terse, with little warmth or humour. Eliezer had never seen his master in such a strange mood. His eyes were mostly fixed ahead of him, as if he had no desire to look around at the land through which they travelled. And once again, Eliezer had the impression that something was weighing heavily on his heart.

On the third day, Abraham stopped them, his gaze on higher ground a little distance away. 'We are nearly there.' He turned to Eliezer, his face strangely impassive. 'You and Jushur are to stay here with the donkey. I will go ahead with the boy.'

'Yes, my lord.'

'Jushur—prepare the fire for the burnt offering.'

'My lord.'

As Jushur struck flint on iron, carefully shielding the fine tinder until he'd coaxed it into flame, Eliezer helped remove the firewood from the donkey.

'The boy will carry the wood. I will carry the fire and the knife.' They were the sole words that Abraham spoke as they prepared for departure. And there was no joy in them. Only when they were finally ready, with a burning torch in Abraham's hand, did he add, 'We will worship and then return to you.' And then they were gone.

Eliezer and Jushur watched in silence as the two started making their way up to the higher ground without a backward glance. When they were far enough away to be out of earshot, Jushur finally murmured, 'Where's the animal for the burnt offering?'

And Eliezer, with a troubled heart, answered, 'I have wondered that also.'

'It was odd that he called Isaac, *the boy*. Is that usual?'

'Not that I've noticed.' And still they watched, until Abraham and Isaac became little more than specks on the mountainside, before disappearing altogether behind a rocky outcrop. By this time, the sun had risen high in the sky, and both men made shelters out of their blankets to shield them from the midday sun. Although Jushur fell asleep quickly, Eliezer could not rest. He couldn't shake off the feeling that something wasn't right. *Abraham's mood had been so peculiar—so unlike his normal self.* And then there was the puzzling question of the lack of a suitable offering. *It wasn't as if Abraham had a bow or snare to kill or trap a goat or a sheep or a gazelle, even if such creatures were up in the mountains.*

With the sound of Jushur's snoring in his ears, Eliezer sat staring at the spot where he had last seen the tiny frames of Abraham and his son, trying to make sense of it all. *Why did this sacrifice to Yahweh feel so different from every other?* And then suddenly—and unbidden—a dark thought entered his mind which he immediately and vehemently dismissed. *It was unthinkable! Abraham would never sacrifice his only son, and Yahweh would not ask such a terrible deed of him!* He was well aware that such practices existed. Servants' talk around the campfire at night had more than once touched on the monstrous rituals performed by some Canaanites, to seek the favour of their gods. *But Yahweh was not like that, and Abraham had no need to gain His favour! Besides,* Eliezer told himself more than once, *Isaac was the child promised by God, the one through whom God's promises were to be carried forward. Yahweh would never require such a thing! And hadn't Abraham spoken of them both returning?* Eliezer assured himself that such a terrible act was inconceivable, given all that Yahweh had said and done. And yet he still felt uneasy. Especially when he remembered Abraham's insistence that his own sons should not accompany them on the journey. *There must be some other explanation, surely!* But try as he might, he could not think of one.

And finally, he saw something. *There it was.* A thin column of smoke, barely visible, rising into the blue sky in the distance. *The deed was done—whatever it was.*

'Didn't you sleep, my brother?' Jushur's question, yawned as much as spoken, provided a welcome relief from his troubled thoughts. Though Eliezer avoided answering directly.

'I rested well enough.'

'Any sign of Abraham and Isaac yet?'

'No. Nothing moves on the mountain.'

Unconcerned, Jushur rose to his feet, stretched and went to the donkey to retrieve one of the waterskins. Eliezer's eyes, however, returned to the same spot: the rocky outcrop on the mountainside. But even as Jushur put his head back and quenched his thirst, Eliezer thought he saw some movement far away. He shielded his eyes and squinted, trying to see better. After several moments he became sure something was moving on the mountain. He stiffened and stared harder. And then, after what felt like an age, the movement resolved into two distinct specks. And Eliezer breathed freely once more.

The difference in Abraham's demeanour when he finally returned could not have been greater. Gone were the distraction and the grim expression, and in their place, peace and joy. 'We have presented our offering to Yahweh, and it has been pleasing to Him,' he proclaimed with a smile.

'Did you find a suitable animal to sacrifice, my lord?' asked Jushur simply. Eliezer waited for the answer.

'The Lord Himself provided the offering—a ram.'

The journey back was again in marked contrast to what had gone before. Conversation flowed, and the mood was cheerful. But on the first evening, as Jushur cooked a lentil stew for them to share, Eliezer casually asked Abraham out of the hearing of the others, 'Did you know, my lord, that Yahweh would provide a ram for the offering when you left us this morning?'

Abraham looked at him for a long while, saying nothing, as if he were weighing up a matter in his mind. And then he said, 'Walk with me, Eliezer.' For a while, they wandered in silence out of earshot of Jushur and Isaac, and then Abraham suddenly said, 'I will not hide it from you.' And Eliezer waited. 'Yahweh told me to offer Isaac as a burnt offering. That was the sacrifice He asked of me.' Eliezer drew in a sudden breath, but did not speak. 'I knew that I had to act immediately, whilst my resolve to obey still held. I didn't trust myself to delay—or to tell anyone.'

'Sarah knew nothing?' asked Eliezer, though guessing the answer.

'I could not tell her. She could not have borne it.'

'So what happened, master,' asked Eliezer quietly, 'for you returned together?'

'When we reached the place, Isaac asked me where the lamb for the offering was.' Abraham, for a moment, seemed unable to speak. 'I told him that God would provide the lamb.' He continued looking steadily ahead. 'We built the altar together, and arranged the wood on top. Isaac was looking around, waiting for the lamb. Then, when it was completed'—Abraham's voice began to crack—'I said to him, *You are the lamb that God has provided.*' He paused, composing himself before he continued. He then took a deep breath, his eyes full of unspilled tears. 'Isaac went pale, but he submitted to me. He allowed me to bind him and lay him on the altar, though he was trembling. I then unsheathed the knife, and raised it to slay him. But the voice of Yahweh came from heaven, telling me not to harm him.'

'It was a test?' whispered Eliezer.

Abraham nodded. 'Yahweh now knows that I withhold nothing from Him.'

They walked in silence once more. After several moments, Eliezer asked, 'And what then? I saw the smoke from the altar.'

'I lowered the knife and began cutting Isaac's bonds. But even as I did, I heard bleating behind me. I turned to see a ram with its horns caught in a thicket. And Isaac, as he sat up, said, *Look father! Yahweh* has *provided the animal!* So we killed it, and offered it to the Lord, kneeling and worshipping. I named the place, *Yahweh provides.*'

'You said when you left us, *We will return.* How did you know that, when you would have slain Isaac?'

'The Lord said that He would establish His covenant with Isaac, and that Isaac would have descendants. I thought that if He could give life to a dead womb, as He did for Sarah, then maybe He could give life to Isaac again. But I did not know. The Lord called me to obedience. What lay beyond that obedience was in His hands.' He paused again. 'But after we had worshipped, Yahweh called to me a second time. He repeated His promises that He would multiply my descendants, to be as numerous as the stars in the heavens and the sand on the seashore. And He also said that all the nations of earth would be blessed through my seed.'

Eliezer marvelled at his master's obedience and the promises given to him—but baulked at the prospect of a God who demanded all.

As he lay on the ground that night, staring up at the innumerable stars which were spread out across the sky like a shimmering shawl, Eliezer pondered the events of the day. *Could it really be that Abraham's offspring would be as abundant as the stars above him? Yet God had created each of those stars, so surely he could multiply children!* And as he was reminded of the greatness and power of Yahweh, he wondered if he would have been able to offer up Asriel— or any of his children—to the Almighty, as his master had done. *God had surely never meant Abraham to kill Isaac. But Abraham had not known that when he lifted the knife.* But there was comfort, too, in his thoughts. *Yes, Yahweh demanded all, but in giving his all, Abraham had received an incomparable promise of blessing from God.* And in the darkness and the quietness of the night, he mouthed a silent prayer: *Good and faithful God, from whose hand I and my family have received bountiful blessings, help me to serve You with the same devotion and obedience as my master, Abraham, whatever the cost.* And although he doubted that he could ever match Abraham's faith, he meant his prayer—every word of it.

Notes

1. *Regarding the incident with Abimelek, it must presumably have happened within three months at most after the destruction of Sodom. Sarah had to be back with Abraham nine months before Isaac was born, which was roughly a year after Sodom was destroyed, given God's words in Genesis 17:21, 18:10,14.*

2. *Sarah would have been eighty-nine or ninety when taken by Abimelek. Given that she died at a hundred and twenty-seven, maybe she was, in that incident, the equivalent of, say, a good-looking sixty-year-old today, i.e. well past the age of child-bearing, but still attractive. Or maybe, given Abimelek's awareness of God's blessing on Abraham's life, and his later desire for Abraham's good-will, taking Sarah as his wife was seen as a way of securing a good relationship with a rich and powerful neighbour.*

3. *We don't know the age of Isaac when Abraham went to sacrifice him. He was clearly old enough to talk and ask questions*

and carry firewood, but still young enough for Abraham to presumably lift him. In this account, therefore, Isaac is taken to be nine years old.

4. Jews take the location of the temple as the place where Abraham offered Isaac, and this story has followed that tradition. It is around 50 miles from Beersheba to Jerusalem, which would fit with the length of journey Abraham made. But it is debated as to whether it is the same place. In 2 Chronicles 3:1 (which is the only other reference in Scripture to Moriah), it is also described as a mountain. One thing that counts against this, however, is that in 2 Chronicles, Mount Moriah becomes the site of the temple, and is therefore part of Jerusalem. If Salem (in Genesis 14:18) does refer to the place that is later known as Jerusalem, then the place of sacrifice probably wouldn't be the remote place that seems to be implied in Genesis 22.

8

'Go to my country and my own relatives and get a wife for my son Isaac.' (Genesis 24:4)

'Find out what goods they bear,' said Abraham to Eliezer, as merchants began to dismount from their camels nearby. 'And ask them if their animals need water.'

At sixty-five, Eliezer was still surprisingly sprightly, even if he was not quite as swift as he had once been. He hurried over to the group of strangers, wondering how far they had travelled. It was not unusual to see a caravan passing close to them at Beersheba. Groups of merchants—on donkeys or with long camel trains—would, from time to time, travel along the Way of Shur, trading frankincense or silverware, fine linen or coloured dyes. Or indeed anything others might be willing to buy with silver or gold. And often they would stop at their settlement as they travelled south to Egypt or north to Damascus or beyond, sometimes watering their animals at Abraham's well.

After a brief conversation, Eliezer returned to his master. 'They would welcome water for their camels, my lord. And they are selling fine gold and silver jewellery—armlets, bracelets, rings, earrings and necklaces—some with lapis lazuli and other precious stones. They also have myrrh and painted pottery from the Land of the Rivers.'

'They have travelled far,' replied Abraham.

'I would see their jewellery,' said Sarah with a smile. 'Isaac may only be twenty-five, but it would not harm to see if there are bracelets or rings that could be gifts for a future wife.'

There was a twinkle in Abraham's eye. 'And my wife could wear those pieces until they are needed for a daughter-in-law.'

'Now that is a good idea, my husband,' said Sarah with a laugh, feigning surprise.

Eliezer smiled. It had been years since he had seen the sadness that had been a constant, brooding presence for so much of her life. *Isaac had brought such joy and laughter into both of their lives.*

The three of them walked together to the camels. 'You are welcome,' his master said to the merchants. 'I am Abraham, and we will bring out food and drink for you.'

But before he could say more, one of the men replied, '*Abraham?* We were asked by a man in Harran to look out for someone by the name of Abram, son of Terah.'

'I am that man,' said Abraham, and Eliezer waited with interest to hear what news the trader bore.

'Then I bring you greetings from your brother Nahor—'

'He lives in Harran now?'

'Yes, with his wife Milcah.'

'She is also my niece, the daughter of my other brother. But what of my father Terah.'

'He still lives, but the days he has left will be few.'

Abraham was silent for a moment, and then asked. 'And what of Nahor? Does he prosper?'

'Milcah has borne him eight sons!'

'Eight? The Lord has blessed him indeed. But come, sit and eat and tell us more.' He glanced at Sarah, and then back at the men, and added, smiling: 'And bring your gold jewellery.'

Sarah wore the jewellery for twelve years. The day of her death was one of great mourning for the whole camp, but none wept more than Abraham and Isaac, with their heads covered in dust and ashes. But there was one matter that needed to be quickly resolved— and that was a suitable burial place for Sarah. When Burrukam and Ninlil had died a few years earlier, they had been buried in shallow graves, outside the camp in Beersheba. The graves were covered with heaps of rocks, both marking them and preventing them being disturbed. But now they were back in Kiriath Arba. *And the wife of a great man deserved better.* Eliezer wondered what his master would do. *Whatever was decided, it would have to be that day.*

The tent flap was pushed back, and Abraham emerged, with the weariness of grief heavy upon him. 'Eliezer, come with me. Bring your three sons with you, and five hundred shekels of silver.'

'Will we be going far, my lord?'

'Into Kiriath Arba to see the sons of Heth. I will see if Ephron will sell me the cave of Machpelah on his land as a burial site.'

'Very well, my lord. I will see to it immediately.'

By the time they left, Eliezer was not only joined by Kemuel, Eldad and Asriel, but also by Asriel's youngest son, Mahaz. 'He will learn from what he sees,' said Eliezer, when Asriel had suggested bringing his twelve-year-old son. 'Abraham will not object.'

Eliezer and his sons stood at the edge of the gathering in the meeting place at the city gates. He recognised most of the family of Heth. They were Hittites, and descended from Canaan. *His master would need tact.* They had been happy—as had Aner, Eshcol and Mamre, some fifty years earlier—for Abraham to dwell among them. But he was still an outsider to them, and allowing him to acquire a permanent plot in what they considered their land would not be something they would do lightly.

Abraham sat with the sons of Heth, drinking barley beer with them, and being offered their condolences. But he soon put the cup down. 'I am a foreigner and stranger among you,' he began. 'Sell me some land for a burial site here so that I can bury my dead.'

'Hear us, my lord,' replied the one who appeared to be the eldest. 'You are a mighty prince among us. Bury your dead in the choicest of our tombs. None of us will refuse you his tomb for burying your dead.'

Eliezer leaned over to Mahaz, and whispered, 'See what they are doing, Mahaz. They flatter Abraham, because they would rather he use their tombs than take any of their land.' Mahaz gave a wordless nod, but then Abraham stood and bowed to them.

'If you are willing to let me bury my dead out of my sight, then hear me. Ask Ephron son of Zohar on my behalf to sell me the cave of Machpelah, which belongs to him and is at the end of his field. Ask him to sell it to me for the full price as a burial site among you.'

'Now see what our master does,' whispered Eliezer to his grandson once more, as murmurs rippled around the seated men. 'The Hittites might not want us to buy land, but Ephron may be very happy to sell it at a good price.

Now watch! See the man with the green scarf round his head?' Mahaz nodded again. 'That is Ephron.'

And Ephron spoke. 'No, my lord, hear me. I give you the field, and I give you the cave that is in it. I give it to you in the presence of my people. Bury your dead.'

'Abraham has the field!' whispered Mahaz excitedly. 'And as a gift!'

'Not quite,' replied Eliezer, as Abraham bowed low once again. 'Saying that is just the custom. Everyone knows he will have to pay, but it does mean Ephron will sell.'

'Hear me, if you will,' began Abraham again. 'I will pay the price of the field. Accept it from me so that I can bury my dead there.'

Ephron gave a little shrug of his shoulders, as if it were a small thing. 'Listen, my lord; the land is worth four hundred shekels of silver, but what is that between you and me? Bury your dead.'

'That is a heavy price!' said Eliezer quietly to all his sons with some disdain. 'Ephron knows our master has no other choice.'

But Abraham nodded, 'I will pay.' He then gestured to Eliezer to bring the silver, which was duly weighed out for all to see.

And Eliezer murmured to himself more than to his sons, 'And so our master finally owns one field in the promised land.'

Eliezer sighed with exasperation. 'Mahaz *is* only fifteen.' Three years had passed since Sarah's death.

'It is never too early to start thinking of a suitable wife for him,' replied Lilith. 'Abraham is sure to give you a free choice—'

'And I will give Asriel a free choice in picking a wife for his own son, when it is time.'

'Silili would make a good wife.'

Eliezer laughed. 'How is it, my wife, that every part of your body tires with age, except your tongue?'

'For the same reason your ears still hear well. Because the Lord knows that there are still things that I need to say and that you need to hear.'

Eliezer laughed again. 'Well, my ears now need to listen elsewhere. I will not keep my master waiting any longer.' And with that, he leaned over and kissed Lilith's grey head of hair and left, to answer Abraham's summons.

He found him standing in his tent, seemingly deep in thought or in prayer. *His master's great age had finally begun to show.* 'You called for me, my lord?'

Abraham studied Eliezer for a few moments before speaking. 'Remind me. How old were you when you first came to serve me?'

'Thirteen years old, my lord. It was two years before you left Harran—'

'When I was seventy-five. Yes, I remember it.' Abraham thought for a moment. 'So altogether you have served me…'

'Sixty-seven years, my lord.'

Abraham gave a little laugh. 'Yes, you were always good at counting.' He paused for a moment. 'And I am now a hundred and forty years old, and you are eighty.'

'Yes, my lord.'

'But ours are not the ages that concern me today. Isaac is forty. That was the age I married Sarah. And I have decided that the time has now come for me to find a suitable wife for my son.' Eliezer nodded, though wondering what Abraham would say next. 'Eliezer—there is no other servant in my household whom I trust as I do you. That is why you have been in charge of all that I own for many years. And you have always served me faithfully.'

'It has been my desire and my pleasure to do so, my lord.'

'But I also trust you because you honour Yahweh. I see it in the way you live and the way you speak of Him.'

Eliezer smiled. 'I have learned of the Almighty through you, my master, and I am in your debt. For I have seen His power and His faithfulness because of you, and I have sought to serve Him, as you do.'

'And that is the reason, Eliezer, I am now entrusting to you the solemn task that I would entrust to no other: that of finding a wife for my son Isaac.'

Not for the first time in his life, Eliezer wondered if he had heard Abraham right. *Why would he not choose a wife for Isaac himself?* 'Master?'

'Yahweh once spoke to me, telling me that, many generations from now, the people of this land will come under His judgment for their sin. And so I will *not* have a wife for Isaac from among them. I am, therefore, sending you on a journey that I am too old to make myself. I want you to swear by Yahweh, the God of heaven and earth, that you will not get a wife for my son from the daughters of the Canaanites here, but will go to my country and my own relatives and find a wife for Isaac there. We know that my brother Nahor moved to Harran and Milcah bore him many children. I will trust the Lord that there will be a suitable wife for Isaac from within the family.'

Eliezer thought for a moment. *Surely he couldn't force a girl to make such a long journey away from her home?* 'Master, what if she is unwilling to come back with me to this land? Shall I then take Isaac back to Harran?'

Abraham answered immediately and forcefully. 'No! Make sure that you do not take my son back there! He is not to leave this land.' He went on, 'Eliezer, you know that Yahweh brought me out of my father's household and my native land. You know that He spoke to me and swore to give this land to my offspring. Now He will send His angel before you to help you, so that you can get a wife for my son from there. If she is unwilling to come back with you, then you will be released from this oath. But don't take Isaac back there.' Abraham lifted up the hems of his robe. 'Place your hand under my thigh now, and swear.'

Eliezer knelt at his master's feet and reached up under Abraham's robe, enacting the sign of a sacred vow. *And through it, his master's line would be preserved.* 'I swear by Yahweh, God of heaven and earth, that I will do all that you ask.' Abraham sighed, as if from relief, once the promise had been made. Eliezer withdrew his hand, aware of the solemn responsibility that had just been placed upon him.

'And now,' said Abraham, 'we will make plans together for your journey.'

Eliezer decided that riding a camel was not the most comfortable way to travel. *Still, at eighty years old, he was glad that he didn't have to walk.* He had left Kiriath Arba some three weeks earlier, retracing the route he had travelled with Abraham sixty-five years earlier. Although this time, there weren't hundreds of goats and sheep to slow them down. Just the steady lollop of camels—ten of them, with six riders.

'Are we nearly there yet?' shouted Asriel.

Eliezer turned his head, raising his eyebrows. 'It is almost as if I am hearing the voice of my grandson Mahaz! Why so impatient?'

'My brother has no patience,' interjected Kemuel, 'because he has no skill with animals! He has never learned to ride a donkey properly, let alone a camel!'

'And you ride it better than me?' replied Asriel.

'At least I didn't fall off the first time the camel rose from its knees.' The three others from Abraham's household laughed loudly.

'But my father hasn't answered my question yet,' said Asriel, clearly keen to divert the conversation away from his lack of prowess.

'Maybe a day or so more? So, yes, we are nearly there.' Eliezer smiled to himself. *Camels might be uncomfortable, but at least they could travel a good distance without needing to stop for water.* There was, however, a more important reason for their choice: camels were a sign of great wealth. *If they wanted to impress the family of a prospective wife for Isaac, then camels were definitely a good place to start. Particularly ten of them.*

Throughout the long journey, the matter that had been uppermost in Eliezer's mind was how exactly he was going to find a suitable wife for Isaac. He had confidence that Yahweh would provide a wife for him. *How could His promise to Abraham be fulfilled unless that was so? But how was he to know the one that was the Lord's choice? That was the problem!* But he remembered what Abraham had told him once—that he could let the Creator know what was on his heart. And so he prayed. He prayed to the God whose power he had seen first-hand. The God who had helped them defeat Chedorlaomer. The One who had twice protected Abraham from his own folly. The God who had met and spoken to Hagar in the desert. The Almighty, who had spoken to his master and done the impossible for him, and who had provided a ram for an offering when Abraham had been tested. And as he prayed, an idea began to form in Eliezer's mind. *A test. He would ask Yahweh to show him the right choice through a test of his own. But what could its nature be?* And as he lurched up and down on the camel, he suddenly knew the answer.

The sun dropped lower behind them as the city of Harran came into view. Eliezer pulled on his reins and brought the camel to a halt. The others followed his lead. 'What is it, father?' asked Kemuel.

'That is Harran. We will be sleeping there tonight.'

'At last,' muttered Asriel.

'There is a well outside the city where the women go in the evening to draw water. We will take the camels there, but then I want you to draw back. Leave me with the camels, and I will put the matter in Yahweh's hands.' *And he would soon see if the God of Abraham was also the God of Eliezer, both hearing and answering his prayer.*

A short while later, Eliezer was coaxing the camels down onto their knees next to the water trough near the well. And as he stood there, alone, he bowed his head and prayed quietly under his breath. 'Yahweh, God of my master Abraham, grant me success today, and show kindness to my master Abraham. Look, here I am, standing beside this well. The daughters of the town will be coming out to draw water. May it be that when I say to a young woman, *Please let down your jar that I may have a drink*, and she says, *Drink, and I'll water your camels too*—let her be the one You have chosen for Isaac. By this I will know that You have shown kindness to my master by answering my prayer.'

Eliezer lifted his head—and started. A girl was already walking towards him, carrying her water jar on her shoulder. *Could this possibly be God answering his prayer even before he had finished it?* He studied her as she walked closer. There was no question about her beauty, and she carried herself with poise. Eliezer reckoned her to be around seventeen or eighteen. He noticed she wore none of the customary jewellery of a married woman. She dropped her eyes as she realised she was being watched. *That was a good sign. She was clearly modest.* She stopped by the well and filled her jar, and as she raised it to her shoulder again, he hurried over to her. 'Please give me a little water from your jar.'

She looked briefly at him, and then dropped her eyes again. 'Drink, my lord,' she replied, quickly lowering the jar and offering it to him.

Eliezer's heart was pounding. *Would she pass the test and be the one Yahweh had chosen?*

He drank, but even as he was passing the jar back to her, she spoke again. 'I'll draw water for your camels too, until they have had enough to drink.'

Eliezer's heart quickened further. She swiftly emptied her jar into the trough, and then ran back to the well for more. He watched in silence as she went back and forth, time and again. *Not just water for them to drink, but enough for ten thirsty camels to quench their thirsts. That was even more than he had asked! Here was a girl of noble character, who would willingly put herself out to serve a stranger. But he didn't even know her name or her family yet!* When the camels had finally finished drinking, she stood by the well, with her jar full of water once more, catching her breath. 'Thank you,' said Eliezer simply.

She smiled at him, 'You are most welcome,' and then bowed to him, and made to leave.

'No, wait,' said Eliezer suddenly, and she looked up, perplexed. He took out a gold nose ring and two gold bracelets from the bag that was slung around his shoulder. *Her family must know of his master's wealth. But who were they? Was it possible that she was related to Abraham?* She was clearly startled as he slipped them onto her nose and wrists, but before she could respond, he asked, 'Whose daughter are you? Please tell me, is there room for myself and those who travel with me to lodge in your father's house for the night?'

'I am the daughter of Bethuel, the son that Milcah bore to Nahor,' she began. And even as Eliezer stared at her in astonishment, scarcely believing what he had just heard, she added, 'We have plenty of straw and fodder for the camels, and room for you to spend the night.'

Eliezer dropped to his knees and bowed down, overwhelmed by how his prayer had been answered. 'Praise be to Yahweh, the God of my master Abraham. He has not abandoned His kindness and faithfulness to my master. He has led me to the house of my master's relatives.' And even as he raised his head, the unnamed girl set down her jar, turned, and began running back to the city.

Eliezer continued watching her. Just as she was disappearing from sight, a voice behind him asked, 'What happened?' Kemuel and the other four had come over to join him.

'I believe the Almighty has granted us success already. He has guided me straight away to the daughter of our master's nephew. Surely there could be no better match!'

'The first one you spoke to—in the whole of the city?' exclaimed Asriel in amazement.

Eliezer nodded, 'Yes, Yahweh truly is the God of wonders, both in the heavens above and on the earth below.'

'Where did she go?' asked Kemuel excitedly.

'She has left her water jar here. She must have run back to her family to tell them what has happened.'

Kemuel shook his head, clearly astounded. 'What do we do now?'

'We wait. The matter is in the hands of Yahweh.'

But they didn't have to wait long. Soon, a solitary figure—a man—was hurrying from the city towards them. 'Do you think this is her father?' asked Asriel quietly, as he approached.

'He looks too young,' whispered Eliezer, not taking his eyes of him. 'He could be her brother.'

The man bowed low to them. 'I am Laban, son of Bethuel, and brother of Rebekah.'

'And was it Rebekah who drew the water for us?' replied Eliezer. 'She did not tell me her name.'

'It is. Now come, you who are blessed by Yahweh,' said Laban. 'Why are you standing out here? I have prepared the house and a place for the camels. Come, follow me— you are most welcome.'

It felt strange to Eliezer, being back after more than sixty years in the house which Abraham had shared with his father Terah. And it felt even stranger to be sitting in the main room of the house, treated as the honoured guest rather than the servant. *How his life had changed since the time he had served his own uncle beer and dates in that very room!*

As the camels were being unloaded and given straw and food, Eliezer quickly discovered that Abram's brother Nahor had died some years before. Even Bethuel's years—despite being far fewer than those of Abraham—hung heavily upon him, and he seemed content to sit back with his wife and leave the talking to his son, Laban.

Rebekah brought a hearty goat stew in to them, with bread and beer, and then left them. But Eliezer held up his hand. 'I will not eat until I have told you what I have to say.'

'Speak then,' answered Laban.

'I am the servant of Abraham,' he began. 'Yahweh has blessed my master abundantly, and he has become wealthy. He has given him sheep and cattle, silver and gold, male and female servants, and camels and donkeys. My master's wife Sarah has borne him a son in her old age. His name is Isaac, and Abraham has given him everything he owns.' Then Eliezer proceeded to tell them of the oath and his journey to Harran, describing in detail the test he had laid before God, and how Rebekah had more than fulfilled his request. And more than anything, he wanted to let them know that he believed that Yahweh's hand had been upon him. So, as he finished telling his story, he said, 'I bowed down and worshipped Yahweh. I praised the God of my master Abraham, who led me the right way, to find the granddaughter of my master's brother for his son.' He then turned to Bethuel. 'Now, if you will show kindness and faithfulness to my master, please tell me. If not, make it clear, so I may know what I must do next.'

Bethuel's rheumy eyes looked steadily back at him. 'This is from Yahweh; there is nothing more to be said.'

Laban rose, left the room, and returned moments later with his sister. 'Here is Rebekah. Let her become the wife of your master's son, as Yahweh has directed.'

And once more Eliezer knelt and bowed his head down to the ground. *Great God, You have shown me once more that You are faithful and good to my master Abraham—and to his servant. Praise be to Your name!* He then raised himself to his feet, and beckoned to his sons, whispering, 'Come with me. We will fetch the gifts before we eat.' They returned, laden, and presented red and blue dyed garments of fine Egyptian linen to Rebekah, together with intricately engraved silver bowls and gold rings and earrings. Her parents and brother were also presented with costly rugs and silverware and perfumes. And finally, Eliezer adorned Rebekah with a stunning gold and lapis lazuli necklace, bought many years earlier, and chosen—and worn first—by Sarah.

Abraham lived not only to see twin boys, Esau and Jacob, born to Isaac and Rebekah twenty years later, but also the first fifteen years of his grandsons' lives. By the time Abraham had breathed his last, Eliezer was a hundred and fifteen years old. *It was as if his master's longevity had somehow clung to him, like flour on the hands after baking bread. But now he was weary. Very weary.* He had buried first Lilith, and then all his sons and daughters. Grandchildren and even their own grandsons and granddaughters now surrounded him. Eliezer leaned on the arm of Mahaz as he watched Isaac and Ishmael—brought together by their father's death—bearing Abraham's body into the cave of

Machpelah, where his master had laid Sarah thirty-eight years earlier.

Despite not being able to remember the names of all his progeny, Eliezer could still remember clearly a single day, over a hundred years earlier, when he had been taken to Abraham—*or Abram, as he had been then.* His uncle had said simply, *You will do well with him,* and had then left him. *How could either of them, that day, have known how his life would indeed be blessed beyond measure through his master! But was that not what Yahweh had promised Abraham? That others—indeed, the whole world—would be blessed through him?* Eliezer's eyes returned to the cave as Isaac and Ishmael emerged. *And what of Yahweh's promise of innumerable descendants? Ishmael had not been the one through whom that was to be fulfilled, and the first of the innumerable descendants could still be swiftly numbered and named—Isaac, Esau and Jacob. And what of the promised land? The small burial plot was the only part of it that Abraham actually owned. And yet his master trusted the Almighty. In faith, he had claimed Canaan for Yahweh, leaving altars of stone scattered throughout the land.* But if there was one thing that Eliezer had learned over the years it was this: Yahweh was faithful. *Faithful and good.*

He lifted his tired eyes to heaven. He had one last request. *God of Abraham, grant me only this final blessing, I beg of You: bring my days on this earth swiftly to a close, that I may follow my master to the place You have taken him. O Yahweh, hear me, I pray!*

And for one last time, God answered Eliezer's prayer.

Notes

1. *Genesis 24 does not say that the servant sent by Abraham is Eliezer, but many commentators think that it may well be.*

2. *This chapter begins with Terah and Nahor still living and Abraham aged 125. Scripture states Terah died at 205, but, as already stated, it is not necessarily clear how old Terah was when Abraham was born. He would have still been living if Abraham was born to him before he was 80. Scripture gives no indication of how old Nahor was when he died, but it can probably be safely assumed that he travelled north from Ur to Harran before he did so, as Harran is referred to as 'the city of Nahor' (see point 5 below).*

3. *We don't know the age at which Abraham married Sarah. It is artistic license here to take it as forty, but it functions in the narrative as the reason why Abraham decides that it is time for Isaac to wed. In the list of the descendants of Shem in Genesis 11:10-26, it seems to have been the norm for Shem's descendants (with the exception of Terah) to father their first children (after marriage) between twenty-nine and thirty-five, so this is a way of simply explaining Isaac's later marriage.*

4. *Rebekah is Isaac's first cousin, once removed, i.e. Isaac and Bethuel are first cousins, though there is presumably a significant age difference between them. We do not know how old Rebekah was when she married Isaac.*

5. *The place to which Abraham's servant is sent is 'the city of Nahor' in 'Aram Naharaim' (Genesis 24:10) which seems to be a name for the general area of north-western Mesopotamia and what is called Paddan Aram elsewhere in Genesis (see also note 1 at the end of the first chapter of Eliezer). Given that Harran is in that area and Nahor possibly joined Terah when he moved from Ur, it has been assumed that this is the*

city in which Bethuel and Laban were living, particularly as Jacob is later sent specifically to Harran, where Laban is said to be living (Genesis 27:43).

6. It seems reasonable to imagine that, if living in Harran, Bethuel and Laban might be in the same house that Terah occupied (if Terah did, indeed, live in a house rather than a tent, there).Certainly Scripture makes reference to a house several times in this story (Genesis 24:23,27,31-32).

7. The Israelites may not have had a well-developed view of the after-life, but the mere fact that they treated the bodies of the dead with respect and care probably indicates that they held some form of hope for a future life.

Asher

Terah

Abraham   Nahor   Haran

Bethuel

Isaac = Rebekah   Laban

Esau   Jacob = Leah   = Rachel
                    (& Zilpah)   (& Bilhah)

(by Leah)   (by Bilhah)   (by Zilpah)   (by Rachel)
Reuben (1)   Dan (5)   Gad (7)   Joseph (11)

Simeon (2)   Naphtali (6)   Asher (8)   Benjamin (13)

Levi (3)

Judah (4)

Issachar (9)

Zebulun (10)   ( ) – order of birth

Dinah (12)

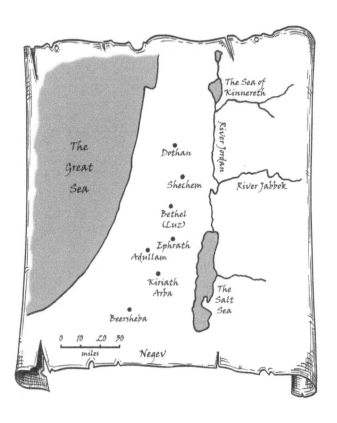

Jacob was angry and took Laban to task… 'Twenty years I was in your household. I worked for you fourteen years for your two daughters and six years for your flocks, and you changed my wages ten times.' (Genesis 31:36,41)

Asher kicked the dry ground, succeeding only in getting dirt between the leather of his sandal and his foot. Apart from his sandals, he wore only a simple, knee-length woollen tunic. His seventh winter had not long passed, and the waxing of the sun's strength did not yet call for his head to be covered against its consuming heat. He lifted his foot briefly and shook it, dislodging the earth, and then picked up a small, smooth pebble. He tossed it, aiming for the elderly goat standing nearby. It hit and then fell from its rather scrawny rump. A kid or a lesser goat would have bolted or at least trotted away. Instead, Asher's only reward was the animal's attention, as it slowly turned its head towards him, regarding him with dispassion whilst it continued to chew the cud. It soon looked away again, as if he were of no importance. *And the stupid goat was right.*

Despite only being seven years old, Asher was already well aware of his place in the family—and it was not one he would have chosen. His mother, Zilpah, was not his father's favourite wife. In fact, she wasn't even a wife, but the maid of one of his two wives. Of the *other* wife—Leah—*not* Jacob's favourite. And he was the younger of his mother's two sons. He may not have been the last of Jacob's eleven sons, but he was certainly the least.

Asher picked up a slightly larger stone, hitting the goat's flank this time. *It was certainly easier when the animals weren't moving.* But again, there was no bleating or sudden flight. Just an unhurried amble away from him. *Stupid goat*, thought Asher for the second time, as it continued to deny him the respect he felt the creature (at least) owed him. Its plain coat marked it out as belonging to the herd of his father's uncle, Laban. His father's flocks were the (supposedly fewer) spotted, speckled and streaked goats. That was the deal. The deal made by Laban, whom he knew (because his older brothers had told him) to be a cunning, lying, cheating, son of a—

'Asher!'

'Ow!' Asher spun round as the hard shrivelled fig that had struck him on the back fell to the ground. 'Stop it!'

'Then stop day-dreaming, you mangy mule,' replied Gad, walking up to him. He was only a year older than Asher, but it showed in both his height and weight. He put his hands on his hips, the stance of their mother's firstborn. 'Why did you leave the tents? You were told not to wander off.'

Asher glared at him. 'Ow!' he yelled, as Gad clipped him round the ear. 'What was *that* for?'

'For throwing stones at the goats. *Again*. I saw you.'

Asher lunged at his brother, catching him off-guard, so that both of them toppled over onto the dirt. It took somewhat longer than normal for Asher to end up in his usual place—flat on his back with his brother sitting astride of him, pinning his arms to the ground and smirking down at him. There were not many who triumphed over Gad. 'Get off!' panted Asher.

'Not until you admit you're a mangy mule.'

A shrill whistle rang out. They both turned their heads towards the sound. Asher, from his supine position, had a sideways view of Leah's eldest—Jacob's firstborn—standing on the top of a small ridge, a little way off. 'You're meant to be finding your brother, Gad,' shouted Reuben, 'not killing him. Get back to the camp, both of you—now!'

'He acts as if he's in charge,' muttered Gad as he released Asher. He's twelve not twenty!'

'That's only—' There was a momentary pause from the ground. '—four years older than you!' Asher silently determined, however, to ask Reuben (when Gad wasn't around) to teach how him to whistle using his fingers. *It was, after all, a mightily impressive sound.*

Despite being Asher's fiercest critic, Gad was also—when necessary—his greatest ally. They were, after all, the only two sons of Zilpah among the eleven brothers. Once on his feet, Gad offered Asher a hand, and pulled him up. 'Come on.'

'What's going on?' asked Asher, trotting a step or two behind his brother, as they hurried back up the ridge.

'Everything's being packed up and all the herds are being gathered. But nobody's telling us why.'

Asher could soon see it for himself. Two out of the four family tents were already lying flat on the ground, their poles and ropes being lashed together, with the other two in the process of being taken down. Asher gawped in amazement, as the only home he had ever known was dismantled.

But it had not been his father's only home. Twenty years earlier, when he had been seventy-six but had (apparently) looked half that age, Jacob had travelled from Canaan to Harran, to find not only his relatives but a wife. He had, through the deceit of Laban, however, ended up with two. He had also fathered sons with both of his wives' maids. And now he had eleven sons and one daughter. All of whom, Asher suddenly realised, were now waiting for him. His father was clearly about to address the whole family. He deliberately avoided Jacob's eyes and glanced around. Leah was standing with her six sons and Dinah, their only sister. Bilhah—the other maid—had her arms around Dan and Naphtali. His own mother stood with her arms folded, glaring at him, her displeasure clear. Rachel, Leah's younger—and more beautiful—sister, stood at Jacob's side. The place of the favoured wife. And Jacob rested his hand upon the shoulder of six-year-old Joseph, his youngest son and the only child of Rachel. Eleventh in line but first in their father's heart. And everyone knew it.

'Today,' began his father, 'we are leaving the Land of the Rivers, and are beginning the journey to Canaan—to my native land and the home of my father, Isaac. God has directed me to return there at once, so our journey will be swift.'

Asher's mind began to wander as his father started giving instructions. *God had directed him? How?* He glanced around again, as if the deity might still be lurking nearby. He saw no mysterious being, but what did surprise him was the absence of Laban's family. *Why weren't they helping or coming to say farewell?* But then he remembered they had departed the previous day with their flocks, to journey to the nearby town where the shearing and wool trading was done. He had visited it once. He then wondered if Canaan would be very different from the lands around Harran, and what they would see on the journey. He began to imagine the fearsome and monstrous lions and bears that his brothers Simeon and Levi had said could tear small boys limb from limb or eat them alive. *He would not be one of those small boys! He would bravely fight them with a bow and arrow, like the ones used by the men who hunted deer. And if his arrows missed, he would throw rocks at the beasts, and they would recoil from him in fear, their enormous legs pounding the earth as they fled, never to be—*

'Oi!' hissed Gad, thrusting his elbow sharply into Asher's side. 'You're meant to be listening.'

But his father appeared to be finishing. '…whilst you will travel by camel. As soon as the tents are loaded onto the donkeys, we will depart. And Yahweh, the God of my fathers, has promised that He will go with us. So be ready—' Jacob's eyes found Asher's. '—*all* of you.' A quick nod of dismissal, and then he was gone.

There was a sudden hubbub of activity and noise, as possessions were strapped to donkeys, bedding was rolled and tied, and waterskins were filled from the well nearby. Not finding (or wanting to find) any particular job to do, Asher wandered around, watching all the activity, particularly the camels being led into the camp. He ambled over to them, making sure he was beyond the reach of their legs. He'd never ridden on one before, and the prospect filled him with a mixture of fear and exhilaration. A hand on his shoulder suddenly yanked him around. Dan, nine years old, glanced about, clearly checking no one was in earshot. He said excitedly, in a lowered voice, 'We're running away!'

'*What?*' exclaimed Asher, wide-eyed.

'Laban doesn't know we're going. Judah overheard Father talking to Rachel and Leah a few days ago. They've been waiting for Laban and his sons to leave with their herds. It's their busiest time, and they'll be working from dawn to dusk with the herds being sheared. They won't know we've gone for days, and by then we'll be far away!'

'But why?'

'Because Laban's a cheat! Judah says that Reuben thinks he won't want us leaving with all our herds. And Laban's sons are saying that Father has taken all their livestock and their wealth.'

'That's donkey dung!'

'I know! It's not Father's fault if Laban tells him that his wages are all the spotted goats and then all the goats go and have spotted kids!'

Asher suddenly felt a little tug on his tunic, and turned to see the pretty little face of five-year-old Dinah. 'Go away!' said Dan forcefully, and Asher stuck out his tongue at her for good measure. But Dinah could give as good as she got. Her small brown eyes hardened and she returned the gesture, before turning and running away towards her mother, Leah. But as eager as Asher was to hear more, it wasn't to be.

'Asher!' called Zilpah. 'Stop wasting time. We're ready to leave now. Dan, your brother can't get onto the camel until you're there. Your mother is waiting for you. Both of you—move!'

Asher trotted over to his mother. A camel was already kneeling down, with Gad on its back. 'Up you get. There's a skin with milk in the saddlebag if you need a drink.'

Asher looked up at his mother, disappointed. 'Can't I have my own camel?'

She put her hands on her hips and raised her eyebrows. It was an expression Asher knew only too well. She shook her head, making the loops of her silver earrings dance. 'You're too small, you've never been on one before, and you have as much chance of steering it in the right direction as a baby lamb.' Gad sniggered.

'But I don't want to go with Gad!'

'It's Gad or me. And look, Dan and Naphtali are sharing a camel. And Issachar and Zebulun. Even Levi and Judah are sharing, and they're two years older than you and Gad. Or you can be like Joseph if you prefer, sharing with his mother.' But it was her next words that decided it for Asher. 'Or little Dinah, sharing with Leah.' Within moments, he was clambering up behind Gad onto the large saddle. 'Hold on tight,' said Zilpah, as the camel began swaying precariously as it rose to its feet. Asher didn't need to be told.

It was ten days later when Laban and his sons caught up with them. They were still some way from the land of Canaan, but were now closer to it (so his father said) than the Euphrates, and they were in hill country. They had pitched their tents for the evening, and the herdsmen were watering and pasturing the flocks. Gad and Asher, together with Dan and Naphtali, were doing what they always did—unpacking the rugs and bedding and laying them out in the tent that they shared with their mothers, the two maidservants.

'It is Laban! He has found us.' At Bilhah's words, Asher and his brothers immediately abandoned their tasks, scrambled to their feet, and hurried over to where Zilpah and Bilhah were standing, at the entrance of the tent.

'He has no sheep or goats to slow him down,' replied Zilpah. 'If he chose to pursue us, he was always going to catch us, sooner or later, however quickly we drove the herds.'

'What's he going to do?' asked Dan eagerly. Never had the boys had so much excitement in so short a time.

'Nothing here belongs to him!' spat out Bilhah.

A hand grabbing his tunic immediately halted Asher's progress. 'Where do you think you're going?' asked his mother.

'I want to see what happens!'

'Your father will not want any of you under his feet when he talks with Laban.'

'But Laban's sons are with him,' whined Asher.

'Laban's sons are grown up. You are not!' His mother's words did not, however, stop either Asher or his brothers watching keenly. As did the rest of the camp. Rachel had perched herself on the top of her camel saddle that had been set down near her tent. To no one's surprise, the conversation between the two men was animated, and Asher didn't need to hear the words to know that it was heated. Jacob gestured angrily towards the tents, and with that both men came towards them, neither looking happy.

Laban stooped and went under the flap of Jacob's tent, whilst the latter stood outside, tight-lipped and arms folded. 'What's Laban doing?' asked Gad, mystified .

'Searching your father's tent, if I am seeing rightly,' answered Bilhah, without taking her eyes off the tent flap. 'And, whatever it is he is looking for,' she continued some moments later as he re-emerged empty-handed, 'he has clearly not found it.'

He then approached Leah's tent, asking her angrily, 'Have you taken them, my daughter?'

'Taken what?' she snapped. 'You will only find what is rightly mine in there!'

'The household gods! *Someone* has taken them,' said Laban, 'and I will find them.' He then disappeared inside her tent.

'Well, you won't find them in there,' called Leah after him, taking Dinah up into her arms, as her six sons stood around her. Simeon and Levi muttered something to each other, but Asher couldn't catch what they said. *But then, his older brothers probably didn't intend him to.*

Once again, Laban emerged frustrated. 'It will be us next,' said Zilpah under her breath. 'Boys! Out of the way.' She and Bilhah shepherded Asher and his brothers out of the shade of the tent and into the late afternoon sunshine, as Laban swept passed them and into the tent. Asher watched with curiosity as he lifted rugs and rummaged through their bags, swearing loudly. The two women folded their arms, and fixed Laban with cool expressions as he once more strode out of the tent without the idols. After Rachel's tent received similar treatment, Laban started delving through the assorted saddles and bags that were still lying around. When he got to Rachel, however, she remained seated.

'Let not my lord be angry that I cannot stand before you,' she began, casting her eyes respectfully to the ground. 'The manner of women is upon me.'

'Your mistress seems unusually indisposed,' whispered Zilpah drily, as Laban swiftly left Rachel, and moved onto the next bag.

'I have never known it to stop her before,' replied Bilhah under her breath. 'And I did not think her monthly time was due yet.'

'Do you think she's stolen them?' whispered Gad, open-mouthed.

'That is not a question for you to be asking,' replied Zilpah sharply. After a pause, however, she added: 'But if someone from this family has taken them, as Laban clearly believes, that person must think that possessing the gods will bring them good fortune.' And Asher caught the knowing look that passed between the two women.

His father's expression, however, was one of growing anger. 'How have I wronged you,' asked Jacob, his voice raised, 'that you hunt me like an animal?' Laban had finally given up his search, clearly frustrated. 'If you have found anything that belongs to your household,' he continued, 'then set it down before us, for everyone to see.' But he had much more to say. As he spoke of his twenty years of labour for his uncle, and the hardships he had endured keeping his flocks, Asher's attention began to wander. The words only told him what he already knew. He started trying to surreptitiously stamp on a nearby spider. The small creature, however, was much quicker and more agile than Asher had imagined and, despite Naphtali joining in, it eventually scuttled, unscathed, beyond their sandals' reach.

And soon, to Asher's surprise, they themselves were beyond Laban's reach too. Despite the initial animosity between Jacob and his uncle, a treaty and a shared meal that evening finally brought peace between them. The following morning, after final blessings, Laban departed. It was the last time Asher saw him. But it was not long before the shadow of divided kin fell across them again.

Asher bit his lip, determined not to whimper. Dan had kicked him in the darkness. It was a game they played most nights, though a peculiarly painful pastime.

They were, of course, supposed to be going to sleep behind the curtain that created the sleeping area at the back of the tent. Zilpah and Bilhah were sitting talking quietly on the other side, by the light of small clay lamps. At night (when he and his brothers weren't tormenting each other), Asher often lay on his mat—before sleep took him—just watching the patterns made by the flickering lamps, as their dim light fell on the thin curtain.

But that was not now. Now they were playing their game. It was simple one. The four boys would kick, flick, pinch or thump one another, and all would do their best to muffle any cries. For any outburst would be greeted by a sharp rebuke from the front of the tent, telling them to be quiet and go to sleep. Or the curtain would be yanked back by the women, when a fight or tears or both ensued— as they did with unsurprising regularity. And if there were fights, Gad would usually come off best, despite being a year younger than Dan. And despite being the same age as Naphtali, Asher would always come off worst.

But that night, as Asher stifled his yelp, they all heard an unexpected voice in their tent—that of Leah. 'Zilpah, Bilhah,' she said softly. 'I have news.' And all four boys instantly stopped—and listened. Asher could just about make out in the less-than-complete darkness Dan holding a finger to his lip, and all immediately and silently rolled onto hands and knees and drew closer to the curtain, not making a sound.

'Come join us, mistress,' said the voice of Asher's mother, equally softly. 'What news?'

'There are few secrets between those who dwell in tents,' replied Leah, and it sounded as if she was relishing her words. 'But I have just discovered one of Jacob's greatest and oldest ones.' Asher held his breath, straining to hear better.

'And you will share it with us?' asked Bilhah eagerly.

There was a pause. 'Do they sleep?' Another pause followed. Asher tried to keep perfectly still. He could hear no sound from any of his brothers. They had long since given up attempting to fool the mothers with their efforts at mimicking snores.

'They sleep,' replied Zilpah after a few moments of silence, and Asher felt a warm sense of satisfaction at having deceived the women.

'Then I will tell you,' said Leah, in little more than a whisper, 'what I have just heard. My sister lies with Jacob tonight—'

'That much we know already, mistress' interrupted Zilpah. 'We saw her enter Jacob's tent after the meal.'

'And you heard them talking in the tent?' asked Bilhah.

'As I said, there are few secrets here,' replied Leah, with a triumphant little laugh. Asher suspected that Jacob's secret was not something overheard by chance. They had grown up knowing the bitter rivalry between the sisters, both for the affection of their father, and for bearing him sons. And his older brothers had taught him the power that comes from knowing the secrets of others.

'My ears harken only to your words, my mistress,' said Zilpah, a thrill in her voice.

'Keep us waiting no longer!' added Bilhah. There was a short pause, and once more, Asher strained his ears.

'We all know that Jacob has a brother,' began Leah. 'An older twin…'

'Esau,' said Bilhah.

'Indeed. But Jacob has barely spoken of him in all the years we have known him.'

'What you say is true enough,' said Zilpah.

'We have always been told that he came to Harran to find a wife,' continued Leah.

'As he did, marrying first you and then your sister. We know that,' said Bilhah.

'Ah. But that is not the only reason he travelled so far!'

'Go on,' said Zilpah.

'He was fleeing from his brother.'

'For what reason?' asked Bilhah.

'He deceived his father, Isaac. I heard it from Jacob's own lips! He told Rachel that Isaac's sight was failing, and he pretended to be Esau, so that he could receive Esau's blessing—the blessing of the firstborn son!'

'Why would he do such a thing?' exclaimed Zilpah.

'Esau had already traded him the right of the firstborn—for a bowl of stew, if you can believe it!'

'To give up the privileges of the birthright so lightly is a foolish thing,' said Bilhah.

'Yes, and Rebekah—Laban's sister and Jacob's mother—had also told Jacob that before he and Esau were born, Yahweh had spoken to her, telling her that the older twin would serve the younger.'

'But that does not excuse deceiving his own father!' said Zilpah.

'No indeed,' continued Leah. 'But Isaac's blessing also made Jacob lord of his brother. And when Esau discovered the deception and that there was no blessing left for him, he planned to kill Jacob.'

'No!' The exclamation slipped from Asher's lips before he could help himself. He was immediately pushed down into the bedding by Gad, who then clamped his hand firmly across Asher's mouth. But the word could not be unsaid. There was a sound of movement and Bilhah's head suddenly appeared around the curtain. Gad immediately let go of Asher, as if he were a firebrand that had burned down to the hand.

'We all heard voices and woke up,' lied Dan. 'We couldn't help hearing what you were saying!'

'Yes, that's right,' added Gad, with a soulful look. 'It wasn't our fault.'

Asher was fairly certain that Bilhah did not believe a word of it, but then heard Leah sigh. 'They might as well know. They will likely meet Esau soon enough.'

Dan immediately crouched down, wriggling his head under the bottom of the curtain, and Asher and the others followed his lead. Four heads swiftly emerged into the lamp-light onto the other side. *And there were the hands on the hips and the raised eyebrows, and his mother regarding him and his brother with a withering expression.*

'So when will we be meeting Esau?' asked Dan excitedly. 'Will Father have to fight him?'

All eyes were on Leah, waiting expectantly. Zilpah and Bilhah both resumed their positions on the red, brown and orange patterned rugs, leaning upon one arm with their legs folded together, as Leah was doing. 'Rebekah had promised to send word to Jacob when his brother's fury had subsided.'

'But no message came?' said Bilhah.

'No message came.'

'What if something happened to her before she could send the message?' suggested Gad, wide-eyed.

Leah shrugged her shoulders. 'All I know is that no news has come from Jacob's home, for good or for ill. But now, travelling to Canaan, he cannot escape either the past or his brother. I suspect that is why he has finally told Rachel the truth. Jacob has heard that Esau is living in the south, in Seir, and plans to send a message to him, presumably to try to gain his favour.'

'Is that wise,' asked Zilpah, 'if he does not know how his brother will receive him?'

Leah leaned in. The other women did the same. 'He said that angels met him today,' she said, lowering her voice.

'Angels!' exclaimed Asher and Naphtali with one voice.

'When?' demanded Dan.

'How your father's God appears to him or speaks to him I know not and he did not say. He said only that the angels of God met him.'

'Well, what else *did* he say?' asked Gad eagerly.

'I chose not to listen any further,' said Leah, with a sudden tartness in her tone.

'Why not?' continued Gad, curious.

There was a pause. 'Because my husband then decided to comfort himself with my sister.'

'But he still might have said something else,' added Asher. He was sure that, if it had been him, he would have stayed there, listening.

The women looked at each other, and then suddenly burst into raucous laughter.

'Other sounds may well have escaped Jacob's lips,' said Zilpah eventually, tears beginning to run down her cheeks, 'but nothing my mistress nor any of us would have wanted to hear!'

Asher liked it when his mother laughed. Her eyes sparkled and her dark hair shook. But he did not understand what was so funny.

Leah's eyes fell on him, and she smirked. 'Your youngest looks bewildered, Zilpah. I will leave you to enlighten him later.'

Discovering a fact about his father before the sons of Leah instilled within Asher a rare—if short-lived—sense of importance. They did, of course, find out for themselves soon enough from the lips of their mother, who would not have her own sons knowing less than the sons of the maids. Jacob's shocking secrets fuelled numerous whispered conversations between Asher and his brothers, and more than once, Laban's name was mentioned. They all knew the story of how Laban had cruelly deceived their father on his wedding night. Jacob had thought he was marrying his beloved Rachel, for whom he had laboured seven years. That had been the bride price he had given Laban for her. But after lying with his bride, the removal of her veil the following morning had revealed the older sister, Leah. Laban had deceived him, saying it was not done for the younger to wed before the older. But for the promise of another seven years of labour, Jacob was allowed to marry Rachel after Leah's bridal week had passed. And yet now they also knew that Jacob, the deceived, had also been a deceiver. *Deceiving his blind and elderly father!* Asher could barely believe what he had been told. *His own denials of throwing stones at goats were surely nothing in comparison!*

But there was something that puzzled him, though it remained unspoken. His father had claimed more than once that Yahweh had spoken to him or appeared to him. *Was this some strange god who overlooked or didn't care how people behaved? How could Yahweh bless Jacob when he had lied to his father so badly?* Asher couldn't make any sense of it, so he gave up trying.

But soon, fresh news stirred the company once more.

'Look!' said Gad suddenly one afternoon, pointing ahead of them.

From his vantage point on the camel—even sitting behind his brother—Asher could see movement ahead of them to the south, further down the slope they were descending. He squinted, shading his eyes from the sun. The blur gradually resolved into trotting camels, their riders clearly travelling with some urgency. As the gap between them closed, he could soon make out the messengers his father had sent ahead to Esau, presumably returning after having met Jacob's brother.

'Make the camel go faster!' urged Asher.

'I can't, stupid!' replied Gad, exasperated. 'Have you forgotten it's tethered to the ones in front and behind?' Asher's early dreams of camel races, with he and Gad beating their brothers, had been swiftly shattered on the first day of their journey, when it became apparent that they were not going to be trusted with even steering their own camel.

'But we won't hear what they say.'

'I know, but there's nothing I can do about it, you idiot.'

When the messengers reached Jacob, at the head of their company, all camels—including Asher's—were swiftly reined to a halt. Although the short exchange that followed was out of earshot, Jacob was soon gesturing, sending servants running towards them.

'Stay where you are, Asher!' Zilpah's sharp words interrupted his efforts to swing one of his legs over the saddle so that he could jump down—a feat he had already performed a number of times, despite the height of the drop from the camel's back. But soon all the camels were kneeling down anyway to enable a more dignified dismount. Rachel and Leah were summoned to Jacob whilst his eleven sons and one daughter were left in the care of Zilpah and Bilhah.

'Eleven brothers separated by only six years, and they expect us to keep them quiet,' muttered Zilpah, shaking her head, as Simeon shoved Levi. Soon the two sons of Leah were locked together, each attempting to wrestle the other to the ground. Asher immediately took the side of Levi, the younger of the pair.

'Kick him, Levi!' yelled Asher, though his words were somewhat lost in the ruckus. Dinah, by now safely in the arms of Zilpah, was shouting for Simeon. The only two who didn't seem to be shouting for one or the other were Reuben and Joseph—the oldest and the youngest—both standing with arms folded, as if they were above it all. And in all the chaos, no one had noticed Rachel and Leah's return.

'Stop it now!' bellowed Leah above the commotion, bringing the wrestling match to a sudden end, though not before Levi had taken advantage of his brother's distraction, swiftly hooking his foot around one of Simeon's legs, and yanking it from under him. Simeon crashed to the ground. Leah glared at Levi, but finally, having the attention of all twelve children, she spoke.

'We will camp here for the moment, but Jacob has told us not to pitch our tents. We will cook and eat, and then sleep under the stars tonight. And we will divide into two groups. I will camp over there, with Zilpah.' She gestured towards a tree some distance away. It was on a gentle, grassy slope that led down to a fast running river—the Jabbok—whose waters flowed westwards, towards the sinking sun.

'And I will camp there, with Bilhah,' said Rachel, pointing in the opposite direction to some bushes, further upstream.

'Why do we have to split up?' asked Judah.

'Because your father said so,' answered Leah sharply.

'But what of Esau?' asked Reuben, saving Asher the trouble of voicing the question himself.

'He is coming—with men. To meet us.' But there was something about the way Leah answered that seemed odd to Asher, as if she were not quite her usual self. But it was soon forgotten in the excitement of something new and different.

'That's right,' said Zilpah, as Asher carefully stirred the large pot of lentil stew that hung over the fire. If there was one thing apart from riding camels (and throwing stones at goats) that Asher enjoyed, it was helping his mother with the cooking. Of course, helping with cooking also meant that food passed through his hands long before the meal, and—when his mother wasn't looking—not all of it made it to the pot. Though he had yet to develop a taste for raw onions or dry lentils. But he enjoyed the smells rising with the steam from the bronze pots, and the aromas exuded by the herbs when he rolled them between his fingers. And once, in an uncharacteristic show of interest in his eighth son, Jacob had shown him how to make a stew like the one they were making now. *He had been in a good mood then. He was not in a good mood now.*

His father seemed to be behaving strangely. Whilst they prepared the meal, he went down to the river and paced around, this way and that, as if he were constantly changing his mind. He then disappeared up into the hills as the sun sank lower in the sky. He hadn't reappeared by the time the food was ready and they were sitting down to eat. However, in the middle of the meal, just as Asher was dipping his bread into the stew again, Dan suddenly asked, 'What's he doing now?' Asher looked up and glanced around. He followed Dan's gaze, and saw that his father had returned and was among one of the nearby herds, counting and separating animals with some of the herders.

Leah glanced up briefly, and said, 'I don't know.' Her eyes soon returned to the large dish of stew, although strangely, she appeared to have little appetite. She held Dinah in her arms, occasionally running her fingers through her dark, unruly curls. Asher and his brothers, however, continued watching their father in fascination. The numbers of animals that were being separated off soon far exceeded the number to which Asher could count.

'There must be something approaching two hundred ewes there,' said Reuben, by now standing to watch, as Jacob sent the animals off with some herdsmen, down toward the Jabbok, even as the sun was finally dropping behind the western hills.

Asher's mother was also on her feet, pointing. 'You see where the river widens down there? That is where it will run shallow. They will cross there.'

'But where is Father sending them?' asked Simeon.

Zilpah glanced over to Leah, but she didn't look up. After several moments, Zilpah said quietly, 'His brother is coming. Maybe he seeks his favour with a gift.'

They continued to watch as further herds were sent across the river as the light faded: rams, male and female goats, camels, cows and bulls, male and female donkeys. *If this was a gift,* thought Asher, *it was a gift fit for a king!* And with all attention on the river, no one saw Simeon and Levi slip away.

Their breathless return was different. 'We spoke to one of the messengers Father sent to Esau,' began Simeon, excitedly. 'They said he's coming with four hundred men!' Asher and several others leaped up.

Leah was also on her feet. 'They are coming to welcome us,' she said angrily, with a forcefulness that surprised Asher.

'But what if they're not?' countered Levi. 'What if—'

'Hold your tongue!' roared Leah, her dark eyes flashing. 'You two have said more than enough already!' Asher wasn't sure he'd ever seen her so furious. *She was even angrier than when the pair had deliberately killed a ewe with a bow and arrow they had made.* 'Now sit down, all of you. You will stay here, and none of you will wander off again. Reuben—go with Zilpah and collect more wood for the fire. No, Asher, you can't go with them. Stay where you are.' Asher closed his mouth. Leah sat down again, glaring at them all until they followed her lead. She pulled Dinah even closer, and nobody spoke.

The sky above them darkened. As the first glimmering stars appeared in the blackness that was gradually consuming the hills around them, Jacob finally emerged from the gloom. Leah rose, but before she could take one step, he spoke. 'We are going to cross the Jabbok, now—this night—and camp on the other side.'

'But it is dark,' pleaded Leah. 'The young ones are tired and the waters will be—'

'My mind is made up,' interrupted Jacob firmly. The light from the fire cast shadows across his face. Again, his expression puzzled Asher. It was almost as if his features were hewn from rock, strangely unmoving and devoid of life. 'Rachel and Bilhah are already packing up. They will wait for us at the water's edge. All of you—on your feet, now.'

Asher and his brothers knew better than to speak whilst their father was with them. He helped them to roll up the rugs and bedding, and tie them to the nearby donkeys, already laden with their cooking pots. The fire was still burning as they left it and walked in silence down to the river.

Reuben carried Dinah, who was virtually asleep, over the shallow ford on his back, while the women held the hands of the youngest four boys. Jacob stood on the bank watching them go, their only light being that of the crescent moon to the west and the firebrand being carried by Leah in her free hand. The waters felt icy as Asher began wading through them with Zilpah. The waters rose above his ankles, to calf height, but did not rise any higher. Although he would never have admitted it, he was glad of his mother's hand to steady him, as his feet wobbled back and forth on the unseen stones of the river bed. Gad and Naphtali hung on to ropes on the sides of the donkeys, which were being led through the waters by Simeon, Levi, Judah and Dan.

Once they had crossed the Jabbok, they turned and looked back. The dark figure of their father was still standing, unmoving and silent, on the opposite bank. He then turned and walked into the night.

'Where is he going?' whispered Judah.

'He wishes to be alone,' answered Leah quietly. 'But we must find somewhere up the slope to bed down for tonight. Boys, pick up any wood that you see on the ground, so we can start a new fire. The night is chilly enough already, and it will be colder soon.'

Asher slept that night under the stars with a large fire burning nearby. The lateness of the night meant that most were asleep as soon as they were lying on rugs with sheepskins pulled over them against the cold. But before Asher slipped into a deep sleep, he heard snatches of something he rarely heard—the two sisters whispering together without animosity.

'…he does not know what he is doing.'

'I know… He cannot make up his mind what is for the best.'

'He is beside himself…' And those were the last words he heard.

All woke early without the cover of a tent to shield them from either the early morning light or its chill. Asher smelled baking bread before he even opened his eyes. His nose also told him that it was cold. His ears, however, informed him that he was not the only one of Jacob's sons awake. He yawned, wriggled upwards and rose to his feet, whilst keeping the sheepskin draped around him. He wandered over to the rekindled fire to join Dan and Judah, who were already warming themselves. Although

233

the sun had not yet risen above the eastern hills, he was the last to rise. The women were all busy mixing dough or baking flat rounds of bread on the metal domes positioned over smaller fires. The nearby quern-stones, still bearing a dusting of flour, told Asher that the women had been awake even earlier, grinding the barley for the bread. He wondered when, if ever, they had slept—until fresh bread and creamy curds from the goat's milk banished the question from his mind.

Another question soon presented itself, however, as they were packing up the camp. 'Jacob returns!' exclaimed Zilpah suddenly.

Asher followed his mother's eyes towards the Jabbok. Jacob was about to cross it, but was leaning heavily upon his staff. 'Why is he limping?' asked Asher.

'I don't know,' answered Zilpah, as everyone stopped to watch him wading across. The sun finally peeked above the hills to Asher's right as Jacob slowly and painfully walked up the slope to meet them. Asher raised his eyes from his limp to his face. *His father was different. He seemed exhausted, but there was something else.* But neither Asher nor any of them were given answers, for Jacob's arrival was not the only one.

Jacob suddenly looked beyond and behind them. 'Esau comes!' he cried. Asher spun round to see a huge company, still some distance away, walking down the hill towards them. 'Quickly, my sons! Stand with your mothers—now! I will go ahead. Bilhah and Zilpah—follow me, a little distance behind with your boys. Then Leah—you follow on, with your sons and Dinah. Rachel—you go to the back with Joseph.' Then he added, 'Yahweh walks with us.' And with that, Jacob was gone, limping towards his brother.

'We're going first!' said Asher excitedly to Gad. He had never before been placed ahead of the sons of his father's wives.

'It only means that if Esau attacks us, you'll be killed first!' said Simeon spitefully. But he felt—and Asher heard—the flat of Leah's hand against him moments later.

'Do not say such things!' she spat out, grabbing Simeon by the neck of his tunic.

'But it's true,' exclaimed Levi, coming to his brother's defence.

'And you two are both cruel and foolish,' she said vehemently. 'You will frighten the young ones!'

'I'm not frightened,' protested Gad.

'Nor am I,' said Asher, though his stomach told him otherwise.

Leah took hold of Levi with her free hand. 'You're coming with me, and if I hear either of you so much as whisper those words to any of the others, I swear you will feel more than my hand!' And with that, she dragged them away from Asher and Gad. And when Zilpah took them both by the hand to follow after Jacob, neither complained. Asher walked close enough to his mother to feel the movement of her legs.

'Your father is right,' whispered Zilpah. 'His God is with us.' But then she felt silent.

As Esau drew closer, Jacob stopped and bowed down to the ground seven times. 'He bows to him as to an overlord,' whispered Bilhah, and Asher's heart began to pound as Esau then broke into a run towards his brother. Asher wondered if he was carrying a sword.

But Esau met Jacob with only an embrace and then tears. Asher had never seen his father weep before, but the brothers held each other and wept as the rest stood and watched. If they spoke, their words were beyond Asher's hearing.

Eventually Esau lifted his head and looked towards them. He released Jacob from his embrace. 'Who are these with you?'

'They are the children God has graciously given your servant,' replied Jacob, who then beckoned to them.

'Bow down when I do,' whispered Zilpah, barely moving her lips, and Asher bowed to the ground as he had seen his father do, when they finally stood before Esau. Leah and her children did the same, followed by Rachel and Joseph last of all. Jacob introduced them in turn to his brother. Esau cast his gaze slowly over them, marvelling.

'But what of all the herds that I met?' asked Esau. 'Why did you send them?'

'To find favour in your eyes, my lord,' Jacob replied. Asher studied the two brothers as they continued to talk. Both, he knew, were ninety-six. He had always been told that the men of their family lived long. *For twins, though, they were quite different.* To start with, he wasn't sure he'd seen anyone as hairy as Esau before. Whilst his own father's hair was fine and dark, Esau's was ruddy and thick—and abundant. Although they hadn't met any bears on the journey, Asher wondered whether, if they had, the bear might have looked a little like Esau. He then changed his mind slightly: *an aging bear, perhaps.* Both heads were streaked with grey. But although their features were different, their faces were alike in one respect: both had been weathered by the elements. *Different, but brothers,* thought Asher. He then glanced around at his own siblings. *Like us.*

It fell to Gad to explain to Asher afterwards that—whilst his mind was wandering—Esau had proposed they all return to Seir together. 'But Father said it would be better for us and our herds to follow more slowly afterwards,' concluded Gad.

'So we're going south, then,' said Asher, pleased with himself for knowing the direction of Seir, and Gad nodded.

But after Esau had departed the following morning, they started following the course of the Jabbok, and Asher knew that the sun on his back meant they were travelling west. When the sun was not far beyond its zenith, however, Jacob announced they were to stop, saying that the Jordan lay ahead of them.

Asher was still pondering their route after the tents had been pitched and he was sent to collect firewood. Although in truth, he spent more time exploring than he did gathering sticks. *Had his father forgotten the way to Seir, or were they going by a different route, or at a later time? Or had he simply deceived his brother once again?* He had no answers. It was as mystifying to Asher as Jacob's story the previous evening. His father's limp—so they were told—was the result of a long wrestling match with a stranger in the night. A stranger whose mere touch had been enough to put Jacob's hip out of joint. A stranger who had bestowed on him a new name: *Israel—he struggles with God.*

One of their speckled goats suddenly emerged from behind a nearby tree, tugging at the grass that grew in abundance near the river. Asher laid his meagre bundle of sticks on the ground, and picked up a nearby pebble. *The stupid goat would run this time!*

'Asher!' Zilpah's voice came from somewhere behind him. 'Put that stone down at once!'

He spun round, attempting to keep his hand out of sight. He adopted a look of surprise. 'I haven't got one!' he lied.

Notes

1. *Asher is listed last in the genealogies of the sons of Jacob (e.g. Genesis 35:22b-26, Exodus 1:1-4), despite not being the youngest.*

2. *All of Jacob's sons (except Benjamin) are born whilst he is the region of Paddan Aram (north-western Mesopotamia). Jacob stays there twenty years (Genesis 31:41), the first seven of which he is unmarried. It appears that ALL of these eleven sons are born within the first seven years of marriage. He first speaks to Laban of leaving when Joseph is born (Genesis 30:25), but then Laban suggests he stays, his wages being any animals born with particular colouring. Jacob subsequently states (in 31:14) that he has worked six years for the flocks he has accumulated. It would make sense that his first intention to leave is, therefore, after fourteen years, when Joseph has been born to Rachel, and he has finally worked off the seven years of labour for each of his two wives. It has been assumed that Dinah is born to Leah early on in the last six years he is there (Genesis 30:21).*

3. *The order of the births of the sons of Jacob has been taken to be the order in which they are recorded in Genesis 29:31-30. Although it isn't necessarily the case that, say, all of Leah's first four children are born before Rachel gives Bilhah to Jacob, it is possible to construct timings for all the children to be born to the four women, keeping the order given, allowing for a minimum of twelve months between two children being born*

238

to the same mother (but, for example, having Dan born to Bilhah only a month after Judah is born).

4. There is no particular reason to suppose that other daughters were born beside Dinah. The same God who could enable a child to be born to barren Sarah, well beyond her child-bearing years, could clearly also grant both abundant fertility and sovereignly direct the gender of children to establish the twelve tribes of Israel.

5. Whilst there are references to lions and bears existing in Canaan, the lions would have been Asiatic ones, which were far smaller than the African variety.

6. The key to determining Jacob's ages at different parts of the story comes later in Genesis, and will be dealt with in chapter (7).

2

Then Jacob said to Simeon and Levi, 'You have brought trouble on me by making me obnoxious to the Canaanites and Perizzites, the people living in this land.'
(Genesis 34:30)

'Where are you going?' asked Asher, as he leant casually on the crook he used to capture errant sheep.

'What is it to you?' replied Dinah, with a toss of her long, dark curls. There was no doubting whose daughter she was. Asher was never sure whether being a son of Leah's maid stood him above or below a girl born to Leah. Whatever the truth, she always behaved as if it were the latter.

'I was only asking,' said Asher coolly.

She eyed him up and down as if he were some donkey being traded by a herder.

He wasn't sure when Dinah had become a young woman, but now, in her fifteenth year, there was no mistaking it. Her body had taken on the generous lines of a woman who was ready to bear children. Her dainty ankles, adorned by gold chains, showed beneath the hem of her deep orange tunic, and a fringed, patterned scarf tied around her waist accentuated the curves of her body.

'If you must know, I am tired of having to listen to eleven brothers who smell like goats and don't look much better.'

'You're going into Shalem?'

'Well I'm not going to talk to the camels!' She sneered at Asher disparagingly. 'I need the company of other women my own age.' She deliberately accentuated the word *women*, as if to remind him she wasn't a girl any more.

'Don't get into trouble,' said Asher as she turned to go. *She was clearly of the opinion that their short conversation was over.*

'I'm old enough to take care of myself,' she said, without looking back.

Asher watched her go. The skirt of her tunic swayed back and forth gracefully as she walked, and he had to admit that his sister had developed into a woman that a man could easily desire. Especially as she had been blessed with features more pleasing than her mother's.

He stared after her idly. *How much longer would it be until his father found him a wife?* He was already sixteen. *But then his father had not found Reuben a wife yet, and he was twenty-one.* The thought was not an encouraging one.

Soon it was hard to distinguish the distant figure of Dinah against the dark brown bricks of the walls of the town. They had already lived near Shalem for several years, after crossing the Jordan into the land of Canaan. They'd pitched their tents within sight of the city, on ground bought for a hundred pieces of silver from Hamor, the ruler of the town.

'You're meant to be watching the sheep, not your sister.' The approach of Reuben, Dan and Gad had gone unnoticed by Asher. His eldest brother's rebuke finally tore his gaze away from her. 'We saw her leave,' added Reuben. 'Why is she going into the town?'

'*I need the company of other women my own* age,' said Asher, in a voice and manner that mimicked his sister.

The others—even Reuben—laughed.

'She goes alone?' asked Gad.

'You know what she's like,' replied Asher.

'Father should not have let her go,' said Reuben forcefully. Dinah was, of course, the daughter of his mother.

'He probably didn't notice,' said Dan. 'After all, how much attention does he pay *any* of us, especially now that Rachel is with child again?' They were in no doubt that Rachel's swelling belly—over fifteen years after Joseph's birth—had brought their father great delight. And everyone knew that Joseph and his mother enjoyed the greater part of their father's affections.

'He should find Dinah a husband!' said Dan, 'That might stop her wanderings.'

'As he should find me a wife,' said Reuben bitterly. 'He has not even spoken of it yet.'

'But he didn't wed Leah until he was eighty-three!' exclaimed Gad.

'Yes, and he's over a hundred now,' said Asher, 'and our great-grandfather Abraham lived until he was a hundred and seventy-five. Men live long within this family.'

'But what if *we* don't,' grumbled Reuben. 'I could die before I lie with a woman!'

'We all could!' added Dan.

'But where will he find wives for us?' asked Gad. 'Father was sent to Harran to find a wife, so he wouldn't marry a Canaanite—'

'That was *one* of the reasons he went there,' interrupted Reuben. None of them had forgotten their father's deception.

'But what about us?' continued Gad. 'Will Father want us marrying any of the daughters of Shalem?'

'He could send us back to Laban to find wives,' suggested Asher.

'He may not want us returning there,' replied Gad. 'But what about Esau's daughters? They are much closer and they are kin.'

And as their discussion continued, Asher glanced over to the town once more. Dinah had disappeared.

'Have you seen your sister?' asked Leah.

Asher shook his head, more interested in seeing what was in the cooking pot for the evening meal. 'Not since she went into Shalem earlier.' As he was answering, Jacob happened to walk into the camp. Joseph was where he usually was—at his father's side.

'I am worried for Dinah,' said Leah before even greeting her husband. 'She has not returned from the town and it is almost dark.'

'She will be safe enough there,' he replied casually. 'Hamor knows us well and it is his city. And you know what she is like. She was probably talking so much with the women there that she didn't realise how low the sun was, and has decided to stay for the night. Do not fret over her.'

Leah glared at him, adding pointedly, 'She is your daughter too.'

'It is too late to go to the town now anyway. The gates will probably already be shut. You can go into Shalem yourself in the morning and fetch her back.'

'You can be sure that I will,' said Leah, her dark eyes filled with defiance.

When Asher went out into the fields the following morning to see to the animals, he fully expected to return later in the day to find Dinah back. What he found, however, was an uproar. His mother was sitting with Leah, clearly comforting her. Judah was talking angrily with the two youngest sons of Leah, who also seemed to be simmering with rage.

Asher wandered over to Gad. 'What's going on?'

'Haven't you heard?'

'Why would anyone tell me anything?' replied Asher sarcastically.

'Shechem, Hamor's son, forced himself upon Dinah and lay with her!'

'He defiled her?' asked Asher, shocked. 'He may be the son of a ruler, but he should not have done that. That is a disgrace!'

'We only found out a little while ago. Simeon and Levi were furious that Father didn't tell them earlier. He knew as soon as Leah returned from Shalem.'

'And Dinah? Was she hurt?'

'We don't know. They're keeping her in the town.'

'They can't do that!' said Asher angrily.

'I know, but Hamor came here instead to talk to Father. He said that Shechem desires Dinah for his wife, and Reuben, Simeon and Levi have gone with Father to talk to Hamor and Shechem in Shalem.'

'Will Father consent to a marriage?'

Gad shrugged his shoulders. 'They are Canaanites. But this is their land—and they have Dinah.'

Asher's surprise at his father's consent to the marriage was exceeded only by his surprise at the bridal price which—if his brother was to be believed—had been set by Simeon and Levi. '*All* the men of the town to be circumcised?' he exclaimed.

Gad nodded. 'That's right—not just Shechem.'

Asher was perplexed. He and his brothers had all been circumcised on their eighth day, in accordance with the practice of their great-grandfather Abraham. But Simeon and Levi—like most of them—had never shown much devotion to the God of their fathers. 'That is strange. When did circumcision become important to them?'

Gad shrugged his shoulders. 'It is, as you say, strange.'

But their bewilderment was short-lived. Three days later, Judah came running into the field where they were inspecting the hooves of the goats. 'You must come quickly!' he said breathlessly. His eyes were wide and shining.

Gad gave the goat he had been holding a slap on the rump. It trotted off. 'Come where?'

'Shalem!'

'What is it?' asked Asher.

'Simeon and Levi have restored the honour of our sister. Find Dan and Naphtali and bring them too. But don't tell anyone else—especially not Father or Joseph!' And with that, he ran off, back towards the town.

When Asher and his brothers reached Shalem, the city seemed strangely quiet. But as soon as they passed through the first set of gates, into the open area which served as the town's meeting place, they were met by Simeon holding a large sword stained deep red, with a lifeless and bloodied body lying close to his feet. Dinah sat nearby, still wearing the deep orange dress. But when she raised her eyes, they were reddened, and it was as if she didn't see them. She then lowered her head wordlessly. Asher stared at the body—he had seen the bodies of older herdsmen when they had died, but this was different. The body was lying face down, the earth stained dark to one side of it. He looked up and met Simeon's eyes. They were defiant and proud.

'He deserved it. They all did.'

'What do you mean?' asked Gad.

'They have paid for their crimes with their lives.'

'You and Levi put the whole town to the sword?' asked Dan, incredulous.

'Just the men,' replied Simeon.

'By yourselves?' asked Asher.

'It wasn't difficult. They were still in pain.' Asher suddenly understood the reason behind their request for circumcision. 'And now everything in the town is ours for the taking.'

Asher looked around, greed awaking within him. Any questions that had arisen in his mind about his brothers' actions suddenly faded like mist in the morning sun. *Of course they were in the right. Their innocent sister had been degraded and defiled by the son of the ruler! All must pay!* And the more they plundered, the less he cared about the blood on either the victims' clothes or his brothers' hands. There was even a strange fascination with the dead. He poked one body with his foot. *How strange that the life of men could be so easily taken—by just one stroke of the blade. No different from their slaughter of goats or sheep when meat was desired.* But he still avoided the bodies of those whose years appeared similar to his own.

He wasn't sure how many men had been slain—the town wasn't a large one—but it still took most of the day to plunder Shalem. Anything that was of any value—clothes, jewellery, weapons, gold, silver, bronze—was taken and loaded onto carts that they had found.

Sometimes there was a shout of glee when an item of particular value was found. The richest pickings were, of course, in the home of Hamor, from where Simeon and Levi had taken Dinah. Goats, sheep and donkeys were rounded up, though Simeon and Levi had ham-strung all the oxen. When Reuben cursed them for their stupidity in laming the animals, Simeon had shrugged his shoulders and replied, 'We don't plough so we don't need them.'

And amongst the plunder were, of course, the women and children. Some were weeping, while others looked as their sister had done. A number were openly hostile. Asher avoided their eyes. But none had any choice but to go with the sons of Jacob.

As they left Shalem for the last time, however, Asher finally heard Dinah speak. Her words were bewildered and to no one in particular. 'He said he loved me.'

Their father was waiting for them on their return. *Clearly they had been missed.* Jacob stared at the women and the plunder and the carts. 'What have you done?' he asked, shaking.

Asher suspected he knew the answer.

'Levi and I have avenged the wrong that was done to our sister!' said Simeon, unafraid to meet Jacob's accusing eyes.

'The men of Shalem have paid for defiling Dinah,' added Levi. 'We have done only what it was our right to do.'

Jacob's fury spilled over. 'You've brought trouble on me!' he yelled. 'I will be a stench to those living in this land. We are only few in number—you know that—and if the Canaanites join together against us and attack, I will be destroyed as will this household! Did either of you think of that?'

But Simeon's eyes flashed. 'Should Shechem have treated our sister as a harlot?' And neither he nor Levi were cowed by their father's words. Jacob seemed to have no answer, so turned and went back to the camp. And at Asher's side, Judah whispered, 'He seems to care more about peace than our sister's honour.'

If Asher—or any of his brothers—had thought that the virgin daughters of Shalem might make suitable wives for them, it was not to be. What happened instead was a gathering of both family and servants some time later, to be addressed by Jacob.

'God has spoken to Father,' said Joseph to those of his brothers who were standing near him, in the lofty tone of one who knows something of importance before others do. 'We are going to be moving on.'

'He would know first, wouldn't he?' muttered Dan under his breath, so that only Naphtali and Asher could hear. Asher wasn't sure whether Joseph had gleaned the information from his father or his mother. Either way, the outcome was the same: smug self-importance. But a hush then fell over the assembly as Jacob stepped forward to speak.

'We are to leave this place and travel to Luz.' Jacob paused, casting his gaze across them all. 'But first, each one of you must get rid of any foreign gods and any tokens of allegiance to those gods. You are to bring them to me. You are then to purify yourselves—wash and change your clothes. We will then depart for Luz, where I will build an altar to the God who has answered me in the day of my distress, and been with me wherever I have gone.'

Soon there was a growing heap at the edge of the camp: idols of wood and metal, clay and stone—some painted and some plain. Gods of the Land of the Rivers, of Canaan and of Egypt, and earrings of gold or silver bound up with those gods. And amongst the strange pile, the household gods that had gone missing from Laban's house. They had suddenly appeared, as if from nowhere, though Dan claimed he had seen his mother, Bilhah, sneaking out with them when she thought no one was looking.

Asher raised an eyebrow. 'And was she doing her mistress's bidding?'

Dan smirked. 'What do you think?' None of them had doubted Rachel had taken them.

Whatever his father's thoughts at the appearance of the idols, they remained unspoken. And after Dan and Gad had dug a deep hole beneath a nearby oak tree, Jacob tossed the recently-cherished treasures into the pit. He then filled it himself, shovelling the earth upon the idols, as if they were—like excrement—a defilement to be buried and concealed for good.

The journey south to Luz took only a few days. Without herds, it would have been less than two. Asher was conscious of his father's fears following the slaughter at Shalem, that the people of the land might band together and rise against them. But any encounters with the Canaanites were, if anything, the contrary.

'It is as if *they* fear *us*,' began Joseph one evening, 'despite how few we are!'

Asher glanced around the faces illuminated by firelight as they ate together. *It was true. The people in the towns they had passed had either avoided them or been swift to meet their requests.*

249

'It is the hand of Yahweh,' answered Jacob. 'He sends his terror upon them.' His eyes fell upon Rachel, whose swollen belly announced that her time was near. 'The Lord is with us and blesses us.' He paused, and then looked up. 'We will reach Luz tomorrow. But we will call it by that name no longer.' Asher was intrigued. 'After I left Beersheba and set out for Harran,' continued Jacob, 'it was near Luz that Yahweh met me. I had a vision there as I slept. The Lord promised this land to me and my descendants, bestowing upon me the promises first given to my grandfather Abraham. And the Lord told me that He would be with me wherever I went, and would bring me back to this land—as He has done. I changed the name of the place to Bethel—*house of God*. And tomorrow I shall build an altar to the God of Bethel.'

'And the Lord has changed your name also, Father,' said Joseph, 'to *Israel*.'

'You are right, my son. I shall also be known as *Israel*.'

But Jacob's God was still a riddle, a mystery to Asher. And the mystery deepened...

It had been more than fifteen years since Asher had heard the sounds of childbirth among the family tents. He hadn't liked them then, at Dinah's birth, and nothing had changed. *They were always the sound of pain.* He had witnessed cows and camels calmly giving birth to their young, and lambs being born to ewes. He had watched and helped with the birthing of numerous kids, as their mothers continued eating grass, giving an occasional bleat, or more if the birth was a difficult one. And it was usually quickly over. But childbirth was different. He had never witnessed one, but he wasn't sure that he wanted to.

The groans, the cries and the screams seemed more akin to a long, drawn-out death than a birth.

They all knew the story, of course. The story passed down from their first father Adam until it reached Noah. The story then handed down after the flood until it was told to Abraham, who told it to Isaac, who told it to Jacob, who told it to them. It was the story of the sin of their distant parents Adam and Eve, whose disregard for the command of God meant toil in the field for men and pain in childbirth for women. And the latest to suffer the curse of Eve was Rachel, giving birth to a new son or daughter for Jacob.

They had been on their way south from Bethel, but before they had reached Ephrath they had pitched their tents when Rachel's travail had begun. Asher had taken some of the animals that morning to find pasture. He had departed to the sound of her cries, but had not expected to be hearing them still on his return at the end of the day. Bilhah emerged from Rachel's tent as he was just putting down his staff. She had a wooden pail in her hand and her expression was grim. 'Asher, quickly! Empty this and fill it with clean water.' She handed him the pail and didn't wait for a reply, disappearing behind the tent flaps as another scream sullied the air. He glanced down. The water was red. *A difficult birth.* But it didn't last much longer.

Even as his youngest brother was drawing his first breaths, Rachel was drawing her last. And with her dying gasps she bestowed on her second son a name: Ben-Oni. *Son of my trouble.* But Jacob named him differently: *Son of my right hand.* Benjamin.

'How is it,' muttered Asher to Gad, as they sat drinking barley beer under the stars two nights later, 'that Father says that Yahweh blesses him, and then Rachel dies in pain and blood and screams?' Gad remained silent, staring into the darkness, so he went on. 'Father rids the camp of foreign gods. He builds Yahweh an altar at Bethel. And—if what Joseph says is true—Yahweh appears to him again at Bethel and speaks with him.' He paused. 'And then Yahweh takes from him his beloved wife.' He took the clay jar of ale from Gad's hand, and then stared up at the stars. They were as silent and inscrutable as his father's God.

The fire near their tents was by now burning low, and the sounds of the camp had died away. The cries of the newborn child had been stilled by the milk of a wet-nurse. The baby's mother now lay in a tomb they had left behind them as they resumed their journey south. Finally Gad spoke. 'Jacob also said that Yahweh first promised him this land just *after* he'd deceived his father.' After a few moments, he added, 'A God who blesses after lies and curses after worship.'

Asher drained the jar. 'Yahweh is a strange God.'

Jacob's grief was still fresh and Benjamin had not even seen his second full moon when the tents of Jacob were disturbed once more.

'He did *what*?' exclaimed Asher.

'Ssshhh!' Gad looked around, and then dragged Asher away from the tents. When he was sure no one was near, he repeated the words to Asher. 'Reuben lay with Bilhah.'

'Is he mad?' said Asher, stunned. 'Why would he do such a thing?'

Gad shrugged his shoulders. 'Father was prepared to see Dinah married, but has still not spoken of wives for any of us yet. You know how Reuben feels about that. Maybe he couldn't wait…'

'And Bilhah agreed to it?'

'Dan did not say that Reuben had forced himself on her. And, after all, our father is becoming old and Reuben is young and strong.'

Asher was silent for a moment. 'And Dan and Naphtali?'

'Furious. But what can they do? Reuben is Jacob's firstborn, and like us, they are only sons of a maid—'

'A maid that Reuben has now lain with,' said Asher. He suddenly added, 'And does Father know?'

'I don't know, but—what was it Leah once said about secrets and living in tents?'

Whatever the exact words, Asher remembered her meaning.

'If he doesn't know yet,' continued Gad, 'he probably soon will. Especially if Joseph finds out.'

Notes

1. *In Genesis 33:18, it says that 'Jacob…arrived safely at the city of Shechem in Canaan' (NIV). However, some commentators argue that it should be translated, 'Jacob arrived at Shalem, a city of Shechem in Canaan', and this is reflected in some Bible translations. The place may be identified as the modern village of 'Salim', which lies only about three miles east of the archaeological site that is taken to be Biblical Shechem. Adopting this translation also makes the narration easier, avoiding confusion with Hamor's son, Shechem.*

2. *We do not know the reaction of Dinah to what happened, although Genesis 34:3 does speak in positive terms of how Shechem treats her after the rape.*

3. *It is not clear how the earrings referred to in Genesis 35:4 relate to the worship of foreign gods. They may have been some form of charm.*

4. *The events of this chapter are assumed to take place shortly before the events of Genesis 37, when Joseph is seventeen years old. This allows Dinah to be into her teens (fourteen), assuming she is born in Harran after the last of the brothers.*

5. *The detail of Simeon and Levi ham-stringing oxen only comes out later in Genesis 49:6. It seems reasonable to assume that it happened at Shalem.*

6. *Ephrath is an earlier name for Bethlehem.*

7. *We're not told of Reuben's motivation for sleeping with Bilhah. Some think it was him asserting his authority or rights as the firstborn. However, Jacob's later words about him being turbulent or unstable or uncontrolled as water (Genesis 49:4) may point to a simple lack of restraint.*

3

Now Israel loved Joseph more than any of his other
sons…When his brothers saw that their father loved him
more than any of them, they hated him and could not
speak a kind word to him. (Genesis 37:3-4)

Asher sat on his haunches and stirred the pot suspended
over the small fire. *Good. The stew wasn't burning.* He
lifted the spoon to his lips, blowing on it and tasting its
contents before adding more coriander seeds from a small
cloth bag. He glanced around. The heat of the day was
dissipating, and his view was no longer blurred by a haze.
The land was losing its winter green.

'We'll have to take the herds north soon, into the hill
country,' said Gad as he sauntered towards his brother.

Asher nodded. 'These lands have even less pasture
now that the sun grows stronger.'

Their journey south from Bethel the previous year
had finished at Kiriath Arba, and with a reunion with
Isaac. He was, to Jacob's joy, still living, though his
mother, Rebekah, already lay in Abraham's tomb. They
had pitched their tents nearby.

Asher, Gad and the sons of Bilhah had been sent by
Jacob to pasture animals a day's journey from the camp.
He had also sent Joseph. Having led the herd to decent
grazing near a stream that still flowed with the winter's
rain, they were attending to their own comforts. Gad

leaned over the bubbling and steaming pot. 'Smells good.'

'Chickpeas, onions, garlic.' Asher smiled slyly. 'And, of course…'

'Meat,' they chorused.

'Alas! We could not save the goat from the leopard,' said Gad in such a sorrowful tone that Asher laughed.

'If you tell Father in that voice, he will know you are lying!'

'But why shouldn't we be allowed meat from the herd. One goat will hardly be missed.'

'Except by Joseph.' That Jacob had taught their younger brother how to write on clay tablets, recording the herds, was a skill that he was always keen to show off.

'And that,' said Gad, 'is why there was a leopard.'

'And how are we going to explain the beer to Father?' Dan had earlier gone to a nearby town to trade the rest of the meat from the goat they had slaughtered for easily hidden silver—and beer.

Gad laughed. 'There won't be any left after tonight.'

'Joseph—go and fetch some more wood for the fire.'

Back with the family, Dan—now twenty—would never have dreamed of ordering Jacob's favourite around. Asher knew that. They all knew that, including Joseph. But there, away from the eyes of their father, it was different. And the sons of Bilhah and Zilpah numbered four, and the son of Rachel only one.

'It's not my job,' said Joseph defiantly.

'You're the youngest, so it is,' taunted Asher, enjoying putting the seventeen-year-old in his place.

'I'm only one year younger than you,' said Joseph. 'And besides, you're only—'

'Only what?' replied Asher, his eyes flashing. He was fairly certain the words *the son of a maid* had been in Joseph's mind before he thought better of it. All four had heard him say it before. Asher looked steadily at his brother as he lifted the jar of beer to his lips again.

Joseph glared back, rose to his feet and stormed off, his fists clenched.

Even before he was out of earshot, they were laughing. 'He was as angry as a pestered hornet,' said Naphtali, almost beside himself, despite his normal reserve. Though the beer already drunk and a large helping of goat stew had lightened all their moods.

When they had finally stopped, Dan said, 'He hates it when he can't lord it over us.'

'*You're only the son of a maid*,' said Asher, mimicking Joseph and reviving the laughter. But his mocking words suddenly troubled him, and he became quiet. He gazed up into the dark sky at the waxing moon. *In a few days it would be full again.*

'What is it, Brother?' asked Gad as they quietened down.

Gad knew him too well. 'The story of our great-grandfather Abraham…' began Asher.

'What of it?' asked Dan.

'He had two sons…'

'Isaac and Ishmael. Yes, we know that,' said Gad, slightly impatiently.

'But in time, Abraham sent Ishmael away. The son of the maid was to have no part in Yahweh's promises—only Isaac, the son of his wife.' They all fell silent.

'You wonder if the same will happen to us?' said Naphtali.

After a pause, Asher shrugged his shoulders. *Maybe Yahweh had as much interest in them as Jacob did.*

The question remained unanswered, however, as the direction of Dan's gaze suddenly shifted. 'He's coming back already,' he said, exasperated. They all followed his gaze. 'And he's only carrying two pieces of wood!'

They watched in silence as Joseph marched up to the fire, threw two sticks onto it, and declared, 'I'm going to get some sleep. You can wake me later and I'll take first watch.' He glared at them. 'And if you want more wood, you can get it yourself.' And with that, he stormed off towards their small tent.

'At least now we can enjoy ourselves properly,' muttered Gad. There was a moment's silence, and then laughter. And Asher's questions were forgotten as the jars were raised.

The first thing Asher became aware of was a dull, intermittent pain. A pain that slowly identified itself with being kicked in the side. And then came shouting that made him feel as if a tent peg were being hammered into his skull.

'Wake up! Get up!'

The sun felt unusually bright—painfully bright—as Asher finally opened his eyes slightly. There was another kick in his side.

'Get up, Asher—now!'

Asher groaned, finally managing to say with some difficulty, 'Stoppit.'

Joseph kicked him again. 'I'll stop it when you get up and start helping with the animals.' Asher forced himself up into a sitting position, squinting up at his brother. The sun made him want to close his eyes again. 'You're as useless as a lame ox! You all are.'

Asher glanced around slowly and painfully. Dan, Naphtali and Gad were still lying motionless nearby, empty jars strewn around them. He thought he could smell vomit. *So much for the goat stew.* The mere thought was enough to make him nauseous. Speaking was too much effort, so he just put his head down between his knees and let Joseph continue his tirade. *Joseph had clearly singled him out as the youngest of the four.*

'None of you woke me. And why was that? Because you were all drunk and insensible as dead donkeys! When I *did* wake up, the moon had already set and the fire was barely alight. I only just managed to light a torch from it to check the goats. I spent the rest of the night watching over them because none of you could be woken. If it wasn't for me, the goats would be scattered across the land by now or ravaged by wild animals. Or by your imaginary leopard.'

'Have you finished?'

'No. If that isn't bad enough, you smell like camel's breath. I'm going to get some more sleep now. You can wake your brothers.' And without another word, Joseph stormed off.

Asher groaned again and closed his eyes.

If Jacob's displeasure towards them—the result of Joseph's tales—was bad enough, his favour towards Joseph was, if anything, worse. It wasn't enough for their father to give him a richly ornamented robe, fit for a king. He had to present it to him whilst they all watched. Both their grey-haired father and Rachel's eldest made no secret of their pleasure. And if a person could be felled by a look, then Joseph would have been slain then and there, ten times over, as he admired the colours, the fringed sleeves and the gold of the robe.

'He really is the chosen one, isn't he,' muttered Judah under his breath. It didn't help either that Joseph had been blessed with exceptionally fine features as his mother had been—and knew it.

'It's as if we mean nothing to Father,' added Levi bitterly.

And Asher knew their words were true. *Their father loved Joseph more than any of them, and wasn't afraid to show it.*

They all started avoiding Joseph even more. Not that he let them.

'I had a dream last night—' began Joseph, still flaunting his robe.

'Yes, I know,' interrupted Judah, as he and Simeon helped Asher and his brother load some donkeys with cheeses and animal skins. They were to be bartered in Kiriath Arba for cloth and for pottery jars to store grain they had recently harvested. 'You already told me.'

'And me,' added Simeon.

'But Gad and Asher haven't heard,' said Joseph.

'And do we care?' murmured Gad.

If Joseph heard the words, he ignored them. 'In my dream, we were all out in the fields binding sheaves of corn, when suddenly my sheaf rose and stood upright. All your sheaves gathered round it and bowed down to it.' He was triumphant, and then added—completely unnecessarily in Asher's eyes—'What do you think it means?'

'It means that one cup of beer in the evening is too much for you,' said Gad with a smirk.

But Judah turned on Joseph angrily. 'Do you actually intend to rule over us?'

'You may think you look like a king in your fancy clothes,' added Simeon, 'but I will only bow down to you when the Euphrates dries up.' He paused for a moment, and then looked Joseph in the eye. 'Oh, but you're probably too young to remember the Euphrates. Aren't you?'

Joseph gave a little shrug, as if he didn't care, and walked off.

It wasn't many days, however, until Joseph was back. 'I had another dream—'

'Really?' said Asher, trying to sound as disinterested as possible as he sat on his small three-legged stool. He didn't even bother turning round to face Joseph, but continued milking the goat. He would have walked away if he had been standing.

'This time the sun and moon and eleven stars were bowing down to me!'

Asher pulled even harder on the teats of the goats, biting back words that would be unwise, and resisting the urge to clout his brother, which would be even worse. *Whatever he did, Jacob would hear of it.* 'I'm busy. Go away.' *He couldn't tell tales about that.*

There was, however, one small consolation when the dream reached Jacob's ears. '…and Father rebuked him,' said Dan with satisfaction, as he sat with Naphtali, Gad and Asher in their tent that night. 'I heard him! He said to Joseph, *Will your mother and I and your brothers actually bow down before you?* He wasn't happy.'

'Joseph just doesn't know when to stop,' said Asher.

'Father seemed happy enough,' said Gad, 'when it was just us bowing down to him in his first dream. He obviously doesn't like it when he's bowing down as well.'

'At least he now knows how it feels,' muttered Asher. And although he hadn't punched Joseph that morning, he allowed himself the gratification of imagining it instead.

Asher's stone hit the goat square on the side. It bleated loudly and ran off.

'Your shot is better than it used to be, Brother,' laughed Gad. 'And faster.'

'I don't think it drew blood this time, though,' replied Asher. It had been some years since a sheep or goat did *not* run from him. Despite the unfortunate animal now being much further away, Asher threw a second stone.

'Another good shot,' exclaimed Gad, as the stone found its mark and the animal and those with it scattered.

And there was no Joseph to tell tales, thought Asher with satisfaction. That their brother didn't do his fair share with the herds was a price they were all more than willing to pay for his absence. Not that Asher's amusements met with the full approval of the rest.

'Stop harrying the herd!' called a voice behind them. 'Can you not act your age for once, Asher?' Reuben went on: 'Sometimes I think you have as much sense as a lamb loitering in a lion's den.'

Before they turned round to face him, Asher rolled his eyes and then mimicked his brother's petulant face.

He knew it too well. Gad snorted.

Before either could speak, Reuben declared, 'We've decided to go on to Dothan.'

'Who's *we*?' asked Gad sharply.

'Simeon, Levi, Judah and I—whilst we were selling the milk in Shechem.'

I might have guessed, thought Asher. He was used to the oldest of Leah's sons making the decisions when they were out with the herds and away from their father. 'What's wrong with staying here?' grumbled Asher. 'This is where we told Father we'd be.'

'The grazing may be better further north, and we're going whether it pleases you or not. It will take little more than a day. Gather the animals and bring them back to the tents. And don't dally.' And with that, Reuben turned and left.

'*We're going whether it pleases you or not,*' said Asher, exaggerating both his brother's tone and expression.

'Sometimes he's almost as insufferable as Joseph,' muttered Gad. 'I think he's even worse since Father allowed him to marry.'

Asher thought for a moment, and then brightened. 'Ah, but going to Dothan does mean one thing.' He smiled slyly at Gad. 'Joseph won't know where we are if Father sends him to check on us.' And Asher found the image of Joseph wandering around Shechem for hours—*maybe days!*—searching for them immensely satisfying.

'Give it back!' shouted Zebulun, as Levi reached down and snatched the jug of beer from his hands. Zebulun jumped up from where he was sitting near the campfire and faced his brother. 'You've already had more than me. Just because you're older doesn't mean you can just drink as much as you want.'

Asher had some sympathy. Zebulun was the youngest of the sons of Leah, and only a month or two older than Joseph. Leah had always claimed that the arrival of her sixth son had barely been noticed by Jacob, with the birth of Rachel's firstborn following so soon after. And to add to his misery, the other sons of Leah also treated him as the last and the least. But what Zebulun lacked in years, he made up for in sheer determination, and he launched himself at Levi as the rest of them looked on with amusement from around the fire.

'Idiot!' exclaimed Simeon, as beer from the jug slopped over him. He leapt up, and clouted Zebulun. 'You've just spilled half of it down me.'

'Sit down, all of you,' shouted Reuben, annoyed.

Zebulun glared at Levi, who promptly downed a long draught from the jug and then held it out to him. *There probably wasn't much left.* Zebulun snatched it and sat back down next to Issachar, born to Leah a year before him. Asher was sitting close enough to hear Zebulun mutter, 'You could have helped me.' *But Issachar was a lazy donkey.*

As Levi took his seat, he continued to taunt Zebulun. 'So, Brother, are you following our father's example, usurping me as he usurped Esau? The younger receiving more than the older?'

'I do not ask for more,' sulked Zebulun. 'Only what is fair.'

'And what is fair, O little runt?' said Simeon, joining in.

'To have the same as you!' shouted Zebulun. He paused, his eyes flashing. 'Just as you would want Father to give you the same as Joseph!' His words had the desired effect. He had jabbed at an open wound. And if there was one thing that united them all, it was a shared hatred of Rachel's son.

No one spoke, until Reuben broke the silence. 'But that will never happen,' he said bitterly. 'Joseph will get more than any of us.'

Simon scoffed. 'You did nothing to secure the rights of the firstborn by sleeping with Bilhah!' It was easier to mention the reckless act with Dan and Naphtali on the first of the night watches with the herds.

'What difference did it make?' retorted Reuben, picking up a stone and hurling it into the fire so hard that glowing embers burst upwards. 'I'm sure Father believes that just as *he* was destined to rule over *his* elder brother, so Joseph is destined to rule over us. Over you, over me, over *all* of us.'

Judah nodded savagely. 'I think Father would be more than happy to give Joseph *everything*,' he spat out, 'and for us to be his servants, grovelling before him and licking the dust off his feet!'

'And Joseph claims to have seen it in his stupid dreams,' said Levi.

Asher often listened more than he spoke when all the sons of Leah were gathered. *After all, he knew his place.* But in the moody silence that followed, and helped by some beer, he jumped to his feet, grabbing the striped rug on which he had been sitting and holding it around him like a cloak. *'I've had a dream,'* he began, in both Joseph's voice and manner. He began strutting around, and his brothers started to laugh and jeer. *'In my dream, we were all out in the fields binding sheaves.'* Asher was getting into his stride.

'*When suddenly all your sheaves gathered round my sheaf and…*
Wait! What is this? They trampled and stamped on it. No, that
cannot be right…'

As raucous laughter filled the night air, Levi cupped
one hand to his mouth and shouted out to Asher, 'We've
all had that dream, Brother!'

Reuben had been right. It hadn't taken too long. Despite Asher's
reluctance to move from Shechem, they had easily
reached the town of Dothan by the following night. As he
continued pitching a small tent not far from the town, he
cast his mind over the provisions still lashed to the donkey.
He had lentils, chickpeas, leeks and herbs. More than enough. It
would make a good meal when Reuben and Issachar returned
from Dothan with fresh bread. He didn't have many raisin cakes
left, but maybe Reuben would bring back figs and olives.

Asher swore as he struck his thumb rather than the
tent peg with the mallet.

'If you watched what you were doing, stupid,' said
Gad, 'rather than day-dreaming, then you wouldn't keep
hitting yourself.'

But before Asher could respond, Simeon called
them. 'Gad, Asher! Come here.' The tone of his voice
intrigued Asher. They were soon standing with all
their brothers, bar Reuben and Issachar. And each was
staring at a person in the distance—a person whose
coloured robe they all recognised long before they could
distinguish the face.

Simeon cursed loudly. 'Here comes the dreamer…'
His voice was cold and hard.

'What's *he* doing here?' said Gad angrily. 'Can we
never be rid of him?'

'He's probably been sent by Father to check up on us all,' said Dan without taking his eyes off Joseph, 'so that he can go back and tell him how terrible we all are.'

'And he's still wearing that nauseating robe,' said Levi. 'Doesn't the swine ever take it off?'

'But how did he know where to find us?' asked Asher. 'He didn't know we were coming here.'

'I don't know,' muttered Judah. 'But he knows everything, after all,' he added sarcastically. 'Or at least he thinks he does.'

'If he's had any more of his dreams,' said Gad, 'I swear I *will* hit him this time.'

'It's not the dreams that are the problem,' said Simeon. 'It's that he wakes up and tells us!'

Asher watched the small figure gradually increasing in size as he drew nearer. *He hated that robe. He knew he was the least among the brothers. But the robe—and the way Joseph wore it—made him feel as if he were nothing. As if he were dirt beneath Joseph's sandalled feet.* Asher suddenly became aware that Simeon and Levi were whispering to each other. He tore his gaze away from Joseph and glanced at them. *They had the same wild look as at Shalem.*

'What is it?' asked Judah.

'Why not make *our* dream come true?' said Levi. It took Asher a moment to remember Levi's words from the previous evening.

'But if we give him a beating, Father will hear about it,' said Zebulun.

'We know,' said Simeon. 'So why stop at a beating?'

They looked at each other in silence for a few moments, letting his meaning sink in. 'You mean... *kill* him?' asked Judah.

'Which of us has not already done the deed in our hearts, imagining him dead?' replied Levi, meeting each eye in turn. Silence. There was no denial.

'He deserves it,' stated Simeon. 'As did Shechem and the rest.'

Asher pictured Joseph lying dead, like the men of Shalem. *The thought was a heady one. An exhilarating one.* Asher told himself that Simeon was right.

Judah added, 'He has done more than enough to bring it on himself.'

'He has indeed,' said Simeon. 'Think about it. He has stolen our father's affections and treated us with utter contempt. Why not let our hatred of him do something more than just darken our hearts?' He paused. 'We are far from home and in a deserted area. No one will know. Has this chance not come to us by good fortune to rid ourselves of him, once and for all?'

'Let us do this, Brothers!' said Levi. 'But we are in this together or not at all.' He glanced round at them again, as did Simeon. There was a pause. Levi looked over to the figure of Joseph, still some way off. 'We must decide now.'

'Together?' said Simeon. And each one gave their assent by a single word or a curt nod.

'He has already taken our father's love,' said Zebulun. 'I do not doubt he will also take our inheritance.'

'That's right,' said Judah. 'Let's be done with him—forever!'

'What about those empty water cisterns over there?' said Gad, pointing to the abandoned storage pits, the edges of which they had already had to haul sheep away from. 'We could throw his body in there!'

'We could say that a lion or a bear killed him,' suggested Asher. 'Or a leopard!'

Dan gave Asher a withering look. 'And then Father would ask why we didn't bring his body back.'

'His robe,' said Asher suddenly, keen to rescue his idea. 'We could rip it up and dip it in blood and take it back to Father like that, saying we found it.' The brothers stared at him with something akin to amazement.

'It is a good plan,' said Simeon. 'And then we'll see what comes of his dreams.'

'What are you talking about?' said Reuben. None of them had noticed his return with Issachar. 'What plan?' The hasty explanation left him aghast. Reuben glanced over at Joseph, getting ever closer, and then back at them. 'Blood is sacred. Do you want that of Joseph on your hands?'

'He deserves it!' said Judah, echoing Simeon. Seven other voices agreed.

'And I am not arguing with that,' said Reuben. 'But we do not have to shed his blood ourselves. All we need to do is throw him in the cistern. He'll never be able to climb out by himself. Then let the heat and thirst of the desert do the job for us.'

'Or maybe a wild animal *will* kill him,' suggested Asher.

Reuben ignored him. 'But our hands will not have spilled the blood of a brother. We must settle this matter now, before he arrives!'

Reuben's words were enough to sow hesitancy in Asher's mind. He longed to give Joseph a beating—and more. *But then again, perhaps it would be better to avoid getting blood on his hands.*

'Maybe it is a better plan,' said Levi eventually, and—it seemed—somewhat reluctantly. 'As long as he ends up dead.'

'But we can still say that a ferocious animal killed him,' said Asher, 'can't we?'

Their decision not to shed Joseph's blood did not mean he was handled gently. 'Jacob sends his greetings,' said Joseph when he finally met them, and in the tone that they most detested.

As if we are just servants, thought Asher, *and he is the only one who speaks for our father.*

And Joseph suddenly found himself surrounded and hemmed in. 'What are you doing?' For once, there was uncertainty in his voice.

Levi spat on his hand, and then wiped it down the precious robe together with the grime and sweat from his palm.

'How dare you!' yelled Joseph. But there was nowhere for him to go.

'You have lorded it over us one time too many,' answered Simeon. 'And now you will pay the price.'

'And no one is going to save you,' added Dan.

'Get his robe off him,' said Levi calmly. And suddenly nine pairs of hands grabbed Joseph and started pulling at the richly ornamented garment. Reuben chose to simply watch with folded arms.

'Stop it! Let me go,' cried Joseph. And for the first time ever, Asher saw fear in his eyes.

'Not so high and mighty now,' said Judah, as he helped wrestle Joseph to the ground, as they continued wrenching the heavy robe from his body, leaving him with only his tunic. Simeon and Levi pinned him to the ground. Asher couldn't resist planting his foot sharply in Joseph's side. He wasn't the only one.

'Let me go,' cried Joseph again.

'We're only bowing down to you,' taunted Levi, with his knee upon one of Joseph's arms. 'Just like you dreamed.'

'Two of you grab his legs,' ordered Simeon.

'What are you going to do to me?' said Joseph, his voice unsteady.

'We've had enough,' spat out Judah, 'and it is time to rid ourselves of you—for good.'

'NO! Please, no!'

It was strange seeing Joseph so distressed. But a wild animal had awoken within Asher. *He hated Joseph.* And now his brother's anguish brought him a savage gratification, as if he were a lion sinking its teeth into its struggling prey and tasting the warm blood. *He was enjoying it.* He gave him another kick.

Four of them picked him up roughly by his arms and legs and carried him, now struggling madly, toward to the cistern. The fear in his eyes had become terror, and he began pleading with them, saying over and over, 'Please don't kill me.'

The stone pit, with its smooth lime-covered walls, had clearly held water once, but not for some time. It was deep enough for Joseph not to be able to climb out, but not so deep that pushing him into it would break his bones. *Provided he landed properly.* But cuts and bruises were inevitable. The cry of pain that resulted was strangely satisfying to Asher's ears. They all looked over the edge and down into the cistern, where Joseph now lay at the bottom, breathing heavily and staring back at them, his cheeks wet with tears of fear or pain or both.

'He's not dead—yet,' said Levi.

And as they turned their backs and walked away, the desperate cries had changed. 'Don't leave me here! *Please!*'

Judah turned to his brothers. 'Let's eat. What are you going to cook for us, Asher?'

'I'm going to check on the sheep,' announced Reuben.

'But the meal will be ready soon,' protested Asher, kneeling beside the small fire, and stirring the large pot of stew that was suspended over it.

'And we found cheese and raisin cakes in Joseph's bag,' said Gad, standing behind his brother.

'Then you can save me some,' replied Reuben, promptly turning his back and leaving.

When Gad was sure he was out of earshot, he muttered, 'What's got into him?' Reuben never seemed to make any effort to hide his bad moods.

Asher shrugged his shoulders and then stood. 'You'd think he'd be as pleased as the rest of us to have rid ourselves of Joseph.' But neither the question nor the faint cries in the background troubled them as much as their grumbling stomachs.

'Isn't it ready yet?' asked Judah impatiently as he walked over towards them.

'It'll be ready by the time you go and tell everyone to come and eat,' replied Asher.

Judah crossed his feet, and promptly sat down. 'Gad can tell everyone.'

Gad stared at him long and hard, fuming. 'You're such a—' He broke off.

'A what?' said Judah, meeting his eyes and refusing to look away.

Eventually, Gad muttered something to himself, and then cupped both hands to his mouth, yelling at the top of voice, 'FOOD'S READY!' He then crossed his arms and his feet, gave Judah a belligerent glare, and descended slowly to a sitting position.

Gad's shout had the desired effect. But they had barely sat down to eat when Simeon suddenly pointed and said, 'Look! Over there.'

Asher stopped ladling stew into dishes, and glanced up. He followed the direction of Simeon's finger. The brothers started to rise to their feet. 'A caravan,' began Levi. 'Ishmaelites, by the look of them.'

'With camels loaded like that and travelling south,' said Simeon, 'I'd guess they're on the way to Egypt.'

'And with all those jars and pots,' said Naphtali, 'they're probably carrying spices.'

They stood in silence for a few moments, watching the traders leading a long line of camels tethered together, with different shaped and sized bundles and pottery vessels lashed securely to the camels' backs and sides.

Then Judah suddenly spoke. 'What do we gain if we kill Joseph and cover up his blood?'

'What do you mean?' asked Levi.

'Why don't we sell him to the Ishmaelites?' There was a moment's silence as they glanced at one another, taking in Judah's suggestion.

'What, as a slave?' asked Asher.

'Why not?' said Judah. 'Just think about it. He will still be out of our lives, and we won't be responsible for the death of our own flesh and blood. He is our brother, after all.'

'A slave in Egypt...' mused Simeon. 'He'll be on his own. He'll never get out of that.'

'How much will we get for him,' asked Gad.

'Twenty shekels of silver is the usual price for a young male,' replied Simeon. 'Two shekels each.'

'What about Reuben?' asked Issachar.

'We can decide for ourselves without him,' said Zebulun. 'He's hardly going to complain when he gets his two shekels of silver.'

'I say we do it!' exclaimed Levi. And Asher added his voice to the chorus of agreement.

'Come with me, Simeon,' said Judah. 'Let's go and speak to them.' He turned to the others. 'If we beckon you over, it means they will buy him. And the rest of you will then need to get Joseph out of the cistern.'

The two hurried over to the caravan whilst the others watched. The Ishmaelites stopped, and after a short exchange, Judah beckoned to them. Levi led the remaining brothers to the cistern, whilst Dan retrieved some spare rope from the tents. Joseph was still shouting when they arrived.

'Good news, Brother,' said Levi, leaning over the edge and peering down. 'We've decided to spare you and get you out of there.'

Clever words, thought Asher. *More likely to make him come willingly. He would probably think they were just teaching him a lesson, and that it's over now.*

Dan tossed one end of the rope down into the cistern, and soon Joseph—bruised, bloodied and with a tear-stained face—was clambering over the edge. The look of relief was short-lived.

'Tie his hands,' ordered Levi, almost before Joseph was standing.

'What are you doing?' said Joseph, as Gad quickly bound the rope round his wrists whilst Asher and the others held him fast. 'I thought you were letting me go?' His fear had returned.

'You're going on a long journey,' said Dan.

Gad pulled hard on the end of the rope, tightening the knot. He gave it a couple of sharp tugs. 'That will hold.' Dan started pulling on the other end of the rope, dragging Joseph forward.

'Where are you taking me?' begged Joseph.

'*We're* not taking you anywhere,' replied Levi. And as the Ishmaelite caravan came into view, he added, 'But *they* are.'

'They examine him like a bullock in a market,' said Gad. He and Asher were watching from a little distance, as Simeon, Levi and Judah haggled with the Ishmaelites. The traders were prodding and feeling Joseph, looking him over from head to toe, even inspecting his teeth. Asher could see the expression on Joseph's face. *Wide-eyed terror, as if he were some defenceless creature, caught in the paws of a lion, knowing its fate, but unable to escape.* Although out of earshot, Joseph was clearly pleading with his brothers. But when silver finally changed hands, it was all over. Joseph stared back at the rest of them, finally struck dumb. *He can't believe what's happening to him,* thought Asher with some satisfaction. Joseph's gaze was only torn away from them when the camel to which his rope was tied started moving and he was jerked forward. *It would be a long walk to Egypt.*

The three sons of Leah rejoined them as the caravan continued on its way. 'What did you get for him?' asked Issachar.

'They offered ten shekels of silver,' said Simeon, 'but we said he was worth thirty, as he was fit, healthy and only seventeen years old. We finished at twenty.'

'So two shekels each,' said Zebulun.

'And they're going to Egypt?' asked Gad.

Judah nodded. 'Yes, they're going there with spices, balm and myrrh. And we checked which way they were going. They're following the Way of the Sea, along the coast.'

'The Way of Shur would have taken them too close to Kiriath Arba,' added Simeon. He laughed. 'We didn't want Father to see his son going past him on the end of a rope!'

Judah laughed with the rest of them, adding, 'Now let's eat.'

Most were finishing their first bowl of stew when Reuben returned—and they heard him before they saw him. 'Where's Joseph?' he shouted. 'What have you done with him?' He looked distressed.

'He's on his way to Egypt,' replied Simeon, 'with an Ishmaelite caravan.' He held up a small heavy pouch. 'And here's your share of what they paid us for him.' He tossed it to Reuben, who let it fall at his feet. His expression hadn't changed.

'What's the matter?' said Judah. 'You didn't want us to kill him, and we haven't.' He glared at his brother. 'Or were you intending to rescue him?'

Asher studied his oldest brother. *Judging by his expression, that was exactly what he had intended to do.*

'How can I look my father in the eye if I go back without him!' shouted Reuben, with something akin to panic in his eyes.

'Let me guess,' sneered Simeon. '*You* thought you could get yourself back into favour with Father by returning Joseph to him!'

'No, I didn't!' replied Reuben, but Asher knew him well enough to know he was lying. And clearly, so did the others.

'It's not our fault that you fell out of favour,' said Zebulun scornfully. 'Or that you could not keep your tent peg in its bag.'

'You have all the restraint of a ram among ewes!' said Judah.

'But I will bear the chief responsibility when Joseph doesn't return,' spat out Reuben, his distress having turned to anger. 'Not any of you!' He glared round at them all.

'Which is why,' said Levi calmly, 'we will do exactly what we planned. We will kill a goat, we will dip Joseph's robe in its blood, and we will take it back to Father. All we need to say is that we found it like that. He can presume what he likes from it.'

Simeon looked around at them all. 'And *none* of us will *ever* speak of this to anyone else. Not to any of our mothers, not to Dinah or any of the servants. Neither Reuben, Levi nor I will speak of it to our wives—and neither will any of you when you wed.' He gave them a moment for his words to sink in. 'It will be to us as it will be to our father: Joseph was killed by a wild animal. He is dead. And that is the end of it.' He looked back at Reuben, and glanced down to his feet. 'Now, pick up your silver, and eat.'

Notes

1. *Although Genesis 35:27-29 speaks both of Jacob returning to Isaac in Hebron and of Isaac's death (aged 180 years), the two events must have been separated by some years. Given that Jacob must have been 120 years old at Isaac's death, this would not have occurred until around thirteen years after Joseph had been sold into slavery.*

2. *Rebekah's death is not spoken of in Scripture. Given she is not mentioned in Genesis 35:27, but is later referred to as being in the tomb with Abraham, Sarah, and Isaac (Genesis 49:31), it has been assumed that she died whilst Jacob was in Shechem. This may also explain why there was apparently no message from her concerning Esau, as she'd promised (Genesis 27:45).*

3. *Twenty shekels of silver was the normal price for a young male slave at this time. It represented around two years' wages.*

4. *The ancient trade route to Egypt from Gilead does pass Dothan.*

5. *It's not clear when the brothers married, but given the reference to Jacob's daughters (plural) comforting him (in Genesis 37:35), it seems reasonable to assume that this includes daughters-in-law and that the older sons are by now married (and Judah is not, it seems, given Genesis 38:1-2).*

4

Then Jacob tore his clothes, put on sackcloth and mourned for his son many days. All his sons and daughters came to comfort him, but he refused to be comforted.
(Genesis 37:34-35)

'Judah has gone.'

Asher stopped stirring the pot and looked up, confused, as his mother walked over to him. 'What do you mean?'

'He has left the camp,' replied Zilpah, as she put down the bowl of barley flour that she had just prepared for the bread to accompany the stew. 'He took all his possessions with him and told Leah he wasn't coming back.'

Asher stared at her. 'But why? And where's he gone?'

Zilpah shrugged her shoulders before squatting down to add water to the bowl. 'As to *where* he has gone, I can give you an answer. He said he was going to stay with Hirah.'

Asher knew the name. It belonged to a man from a town to the north-west whom they'd met in Kiriath Arba, and with whom Judah had struck up a friendship. 'He is going to Adullam?'

'He was heading in that direction.' Zilpah started mixing the dough. 'But as to *why* he left…' She let her words hang in the air, and then added, 'Maybe he thinks he should be married by now, and wants to find himself a wife. Maybe he has fallen out with his brothers. Maybe he is restless. I do not know and neither does Leah. Only God Himself knows.' She then glanced up and looked across the camp. 'But it is as if he has lost another son.'

Asher's eyes drifted to the figure who sat alone, cross-legged, in the entrance to his tent. Jacob was staring, as if his vision was fixed on some faraway point. But there was nothing to see.

It was nearly two months since they had returned from Dothan. *It had been far easier talking of deceiving Jacob with the bloodied robe than actually doing it. Not that deceiving Jacob had been difficult; watching his reaction had been far harder.* Jacob's grief was like nothing Asher had seen before, not even when Rachel had died. He had torn his clothes, put dust on his head and donned sackcloth. These were to be expected. But the sobs that wracked his aging body and the cries of anguish that tore the soul testified to a sorrow so deep it was crushing him. Nothing that any of them said or did to try to comfort him made any difference. And when the month of mourning for Joseph had passed, Jacob showed no signs of laying aside his grief.

Asher didn't know his brothers' feelings, only his own. The ferocious beast that had awoken within him at Dothan had gone. In its place, however, was a dark, nameless creature whose incessant whispering gave him no peace. And he couldn't wipe away his father's words from his mind: *in mourning I will go down to Sheol to my son.* But Asher knew the truth. *Joseph wasn't in Sheol, the place of the dead. He was—as far as they knew—still very much alive in the land of Egypt.* It was a truth that *he* would have to take with him to the grave.

There was only one place that Asher could freely speak about Joseph, and that was out in the fields with the flocks and with Gad—well away from the tents and from ears that might overhear. The cooler weather and the autumn rains meant that good pasture could be found closer to hand, and several days after Judah's departure, they found themselves together and alone.

'Stupid sheep,' said Asher, as he tried to lift an animal from a small pit into which it had fallen.

'Here, let me help,' said Gad, kneeling down at his side. Together they hauled on the fleece of the distressed creature, whose loud bleating in their ears did not make the task any easier.

Asher swore under his breath, having grazed his arm on a jagged rock as they finally pulled the sheep out of the hole. The animal gave a little shake of its coat and a wag of its tail, and trotted off, with no harm done. Asher bent his arm, and looked down to examine it. Blood had already begun to seep from the shallow wound. 'You'll live, little brother,' said Gad without pity.

They stood for a few moments watching the sheep as it rejoined the flock. Without taking his eyes off it, Asher said, 'Why do you think Judah left?' The question had stayed in his mind.

Gad let out a long breath. 'What do *you* think?'

One of them was going to have to be the first to speak the name of Joseph—or at least allude to him. 'Do you think it's because of Father?'

'Because of his grief, do you mean?'

'Yes. Maybe he couldn't bear watching him every day.' Asher paused. The liberated sheep was calmly tugging at grass again. He turned to Gad. 'It is hard to see him day after day and to know…' He broke off.

'To know we caused it?' offered Gad. 'And that he is grieving for one who yet lives?'

Asher nodded in silence. The truth was he felt wracked with guilt and regret. Getting rid of Joseph was a bad enough crime. But causing their father such unremitting pain was almost worse. *Even if it was their father's treatment of Joseph that had been the start of it.* Asher said simply, 'I didn't think it would be like this.'

'I don't think any of us did. And maybe it is not surprising that Judah feels it worse.'

'But why?' began Asher. 'He was the one who suggested selling Joseph. If it hadn't been for him, Joseph would be dead.'

Gad looked at him almost pityingly. 'Sometimes I think you are slower than a slug on sand.'

'But it *was* Judah who had the idea—when he saw the caravan!'

'Yes, but you are forgetting that Reuben was planning to rescue him. Which he would have done if we hadn't sold him to the Ishmaelites! If Judah hadn't suggested it, Joseph would be back at the camp with Father even now—'

'And we would be in trouble,' protested Asher. Although a voice deep inside shamed him for saying the words. *The trouble would have been deserved.*

Gad eventually added quietly, 'But we are no less guilty than Judah. We all agreed.' And with that, he walked away.

It wasn't only Judah's life that changed, however. Soon, both Gad and Asher were married to granddaughters of Esau, with tents of their own and then children of their own. It was the same for all the sons of Jacob, save Benjamin. He was barely walking when they had returned from Dothan. In the absence of Joseph—and his mother, Rachel—Benjamin had taken pride of place in their father's affections, and seemed to be his only solace. Asher wasn't surprised. But what did surprise him was his own growing affection for the lad. He wasn't sure if it was Benjamin's youth or smiles—or his own guilt over Joseph or the fact he brought some joy to Jacob. Whatever the reason, he found he could not hate Jacob's new favourite.

As the years passed, Isaac finally died, aged a hundred and eighty, and Jacob and Esau buried him in the tomb of his father, Abraham. But life continued and there was always work to be done. The flocks needed Asher's constant attention and care: there was grazing to be found and herds to be led to both food and water. They needed milking, or treating if sick or injured. Those giving birth often required help, those that had wandered away or got into trouble needed retrieving, and all had to be protected both by day and by night from creatures that preyed upon them. His hands were never idle. Almost never.

'Are you going to do something with those lentils, or are you just going to stand there staring into the air?'

His wife always seemed to catch him when he was daydreaming. Asher turned to Ijona. 'I was just thinking…'

She raised an eyebrow, as if she didn't believe him. 'Thinking about clouds or about adding the lentils to the pot?' She rested a hand upon her swollen belly. It would be their fifth child, though the second birth had been twins. She didn't wait for him to answer. 'And when you

283

have added the lentils, maybe you could find your sons. I swear they find it easier to wander off than a horde of witless sheep!'

Asher smiled, bent down and emptied the bowl of lentils into the bubbling pot, giving it a stir. 'I will now hunt for the lost sheep as you ask,' he said as he straightened up again.

'And make sure Imnah isn't throwing stones at the goats again.'

He didn't have to look far. He found Imnah, Ishvah and Ishvi running around madly with four of their cousins—all sons of Gad. They had clearly made up some game that involved sticks and some object (the nature of which was not clear) that they were hitting. It also involved a lot of shouting—some of it at Beriah, Asher's youngest. At three years old, he appeared to be hindering rather than helping their game. But there was someone else there too: their uncle Benjamin. Asher stood and watched for a while. Benjamin suddenly darted into the midst of the mayhem, weaving his way between the players. He scooped Beriah up, both saving him from being knocked flying by the recklessness of his brothers and cousins, and causing him to scream with delight, as he swung him round in the air. Benjamin delivered him safely to the edge of the game, with Beriah crying out, 'More, more!' His uncle threw him up into the air and caught him. There were more screams of delight and calls for him to do it again. That Benjamin was a favourite of both his sons and his nephews—*all* of them—was not in doubt. He was the youthful, unmarried, good-looking uncle who played with them. He was, at seventeen, not much older than the oldest of Jacob's grandsons. *The same age as his brother had been when they sold him.* And every time Asher looked at him, he seemed to see more and more of Joseph in him.

He surveyed his own sons once more, and tried to imagine how he would feel if he lost one of them. *It was unimaginable. Unthinkable.* And he knew that however much they fell out with each other—and they did—for Imnah to want to kill Ishvah, Ishvi or Beriah… It would break his heart. Becoming a father had only deepened his feelings of guilt. It had also made him think, as never before, of the God of Abraham, Isaac and Jacob. *Yahweh had seen what they had done, even if their father had not.* And yet, once more he was puzzled. *What they had done was wrong. Very wrong. And yet Yahweh was blessing him. He had a wife, four healthy boys and another on the way. He had done nothing to deserve them—and everything to have them denied.* At least he knew one thing. He had wronged a son of Rachel once, and would not do so again.

'It's a girl!'

Asher stared at Maka, Gad's wife, who had been assisting the midwife at the birth of his fifth child. 'What do you mean, *it's a girl*?'

'What do you think I mean? It's not a boy!'

'But how can that be?' Asher was stunned. He knew, of course, that girls were born. *But just not in his family.* Jacob had had twelve sons. *Admittedly, he did also have one daughter—his sister Dinah. But none of his brothers had had girls. Reuben had four boys, Simeon had three so far, as had Levi, Issachar and Naphtali. Zebulun had two. Gad had five and Dan had one. And Judah? They had heard there were sons. But none of them had one single girl. Not one. Longevity ran in their family, but so did having sons.*

Maka folded her arms and cocked her head. 'I have not come out to answer your questions, Asher, but to tell you that you have a girl. Just consider yourself blessed that you will have a daughter who will be the envy of all your brothers.' She huffed, unfolded her arms, and added, 'Now, do you want to see her or not?' And with that she turned, pushed the tent flap aside and went in. Asher shook himself and followed.

Ijona was lying back against cushions, her hair damp and matted and her face wet with sweat. But she was smiling. She cradled the baby, wrapped in a blanket, in her arms. Beside her, Zilpah and the midwife were clearing up the trappings of birth. His mother, her dark hair now streaked with grey, smiled at him. 'You have been blessed, my son.' Asher walked over to his wife and knelt down beside her, kissing her forehead. He then gazed down at the bundle, and into the little face. The baby's eyes were closed, but just then, the mouth opened and gave a little yawn. It was a picture of peace.

Asher couldn't help it. He folded back the blanket slightly and looked. Ijona laughed, 'It *is* a girl!'

He replaced the corner of the blanket, smiling. 'It is.'

'Her name is Serah.'

'It is a good name,' said Asher, 'and she is beautiful.' He then laughed. 'And what will our boys think of having a sister?'

'They will be proud to have something that none of their cousins have. And I think they will love her very much.'

She was right.

But Asher's joy was never entirely unsullied. There was always a small dark cloud in an otherwise clear sky.

Everything was tainted. It was as if a drop of jet black pitch had fallen onto his tunic, and nothing he could do could remove it or hide its stain.

'You look as sour as yesterday's milk,' said Ijona one morning. 'What troubles you?'

'It is nothing,' replied Asher. It was what he always said. But Serah's smile, as she waddled over to him, arms outstretched, banished the cloud—at least for a while.

It was only when Asher was out in the fields again that his mind returned—as it often did—to Joseph.

'And how is my niece today?' asked Gad, as he wandered over to him. Maka had been right. His brothers did envy him. Although they delighted in their numerous sons, they seemed to be constantly asking after his daughter.

'Ah, she grows more beautiful every day—'

'She is not yet two!' interrupted Gad with a laugh.

'But I am already sure that a day will come when her cousins will be fighting over her.'

Gad laughed again. 'I do not doubt it, Brother.' They fell silent for a few moments, staring out over the herds.

'It is a blessing to have children. And even Ijasaka is already with child.'

'It looks as if she will bear Benjamin his first child exactly nine months after they wed!'

'He did not waste any time,' said Asher.

'And maybe she will bear twins, as both our grandmother and Ijona did, so that Benjamin can begin to catch us up.' Asher smiled at his brother's suggestion, but then became silent again. 'What is it?'

He could hide little from Gad. He had been wondering about Joseph, and whether Egyptians allowed their slaves to marry or have children. 'Do you still wonder what happened to him—to Joseph—when he got to Egypt?'

'Often,' replied Gad, suddenly taking great interest in some stones on the ground. His pushed one of them to the side with his foot. 'And I wonder where he is now—or if he has even survived the life of a slave.' He paused, and then continued. 'It would not have come easy to one who was used to being served. He would not have found bowing to others to his liking.'

'You are right, Brother.' Asher wondered whether Joseph's arrogance had made his life as a slave short-lived. But then he remembered his expression of terror. *You could not be arrogant when you feared for your life.*

'Gad!' Maka's distant cry from the tents broke into his thoughts.

'You had better go. You would not want to incur the wrath of a wife.'

'That I would not,' said Gad with a wry smile, and left.

But Asher could not shake Joseph from his mind. He tried to imagine, as he had done many times over the years, how life would be for him, if he still lived. *What would it have been like to suddenly be surrounded only by people whose language you did not understand? What would a slave in Egypt be called upon to do, when there was no choice but to obey?* He did not know much about Egypt, but the accounts of travellers had told of magnificent pyramids. He'd heard they had been built more than five hundred years earlier as tombs for their kings. And then there was the great stone creature in the sand, with the body of a lion and the head of a man. *Maybe Joseph was labouring on some huge Egyptian edifice. Or maybe he was scrubbing the marble floors of some rich noble.* Asher looked at the wide open lands before him. *What must it be like to have your freedom taken away, and to be taken from all those you love? Though he and his brothers would hardly be among those Joseph loved. He must hate them all.*

As Asher moved ever closer to his fortieth year, the family of Jacob continued to change, but not only through the increase of the next generation. The day came when Leah died, and then—only months later—his own mother. *As if she were following her mistress faithfully into Sheol, to serve her there.* Jacob buried Leah in the family tomb where his mother and father lay. Zilpah's resting place was more humble. And although Jacob's grief for Joseph had mellowed as the years had passed, he was never as he had been before, and his years—approaching a hundred and thirty—weighed heavily upon him.

But the passing of the years also brought the start of a drought, and with it, Judah's return. Beside him walked a son, Shelah, and a daughter-in-law with twin boys in her arms. But she was not Shelah's wife and neither were the boys his.

On the night of his return, the brothers did what they had not done for many years. They all ate together with their father—without wives, without children. A father and his eleven sons. Asher slaughtered a calf, for their meal was to be a celebration. Judah had been away for over twenty years.

As Gad helped him to prepare the animal—*he would roast some of the meat, and make stew from the rest*—his brother suddenly said, 'He looks as if he bears the weight of the skies.'

Asher glanced up from cutting the meat. Gad was looking over to where Judah was speaking with Simeon and Levi. *It was true. He appeared weary and burdened. If he felt joy at being back, it did not show.* 'No doubt we will hear his story.'

'No doubt.'

Both returned to their task, and Asher was kept busy preparing not only the meat, but also other dishes of lentils and vegetables, whilst Ijona and Maka baked bread. And as the brothers gathered that night, Asher happened to overhear Judah speaking to Reuben. 'He is like his brother.' He was staring at Benjamin.

Judah's story was not an easy one, but he told it with candour. 'My wife bore me three sons,' he began. 'You have all met Shelah, but he was born last. The eldest were Er and Onan. When Er was of age, I found him a wife— Tamar. She was the girl who returned with me.' Apart from Judah's voice, the only sound was the crackling of the fire around which they were seated. Every eye was on Judah, but he was avoiding their gaze by studying the dust. 'But Er was wicked in the sight of Yahweh, and before he had offspring, Yahweh put him to death.'

So Judah had lost a son. Maybe he would know better than any of them how Jacob felt. But Asher was surprised to hear his brother speak of Yahweh. The name of their father's God had not been on his lips before he left.

Judah continued. 'I told Onan to lie with Tamar and fulfil his duty to his brother.' It was a custom with which Asher was familiar: any resulting son would be considered the offspring of Er, and therefore Judah's heir along with Onan. 'Onan lay with her, but whenever he did, he spilled his seed.'

Judah paused, and Gad leant over to Asher, saying under his breath, 'He did not want his inheritance divided.' Asher nodded.

Judah went on, still not meeting their eyes. 'That, too, was an evil before Yahweh, and He also put him to death.' How both his sons died was left unsaid. He went on. 'Shelah was young, and I told Tamar to return to her father's house until he was grown and she could be his wife.' He finally looked up. 'But when he was of age, I did not give her to Shelah. It was my duty to do that for my widowed daughter-in-law. I broke my word and did her a grievous wrong.' He paused again, as if in deep thought.

Once again, Asher was surprised by the admission of guilt. *That was not the Judah he knew.*

Judah continued. 'My wife died, and after my time of grieving I went with Hirah to Timnah to get my sheep sheared. On the way, by the town of Enaim, I saw a woman veiled as a shrine prostitute, as is the custom of the Canaanites. I do not believe, as they do, that lying with them makes the land fertile, but I missed my wife and I slept with her anyway. I gave her my staff and my seal threaded on its cord as a pledge of payment, but when I sent Hirah back to the town later with a goat to pay her, she could not be found, and he was told there were no shrine prostitutes there.' Asher's gaze stayed on Judah. The air was as quiet as the depth of night. 'We returned to Adullam, but I found out three months later that Tamar was with child. She was clearly guilty of sin and I called for her to be brought out and put to death. I wanted her burned.'

Asher was shocked. *The penalty his brother had demanded was extreme.*

'But as she was being brought out,' continued Judah, 'she produced my staff, seal and cord, and said that they belonged to the man whose child she carried. And I understood. She finally had the offspring that I had promised but had not given—not by Shelah's seed, but by mine.' He paused a final time. 'She was more righteous than I. Any guilt was mine.'

There it was again, thought Asher. *He owned his sin.*

'I did not lie with Tamar again,' Judah went on, 'but the twin boys—Perez and Zerah—are mine.'

Silence followed, broken only when Jacob spoke at last. 'Then they are also my grandsons and will have my blessing.' His words welcomed his son Judah back into their midst and became the sign for all to begin talking. And many more tales were told that night.

Gad helped Asher dismantle the spit on which they had roasted joints from the calf. The bronze rod had been stripped completely of its meat. 'It was a fine meal, Brother,' said Gad. 'You honoured Judah with a feast.'

Asher smiled as they laid the pieces of metal down on the ground. He glanced over at Judah who was speaking with Issachar and Zebulun. 'He has changed.'

'We all have,' replied Gad. 'And he certainly had a story to tell.'

Asher picked up a cup of beer to quench his thirst and drained it. As he put it down, he suddenly asked Gad quietly, 'Do you think the death of his sons was the judgment of Yahweh—for the sin against Joseph?'

Gad shrugged his shoulders. 'He said they died because of their own wickedness—not his.' After a moment, he added, 'And why should Yahweh punish Judah and not us? We all share the guilt.'

Asher's brow furrowed. *Judah had believed that his sons' deaths were God's doing. But why hadn't Yahweh punished them for their sin against Joseph?* He lifted his eyes to the vastness of the night sky. And another question rose in his mind, though he was almost afraid to voice it. He kept his eyes on the stars. 'Do you think that God may yet punish us?'

There was a pause. 'I have asked myself the same question.'

Notes

1. *Scripture does not tell us the names of the brothers' wives. However, there is a text called the Book of Jubilees, which parallels some of the material in Genesis and does give names for the wives. It was probably written in the decades before 100BC. It does not have the authority of Scripture, but is thought to include a large amount of tradition. In the absence of any other names for the wives, it seemed reasonable to use the ones from the Book of Jubilees. It might be that there is some truth in the names, handed down through the years; that they are granddaughters of Esau is simply a guess. However, given that Jacob knew that Esau's Canaanite wives had displeased their father, maybe it is not an unreasonable guess that the wives for his own sons came from within the extended family, especially given that both Genesis 38:2-3 and 46:10 make a point of noting when two of Jacob's sons have children by Canaanite women.*

2. *The assumption that Asher had twin boys was based purely on the similarity of two of his sons' names. The same could also be true of two of Gad's sons.*

3. *Both Genesis 49:17 and 1 Chronicles 7:30 mention that*

Asher's sons had a sister named Serah, and Numbers 26:46 specifically states that Serah was Asher's daughter. He is the only one of Jacob's sons who is recorded as having a daughter. Some Jewish tradition contends that she was not the only girl, but that she was mentioned because she was a heroine who performed great deeds. But given she is only mentioned in Scripture in the above three verses, it may be that she was, in fact, Jacob's only granddaughter out of a total of fifty-four grandchildren. However unlikely this may seem, God has already (in the cases of Abraham and Jacob) intervened in the genetics of His people. Given the families were established through the men, it seems that God—within only two generations—firmly established His people, the sons of Israel, as a sizeable people-group. Serah being the only girl may, however, be an incorrect assumption.

4. *We know that Leah dies before Jacob goes to Egypt (from Genesis 49:31), as Jacob later asks to be buried back in Canaan in the tomb in which he buried her (and in which Abraham and Sarah, Isaac and Rebekah are already buried).*

5. *Judah's time away was probably around twenty years, with a maximum of around twenty-two years, given that this is the likely time between Joseph being sold into slavery and the first trip to Egypt. This does allow time for Er to grow up and be of marriageable age (possible mid- to late-teens), and for a gap before Shelah also reaches that age.*

5

When Jacob learned that there was grain in Egypt, he said to his sons…'I have heard that there is grain in Egypt. Go down there and buy some for us, so that we may live and not die.' (Genesis 42:1-2)

The drought that had driven Judah back home became a famine. The fields of barley they had planted after the summer had failed. Both the autumn and spring rains had been as elusive as a jackal in daylight, and caring for the herds was becoming ever more difficult.

'It is as well that the goats eat mostly anything,' remarked Gad, as he and Asher walked back to the camp together in the lengthening shadows.

'In that, they are more fortunate than the cattle,' answered Asher, 'and more fortunate than us.' They both cast their gaze around the surrounding countryside. The hills around Mamre that were usually green in late spring were dry and brown, save for some bushes dotted around and the trees—the oaks and olives, the cypresses and tamarisks. All had roots that were able to draw water from greater depths. 'The drought shows no sign of ending,' added Asher.

'And it's unlikely to do so now until the autumn rains—unless they fail again.'

'What are we going to do?'

'How should I know?' answered Gad impatiently. 'I cannot put clouds full of rain into the sky!'

'But no one has grain to spare in Kiriath Arba, however much silver you wave at them.'

'You cannot eat silver.'

They fell silent. The whole land seemed to be suffering with the same affliction, from Beersheba in the south—which was dry enough anyway—even to Damascus in the north, where they might have expected it to be greener. They had heard rumours of Egypt faring better. But any mention of Egypt only brought back unwelcome memories. *Maybe that was why none of them mentioned the place. Even if it had grain.*

'Your father wishes to see you. All of you,' said Maka, as they approached the tents. Asher went towards his, and she added, 'Now!'

The rest of their brothers were already gathered, sitting in the entrance to their father's tent, which still had all its flaps rolled up in the vain hope of a cooling breeze. Dan and Benjamin shuffled slightly to give them space, and they joined the circle seated on patterned and colourful rugs in the front of the tent.

Asher glanced round at his brothers. Reuben, the eldest, was now forty-five, and Zebulun—a year younger than him—was thirty-nine. Benjamin was in his twenty-fourth year. *The last time they had been gathered like this was at Judah's return.*

'I have made a decision,' began Jacob. 'Every one of you knows how low our stores of grain have fallen, and that this drought and famine afflict the entire land.' His stern expression excluded none, as it swept across them all. 'And yet none of you have looked beyond the borders of Canaan for our deliverance. Instead, you simply stare at each other and do nothing!' Asher shifted uncomfortably.

'I have heard that there is grain in Egypt. So I am sending you there to buy some, so that we might live and not die.'

'You are sending all of us?' asked Judah.

'The more of you go, the more can be brought back,' he replied. 'And many of the animals also need grain. So all of you will go. All except Benjamin.'

'Father, I would go with them too!' said Benjamin, clearly eager to help. 'I am of age.'

'You are *not* going,' said Jacob forcefully. 'And you will speak of it no more.'

But Asher understood. *He had lost one son of Rachel, and would not risk losing the other.*

The terrain slowly changed as they made their way south along the Way of Shur towards Egypt. The parched land of Canaan melted into the barren lands of the Negev, south of Beersheba, and then, eventually, as they turned west, the land of Egypt came into sight. It had taken them from full moon to new moon. They'd left behind the oaks and olive trees of Canaan; the much sparser trees of Egypt were mainly palms. But the land was not as they had expected. Despite having grain, it also had a famine. The annual rise of the Nile had not happened that year— the southerly lands in which it rose were thought to have also suffered a drought. The fertile land around the Nile was as dry as Canaan.

'How is it that Egypt has not only grain for itself but enough to sell to others?' asked Simeon, clearly baffled, as they led their donkeys into the city to which they had been directed. Its bounty did not stay a mystery for long.

Among the voices that spoke in strange tongues, they heard the familiar accents of Ishmaelite traders. One by the name of Kedar began explaining it to them. 'Their grain is as plentiful as sand. This is the second trip I have made here in only a few months.'

'But how is that so when there is drought here also?' asked Reuben.

'Ah! But *this* drought followed seven years of plenty—exceptional plenty,' replied Kedar. 'And in those years they stored up huge amounts of grain—so much, that it is said that they ceased keeping records because it was beyond measure.'

'It almost sounds,' said Judah, 'as if they knew the famine was coming.'

'Some say they did.'

Asher was intrigued. *How could anyone know that?* He would have dearly loved to question Kedar further, but Simeon's question was out before Asher even opened his mouth.

'And they will sell grain to any who come?'

'They do so gladly for now,' said Kedar.

'And where must we go?' asked Levi.

Kedar turned his face westwards and gave a nod in that direction, towards a large building that rose above all others around. 'That's where you'll find both the grain and the man you will have to petition. He is second only to Pharaoh, so I suggest you kiss the dirt that he walks on.'

As Kedar disappeared down a narrow street with his laden donkey, Asher and his brothers led theirs towards the building that far exceeded in size any they had encountered before.

The mudbrick houses around them were not so dissimilar to those in Canaan—unlike the appearance of those who occupied them. Their own coloured and patterned woollen garments and bearded faces stood out among the clean-shaven men dressed in plain white linen. And when words slipped from the lips of the darker-skinned men, the difference was yet more stark. The presence of barefooted Egyptian guards carrying spears with copper heads did nothing to make Asher feel more at ease in the strange land. They also bore large wooden shields, covered with mottled animal hide—square at the base but with a pointed arch at the top. But he was glad of his brothers, glad that he would not have to speak, and glad that he would not have to do anything but kiss the ground before the Egyptian vizier. And for a moment— just one moment—the face of Joseph from twenty-two years earlier rose, unbidden, in his mind. *He had been alone when he had arrived in Egypt.* But the image was swiftly gone as they passed beyond the last of the mudbrick homes and faced the vast storehouse on which their futures depended.

An official who spoke their language directed them to where they were to leave their donkeys and also to where they were to wait. 'We are not alone in travelling from Canaan,' said Reuben, glancing around, as they joined a line that was slowly moving forward. It was overseen by more Egyptian officials, whose eyes darted in every direction and whose mouths were swift to bark out commands to any who stepped out of line. Asher gazed at the unfamiliar scene as they waited silently. *His brother was right.* Although most were Egyptians, garments of orange, green or brown were scattered amongst the bare chests and white skirts.

But the man whose presence both demanded and drew their attention was the one standing on the dais towards which the line was moving. All bowed before him and it was not difficult to see why. Asher could not take his eyes off him. The linen that was wrapped around his waist, and which fell down to his calves, was not like that of others. It was not only held in place by a rich belt of gold and blue fabric, but was of such a fine quality that light could be seen through it when he moved. Although Asher had already seen the dark lines that both marked and widened the eyes of many Egyptians, the vizier's eyebrows were also blackened and his eyelids painted a bright green. He was also clean-shaven, but an elaborate black wig, adorned with coloured beads, was upon his head. There were gold bracelets on his arms and rings on his fingers. But the most stunning feature of his appearance was the wide neck collar that covered part of his chest and shoulders. It was gold, interspersed with turquoise and the blue of lapis lazuli. It was difficult to guess the man's age. *Maybe his years were not so different from their own.*

Asher felt an elbow in his ribs. 'Don't stare!' hissed Gad. He swiftly dropped his eyes, although not before he had glanced round and spotted an official glaring at him.

Suddenly a voice behind them, thick with accent, whispered, 'You look because man—' There was a pause. '—because man very fine.' Both Gad and Asher turned to see who had spoken. They were, of course, at the back of their group. A smiling Egyptian faced them. 'He Zaphenath-paneah,' he continued in a lowered voice. 'He very, very great man.' His eyes flitted around, watching the officials, whose attention was, at least for the moment, elsewhere. 'He rule eight year.' He paused and cast his eyes to the ceiling for a moment. 'Nine year? Wife Asenath. Very great family. She very fine. Father

Potiphera. He priest in On—also big city.' His eyes moved from Asher and Gad to the vizier and back to them. 'You bow!' They nodded and smiled in reply. And Asher—the least of the family if not the last—felt his mouth go dry. *He was about to meet one of the most powerful men on the face of the earth, and certainly the greatest he had ever set eyes upon.*

As the line ahead of them shortened, Asher fiddled with the bag of silver in his hand. They each carried one. He occasionally stole glances across at the dais. And if he had had any doubts about the standing of the man before him, the abundance of spear-carrying guards nearby dispelled them.

'You go now,' said a man whose wig—*if wigs were anything to go by*—indicated a higher rank. Asher made sure he kept his eyes on the ground, and when the others in front of him knelt down, so did he, bowing his head down until it touched the earth.

'Stand!' said a voice. As Asher looked up, he realised the command had come from an official at the vizier's right hand. They all obeyed. The role of the official soon became clear.

Asher's eyes kept darting up and down. The vizier was staring at them. And staring in a manner that only heightened Asher's unease. The ruler snapped out some words, and though the meaning of them was lost on Asher, the harsh tone was not. The official at his side translated his words. 'Where do you come from?'

'From the land of Canaan,' Reuben replied, making sure he addressed the vizier rather than the interpreter, 'to buy food.' The official turned to the vizier and spoke in Egyptian. *Presumably repeating their words.*

The response was swift and the tone severe. And when the translation came, Asher's disquiet became fear. 'You are spies! You have come to see where our land is unprotected.'

'No, my lord,' Reuben answered. 'Your servants have come to buy food.'

'We are brothers,' said Simeon, 'we are all the sons of one man.'

And before their words could be translated, Judah added, 'Your servants are honest men, not spies.'

Asher did not have to understand their language to know that the Egyptian did not believe them, and the interpreter repeated his accusation. 'No! You have come to see where our land lies open before you.'

Asher felt sick. *They were in a foreign land and at the mercy of the powerful man before whom they stood.*

Reuben spoke for them again, pleading, 'We are just brothers, not spies.'

The next words from the vizier were unexpected, however, and were spoken less harshly. 'Does your father still live?'

Reuben was momentarily taken about. 'Yes, my lord.'

Another question followed. 'And do you have another brother?'

Reuben replied, 'Your servants were twelve brothers, my lord, the sons of one man who lives in the land of Canaan. The youngest has stayed with our father, and one is no more.'

As inexplicably as the harshness had lifted, it returned, strengthened. 'It is just as I said. You are spies!' Asher's heart was racing as the vizier spoke again through the interpreter. 'This is how you will be tested: as surely as

302

Pharaoh lives, you will not leave this place unless your youngest brother comes here.' Another command was barked out. 'Send one of your number to get him. The rest of you will be kept here in prison, so that your words may be tested to see if you are telling the truth. If you are not, then as surely as Pharaoh lives, you are spies!' And Asher could guess the fate of a spy.

Before they could respond, the ruler gave another angry and unintelligible order—but this time, not to them or to the interpreter. The guards who had been standing nearby suddenly moved towards them.

'What's happening?' whispered Asher urgently to Gad.

'He is doing as he said,' answered Gad, wide-eyed, and within moments they found themselves facing the tips of spears. The ruler continued to give orders to the guards, and it soon became clear that he wanted them separated. There was not even time for them to speak again before they were marched away. Asher's eyes met those of the man who had stood behind them in the line. *He pitied them.*

Asher's stomach complained loudly once again. It was only his second day in the cell but already he was dreaming of the stews and bread that he cooked at home. Although food was brought in, it was barely enough to keep a man alive, let alone fill his belly.

He was not the only one confined in the cell. *Not that the others were company.* They talked among themselves and their language was not his own. So Asher found himself alone with his thoughts—and they brought him no comfort. *Had the vizier already sent one of his brothers back to*

303

Canaan? If it was Reuben, would his father take notice? He had never forgotten how his firstborn had betrayed his trust by sleeping with Bilhah. Would Simeon or Levi fare any better? Their rash slaughter of the men of Shalem meant their father questioned their judgment. But even if Judah spoke for them, would their father be willing to send Benjamin to secure their freedom? It was a question whose answer was by no means certain in Asher's mind. And in his darker moments he wondered if he would ever see Ijona or his sons or his beautiful Serah again.

But this was what they had done to Joseph. It was a thought that haunted him for much of the time. *They may not (with the exception of his brief time in the cistern) have put him in a prison cell, but they had seen him bound and his freedom taken. They had sent him far away from those he loved, with no hope of return. And they had exulted in doing so. And what had been his crime? Yes, he was an arrogant braggart with a head the size of an ox. But it scarcely warranted their treatment of him—their own flesh and blood.* And though it was painful to acknowledge, Asher knew that it was hardly Joseph's fault that he had their father's favour. *He hadn't chosen to be born to Rachel. And was flaunting his coat so much of a crime?*

As he lay down to sleep that night on the hard floor of the cell, he could not escape the thought that Yahweh was finally punishing them, paying them back in kind. *They could hide their sin from their father, but not from Him. And if He was paying them back, then what lay ahead?* And not for the first time, he silently prayed to the unseen God of his fathers. But this time he begged, as if his life depended on it—for he believed that it might. *O Yahweh, God of my father, Jacob, my grandfather Isaac, and my great-grandfather Abraham. You have seen my grievous sin. Please do not hold it against me.* He paused. *Against us.*

304

It was on the third day that Asher's fortunes changed. He heard the bolts on the other side of the wooden door being drawn. Then it opened. A man flanked by two guards with spears stood in the doorway. He glowered at Asher and barked out a command in Egyptian.

Hope and fear both rose in Asher's heart. 'What?' he replied, adding, 'I don't understand.'

The incomprehension was mutual. The man pointed at Asher and repeated the words, yelling. One of the other prisoners shouted at him derisively, and then shoved him towards the door.

Once outside, there was, however, a small grain of comfort. His brothers were also being taken from their cells. There was no chance even to whisper before they found themselves, once more, bowing before the vizier. The order to stand was given. As before, the Egyptian fixed them with his gaze. Asher swallowed hard and looked down at his feet.

The ruler began to address them again, but this time the tone was different—more conciliatory. Asher waited more in hope than in fear for the translation. 'Do this and you will live, for I fear God,' began the official. 'If you are honest men, let one of your brothers stay here in prison, while the rest of you go and take grain back for your starving households.' The vizier spoke again, insistently. The official continued, 'But you *must* bring your youngest brother to me, so that your words may be shown to be true and that you may not die.' Then the vizier stood in silence, with his arms folded across his chest.

It took Asher a few moments to realise what was happening. *He was waiting for them to choose who should stay!*

But that was not what they spoke of first—and suddenly it was as if the vizier was not there. Asher quickly realised he had not been the only one troubled by guilt in the cells.

'This is all happening because of our brother,' began Levi, his face strained. 'We're finally being punished.'

Dan shook his head slowly. 'We saw how distressed he was when he pleaded with us for his life, but we wouldn't listen.'

'Levi's right,' added Simeon, looking pale. 'It is the reason why this distress has come on us.'

'Didn't I tell you not to sin against the boy?' replied Reuben angrily. 'But you would not listen! Now we must give a reckoning for his blood.'

There was a pause. *What Reuben said was true.* Asher suddenly noticed that the vizier had, for some reason, turned his back on them. He was only glad that the ruler could not understand their guilt-ridden words. *Had that been the case, he might not have chosen to be so lenient.*

'But what are we going to do?' asked Judah eventually.

There was another pause. 'I will stay.' They all turned to look at Simeon. He did not give a reason. He did not have to.

Reuben was the eldest, but if any of them carried less blame, then it was him. So the one who carried the greatest responsibility was the next in line—and that was Simeon. For once, Asher did not mind being the last, and none of them argued with their older brother. *They had no choice,* thought Asher. *They were at the mercy of the vizier, and he was, at least, allowing the rest of them to return—and with grain.* He watched as the vizier turned back to face them. There was something strange about his expression that Asher couldn't fathom. Simeon stepped forward and repeated his words.

The vizier replied through his official. 'Bring your youngest brother to me. If you do, I will give you this brother back and you can go freely in this land.' Then a nod from the ruler brought the guard forward, but not before they had all murmured their thanks to Simeon or rested their hands on his shoulders.

As he was being taken from them, Levi hurriedly whispered to him, 'We will not abandon you. We *will* return.'

Asher was not the only one dumbfounded when they discovered that their silver had been generously exchanged not only for bulging sacks of grain but also for ample provisions for their journey home. But still they chose to put as much distance as possible between themselves and the city before stopping for the night.

'How is it,' began Dan, as they sat down to eat the best meal they had enjoyed for many months, 'that the man could change from being hostile to being generous towards us in so short a time?'

'Maybe he was just trying to frighten us to begin with,' said Gad.

'I was frightened enough *before* he put us in prison for three days,' admitted Asher with a little smile. Others nodded. *He hadn't been the only one.*

'But he did not have to send us away with bread and beer,' said Reuben.

'And the rest,' added Asher, whose knife had chopped the onions, garlic and vegetables that he'd added to the pot with the lentils.

'But he still took Simeon,' said Levi quietly, silencing them all.

An image of the vizier arose in Asher's mind. *Maybe, as he had been generous to them, he would hold their brother in a better prison.* He pondered the idea for a moment. *Did such a thing even exist?*

'We cannot tell Father that we were locked up for three days,' said Reuben suddenly, breaking the silence. 'He will never let Benjamin return with us if he thinks it will put him in danger.'

'Are you suggesting we lie?' asked Zebulun.

'No, only that we are careful about what we tell him.'

'But what are we going to say about why Simeon isn't with us?' said Levi sharply.

Reuben had no answer, but Judah spoke. 'Our brother is right. We can tell Father that the man spoke to us harshly and demanded to see Benjamin to prove our words were true, and that Simeon has had to stay until we return with him. But we don't tell him that Simeon is in prison...or that he threatened us with death.' They all sat in silence for some moments. 'So that's agreed,' said Judah. No one argued with him.

Asher stared at the empty cooking pot that sat in their midst, and then glanced over at the donkeys. *The animals also had a long journey ahead of them and needed feeding too.* He rose to his feet. 'Donkeys can't eat lentil stew, even if any were left.'

As he walked over to his beast, Gad shouted out behind him, 'Will you feed mine too?' A chorus of *And mine* followed. Asher smiled wryly to himself, and without looking back, shrugged his shoulders. He opened the hessian sack that had been on his donkey and put his hand inside. He looked down, puzzled. For amongst the smooth-flowing kernels of barley, he felt something else. And there, lying at the top of his sack, was a familiar pouch. He pulled it out, heart thumping, and tugged on the drawstrings with a finger to open it. He peered inside. The silver he had taken down to Egypt was there—all of it. *What was God doing to them?* 'Look at this!' he called in a trembling voice.

Jacob had seemed satisfied by their story, shorn also of any mention of the unexplained silver. *If all went well, they would be able to return to Egypt to free Simeon without delay.* But Asher's optimism was as short-lived as mist on a summer's morning.

'Come here quickly,' shouted Dan. Asher and Gad left the donkeys they had been attending, and hurried over to where Dan, Naphtali and Issachar were emptying the sacks of grain into the brick-lined pit in the ground. Their pace was quickened by the tone of alarm.

'What is it?' asked Levi, as he, Reuben and Judah also joined them, with Zebulun not far behind.

'Look,' said Issachar as he held up one of their pouches of silver.

'Yes, Asher found it in his sack,' whispered Gad impatiently, conscious of their father's approach, as he laboured towards them, leaning on his staff.

'But this isn't from Asher's sack,' said Dan. 'It was from an unopened one.'

'Are you sure?' asked Asher. Dan rolled his eyes.

'Open the others—quickly,' ordered Reuben. And as each sack was ripped open, there was the same unwelcome sight.

'What is this?' said Jacob. 'What have you found?'

'The silver we took to Egypt,' replied Judah, his face pale. 'It has been put in each of the sacks.'

Jacob was visibly trembling as he stared at them. 'What is the meaning of this?'

Reuben shook his head, 'We do not know.'

Questions streamed into Asher's mind. *Who had put the silver there? Why would anyone do that to them? Would they now be accused of stealing if they returned to Egypt?* He suddenly felt the hairs on the back of his neck bristle. *Was this Yahweh's doing—His further judgment in some way? If they couldn't return to Egypt they might starve if the famine continued. But if they went back, would disaster await them?* It soon became clear that he was not the only one to consider this possible fate.

'You have bereaved me of my sons,' wailed Jacob as the old grief re-emerged, as unwelcome as a fox among the flocks. 'Joseph is no more, and Simeon is no more. And now you would take Benjamin too. All these things have come against me!'

Reuben laid his hand upon Jacob's arm. The old man raised his eyes. 'If I don't bring both Simeon and Benjamin back to you, you may put two of my sons to death.' He looked pleadingly at their father. 'Entrust Benjamin into my care, and I will return him to you.'

But Jacob would not be moved. 'My son shall *not* go down to Egypt with you,' he said, shaking. 'Joseph is dead, and Benjamin alone is left. If harm should befall him there, you will bring my grey hair down to Sheol in sorrow.' He shook his head and, as if to himself, whispered, 'He shall not go.'

Notes

1. *Although specific pharaohs are named elsewhere in Scripture (e.g. Jeremiah 44:30 refers to Pharaoh Hophna and Jeremiah 46:2 to Pharaoh Necho), the practice of Egyptian rulers was not to name their enemies in their written records. Traditionally, Moses has been considered as the main author of Genesis-Deuteronomy. Having been brought up in an Egyptian court, he could be expected to follow the same practice, hence the lack of any specific name for Pharaoh (in both this story and that of the Exodus).*

2. *Without specific, historical references in the story, it is impossible to associate it for definite with any specific pharaoh. However, dating within the Bible itself (see notes in Chapter (7) below) may point to Joseph serving under two different rulers.*

3. *There is some debate as to whether the title of vizier is appropriate. However, because it is historically feasible (and a vizier was like a prime minister), it is a convenient term to use here.*

4. *It is unusual for rains to fail in both the Levant and Sudan (where the Nile rises), but this particular drought obviously affected all of that region of the world.*

5. *More detail is given in Genesis 43:7 about their first audience with the vizier, and this has been incorporated into this chapter.*

6. *We don't know which of the brothers found the silver on the way home (Genesis 42:27). But 'One of them…' could easily be applied to Asher (as the least of them and one who probably would not to be named).*

7. *The Bible does not describe the brothers being held in custody separately. But if they had been held together, then surely they would already have had their conversation about being*

punished. Being separated would also mean that they would know more fully how Joseph must have felt. See also the note below.

8. *Although prisons were rare in the ancient world (there is nothing, for example, in Old Testament law about prison sentences for any crime), Egypt is known to have had them. An Egyptian papyrus (from roughly the time of Joseph) speaks of Egyptian prisons and indicates that they could have both 'cell-blocks', similar to a modern prison, and 'barracks' for larger numbers of prisoners who were forced labourers for the government.*

6

'God has uncovered your servants' guilt.' (Genesis 44:16)

'We should have returned sooner,' muttered Levi, as the landscape around them became dotted with palm trees once again. The Egyptian city came into view in the distance, shimmering in the haze above the sandy ground, silvered by the heat of the sun. He and Simeon were two of a kind, and of all of them, he had missed their brother most keenly in the months since they had returned from Egypt.

'We didn't have a choice,' said Judah. 'Father has only let Benjamin come now the grain has run out. To persist in refusing would have meant watching him starve.'

'And not only him,' added Asher quietly.

Judah's persuasion and his personal guarantee of Benjamin's safety had finally allowed their return to Egypt, and Jacob's final words echoed in Asher's mind: *May God Almighty grant you mercy before the man...* The words had become his frequent prayer on the journey down.

Asher stared at Benjamin as he walked alongside Reuben ahead of them, both leading their donkeys. He prayed silently once more. *Have mercy, Yahweh. Save us from disaster. Although we deserve it, Benjamin doesn't.* He knew their father would not survive his loss.

The petitioners' line in the granary was moving slower than the sun across the sky. But Benjamin seemed

313

fascinated by every sight and sound of the unfamiliar land, and stared at the vizier as Asher had previously done. Asher's mouth felt as dry as a wadi in summer, and the sweat on his palms had nothing to do with the heat of the morning. He fingered his pouch once again—this time holding twice the amount of silver, not only to buy grain but also to repay what they had found in their sacks. They also each carried a gift for the vizier from the produce of Canaan and beyond.

As their knees and foreheads once more touched the earth before the vizier's dais, Asher barely dared breathe. *Would they be accused of stealing the silver? Surely they were about to face either death or salvation.*

But Asher was wrong. When the command to stand was given, they waited nervously to be addressed, but it was not to them that the vizier spoke. After staring at them for some moments, he called another official to him, and gave orders, pointing at them as he did so. Before they had any chance to petition the ruler or present their gifts, they found themselves being ushered out of the huge hall by the official. But this time they were not being directed by the heads of spears.

'I am the steward over the house of Zaphenath-Paneah,' began the Egyptian, as they reached the area outside where they had tethered their animals. He spoke their language but with a heavy accent. 'At noon, you are to eat dinner with him. Follow me, and bring your donkeys.' They complied; they had no choice.

As they followed the steward through the streets of the city, they silently exchanged looks of bewilderment and fear. Asher began to wonder if it would be a better idea to mount their donkeys and flee.

'This is because of the silver in our sacks,' said Gad so quietly only Asher could hear.

Asher nodded, and whispered back in a shaky voice, 'He must be taking us away from the crowds to attack us!' He could not think of one reason why the invitation would be genuine.

'He is only one and appears unarmed,' replied Gad, ashen. 'It will be different when we reach the vizier's house. There, we will be at their mercy. They'll take our donkeys and make us their slaves!'

'Shouldn't we try to escape?'

'Their chariots would outrun us…'

Asher fell silent. His lips continued to move, however, as, over and over, he repeated his father's prayer: *God Almighty, grant us mercy…*

An imposing two-storey brick house soon stood before them. But directly they stopped by the entrance, Judah nudged Reuben. 'Go now,' he whispered urgently. Reuben hurried over to the steward, and began his petition, holding up his pouch of silver as he did and pointing back to them.

'He's explaining about the silver in the sacks,' said Judah under his breath. Asher waited, his mouth dry.

The steward suddenly turned and approached them all. He smiled. 'Your God, the God of your father, has given you treasure in your sacks. I received your silver.' With that he smiled again, turned, and disappeared into the house.

'How is that possible?' murmured Gad. No one even attempted to answer.

The hope born of the astonishment in Asher's heart only grew when the steward returned with Simeon. Levi was the first to embrace his brother. *Surely they would not restore Simeon if they intended them harm?* And Asher began to believe his prayer for mercy had been answered, though he knew it wasn't deserved. *But then again, wasn't that the nature of mercy?*

'Your donkeys will be taken care of,' continued the steward. 'Now come inside and refresh yourselves.' And taking their gifts for the vizier, they followed in silence.

Asher's bemusement swiftly melted into awe. He had never been in a building like it. The walls inside were smooth and plastered. Painted columns decorated with lotus flowers supported the roof, whilst the floor was covered in patterns made by coloured tiles. They were provided with stools to sit on in a courtyard, and with bowls, water and towels for washing their feet. They sat among pomegranate trees in huge earthenware pots, and unfamiliar red and blue flowers. The water in Asher's bowl was deliciously cool, though it did not remain clear for long, as his feet were relieved of a long journey's dust. They said little, conscious of the presence of servants, even though the steward had, for the moment, left them. And when they did speak, it was in hushed tones.

'You look well,' said Levi to Simeon. 'Were you kept here?'

Simeon nodded. 'It was not like the prison we were in before, though. There was a window high up in the cell wall, and sufficient food. I was allowed to wash.' He paused, and then added, simply, 'It was not terrible.' He went on, 'Besides, there are a few slaves here who speak in our tongue.'

There was another short pause—a pause in which the memory of Joseph flitted through Asher's mind. *He could not be the only one thinking of him.* The shadow passed.

Simeon continued. 'And they told me about the house when they brought me food and water.' An expression of wonder lit up his face. 'It has over thirty rooms! There are separate areas for the master, for his family—he has two sons—and for his guests. The house even has rooms for bathing in.' Simeon glanced around and lowered his voice even more. 'And for relieving yourself, if you can believe it!' It was a long time since Asher had seen such a grin on a brother's face. He continued, 'They say there is also a spacious garden laid out behind the house, with a large pool surrounded by palm trees, and with vines, shrubs and flowers. They say they have never seen its like.'

'But we have been told,' said Levi, 'that we are all to eat here at noon with the vizier. Why would he do that?'

'Eat with him?' exclaimed Simeon, incredulous. 'Do not ask me to explain it. I have not even seen the man since I was taken from you all.'

'Whatever the customs of Egypt, it seems he means us no harm,' said Reuben.

Judah nodded, casting his gaze around their gracious surroundings. 'I see no guards with spears.' And then he added softly, 'You do not wash men's feet before you kill them.'

They shared such news as they had with Simeon until the sun stood nearly overhead in the courtyard. 'It will be noon shortly,' said Judah. 'We should prepare ourselves and the gifts we have brought.' The responsibility that he was bearing for Benjamin before their father seemed to have stirred him to lead. 'It will be better if the gifts are divided between us.'

Levi nodded, 'They seem paltry enough as it is amongst this grandeur.'

Asher found himself carrying a bowl of almonds, whilst Gad carried pistachios. Others held jars of balm and honey, whilst the eldest bore the valuable myrrh and spices, bought from caravans from the east passing near Kiriath Arba. There was not, however, time for him to become nervous again. Almost as soon as they had arranged themselves, the steward reappeared and they followed him once more in awed silence.

The room into which they were led through carved wooden doors was even more lavish. Its plastered walls were decorated with colourful murals. The ceiling was supported by more painted pillars, covered with the strange Egyptians characters used for writing. Asher briefly wondered what tales were being told or which gods praised. Depictions of palm leaves, vibrant blue scarabs and bright yellow suns were scattered among the symbols, and painted lotus buds and flowers embellished both walls and pillars.

Although others also appeared to have been invited to the meal, Asher's eyes were quickly drawn to the vizier. A woman stood near him, dressed in fine white linen, which hung in soft folds from her shoulders to her ankles. He assumed her to be his wife. She also wore a black wig, though hers was longer, and a gold and blue neck collar and other jewellery adorned her. By her side stood two boys, whom Asher took to be his sons. They wore white linen skirts like their father, but their heads were shaved, apart from a woven braid of dark black hair which hung to one side. Asher judged them to be around eight and five.

The official at the vizier's side invited them to approach him. After presenting the gifts—which were swiftly passed into the care of servants—they bowed to the ground, until their heads were touching the cool, coloured tiles. Once on their feet again, the vizier spoke directly to them, his tone gracious and kind. He studied each one of them as his words were translated. 'How is your aged father of whom you spoke? Is he still living?'

'Yes, my lord,' replied Judah. 'Your servant our father is still alive and well.'

The vizier turned his eyes on Benjamin. 'Is this your youngest brother—the one you told me about?'

'Yes, my lord,' said Judah.

'God be gracious to you, my son.' The words were scarcely translated, however, before the vizier—without a word—hurried from the room. Asher found the uneasy silence that followed almost unbearable. He dared not look at his brothers—let alone speak to them—for fear of causing offence, though he longed for a reason for the inexplicable departure. His eyes darted around all he could see without turning his head. The younger of the boys turned his face upwards to his mother and spoke with the tone of a question. Whatever her answer, the boy seemed satisfied, and returned to staring at them all with obvious and unabashed curiosity.

The uncomfortable silence continued for some time, and was only broken by the eventual sound of the door opening, heralding the vizier's return. He swiftly gave some instructions to his steward, which were the signal for the meal to begin. As the vizier and his family took their seats at a table facing their guests, the steward approached them, indicating a table nearby. 'It is our custom,' he began, 'to eat at separate tables.' Which Asher took to mean that Egyptians would not eat with foreigners. He did not blame them. In their presence he felt as refined as a goat's turd. 'Come this way,' the steward continued, leading them towards a long, lower table, whose stools all faced the table of vizier. A servant was already lighting cones of fat along the table, from which floral scents began to rise. 'Please—sit here,' said the steward to Reuben, indicating the stool at one end. He then nodded to Simeon. 'And here,' directing him to the next stool. When Levi followed, Asher felt the hairs on his nape beginning to bristle, and when Judah and Dan were fourth and fifth he turned to Gad, who seemed as astonished as he was. *They were being seated according to their age! How could the Egyptians possibly know that?* After Napthali and Gad, Asher was shown to the eighth stool. Issachar, Zebulun and finally Benjamin, at the far end, completed the table.

Asher glanced around. *They were all astounded.* He looked towards the table of the vizier, but swiftly looked away when he realised he was looking in their direction. 'How do they know the order of our birth?' he whispered to Gad.

'Maybe Simeon told them,' he said, and then turned to Naphtali to pass the question along the line.

A few moments later, the reply came back. 'Simeon swears he didn't tell them,' whispered Gad back to Asher. The mystery remained.

But soon none of them cared, as the flow of food and beer began. The vizier's table was laden with the privileged fat of a drought-stricken land. Joints of roasted ox, and of duck and goose. Pots of stewed lamb, and plates of grilled fish. Vegetable dishes of long-shooted green onions, garlic and celery. Breads made from wheat and flavoured with coriander. Food was brought to them from his table, and the only other mystery to them was why Benjamin's portions were five times the size of their own. But there was more than ample for all, and any puzzlement was short-lived, drowned in the flow of beer from cups that were only ever empty for the short time it took for a servant to refill them. Musicians played harps, lutes and tambourines as they ate. In any season, it would have been an exceptional feast. But after months of meagre, famine-wrought meals, it was beyond extraordinary.

'You must learn how to make these, Asher!' exclaimed Gad as he took another bite of a cake baked with dates and sweetened with honey. Platters had been brought to their table piled with sweet breads made with fruit, and bowls of dates, pomegranates, figs and grapes.

Asher smiled. He was too full of beer to be bothered to reply. *At least the famine in Canaan could be forgotten for a day.*

Asher's head throbbed. The morning had come too quickly for his liking, as had the time of their departure. He opened his mouth to say to Gad, *My head hasn't felt this bad since…* but shut his mouth suddenly as he remembered the occasion. It had been twenty three years earlier, when his youngest brother's foot had woken him. *Had it really been that long?* Time had done nothing to dull his memory of the events of that year.

Their host had provided them with a large room for the night, and shortly after dawn, they were sent on their way with as much food as they could carry. Their mood could not have been more jubilant as they led their donkeys through the city streets and out through its gate. Asher could scarcely believe their good fortune. *They had kept Benjamin safe, Simeon had been returned to them, and they had enough grain to last them months—with no reason now not to return to Egypt if the famine outlasted the grain. Their trip could not have gone better.*

'Who are they?' asked Naphtali suddenly. Asher glanced over his shoulder and back towards the city, and suddenly felt his stomach twist into a tight knot. For what he saw looked very much like the vizier's chief steward, riding on a chariot towards them, accompanied by a band of guards.

Gad called out sharply to those at the front. 'Reuben, Judah!' He had also seen the approach of the Egyptians. In a moment, all had stopped and were facing the city with apprehension.

'What do they want?' murmured Judah as he joined them.

'We will find out soon enough,' replied Dan.

Asher's heartbeat quickened, and he found himself praying again for Yahweh's mercy. *What wrong had they possibly committed?*

All fell silent as the chariot reached them. The steward reined the horses to a halt, his face stern. A sense of foreboding arose within Asher, and the guards forming a circle around them deepened his dread.

'Why have you repaid good with evil?' began the steward harshly. 'The cup you have stolen—is it not the one my master uses for drinking and for divination?' He glared at them all. 'This is a wicked thing you have done!'

'Why do you accuse us like this, my lord?' protested Judah. 'Your servants would not do such a thing!'

'We even brought back the silver we found in our sacks, my lord,' said Reuben. 'I offered it back to you, but you would not take it. So why would we steal silver or gold from your master's house?'

'You may search all we have,' continued Judah, sweeping his arm across them all in invitation. 'If any of us, your servants, is found to have it, he will die—and the rest of us will become my lord's slaves.'

The steward nodded. 'Very well. Let it be as you say. But only the one who has taken it will be my slave—the rest of you will be free from blame and free to go.'

Judah went to his donkey, unstrapped the sack of grain, and began lowering it to the ground. They all followed his lead. Asher knew that none of them would have taken the cup, even if they had had the opportunity, which he was sure that they hadn't. But he remembered how their silver had mysteriously appeared in their sacks before—and his breathing became ragged.

The steward started with Reuben's sack, and—as at the feast—searched the sacks in the order of their ages. Asher looked aghast, as the steward held up a small pouch that clearly contained coins from the mouth of Reuben's sack. But the steward seemed unconcerned; he replaced the pouch and moved onto Simeon. Another pouch was found, but no cup. He continued along the line, finding pouches in every sack, but acting as if the silver was theirs. Asher barely dared to breath as he came to the eighth sack—*his sack*. The steward rummaged through the grain, recovered yet another pouch of silver, but soon gave a little grunt and moved on to Issachar's sack. By the time he reached Benjamin and the last sack, Asher was beginning to breath freely again. *The silver was—like the previous time—a mystery, but it had all been a dreadful mistake about the cup.* But Judah's cry of anguish instantly drove any relief from Asher's breast, as the steward held up an ornate silver cup. Judah tore his tunic in grief. They all did.

'I did not take it! I swear!' implored Benjamin, terrified.

'You will all return to the city to hear my master's judgment,' replied the steward sternly. They had no choice but to obey.

The vizier was with his attendants in the room in which they had feasted the previous afternoon. They threw themselves on the ground before him, awaiting his words. Asher felt the cool, unyielding tiles beneath him. *Yahweh! Why do you bring this disaster on us?* But the answer had been etched on his heart for twenty-three years.

A harsh command was given in Egyptian, and they were told to stand. Every eye in the room was upon them. Asher glanced briefly at Benjamin. He was pale and his eyes were darting in all directions. *He was only in his twenty-fifth year. They could not abandon him!* Asher silently cried out once more to heaven for mercy, but he did not see any mercy in the face of the ruler as he spoke, and he waited fearfully for the words to be translated.

'What is this you have done? Do you not know that a man like me can find things out by divination?'

It was Judah, with the responsibility for Benjamin's safety, who replied. 'What can we say? How can we prove our innocence? God has uncovered your servants' guilt.' And the guilt had a name: *Joseph.* His brother continued, 'We are now my lord's slaves—we ourselves and the one who was found to have the cup.'

As the vizier spoke again, Asher knew that Judah's words were fitting. *They were standing together—with Benjamin. They had abandoned their father's favourite once. They would not do so a second time.*

'Far be it from me,' began the vizier's words, 'to do such a thing! Only the man who was found to have the cup will become my slave. The rest of you, go back to your father in peace.'

Judah stepped forward towards the vizier, pain in his eyes. 'Please, my lord, let your servant speak. Do not be angry with your servant, though you are the equal of Pharaoh himself.' Judah paused to allow his words to be conveyed to the ruler.

Asher's heart was pounding. *Please, Yahweh. Let him be heard!* And it seemed as if his desperate prayer had been answered when the Egyptian nodded.

And so Judah began to tell the story of their father's love for Benjamin and for his lost brother, stopping after every painful truth for his words to be translated. He spoke of how Jacob had not wanted Benjamin to go to Egypt, fearing his loss, and how returning without him would send their father to the grave in sorrow. He told how he had guaranteed Benjamin's safety to Jacob. *Judah, out of all of them, knew the pain of losing sons.*

Asher's eyes were fixed on the vizier—longing to see some sign of understanding, of compassion, of mercy. But his expression remained inscrutable.

Judah held out his arms to the vizier, offering himself. 'Please let your servant remain here as my lord's slave in place of the boy, and let him return with his brothers.' He paused for the interpreter once more, and then added, 'How can I go back to my father if the boy is not with me?

No! Do not let me see the misery that would come upon my father.'

To Asher's utter amazement, the ruler did not wait for the translation, his face suddenly contorting in pained desperation. He cried out some words, and before Asher even had time to fear their meaning, every servant was scurrying out, closing all doors behind them. Judah backed away to stand with them, and they all looked at each other in utter bewilderment, too stunned to even voice their confusion. But the sound of weeping instantly drew them back to the vizier. Asher stared, dumfounded, at the Egyptian. Deep sobs wracked his whole being, carrying the black lines around his eyes down his cheeks in his tears. He appeared to be trying to say something, but could scarcely breathe enough to form the words. But when they finally came, they needed no translating.

'I am Joseph!' He gasped, struggling for air. 'Is my father still living?'

But no one replied. Asher felt only terror. *How could this be Joseph?* And the memories of all they had done to their brother came tumbling into his mind once more.

Each of them froze—all as still and silent as the columns around the room.

But the man—the man who now unbelievably, shockingly, alarmingly, appeared to be Joseph—spoke again, beckoning them towards him. 'Come close to me.' Asher edged hesitantly forward with the rest, fearful, open-mouthed and staring. 'I *am* your brother Joseph, the one you sold into Egypt!' And Asher finally saw, within the shaven, tear-stained and black-streaked face, familiar eyes.

Asher suddenly glanced across at Benjamin. His expression was one of deep shock. *Not only was he meeting the brother he had scarcely known and had thought was dead, but he was finding lies exposed. Would he hate them too? And what if Joseph wanted revenge? They were in his power!*

'Don't be distressed or angry with yourselves for selling me here,' continued Joseph, expressing perfectly the feelings that were now churning within Asher's heart. A smile was beginning to spread across Joseph's face, and his reddened eyes became bright. 'It was to save lives that God sent me ahead of you!' He continued, 'For two years now there has been famine in the land, and for the next five years there will no harvests. But God sent me ahead of you to save you.' He paused, looking around at them all with a face full of joy. 'Don't you see? It was not *you* who sent me here but God. He made me father to Pharaoh, lord of his entire household and ruler of all Egypt. It is all *His* doing!'

Asher could barely take in the words that were falling upon his ears—as unbelievable as snow in the midst of summer heat. The truth was almost too great, too profound—*yes, too good*—for Asher to grasp. *This was all the doing of Yahweh? But how could Joseph say that? Even if it were true, their actions had been evil.* Joseph's words washed over him, as he stared at his brother. And a distant memory stirred in him. A memory of sheaves and stars in a dream bowing down. *They had come true!* Although those dreams had been relayed with arrogance and received with anger, Asher knew that the man who stood before them now was not that Joseph. *And they were not those brothers.* They had all changed. And the figure who was speaking suddenly came into sharp focus again.

'…and bring my father down here quickly.' Joseph stopped speaking, and then stepped forward to Benjamin, threw his arms around him and sobbed. And the other son of his mother embraced Joseph, weeping.

'But how did you find us in Dothan?' asked Simeon, amazed. 'We were supposed to be in Shechem.' They were sitting around Joseph's table, but now it was laden again with bread, meats, dishes of fruit and platters of sweet cakes and fruit-rich breads. There were jugs of beer on the table, but this time they served themselves. The servants had been dismissed and they were alone. And Joseph was telling his story.

'I was searching for you near Shechem,' answered Joseph. 'But a man asked me who I was looking for—and he had overheard you talking about where you were going. It was the hand of Yahweh guiding me!' He paused, but then drew a curtain over the crime that followed. 'Once in Egypt, I was bought by the captain of Pharaoh's guard—his name was Potiphar. But the hand of the Almighty was on me again, and I prospered there. I learned the language, and, in time, I was put in charge of his household and all he owned. And Yahweh blessed everything he had.' A shadow passed across Joseph's face. 'But his wife wanted me to lie with her. I did all I could to resist her, but one day she caught me alone. I had to flee from her, and she then accused me of trying to force myself on her.' None of the brothers spoke as Joseph paused. 'Her accusations should have brought me death, but I was put in prison instead. Maybe Potiphar didn't believe her. I do not know. But I *do* know Yahweh was with me.' And much to Asher's surprise, Joseph smiled. 'I could not have seen, however, how Yahweh was going to use those years in the dungeon.'

Years! Asher was stunned. He had found three days in prison difficult enough. And yet there was no hint of bitterness in Joseph's words. And still they listened in silence.

'The Lord blessed me again, and the prison warder eventually put me in charge of all those held there. And the Lord brought across my path two servants of Pharaoh. They both had dreams, the meaning of which was given to me by God for them. One was restored to the position of Pharaoh's cupbearer. I asked him to mention me to Pharaoh, as I was innocent of any crime. But he forgot and two more years passed.'

Asher drew in a breath sharply, but it went unnoticed.

'But then Pharaoh was troubled by dreams which none of his advisers could interpret,' continued Joseph, 'and the cupbearer finally spoke of me to him, suggesting that I could help. I was brought before Pharaoh, and Yahweh revealed to me that his dreams foretold seven years of plenty followed by seven years of famine. But Yahweh also gave me wisdom to know what should be done. And because of that, Pharaoh put me in charge of the whole land of Egypt. The seven years of abundance came soon, and now we have had two years of the famine. There will be five more years. And that is why my father and your families must now join me here in Egypt. I will give you the best of the grazing land in Egypt, not far from where I am in the Royal Courts, and you will have plenty.' He voice suddenly became triumphant. 'Yahweh has woven the threads of many stories together to fulfil his purposes. And this—' He reached out and took the hands of Benjamin and Judah who were nearest to him. '—has been His plan from the start. God has blessed me, as you can see. And now He has multiplied my joy by restoring you to me.' Joseph smiled at them once more, with no hint of bitterness, and then concluded, 'Only one more thing will make that joy complete—to see my father again.'

And when Joseph sent them on their journey back to Canaan, with carts for their families to return in, he bade them farewell with a smile on his face. And there was a glint in his eye, as he added: 'Don't quarrel on the way.'

Notes

1. *We don't know how long Joseph was in prison for—only that the total time in Potiphar's service and jail is approximately 13 years. He is seventeen when he is tending the flocks with his brothers in Genesis 37:2 (presumably shortly before the incident later in the chapter when he is sold into slavery), and is thirty when he enters Pharaoh's service (Genesis 41:46).*
2. *Joseph will only have learned that Reuben didn't consent to his being sold into slavery on the first visit of the brothers to Egypt, when he hears Reuben remonstrating with them.*
3. *Joseph's actions remind the brothers of their former sins. He forces them to relive their past, in putting them in prison and threatening them with slavery. He tests them by giving them the opportunity to do to Benjamin what they did to him—to abandon their father's favourite and serve only themselves.*
4. *The references to Joseph's cup being used for divination may simply be to put pressure on the brothers, rather than implying that this was something Joseph practised.*
5. *Nomads like Jacob and his family would not normally own carts, hence Joseph's provision of these for the children and wives on the long journey.*

7

*Now the Israelites settled in Egypt in the region of
Goshen. They acquired property there and were fruitful
and increased greatly in number. (Genesis 47:27)*

Jacob ran his fingers over the rough stones, as he leaned
on his staff. 'My father, Isaac, built this altar here in
Beersheba.' He seemed, for a moment, distant, as if
recalling a life long past. He tore his gaze away from the
pile of stones that had once formed a square, and looked
at his sons. After the news about Joseph, Asher had seen
the years roll off his father like a heavy winter's fleece at
shearing. He was free at last from the grief that had both
aged him and weighed him down for more than a score
of years. Jacob continued, 'Yahweh appeared to my father
here and spoke to him. I watched him sacrifice to the God
of his father, Abraham.' He paused for a moment, casting
his eyes upwards, his brow furrowed. 'That must be nigh
on a hundred years ago.' He looked at them all again. 'And
now, today, we will restore the altar, and sacrifice again to
Yahweh, the God of Israel, as we prepare to leave the land
He promised to Abraham and his descendants—the land
He has promised to us.'

Ten pairs of hands soon had the heavy stones back in
place, as Jacob and Benjamin went to inspect the flocks
and pick the choicest animals for the offering. The task
complete, Asher paused, breathing heavily from the

exertion, and studied the landscape. Beersheba was at the southern border of Canaan and usually fairly dry anyway. Now, in the drought, it was little better than a desert. *Would they ever see this promised land again?* He didn't know. But the hand of Yahweh was on their family. The God who had once felt as distant as the stars, now seemed closer, like a mountain on the horizon—beyond the immediate reach of an arm, but unmistakably there.

The following morning dawned with another cloudless sky. Before they left, however, Jacob gathered everyone around him. Asher stood with Ijona, their four sons and daughter. Serah was by now a beautiful eight-year-old, and, despite the passing of the years, she remained Jacob's only granddaughter amongst the fifty or so grandchildren. The young among them shuffled and squirmed, their eyes drifting around as Asher's had done almost thirty-five years earlier, when Jacob had addressed his much smaller family, as they had prepared to leave Harran for the land of Canaan.

'Last night, God appeared to me in a vision,' began Jacob. The shuffling and murmuring ceased. The eyes of all but the youngest were upon him. 'He spoke to me, telling me not to be afraid to go down to Egypt. He said that He will be with us and will surely bring us back again. But that may not be for some generations. For the God of my fathers also told me that, in Egypt, He will make this family into a great nation. And finally He assured me of my dearest wish—that my own son Joseph will close my eyes when my days on this earth are at an end.' Jacob paused, casting his eyes over each of his sons as they stood with their families. Asher was, as always, last. But he didn't mind. For his father's words had finally answered the question that had haunted him for so many years. *The sons of the maids were not going to be sent away. They would be counted among the sons of Israel.* 'So now,' concluded Jacob, 'we will leave this land with Yahweh's blessing.'

Once more, they followed the Way of Shur towards Egypt, though their progress was slower than before, with loaded carts and herds of livestock. Jacob sent Judah ahead of them to Joseph for directions. Joseph had told them they would live in the land of Goshen. It was the eastern region of the wide fertile land, where the mighty Nile river spread out to the east and west, dividing into a number of smaller rivers which carried its waters into the Great Sea to the north. But where exactly they should go was unclear.

Asher watched Judah's departure. *It was strange that the one who now had their father's trust and respect was the very person who had suggested selling Joseph into slavery. Not that Jacob knew that—or the part they had all played in his captivity.* Joseph had insisted before they'd left Egypt that he would be the one to tell his father, understanding more fully than any, the hand of Yahweh in all that had happened.

Asher suddenly felt a hand thrust into his own. He looked down to find Serah at his side, happily swishing the hem of her tunic around her knees, as she twisted this way and that, in the way that his boys had never done.

'Are you tired of sitting in a cart?' asked Asher, raising an eyebrow.

'I'm tired of the boys!'

Asher smiled. 'And so you have decided to walk with your father for a while?'

She nodded, and then her brow furrowed. 'The boys aren't always very nice.' She paused. 'Sometimes they even throw stones at the sheep.'

'Really?' replied Asher, feigning surprise. He then added after a moment, 'Not the goats?'

'No, they throw stones at the goats as well,' she replied, adding solemnly, 'I would never do that.'

'I'm sure you wouldn't, my little princess,' said Asher, suppressing a chuckle. 'I'm sure you wouldn't.'

Asher stopped and cast his eyes around their new home. Gone were the hills with which they were familiar. In their place was flat, open ground, close to the most easterly of the rivers into which the Nile had divided. Although the earth was dusty, palm trees were scattered liberally across the landscape. If it had not been for the drought, Asher was sure the land would have been green and lush. But whilst crops might for now struggle, the deeper rooted bushes would still provide some grazing, and there was grain for the animals if the grazing failed. The river, though low, could still provide water for the animals. *Their lives would be easier here.*

'We might not have to move our flocks much, if at all, during the year,' said Gad, as he came alongside Asher.

'Is my brother considering the comforts of life in a house in his old age?' asked Asher, with a sly smile.

'Do not mock me!' retorted Gad, folding his arms and adopting the stance of the firstborn. 'You will always be only a year younger than your brother!' He paused and gazed around. 'Still, it is a thought. If we are not moving with the herds, it might not harm to have buildings of our own.'

Asher glanced over to their carts, which had also stopped. He watched as their father was helped down from a cart. 'He almost has the air of a child,' said Gad. 'His eyes dart this way and that in wonder.'

Asher smiled. 'He looks for Joseph.'

'From what Judah said, he will not have much longer to wait.'

They were still erecting their tents when Serah called out, 'Look, Father!' Still with a mallet and tent peg in his hands, Asher turned and immediately saw the reason for her cry. A cloud of dust was rising from the ground to the south-west. It was clear that others were coming towards them, and that it wasn't by foot. Asher raised fingers to his lips, and gave a shrill whistle, gaining the attention of the others at their tents nearby. Soon the whole family—over seventy of them—were standing together, watching the approach of Joseph. His chariot was flanked by mounted guards and men whom Asher assumed to be his brother's servants—or some of them. And at the front of those who waited stood Jacob: leaning on his staff, but standing tall, for the arrival of Rachel's firstborn.

The driver brought the chariot to a halt several paces from Jacob, and Joseph stepped out from under the shade held aloft by another servant. He was still dressed as an Egyptian prince, and as Jacob had never seen him. But it was as if their father did not notice. There was no hesitation. Father and son embraced, holding each other and weeping, as the unspent tears of prolonged grief spilled out with those of joy. And when they finally stood apart, it was Jacob who spoke first. 'Now I am ready to die, since I have seen for myself that you are still alive.'

Asher could scarcely believe he had been chosen to appear before Pharaoh. Ijona had washed the new clothing that Joseph had given him (as to all his brothers) when first reunited. Asher had never had clothes made from linen, and they were much finer—in every sense—than anything he had ever possessed. Ijona had also trimmed his beard and hair, and had scolded him when she had still found dirt beneath his fingernails, despite his best efforts at washing thoroughly.

'I think you will now not shame me,' said Ijona, looking him up and down.

'My sons will not recognise me,' replied Asher, as he smoothed the long, white linen tunic. He had to admit, however, it was much cooler and more comfortable than his usual woollen clothes. 'And my brothers will probably laugh at what you have done to me.'

'Make no mistake,' said Ijona, with the air of one who knows she is right, 'Hezaqa, Egla and Ijasaka will be ensuring that their husbands do not shame them either, and Tamar will take care of Judah.' She paused, adjusting the belt around his waist. She then stood back, scrutinising him for a final time. Satisfied, she then stated, 'Joseph has chosen carefully and fairly.'

'How so?'

Ijona rolled her eyes. 'That your mind still wanders far and wide is no wonder to me. The wonder is that it so rarely strays into the land of perception.' Asher grunted, and Ijona continued, 'In picking brothers to appear with your father before Pharaoh, he has chosen his brother,

Benjamin, as all would expect. But has also chosen two sons of Leah—Judah and Issachar—'

'Ones who have not incurred the displeasure of their father…'

Ijona nodded. 'And he has chosen the oldest son of Bilhah and the youngest son of Zilpah—you.' She waited for him to acknowledge—and agree with—her thoughts. He gave a grudging nod. 'And now it is time for you to go.'

Asher leant over and kissed his wife. 'I will try not to disgrace you.'

'Then leave any speaking to Judah,' she replied with a smile and with folded arms.

If Joseph's house had been grand, it was nothing compared to the palace of Pharaoh. Although still built from brick, and with walls similarly graced with colourful paintings and symbols, its scale was vast and its servants numerous. Jacob leant on Joseph's arm as he led them towards the heart of the palace through long, cool halls, tall columns lining their way with carved lotus flowers and leaves sprouting at their tops. Their new soft leather sandals barely made a sound on the tiles that dazzled with their colourful patterns. And once again, Jacob's face was one of child-like wonder.

'Don't forget what I told you,' said Joseph, lowering his voice and turning his head to face them, as he finally stopped outside a large wooden door, flanked by guards. 'Pharaoh is well-educated and will likely speak to you in our language. When he asks, tell him you are shepherds. Egyptians detest them, and Pharaoh will then be happy for you to live apart in Goshen.' He waited for them to take in his words before turning to the front again. He nodded to the guards who opened the doors.

The audience with Pharaoh largely passed in an over-awed blur for Asher. He couldn't help marvelling at the striking blue-and-gold striped nemes covering the ruler's head, and the gold cobra that stared out at them from his forehead. As Ijona had suggested, he left all speaking to others. It was only when Jacob was presented and Pharaoh's attention was no longer on them that he breathed more freely.

'How old are you?' Pharaoh asked Jacob.

'The years of my pilgrimage are a hundred and thirty,' answered Jacob. 'My years have been few and difficult, and they do not equal the years of the pilgrimage of my fathers.'

Asher studied the face of the ruler. *Was he imagining it, or was Pharaoh in awe of his father?*

Whatever the truth, it was Jacob who blessed Pharaoh before they left his presence. 'May God give you of heaven's dew and of earth's richness,' finished Jacob, 'an abundance of grain and new wine.'

And after the doors were closed behind them, and they were retracing their steps, Asher overheard Joseph saying to Jacob, 'It was a fitting blessing.'

His father smiled as he turned towards Joseph. 'Words with which my father, Isaac, blessed me. And Pharaoh will indeed be blessed by the God of Abraham, Isaac and Jacob.'

'Joseph's words were true,' said Gad, before taking a mouth of fruit-laden bread. Asher had baked it to finish the evening meal they were sharing with some of their

338

family. Lights in little clay lamps flickered around them, as they reclined together at the front of their largest tent.

'Which ones?' asked Asher.

But Gad's mind had been diverted by the sweet, cake-like bread, filled with dates. 'This is your best effort so far,' he said contentedly, leaving Asher's question hanging.

'Your father said much the same thing about the bread,' said Ijona smiling.

'It is true,' added Maka smiling. 'Jacob cannot get enough of Asher's treats.'

'Ha! Are you stealing our father's favour in his old age?' joked Gad, before taking another generous bite.

Asher grinned, deepening the creases around his eyes. 'I would not dream of it.'

Gad paused to swallow the rest of his mouthful before speaking again. 'Your baking may soon be as good as that of Joseph's house. It has only taken you ten years!' he added with a laugh.

'That's your last,' warned Ijona, as the hand of her second grandchild slid towards the wooden platter in the centre of the rugs on which the two families were seated. Malkiel, the younger son of Beriah, had already taken two pieces of the sweet treat.

'You still haven't answered my question,' said Asher. 'Which of Joseph's words do you refer to?'

'When we first arrived,' continued Gad, 'he told us that Egyptians detested shepherds.' His hair now showed flecks of grey, as did the head of Asher. 'Whether it is because of the animals we tend, or because those in houses mistrust those who dwell in tents, I do not know. But they stay away from us.'

'We have known that for a long time,' replied Asher. 'You tell us nothing new!'

'But I have been thinking,' said Gad. 'Maybe it is part of Yahweh's plan.' All the brothers spoke of their father's God far more than they did in their youth.

'Meaning?' asked Maka.

'Yes, please explain, Uncle!' said Beriah. Asher's fourth son was sitting with his wife, in whose arms Malkiel was now restrained, with the youngster's brother, Heber, sitting cross-legged next to them.

'It has been—*what*?—five years since the famine ended, and yet we remain in Egypt—'

'As Father said we would,' interrupted Asher.

'Yes,' replied Gad. He then cast his eyes over to Beriah, and then to his own son Shuni, who had recently married Serah. 'But had we remained in Canaan, how could we be sure our sons and daughters would not intermarry with the tribes living in that land, so that we became no different to them?'

'You are right,' said Ijona. 'After all, Judah married a Canaanite.'

'And Simeon lay with another who bore him Shaul,' said Maka.

Gad nodded. 'Though at least his wife was not of Canaan.' After a moment, he continued, 'Here we can become the nation that Yahweh promised our father. Separate from both Canaanites and Egyptians—the people of Jacob.'

Asher turned to his two grandsons. 'Do you know the other name that Yahweh gave to your great-grandfather?'

Heber answered. 'Israel.'

'That's right,' said Asher with a smile. 'We are the people of Israel.'

It was after seventeen years of living in Egypt that Asher received the summons he knew would one day come. In two years he would turn sixty, but he remained strong and his eyes were still sharp.

'Your father has called for you,' said Ijona as soon as he arrived back from tending the flocks one day. No explanation was needed. They all knew that Jacob, now only three years off a hundred and fifty, had been ill, and that his days were likely numbered.

Asher nodded. 'I will go immediately.'

Ijona handed him a skin of milk. 'Here, have a drink before you go.' As he lifted the skin to his lips, she went on. 'Joseph came to the camp with his sons earlier in the day to see Jacob. He is still here, and waiting for the rest of you to join him.'

After refreshing himself with the familiar, slightly sour-tasting milk, Asher handed it back, wiping the back of his hand across his mouth. 'He will have wanted Father's blessing on Manasseh and Ephraim.'

'Take this cake of figs,' she added, handing him the pressed fruit. 'You can eat it as you go.'

Asher soon found himself walking towards their father's tent with Gad, whose tents were near their own. 'Did you hear about Joseph's sons?' said Gad as they walked side by side.

'Only that they were taken in to Jacob,' replied Asher, taking a mouthful of the figs.

'Jacob has said that they will both be reckoned as *his* sons, and that in the future, the territory of Joseph's descendants will be under their names—Ephraim and Manasseh.'

Asher's brow furrowed, as he chewed over both Gad's words and the figs. He swallowed. 'So there will be a double portion for the descendants of Joseph.'

'Exactly. The right of the firstborn—the double portion—has gone to Joseph, not Reuben.'

'I suppose that should not be a surprise. Father has never forgotten the disrespect Reuben showed in lying with Bilhah.'

'But that's not all,' continued Gad. 'Jacob's blessing also put Ephraim before Manasseh—the younger above the elder.'

'As was the case for him and Esau,' said Asher. 'And with Father's blessing, it shall come to pass.' He then fell silent.

'What is it?' asked Gad, turning towards his brother.

'Will there be a blessing for the sons of the maids?' he murmured, and popped the rest of the cake in his mouth.

The twelve of them stood near the bed on which their father was sitting, supported by richly coloured pillows of fine Egyptian linen. His sight was failing and he called them closer. 'Gather round,' he said in a voice cracked by age, 'so that I can bless each of my sons, and tell you what will happen to you in the days to come.'

His father blessed the sons of Leah first, though not all his words would have been welcomed, especially by Reuben. 'Turbulent as the waters, you will no longer excel, for you went up onto your father's bed, onto my couch and defiled it.' Asher glanced at Jacob's firstborn— he could not meet their father's failing eyes. Simeon and

Levi's fury and violence had not been forgotten either, as Jacob turned his gaze onto the inseparable pair. 'I will scatter them in Jacob and disperse them in Israel.' But it was his father's words to Judah that left Asher both amazed and puzzled. That he now enjoyed his father's trust and favour was no secret, but the blessing was rich and wide. 'Judah, your brothers will praise you; your hand will be on the neck of your enemies; your father's sons will bow down to you...The sceptre will not depart from Judah, nor the ruler's staff from between his feet...'

Hadn't Yahweh given Joseph dreams of them all bowing down to him? And yet his father was now speaking of Judah as the one to whom his brothers would bow. But there was no time to ponder the words further as his father moved on—to Zebulun and then Issachar.

But Jacob's next blessings were not for Joseph and Benjamin. First and not last came blessings for each of the sons of the maids. He spoke of Dan providing justice, and of his brother, Gad, fighting back. *Hadn't he, in their childhood fights, always triumphed?*

But before blessing Naphtali, his father's watery eyes, with their loose lids, fell upon him. 'Asher's food will be rich; he will provide delicacies fit for a king.'

Asher smiled and his heart soared. *He was included. The descendants of the least of the sons of Jacob might not be rulers, but they would live well and be sought by those who held the sceptre.* And that was blessing enough for him.

The journey back to Canaan could not have been more different to their slow move to Egypt. Neither children nor their flocks were with them this time. Instead, the sons of Jacob were accompanied by court officials, Pharaoh's dignitaries and the whole of Joseph's Egyptian household. Chariots and horsemen led them and flanked them. Asher had never seen such a huge or exalted company. It would have honoured any king in his death, but it was all for his father.

On the day he had blessed them, he had also instructed them to bury his body in the tomb of Abraham. And after delivering his solemn charge, he had drawn his feet up onto the bed, breathed his last and died. Joseph had had his body embalmed so they could fulfil their father's wish, and return him to the land promised by God to Abraham and his descendants. Before they left, he was mourned for a period of seventy days by the Egyptians—only two days short of that for a pharaoh. And, after the dignified journey back to Canaan and to Kiriath Arba, they finally laid Jacob with Leah in the tomb of his fathers—the cave in the field of Machpelah that Abraham had bought from Ephron the Hittite, a hundred and seventy years earlier.

But the return journey to their tents in Egypt was not without dread. 'What if Joseph still bears us ill will?' began Levi, as the brothers walked together. Though he had been beside them as they had accompanied Jacob's body, Joseph was now in a chariot and going ahead of them with Benjamin.

It was a question that had also haunted Asher. *Might not Joseph's attitude towards them change now that their father had gone?* He knew Gad had similar fears.

'He might have shown favour to us for our father's sake,' said Zebulun. 'What if he now wants to pay us back? We are at his mercy in Egypt.'

The question hung in the air for several moments as they walked on in silence, the hills of southern Canaan once again disappearing behind them. Asher eyed the horsemen with spears who still flanked them. *One quick order could be the end of them all.*

'What if we speak to him in our father's name?' began Simeon hesitantly. 'Joseph would honour what was said, even if he was not sure it came from Jacob.'

'What do you mean?' asked Dan, staring at him.

It was Levi who continued however. 'We could say that Jacob asked him to forgive us for our sins against him…' There was another long silence. Asher did not like the idea of deliberately deceiving their brother. *But maybe their survival depended upon it.*

All had, in the end, reluctantly agreed to send a message to Joseph, written in the script of the Egyptians. All except Benjamin went together to his house, and presented the message to the chief steward whilst they waited outside.

It had been many years since Asher had felt fear. In their new home, they had lived under Joseph's protection. There had never been any worry over food or of attack. Egypt was strong, and its mighty army with its fast chariots was deterrent enough for any raiders who might seek to profit through force. *But now that same might could be used against them.* Neither he nor his nine brothers spoke as they waited for Joseph's response. It wasn't long in coming.

The steward dressed in the familiar white skirt came out to them. 'Please follow me,' he said. 'Zaphenath-Paneah will see you.' The Egyptian led them past a now familiar courtyard and through the house. Asher glanced at the symbols on the walls and columns that had once seemed so strange. Now he even knew what some of them meant. The steward opened a door for them, but did not follow them in. The door was closed behind them and they found Joseph standing alone.

Asher couldn't meet Joseph's eyes as they approached him. They all threw themselves down before him, as they had done seventeen years earlier, when the silver cup had been found in Benjamin's sack. And Judah uttered the same words as he had done then: 'We are your slaves.'

A small cry of pain came from the man who stood before them. Asher lifted his head, bemused. It was then that he saw the tear stains streaking his brother's face.

'Stand, my brothers,' said Joseph, in a gentle voice. 'Don't be afraid.' And Asher's fears began to drain away, like an autumn shower on thirsty ground. He clambered to his feet, his long linen tunic slightly clammy from his sweat. 'Am I in the place of God?' his brother continued. His face finally broke into a smile. 'Have you not understood yet? You intended to harm me, yes, but God intended it for good—to bring to pass all that is happening today, the saving of many lives.' Joseph held out his arms to them—in welcome, in reconciliation, in love. 'So do not be afraid.'

Asher stared up at the stars that filled the night sky, the tiny points of light shimmering like the innumerable reflections when the sun fell on ripples in the Nile. The sight filled him with a sense of wonder, the brighter stars forming the same patterns he had seen in his childhood in Harran, and then in the years in Canaan. *The stars were the same here, and so was Yahweh.* A sliver of moon hung low in the sky to the west. *There were so many wonders in the Creator's world.*

But then Asher thought of his life in Egypt, and he glanced around at the tents of Jacob, many of them gently illuminated by the oil lamps inside. And he knew, without a doubt, that the greatest wonder of all was the Creator Himself. The way He had worked through their terrible sin to bring undreamed-of good was beyond his ability to comprehend. He gazed up to the heavens once more in utter awe. And it felt to Asher, at that moment, as if the God of Abraham, Isaac and Jacob were looking down on him. The vast and mysterious God whose ways and purposes were beyond imagination beholding one whose path on the earth was like that of an ant. And yet he felt bathed in a Presence that knew him. *A God who noticed and blessed even Asher, the youngest son of the least important maid.*

He heard the swish of the tent flap behind him, and another presence made itself known beside him. 'Are you coming in?' asked Ijona in a soft voice. 'It is getting late.'

Asher took one last lingering look at the dark sky as peace filled his heart, and he let out a deep breath slowly. His hand found that of his wife. 'Yes,' he said, 'it is time to rest.'

Notes

1. *We don't know where Pharaoh or Joseph were based when his brothers come to Egypt. If, based on the datings below, it is assumed that Joseph was taken to Egypt around 1900 BC, it may be that Joseph was living in the new capital city that was founded during the Twelfth Dynasty, which lay between Memphis and Meidum, though its exact location is not known.*

2. *1 Kings 6:1 is an important reference for Old Testament chronology: 'In the four hundred and eightieth year after the Israelites came out of Egypt, in the fourth year of Solomon's reign over Israel...he began to build the temple of the LORD.' This dates the Exodus to 480 years before the fourth year of Solomon, which is widely accepted to be 966 BC. This places the Exodus around 1446 BC—the so-called Early Date for the Exodus. Exodus 12:40 states, 'Now the length of time the Israelite people lived in Egypt was 430 years,' (although there is some textual variation). This would put Jacob's arrival in Egypt 430 years before the Exodus, i.e. around 1876 BC. This dates the story of Joseph to the Middle Kingdom, rather than the Hyksos Period which is sometimes argued. He may, therefore, have served under two great rulers, Sesostris II (1897–1878 BC) and Sesostris III (1878–1843 BC).*

3. *The events of this chapter hold the key to determining Jacob's age in other parts of the story:*
   - *Jacob is 130 years old when he appears before Pharaoh on his arrival in Egypt (Genesis 47:9).*
   - *Joseph enters Pharaoh's service when he is thirty (Genesis 41:46).*
   - *The brothers arrive for the second time after two years of famine (Genesis 45:6), i.e. nine years after the years of*

abundance start, and Jacob comes to Egypt (aged 130) shortly after that.

- *Joseph's age on his father's arrival depends on how soon the seven years of abundance begin following Pharaoh's dream (Genesis 41:32). Here it is assumed it starts when Joseph is thirty-one (which might only be a few months later), making Joseph forty when his father is 130.*
- *Joseph is sold into slavery when he is seventeen (i.e. when Jacob is 107). Other dates can be worked backwards from this.*

4. *We don't know how Jacob is eventually told about the brothers' treachery. Here it is assumed that Joseph tells him.*

5. *It is not clear if Pharaoh is able to address Jacob and the brothers in their own tongue. It is assumed in the story that he speaks to them directly, and not through an interpreter.*

6. *How the brothers sent a message to Joseph after their father's death is not made clear. Presumably it would have been verbally, through an intermediary, or via a written letter. The latter has been chosen here.*

7. *It is not clear when the Israelites changed from tents to houses. Genesis 47:27 speaks of 'property', but this is likely to refer to possessions. However, they were certainly living in houses by the time of the Exodus (Exodus 12:7,13).*

8. *Leah may have been the unloved wife, but the kingly tribe of Judah came from her, as did the Levites (and hence the priesthood). She was the ancestor of Jesus, and she, rather than Rachel, lay in the family tomb with Jacob.*

9. *When the Promised Land is divided up after the conquest, portions of land go to the tribes of Ephraim and Manasseh rather than Joseph, as intended by Jacob. See below.*

10. *Reuben loses the rights of firstborn. 1 Chronicles 5:1 states: 'The sons of Reuben the firstborn of Israel (he was the firstborn,*

but when he defiled his father's marriage bed, his rights as firstborn were given to the sons of Joseph son of Israel)'. Also, no prophet, judge or king is ever recorded as coming from his tribe.

11. The blessing on Simeon and Levi included the words, 'I will scatter them in Jacob and disperse them in Israel.' This was fulfilled in different ways for the two tribes, with the Levites living in the Cities of Refuge scattered around the Promised Land, and Simeon's allocation being enclosed within the land of Judah.

12. There is a final comment on Asher in the genealogical listings in 1 Chronicles: 'All these were descendants of Asher—heads of families, choice men, brave warriors and outstanding leaders' (7:40). Asher may have been the last listed among the sons of Israel, but he was certainly not the least.

Bibliography

Clive Anderson, Brian Edwards, *Evidence for the Bible*, (Day One Publications, 2013).

John D. Currid & David P. Barrett, *ESV Bible Atlas*, (Crossway, 2010).

J. D. Douglas (Ed.), *The Illustrated Bible Dictionary*, (IVP, 1988).

E. W. Heaton, *Everyday Life in Old Testament Times*, (Batsford, 1966).

John A. Heck, *Everyday Life in Bible Times*, (BakerBooks, 2013).

Derek Kidner, *Genesis*, (IVP, 1981).

K. A. Kitchen, *On the Reliability of the Old Testament*, (Eerdmans, 2006).

Lorna Oakes, Philip Steele, *Everyday Life in Ancient Egypt & Mesopotamia*, (Southwater, 2005).

Nick Page, *The One-Stop Bible Atlas*, (Lion Hudson, 2010).

Daniel C. Snell, *A Companion to the Ancient Near East*, (Wiley-Blackwell, 2007).

Chris Sinkinson, *Time Travel through the Old Testament*, (IVP, 2013).

J. A. Thompson, *Handbook of Life in Bible Times*, (IVP, 1986).

John H. Walton, Victor H. Matthews, Mark W. Chavalas, *The IVP Bible Background Commentary – Old Testament*, (IVP, 2000).

Gordon J. Wenham, *Word Biblical Commentary – Genesis 1-15*, (Word, 1991).

Gordon J. Wenham, *Word Biblical Commentary – Genesis 16-50*, (Word, 1994).

Various authors, *Explore Bible Notes*, (The Good Book Company).

In addition to the above publications, numerous online articles have also been used, which are too many and varied to list. The subjects have, for example, included: sunrise and sunset times in various locations at various times of year; phases of the moon; the stability of various shapes of ship; ancient languages and early writing; ancient Mesopotamian, Egyptian and Canaanite names; the milk production of cows, and the milking of goats and sheep; bartering, deforestation and literacy in the ancient Near East; the weight of heifers; sickles and Bronze Age woodworking; bitumen in the ancient world; ziggurats; the speed of travel by camel; ancient Egyptian make-up and wigs; lighting fires using stones; camel saddles; the rate at which various animals breed—notably rabbits.